The Wicked One

"Eva . . ." Lucien spoke at last, his voice like cognac, like black velvet, like the night that pressed in from outside. "I had hoped I had not seen the last of you."

"I can assure you, Blackheath, that you have not."

"And now I shall see *all* of you, I think. Every bit of you. Ah, what delights the night promises . . ."

Her smile faded. Her lashes lowered over dangerously glittering eyes, for he was deliberately baiting her, and she did not like it. But he only turned his back on her and moved to stand before a full-length mirror, watching her in its reflection.

Eva looked into the mirror and met that unflinching gaze. "So, Blackheath," she purred, "will you make this difficult or will you concede? The choice is yours."

"My dear lady, I should think my choice is obvious." His gaze moved briefly over her. "Especially when one considers what life is apparently offering."

DANELLE HARMON

THE WICKED ONE

AVON BOOKS

An Imprint of HarperCollinsPublishers

This is a work of fiction. Names, characters, places, and incidents are products of the author's imagination or are used fictitiously and are not to be construed as real. Any resemblance to actual events, locales, organizations, or persons, living or dead, is entirely coincidental.

AVON BOOKS
An Imprint of HarperCollins*Publishers*
10 East 53rd Street
New York, New York 10022-5299

First Avon Books paperback printing: January 2001

Avon Trademark Reg. U.S. Pat. Off. and in Other Countries, Marca Registrada, Hecho en U.S.A.
HarperCollins® is a trademark of HarperCollins Publishers Inc.

Printed in the U.S.A.

10 9 8 7 6 5 4 3 2 1

For Emma

Chapter 1

Blackheath Castle
Berkshire, England
Winter 1777

He was coming.

The darkened bedchamber was still. Eerily so. Outside, faint through the ancient walls, she could hear the night wind howling around the castle turrets. The solitary candle flame twisted and writhed against the winter drafts that managed to creep, unseen, through the leaded casement windows. But somehow, with some deep, primal part of herself, she sensed his presence. Knew that he had finally arrived . . . was now approaching. Then, faintly discernible over the wind, the rising tattoo of her heart, she heard them.

Footsteps.

His footsteps.

Coming, now, up the spiraling stone stairs of this ancient tower.

Her senses heightened. Her heartbeat quickened. Sitting cross-legged on the huge medieval bed in the near darkness, her heavy skirts fanning about her hips, she became keenly aware of every sensation: the icy air against her skin . . . the way his fine linen sheets felt against her calves, her feet, naked beneath her petticoats . . . the way the lone bedside candle seemed to shrink back in nervous anticipation. She caressed the butt of the pistol, savoring the comforting weight of it in her hand. Her breath, hanging thick as fog in her lungs, stirred in small, silent exhalations. She tensed like a cat poised to strike down her prey.

Any moment now. . . .

And yes, there it was, the sound of his tread coming up those last few stairs as he made his way, unsuspecting, to his apartments, the footfalls louder now than the wind outside that had been her companion since she'd scaled, by way of a rope and her own wits, the parapets, the window ledge, the very walls that had been able to hold at bay cannonballs during the civil war, besiegers from the Middle Ages—but had been unable to keep her, one furious, determined woman, out.

But she was driven by purpose. She had come for one thing, and she would not leave without it. He had fooled her once, this man, his diabolical machinations nearly costing her her position at the French court and jeopardizing her standing among the American contingent in Paris—all of whom were working to secure France's aid in the fight for American independence.

She had worked hard to gain respect and prominence in a political arena dominated by men, but he had threatened that—and now she would threaten him.

Her adversary was a worthy one, a dangerous one, a man purported to be one of the deadliest duelists in England. He had a reputation for cunning. He had secured a formidable backing among his peers at a young age, had steered older men to attain his goals when his own youth should have hampered him, had been a subtle, sinister presence who was quite likely behind or at least involved with the British spy ring in France—a spy ring that had always been one step ahead of the Americans' own cleverly laid plans. No sane person would make an enemy of the Duke of Blackheath. Especially now that he was in the true height of his power. . . .

She squeezed the pistol lovingly. He would not emerge victorious *this* time. Oh, no. She had the element of surprise.

And she—a slow, feline smile curved her lips—had the cunning superiority of her gender.

Now he stopped just outside the closed door. Her eyes narrowed. She steadied the small weapon. The door latch was lifting. She passed her tongue once, twice over her lips, her blood beginning to hum, her smile becoming one of anticipation. She fixedly watched that slim piece of metal rising. Never taking her eyes off it, she reached out with her free hand and gripped the bottle she had stolen. Then she brought the gun up, sighted down her arm, and trained the weapon right where his heart would be when he came through the door.

It opened on a well-oiled sigh, spilling faint light into

the cold, gloomy chamber; outside, the moan and whistle of the wind was suddenly louder. A sense of danger pervaded her bones. Screamed through every nerve. And there he was, a taper in his hand, his tall form backlit by a torch set into the stone wall behind him.

Her finger froze on the trigger, and her breath stuck in her lungs at the sheer magnificence of him.

There was that same unsmiling face, glowing like Satan's in the candle's flickering light, its orange flame picking out the lofty cheekbones, the chiseled mouth with those hard, sculpted lips, the compelling profile with its noble brow and razor-straight nose. His hair was as one with the darkness around him, no powder, no pomade, just thick black waves swept back off his brow and caught at the nape with a bit of velvet.

He was watching her.

Watching her with eyes as still and deadly as a cobra preparing to strike.

The candle in his hand flickered. In vain, the meager flame tried to find softness in a face that was as severe and unforgiving as the stone walls she had scaled, the little tongue of fire finally giving up and shrinking down in cringing terror, the wax running like a tear down the long taper.

Her smile became malevolent.

"Ah, Your Grace. I have been waiting for you. You see"—she held up the aphrodisiac, her voice preternaturally calm—"I found a little bottle in your safe there, and since I cannot afford another error, *you*—like it or not—are going to sample it prior to my departure."

For a long moment, he remained perfectly still, his expression betraying nothing of what was going on behind that inscrutable black stare. And then his lips curved in the faintest of smiles as, putting down the candle, he began to move toward the bed.

Toward her.

Of its own accord, the door swung slowly shut behind him. She steadied the pistol and pulled the hammer back to full cock. Even the ominous click failed to check his approach, or put a glint of apprehension in eyes as black as nightshade. His cravat was the only light on his form, bubbling up like a frothy white fountain beneath his chin, emphasizing its dark perfection, its haughty arrogance, the faint smudge of inky bristle that shadowed his jaw. His waistcoat fitted a torso of classic form, and long, straight legs, the thighs hardened by years in the saddle, the calves enclosed in riding boots spattered with mud, gave him the commanding presence and height of a born ruler.

And now she saw his fingers moving down the buttons of that waistcoat, freeing them, one by one, as he approached.

The pistol had gone sweaty in her hand. He was eight feet away now ... six ...

Her eyes narrowed. She itched to squeeze the trigger, to send a ball ripping through the fabric of his body as his cleverness and deceit had ripped through the fabric of her life. But he ignored the gun, pausing just short of the bed, pulling the waistcoat off, and carefully laying it across the back of a chair.

"Eva de la Mouriére," he said at last, his voice like cognac, like black velvet, like the night that pressed in from outside. "I had hoped I had not seen the last of you."

"I can assure you, Blackheath, that you have not seen the last of me."

"And now I shall see *all* of you, I think. Every bit of you. Ah, what delights the night promises. . . ."

Her smile faded. Her lashes lowered over dangerously glittering eyes, for he was deliberately baiting her, and she did not like being baited. But he only turned his back on her and moved to stand before a full-length mirror, watching her in its reflection, gauging her reaction from over his shoulder as he slowly began to undo his stock.

Eva looked into the mirror and met that unflinching gaze. "So, Blackheath," she purred, "will you make this difficult, or will you concede? The choice is yours."

He lifted his head to undo the final knot beneath his chin. "My dear lady, I should think my choice is obvious." The mirrored black gaze moved briefly over her breasts . . . down the length of her torso . . . took in her seductively curving hips, until an answering, unwanted response fired her own blood. "Especially when one considers what life is apparently offering."

"What life is offering is a choice between this"—she raised the bottle—"and this"—she tipped the gun, never changing its aim. "If it would not deny me the chance to prove that this is the real aphrodisiac, *my* choice would be to put a ball through that conniving black heart of yours."

"Ah, but you do not have a choice. May I remind you, madam, that you just relinquished that advantage to me?"

"Don't play games with me, Blackheath. Your deviousness has cost me dearly, and I'm here to take my revenge." As he merely raised a brow in amusement, it was all she could do not to squeeze the trigger and kill him where he stood. She met his reflected gaze, glare for glare. "That wasn't the *real* aphrodisiac your brothers were carrying in that bottle the night I ambushed them on the road near Maidenhead, was it? Oh, no. It was a substitute. You gave them a clever substitute, and caused me to steal something that sickened and nearly killed the king of France." She swallowed hard, trying to get a rein on her fury. "You damn near destroyed my life."

He pulled the long white strip of silk from his neck and dangled it between thumb and forefinger, watching her with a faintly amused smile. "*Caused* you to steal something? Do you not enjoy free will like the rest of us, madam?"

Green eyes narrowed to dangerous slits. "You made a fool of me, Blackheath, and I will see that you pay for it."

He shrugged. "Ah, then, let that be a lesson to you. Highway robbery is, after all, a hanging offense."

"So is murdering an English peer, but I can assure you that I find it no deterrent. Now get on with it and undress. Better yet, I think I'll have you simply unfasten your breeches, as I doubt this will take but a moment."

His eyebrows rose. "I beg your pardon?"

"You heard me."

"My dear lady." His reflection smiled at her, but it was a patronizing, faintly indulgent gesture that made her want to sharpen her claws on his face. "I can assure you that haste and pleasure do not make appropriate bedmates"—his eyes were gleaming now above that slow, deliberate smile—"if you'll pardon the expression."

"I am not here to take or give pleasure, and I can assure you, I do not couple with dead bodies, as that is what yours will be if you so much as attempt to take liberties with me. Oh, no, Blackheath. I am here only to make sure that *this* time I have possession of the real aphrodisiac, and that it does everything it is supposed to do."

He was still watching her in the mirror, dark eyes hypnotizing, fascinating, magnetic above that sarcastic little smile. "And what, my dear, is it supposed to do?"

"Seduce you."

The smile broadened. He stretched out his arm, and the stock, a white ribbon in the darkness, floated lazily down to join his waistcoat, still draped over the back of the chair. "Ah, of course. Seduce me."

The way he said the words—caressingly, almost invitingly, a velvet command—sent an unexpected arrow of heat through her blood that found its mark at the junction of her thighs. Her mouth went dry. Her pulse quickened. She had come here to steal the aphrodisiac, to humiliate this man . . . but the idea of seducing him and, best of all, mastering him, was a heady thought indeed. For a moment, her calculating eyes settled on the bare oval of skin at his throat, then roved down his torso, assessing him as men had assessed women throughout the ages and finding him blessed in form as well as face. But no. She would not respond to her body's carnal demands. She would not give Blackheath the satisfaction; let him want her, let him covet her, let him hate her, even—but he would never have her . . . not on his terms.

It was obvious he had other ideas. In the mirror, she could see his hands at his throat now, unbuttoning the collar of his shirt, chin raised and his eyes—black, compelling, heavy-lidded eyes—still watching her. There were promises in those eyes. A dangerous heat that made her own body respond in kind. And now, as casually as if he were undressing before a wife instead of the one person in the world poised and more than willing to shoot him, he pulled his shirt free of his waistband, bunched its tails in his fists, and dragged the garment up and over his head.

Muscles in his back rippled, glowing tawny in the faint candlelight, skating over powerful shoulders. Lord, he was gorgeous.

He stood watching her in the mirror, the shirt hooked over his forefinger.

"And now, my dear?"

"Face me and drop the breeches," she snapped, wanting to humiliate him. "Let's see if the rest of you measures up to what you've already bared."

He merely smiled.

She shifted forward on the bed. "I *said*, drop the breeches. Like it or not, Blackheath, you will imbibe this potion, and your body will prove whether or not it is the *real* aphrodisiac before it is tried on someone far more important than you."

He gave an overly dramatic sigh. "In that case, I fear I don't quite see the point of this little . . . exercise," he murmured, releasing the shirt. It whispered down over the chair, hung there a moment, and then slid to the floor in a pool of fine white lawn. Blackheath did not stoop to retrieve it. Nor did he bother to turn around, as though he did not respect the danger she presented. His studied nonchalance stoked Eva's fury—even as it filled her with desire. What infuriating arrogance! What unbelievable egotism! What . . . beautiful arms, hard and strong and slightly bulging where they met those handsome shoulders—

"For you see," he continued, with maddening logic, "arriving home to find a strange and beautiful woman waiting in his bed is fantasy incarnate for any man. The mere sight of you, madam, and the knowledge that I will soon have you, is more than enough to arouse me. I ask you, what good is a love potion, and what does taking it prove, when a man already wants a woman?" At her look of stony wrath, he merely gave a chiding smile. "Really, if it's a reaction you're looking for, I daresay you would be far better advised giving it to one of the statues downstairs."

Eva's smile faded. Her face went flat and hard. She began to swing her legs off the bed.

"Or," continued Blackheath, in that same calculatedly mocking tone, "taking a dose of it yourself. After all, you seem far less willing than I to indulge in a night of bedplay . . . though I can certainly remedy that particular reluctance—*without* benefit of an aphrodisiac."

That did it. Eva slid off the bed, came up behind him, and put the pistol to the base of his skull, her mouth two inches from the warm, deadly metal as she raised herself on tiptoe to hiss into his ear, "Are you ready to get down to business?"

"I am more than ready. It is *your* readiness, madam, that is in question."

Snarling, Eva shoved the pistol hard against his head. In the next instant, she found herself flat on her back and gasping for breath as she stared up at the hangings of his bed, her body crushed beneath the splendid weight of his, her arms pinned flat to the mat-

tress over which he'd shoved her in that one lightning-
fast movement that had knocked the wind from her
lungs.

Stunned, she glared up at him, her heart pounding.
He had bested her.

Imagine!

He smiled down at her, but his eyes were not
amused; they were glittering now, cold, deadly . . . and
reflecting the desire she, too, felt but refused to fully
acknowledge. His mouth lowered, and she flung her
head to one side to avoid the sudden, seductive whisper of his lips against her cheek.

"You know what they say about women who play
with fire," he murmured.

"I am not playing."

"How unfortunate, I am."

"This is *not* a game, Blackheath," she gritted from
between clenched teeth, glaring toward the window
where her canvas bag sat ready by her escape route.
Escape. She quivered as his lips, so warm, so demanding, brushed over the curve of her jaw, igniting unwelcome fires, threatening her resolve.

"Ah, but it is . . . and I can assure you, my dear, that
I will win it. As the outcome is inevitable, why don't
you relax and enjoy yourself?"

"I cannot enjoy the attentions of a scoundrel who
nearly ruined my life. Why don't you just admit you
switched that potion, Blackheath?"

"Ah, but with pleasure. It was necessary to keep it
safe, you see. My brother Andrew is a bit of a . . . hot-
spur. I could not entrust something as valuable as the
world's first proven aphrodisiac into his keeping—
even if he *did* invent it. My intentions were only to

fool him into thinking he was carrying home the genuine article. The fact that you were fooled as well, and that your own no doubt treasonous plans sabotaged by my actions, was merely an unforeseen boon."

"I am an American," Eva hissed. "Though you pompous Englishmen may consider my intentions *treasonous*, my countrymen would call them patriotic."

"My dear girl. When are you Yankees ever going to acknowledge that America is not a *country*, but a group of colonies?"

Eva trembled with fury. But he was crushing her, pinning her helplessly to the sheets, the mattress. She felt him pull the bottle from her fingers and place it on the bedside stand—out of reach, out of harm's way. She could not move. Could not even get her knee up to crush his groin and destroy any and all chances of his ever siring the sixth duke. And now he had pulled back to gaze down at her, triumphant, the hunter admiring his kill before devouring it, one palm cupping the side of her face and forcing her to look up and into those magnetic black eyes.

Her breasts fired in response. She could feel the nipples, tight and hard, against her chemise, her stays, her gown. And she could feel his arousal pressing against her pelvis, even though breeches and skirts separated them.

Think, Eva . . . fast!

The pistol.

She tried to raise her arm, but no, he was still one step ahead of her and had anticipated her movement. His fingers closed over her hand, gently forcing it back down to the sheets, the thumb teasing the sensitive inside of her wrist, rubbing gently, stroking, drawing little circles there until she was no longer trying to turn away, until the pistol, and her desire to empty it into him, were the furthest things from her mind.

Her fingers relaxed. The pistol slid from her grasp.

"So, madam," he murmured, dragging her hand up to his mouth and kissing each knuckle, one by one, as his dark gaze held hers from over the top of each. "Shall we get on with this . . . seduction, or shall I send you home like a good little girl and leave us both wondering what might have been?"

He was dipping his tongue between the root of each finger now, causing involuntary tremors to rake her body, causing her nipples to pucker and ache for wanting him . . . causing her senses to grow thick, vitreous, and dulled. Eva desperately sought the fury that would protect her—and found only helplessness.

Panic.

She glared up at him. Up into those black, black eyes. It was said that the eyes were the mirror of the soul, but Blackheath's soul was a well whose bottom was miles down. She could read nothing in those eyes. Nothing. And then he brought her hand to his lips, pressed his mouth to her palm, and touched the point of his tongue to it.

Eva caught her breath. And what remained of her resolve. *Don't break eye contact with him! Don't let him know how your body is responding, and for God's sake, don't let him know how frightened that response is making you!*

But he knew. And she knew he knew, because now he was smiling in triumph, touching his fingers to the curve of her bottom lip, rubbing it, massaging it, and coaxing the response he wanted from her with a skill that had her very skin burning the clothes that lay, damply now, against it. He was the master. He was the wolf. And this was a game of seduction, all right, but *she* was the one being seduced. The one who had been rendered helpless. She fought for control, but it fled her as he touched two fingertips to his tongue and brought them, wet now, back to her mouth, tracing the proud bow of her upper lip until Eva's gaze went glassy with desire.

His lashes lowered, and bending his head, he kissed her.

There was no help for it. No help for her. Her arms wound around his neck, her mouth parting beneath the insistent pressure of his in sweet defeat. And sweet, it was. Sweet, the feel of his tongue tracing her lips, teasing them more fully apart, now slipping between them to taste the inside of her mouth. Sweet, the sensation of melting straight down into the bed while her body evaporated into steam. Sweet, the languid heat that consumed her, until her hips tilted up, pressing against his arousal, and her legs drifted apart in unspoken invitation.

Take me.

He dragged his mouth from hers, began kissing a trail down her neck. His hand was on her breast, cupping it, smoothing it, the thumb grazing the nipple through fabric that stood no chance against his attentions. She felt his fingers slip beneath the bodice, beneath the chemise, popping the hardening nipple free to caress and tease it. Long, masterful fingers that knew exactly what they were doing. Oh, dear God. Oh, Lord, help her! No man should have this sort of control over her! Fear mingled with desire. She twisted away, her breath coming hard.

"I've changed my mind. Let me up now, Blackheath, or you will regret it."

"If I let you up now, we will both regret it."

"I'm warning you, Blackheath."

"Of course you are, my dear." But he ignored the narrowing of her eyes, the mixture of fear and desperation that lent them a cold emerald glitter in the faint light. He was too focused on conquest. On mastery. And on her nipple, around which he was tracing little circles of fire with his finger.

"Blackheath—"

He lifted his head then and smiled. "But since we are on the subject of warnings, I think it's time I issued one of my own."

"What," she scoffed, reclaiming some of her bravado, "to stay out of the bedchamber of the big, bad ducal wolf?"

His eyes were the cobra's again, black, dangerous, ruthless—and without soul. "If you ever again lay a hand against any member of my family, I will find you—and I will ruin you more thoroughly than you can even begin to imagine."

His words iced her spine. She stared at him, her pulse thudding in her ears as she tried to find something to say.

"While I admire ingenuity, I despise the means by which you carried out your little robbery of the aphrodisiac," he continued. "You may think highly of your own cleverness, your ruse of a disabled carriage to lure my brothers into stopping to help you, but how did you repay their kindness? By striking Charles down and leaving him unconscious in the road in the manner of the crudest highwayman. You might have killed him." The black eyes grew savage. "You might have killed Andrew as well, had he not acted with such a cool head. Perhaps you do not know me very well, madam, but I can assure you that I do not take kindly to anyone who threatens or inflicts harm upon my family."

She seized his hand, shoving it away from her breast and gripping it ruthlessly hard. "If your family lacks the good sense to be off the roads after dark, then they got what they deserved."

"And if you, my dear, lack the good sense to stay out of a man's bedchamber, then you will get what *you* deserve . . ."—his gaze flickered to her nipples, which were standing tautly beneath the fabric of her gown— "and, I might add, now seem to want."

Incensed, Eva reached blindly for the pistol, but it was gone, swallowed in a tangle of sheets, a hard lump separated from her questing fingers by soft linen and too many bunches and folds.

"Now shall we dispense with words and carry on with . . . physical contact?"

She smiled. "What a divine idea."

And managed to get her knee up.

It did not catch him in the groin as she had intended, but at the V of his ribs in a solid blow that doubled him up and punched the breath from his lungs in pained surprise. It was all Eva needed. She shot out from under him, shoved him mightily onto his back, and, straddling him with her body, pressed her thumbs down hard into the base of his windpipe.

He blinked up at her in disbelieving astonishment.

"I can turn the tables as easily as that," she snarled, glaring triumphantly down into his eyes. "And don't you forget it."

He swallowed—or tried to.

"My late husband *le Comte* spent two years in the Orient as governor of a French outpost," she added in a low, menacing voice. "When I wasn't covering for his incompetence by performing his political duties for him, I was learning all I could from the natives— including the best ways to disable a man and defend myself if the need ever arose. Cross me again and I'll kill you."

"My dear lady, if that is your intention, I implore you to use the pistol," he managed with rueful sarcasm. "Strangulation is a most . . . ignoble . . . way to die."

She did not remove her hand. He did not move his body. For a long, charged moment they simply stared at each other, she on top, he on the bottom, neither willing to break eye contact first, neither willing to back down.

And then, despite herself, Eva's gaze flickered to that handsome, chiseled mouth still wearing its faint smile. To her thumb, pressing into his throat. How could she not admire him? He would let her kill him before giving her the satisfaction of coughing, choking, or even letting his eyes water.

She was done here. They had each won a round in this dangerous game of cat and mouse, but in the end the game would go to her. She would have the last laugh. Eva loosened her hold on him, but let her fingers remain on his throat, lightly stroking the angry red mark her thumb had left in lingering warning.

He lay half atop the pillow, his face mostly consumed by shadow—but she could see those devilish black eyes, glittering, watchful, appreciative. . . .

Triumphant.

"Really, madam . . . had I known that being on top would convince you to stay, I would have suggested it far sooner."

Eva lost control of her temper. Snarling, she tried to leap off the bed, but her foot tangled in the sheets and she crashed to the floor, arms flailing, one hand trying to break her fall. The sheets went with her, and there— oh, thank God!—was her pistol, skittering across the cold, cold floor.

She snatched it up just as Blackheath leaped off the bed in pursuit, then she turned and fired.

The report cracked through the room. She saw the aphrodisiac explode like a bottle of blood, and then real blood, the duke's blood, running down his leg as he staggered, took two desperate steps toward her, and fell, still pulling himself after her.

"*Eva-a-a-a!*" he roared.

The game was over; there was no reason to remain. Grabbing her canvas sack, Eva leaped to the window, shoved it wide—

And vanished.

Chapter 2

He gained his feet.

Lunged to the open window and leaned out, gripping the sill, the drapes blowing back past his thunderous face.

Nothing, except for a swinging rope and there, far below on the grass, movement; a moment later, he heard hoofbeats and she was gone.

The door burst open behind him.

"Your Grace! I beg your pardon for disturbing you, but I could swear I just heard gunfire! Are you all—"

Lucien turned from the window.

Phelps, his valet, took one look at the duke's leg— and, paling, leaned against the doorframe for support. At a curt look from his master, he left the room and pounded down the stairs.

Wordlessly, Lucien moved to a chair, sat, and, reaching into a nearby drawer for a knife, proceeded to slice open the side of his breeches just above the knee. A jagged shard of glass the length of his forefinger was deeply embedded in his outer thigh, protruding from the fabric. Blood ran everywhere, pulsing down the leg of his breeches, overrunning the purplish blotches of the aphrodisiac like a rising flood. Extracting his handkerchief, he gripped the wicked fragment and slowly began to pull, never flinching as the glass tore through muscle and skin on its way out, the tissue closing back around the shard as he gradually worked it free.

Blood welled more quickly now. Red-hot pain blazed up his leg. But it was his loins that were on fire.

Unquenchable, agonizing fire.

He bent to retrieve his stock and was just tying it around his thigh over the wadded handkerchief when Phelps returned, one of the upstairs chambermaids in tow.

"Your Grace, I've sent a footman for the doctor. The butler is on his way up now."

But the maid was staring in horror at the duke's leg. "Your Grace! Lord save us, what 'appened to ye?"

"There was an intruder," Lucien murmured, gazing into the black rectangle of darkness into which the Comtesse de la Mouriére had disappeared. Out of the corner of his eye, he saw Phelps gesture to the girl to get started on the broken glass and spilled liquid that littered the floor. "Leave this," he added, "and go back to bed, both of you."

"An intruder?" the servants repeated in surprise.

"But how on earth did he scale—" Phelps started, before another look from his master cut him short.

The duke got to his feet. "Saddle Armageddon."

"But Your Grace, you—you're injured!"

"And call out the hounds. Now."

Phelps looked about to protest; but he knew better than to question his master's orders, especially when the duke was in the sort of cold fury his set, hardened features currently proclaimed. Bowing, he headed back downstairs to convey the orders, the frightened maid just behind him. Lucien waited until they were gone, then he staggered out of the room and began his own painful journey down the tower's spiraling stone stairs. He was halfway down when his sister, Lady Nerissa de Montforte, came charging up at the head of a column of alarmed servants, a hastily donned dressing gown around her willowy frame.

She saw his bloody leg and stifled a scream. "Lucien!"

"Go back to bed, Nerissa."

"What has happened?"

"I said, go back to bed."

She tried to block his way, to no avail. Servants milled about, some running forward to assist him. He waved them away, ordering them to search the grounds and calling for his hat and greatcoat. He heard his orders being relayed, heard Phelps pleading with him to wait for the doctor, heard others vowing to rout and destroy the intruder: "What did he look like?" "Where did he go?" "What should we do, Your Grace?" But Lucien paid them no heed, gripping the stair rail with a clenched white hand as he staggered down the last few stairs, ignoring the confusion, ignoring his pain, ignoring, even, his sister as she flew after him and gripped his arm.

"You are *not* riding that beastly horse," she declared, as he shook her off and found his pace despite the pain biting at his thigh.

"I told you, go back to bed, Nerissa."

"You need a doctor! You need stitches! You need rest!"

They were downstairs now, moving at considerable speed across the Great Hall, where ancient suits of armor with slitted, visored eyes stared out across the torchlit gloom in silent disapproval. Nerissa hurried after her brother. An army of servants swarmed after both of them, desperate to keep their master from bringing more harm upon himself. But Lucien only continued toward the great medieval door, leaving a trail of blood on the polished marbled floor.

He pulled it open and was gone.

Eva de la Mouriére gave the hired horse her head, sending the gray mare flying across the downs. It was starting to rain; she felt it stinging her face, dampening the mare's hide and bringing the mingled scents of horse sweat and wet leather up from the racing animal. She knew Blackheath would not be far behind her. He would never let her escape so easily, and indeed, she would be disappointed in him if he let her go without a fight. Bunching the reins in one hand, she loosened her hair, reveling in the thought that he might chase her, but would never catch her.

She had won.

Won!

She shook her head and laughed, letting the rainy wind catch her flying tresses, exhilarating in the power of the horse beneath her, the knowledge that she had bested the man who, according to popular opinion, could not be outfoxed. Ah, revenge was sweet! Never mind the sharpness of the stirrup irons against her bare and freezing feet; never mind the scraped knees and broken fingernails. And never mind the loss of her boots, abandoned upon her hasty escape at the base of the tower where she'd left them earlier in order to scale the walls.

The prize was worth it.

And right now, that prize was safely tucked in her saddlebags.

Another peal of laughter escaped her. How long would it take Blackheath to realize that this time, *she* had tricked *him*? How soon before he found that the bottle she'd used for target practice contained no love potion at all, but the substitute that he himself had made—a substitute that had kept poor King Louis of France mated to a chamberpot for the better part of a day?

From far behind, she heard the distant baying of hounds. They would never catch her now. Whooping with delight, Eva sent the mare flying over a low brook and disappeared into the night.

The search turned up nothing, of course. The Duke of Blackheath sent the mighty Armageddon galloping over the downs and along the Ravenscombe road, following hounds whose excited baying dissolved into confused yaps and whimpers when they lost the scent near a coaching inn five miles south of Lambourn.

There, he pulled the black desert-bred stallion up short as the dogs milled about in confusion. The innkeeper, summoned from his bed, came running out in his nightcap, bowing and scraping and, in response to the duke's terse queries, apologizing for his inability to help. Lucien set his jaw. The clever witch must have changed horses, he thought, allowing none of the frustrated fury that made his heart pound with something almost like violence to mar his expression. He turned away and stared off into the darkness, ignoring the innkeeper's pathetic attempts to placate his anger. There was no scent left to follow.

She was gone.

Disappeared into the night.

Even as he loathed her, he admired her. Wanted her. Craved her with every cell in his body. His loins throbbed with unrequited lust. His memory burned with the feel of her breast in his hand, the pliancy of her lips beneath his, those incredible, slanting green eyes, flame-red hair, and fatally beautiful smile.

His mood savage, he turned back toward the castle.

He would find her, by God, and when he did, he would have her.

"I declare, Lucien, why you don't let Dr. Highworth do that is beyond my comprehension," scolded Nerissa as she tipped brandy into a glass and stood waiting while her brother pulled the last stitch through his own leg. Upon returning, her brother had sent the doctor away, trimmed away the bloody flaps of his breeches, and proceeded to stitch the gaping flesh shut himself, his face like stone, no wince, no hiss of pain ever escaping his hard, set lips. Nobody but Lucien could sew up his own flesh without fainting dead away on the floor. Nobody but Lucien could do it without benefit of spirits, laudanum, or even a grimace of pain.

"I thought I told you to go to bed."

"Now, Lucien, you know that there is no way I could sleep knowing you were racing about the countryside losing gallons of blood."

"It is hardly gallons, and now that I have returned, I think you should be in your own rooms, not mine. This is inappropriate."

"You're my brother, for heaven's sake, not my betrothed."

"Ah, yes." He looked up, his eyes glowing with banked anger—and something dark and calculating that immediately made her tense with wariness. "Speaking of which, when are you and Perry going to announce your nuptials?"

Nerissa gaped, then hastily turned away, knowing her brother's all-seeing gaze had already caught her evasive gesture. "I'll announce it when he asks me for his hand."

"I am tired of waiting for him to make up his mind."

"Come, now, Lucien. Surely you must know that Perry's young, and still has wild oats left to sow—"

"His fields were planted long ago. He is the Earl of Brookhampton, and neither of you are getting any younger. I will speak to him."

"You will not!"

"I will."

Nerissa's eyes flashed. "I will not have you interfering in my life the way you did our brothers', Lucien! You orchestrated Gareth's and Juliet's affairs so they had to get married. You all but dragged Charles and Amy to the altar. And I can't even begin to forgive you for your cunning in trapping Andrew and Celsie into wedlock. Who gave you the right to play God?" She shook her head. "Oh, no. I won't have you working Perry and me like puppets. What is between us is our own business, not yours."

"As your brother and head of this family, any business of yours is also business of mine."

"And I will thank you to stay out of it!"

Black eyes, devoid of all expression, met angry ones of Wedgwood blue.

"Besides," Nerissa added, nervously fingering the lace at her elbow, "I'd sooner remain on the shelf than suffer one of your—your *manipulations*."

"I only manipulate people for their own good."

"For their own *good*?"

"Yes."

Her face flamed with anger. "Why, that is the most arrogant remark I have ever heard! I know my own good, Lucien, and I won't have you moving Perry and me about like pawns on a chessboard just to suit your own purposes!"

He only smiled as he finally set the needle aside and reached for the glass of brandy she still held, its stem perilously close to shattering in her clenched hand. "Do give me that, my dear. You are about to cut yourself."

Nerissa relinquished it, and watched as he downed

the spirits in one fluid motion. Despite his stony expression, she sensed a roiling fury beneath his still surface, a coiled, savage tension that boded ill. Though she suspected it was directed at another—the intruder, no doubt—Nerissa didn't care to be the current focus of it when the true target was long out of reach. Best to extricate herself from this situation before it deteriorated any further.

"Since you are in an obviously foul temper, I am going back to bed," she said with as much calm as she could muster. "But I'll leave you with one last warning, Lucien. I want you to stay out of my affairs. Leave Perry and me alone."

He smiled, but it was a dark smile, and there was a calculating gleam in his eyes that Nerissa knew all too well. "Of course, my dear. Now go to bed. You have had enough excitement for one evening, I think."

He stood, bowed, and saw her out of his chambers.

Lucien watched her go, his gaze hooded. She was wary now; nervous as a rabbit. He had no intention of staying out of her affairs, of course. And she was right: He was in one hell of a foul temper, a temper that craved action, any action—but, having been thwarted, now growled and paced like a caged beast within him, demanding satisfaction.

Demanding *Eva*.

He summoned Phelps and silently allowed the valet to ready him for bed. Then he deadened the agony in his leg with another shot of brandy, slid beneath the cool, crisp sheets, and lay there in the darkness, thinking . . .

Of red hair and slanting green eyes . . . of breasts crowned with coral nipples . . . of seductively flaring hips ... of skin as white as a virgin's virtue. Sleep would not come early if at all tonight, but given the nightmares that awaited him there, he was in no hurry to embrace it.

He stared up into the darkness.

I will have you, Eva. You may depend upon it.

Chapter 3

~~~

"I don't *know* who the intruder was. Lucien refuses to discuss it," said Nerissa, sidling closer to her beau, Earl Brookhampton, as he expertly steered the horse and phaeton around a chalky puddle of mud glazed with ice late the following morning. Low, scudding clouds were roiling up and over the downs and she could see her breath in the damp air. She was glad she was wrapped in wool and ermine and a hot brick toasted her feet, for it felt cold enough to snow and probably would, by nightfall. "The only thing they found was the intruder's boots, and the rope by which he scaled the tower wall. Why, I've never seen Lucien in such a cold rage!"

"Fellow must've had a jolly good store of courage to even attempt such a thing," said Perry, looking up at the darkening sky. " 'Tis dangerous enough to scale the tower, but to confront Lucien—*Lucien*, of all people!—as well? That intruder must have had a death wish!"

"He'll wish he *was* dead when Lucien finally catches up to him! Especially since that troublesome aphrodisiac that Andrew invented was destroyed in the attempt. Lucien is furious!"

Nerissa rested her head against Perry's shoulder. The dampness had brought curl to his tousled blond hair. The wind had bitten into his cheeks, his eyes were as cool and gray as the sky above, and he had never looked more handsome. She sighed. Oh, how she wished they were already wed, how she wished she could experience the delights of the marriage bed under the tutelage of his warm and capable hands! She let her heart's wish show in her eyes, and in the next moment he leaned close, cupped her jaw with his fingers, and pulled her head close to his. She closed her eyes, welcoming the familiar taste and touch of his tongue against her own, the feel of his lips, hard where hers were soft, demanding where hers were pliant.

But the horse was still moving.

The kiss could not last.

A bump in the road broke it, and reluctantly, they both pulled away, Nerissa passing her tongue over her lips as though to seal in the warmth of Perry's kiss.

He redirected his attention to the road. "If only Lucien hadn't meddled in the first place, the aphrodisiac would still be safe."

"Yes, well, we all know that Lucien will meddle as long as there is air to breathe. I suppose it's all just as well, though. That potion was far too dangerous. I mean, look how much trouble it got Andrew and Celsie into!"

"I'll say it did." Perry glanced overhead at the incoming clouds, reached into his pocket, and extracted two sweets, giving one to Nerissa and popping the other into his own mouth. "Poor Andrew would still be a free man if it weren't for that blasted stuff."

"Uh, Perry, I think there's something you should know."

He turned and raised a brow.

"Lucien is growing impatient with us. He's threatening to take matters into his own hands if we do not set a date soon."

Perry's face drained of color, and he nearly choked on the sweet. Nerissa pounded him across the back, and turning his head, he spat the candy out onto the muddy ground.

"Bloody hell," he swore.

"Perhaps we should just set a date so he can't manipulate us like he did my brothers. . . . Wouldn't it be wonderful if I were the only one in my family he *couldn't* force into marriage?"

Though her tone was light, cajoling, Perry felt as though someone had just iced his spine. It wasn't that he didn't adore Nerissa, whom he had known since childhood; it wasn't that he didn't want to marry her.

He just didn't want to marry her *now*.

He was only midway through his second decade; there were too many adventures to be had, too many seeds to be sown, for him to think about settling down and marrying! And now Lucien, that master manipulator, that Machiavellian monster who had controlled so many other lives, was eyeing him and Nerissa as his next victims? *Oh, God and the devil, help us!*

He stared straight ahead as he turned the horse toward Blackheath Castle, unable to look into her eyes, so blue, so eager, so hopeful. "I, uh, don't think we should act just yet," he said lamely. "There is nothing your brother can do to force our hands. Besides, I—well, I'm not yet ready to settle down. . . . I'm not ready for the demands of being a husband, being a father. . . ."

"Don't you love me?" she asked playfully.

"Of course I love you, Nerissa." He leaned over and kissed her even as he flicked the reins to get the horse to go faster; this was a conversation he was *not* inclined to have, and the sooner he got her home, the better. "But I'm young. You're young. Marriage is a lifelong commitment and shouldn't be something two people rush into."

"Young? I'm nearly twenty, you're halfway to thirty, and you've been giving me the same answer for the last two years." She lifted her chin and stared off over the downs, watching a flock of sheep grazing in the distance. "Why, a woman could get tired waiting for you to have your fun, Perry. A woman could decide that she, too, needs some *fun*, and start seeking it elsewhere."

"And what is that supposed to mean?"

Her smile was distant. "Exactly what you think it means."

Suddenly irritated, he pulled the phaeton up sharply before the castle's main entrance. What was it with women, always pestering, always nagging, never happy until they had a ring on their finger? Wasn't a promise good enough?

"Listen, Nerissa, if you simply want to show off a ring for your friends, I'll go to London and buy you—"

"Perry, you don't understand. I don't want jewelry. I want *you*."

"But Nerissa, I—"

She looked down, pretending an interest in her fur muff. "No, no, I shall not nag you, you've made it clear as crystal what your priorities are."

"Dearest, you're just eager to get married because you've seen three of your four brothers wed, and you're feeling left out." Her face hardened, and he heard his tone grow desperate. "It's not that I don't love you, Nissa, I just need time to . . . well, to have my adventures before I settle down to a life of—of, well, boring domesticity. . . . Oh, hell—"

She stiffened, looking straight ahead with a bleak expression in her eyes. A footman approached and took the horse's head. Perry, cursing under his breath, jumped to the ground, reached up, and helped Nerissa from the phaeton. She merely slew him with a hurt look, pulled her gloved hand from his, and strode angrily toward the castle.

"Nerissa! At least let me see you safely indoors!"

She paused only long enough to toss over her shoulder, "Good day, Perry. Come back when you've had your fill of *adventure*."

She swept inside, leaving him gritting his teeth in frustration.

Women!

Neither of them noticed the slight movement of the drapes at the library window.

"More candles, Puddyford," murmured the Duke of Blackheath, as he stood at the window watching

Nerissa's and Perry's return with a deceptively absent stare. "It grows dark in here."

"Yes, Your Grace." Obediently, the servant lit more tapers, casting a quick glance at his silent, preoccupied master before hurrying out past Sir Roger Fox, Esquire, who sat near the hearth contemplating a glass of port.

Fox waited until the servant had gone, then looked up at the duke, whose broad back was silhouetted by the gray light coming in from the window. "So," he said, "you want me to have our Parisian contact abandon his surveillance of the French court and concentrate on watching the activities of this"—he smiled—"woman, instead?"

"It is of more importance to me at the moment."

"Yes, but is it of more importance to Britain? As we all know, the only reason the Americans are even *in* Paris is to stir up trouble, to try and bring French strength in on their side of this confounded war. We must remain one step ahead of them, otherwise we'll find ourselves fighting the damned Frogs as well as the Yankees."

The duke did not turn from the window. "This woman is dangerous, at the forefront of the Americans' activities, and I will continue to thwart her efforts as long as I draw breath."

The duke let the drapes fall shut and returned to the fire, a look on his face of smug triumph.

"What is it?" Fox asked, frowning.

"Perry has just brought Nerissa home, and all appears to be exactly as I suspected it would be."

"Meaning?"

"Oh, just the predictable argument between my two little birds of paradise," Lucien drawled, reclaiming his

chair and pouring himself a glass of port. A slamming
door heralded Nerissa's entrance, and both men heard
the spray of gravel outside as Perry sent the phaeton
thundering away from the castle at what sounded like a
suicidal pace. "So, my dear Fox. Did you carry my letter
to Lord Islington in London?"

"Yes, and I negotiated the sale of his Spanish estate
to a certain Don Eduardo Mendoza, too—though I
must confess, the whole business fills me with trepida-
tion, Lucien. I can't imagine what you'll do with a
Spanish estate, nor why you feel the need to invent a
false identity under which to buy it."

Lucien was gazing into his glass, smiling. "Ah, but
that Spanish estate will suit my needs nicely, I think. I
really did have to do something about my sister's
hopeless . . . *situation*."

"Some diabolical plan up your sleeve to get your
last sibling married, then?"

"It is for her own good."

"For the love of God, Lucien, one of these days
you'll go too far and your scheming machinations will
come back to haunt you."

"Oh, but I think not," the duke murmured. "After
all, my dear Fox—I have a perfect record."

A week later, Lucien was at his correspondence
when Nerissa burst in.

"Lucien!"

He turned, quickly schooling his face into bland
inquiry, brotherly concern, banishing his triumph to a
place where she would never find it. His sister was as
distraught as ever he'd seen her. "You must do something!" she cried. "Perry's off to Spain—*Spain*, of all

places—and I'm afraid he'll never come back after the way I treated him!"

Lucien felt a savage stab of delight. So, his instructions had been followed to the letter, then. . . . Good.

"My dear girl," he said, putting an arm around her shoulders and drawing her nearer the fire. "Sit, and take a glass of Madeira with me while you tell me exactly what happened."

Nerissa was too upset to sit, though she hastily accepted the glass her brother offered her and downed it with an ease that brought a frown to his deceptively mild countenance. She began to pace, blinking back tears of anger and frustration.

"He got a letter yesterday, from a Don somebody-or-other in Spain . . . a solicitor for the estate of some client who died intestate. Well, this client had no heirs, and his closest living relative turned out to be Perry, of all people! I never knew that Perry had relatives in Spain! What other secrets does he harbor, what other surprises does he have in store for me? And now this Spaniard wants him to come at once to inspect the land and house, and determine what is to be done with it. Oh, Lucien, what am I to do?"

"Do?" Lucien smiled cajolingly. "Really, my dear, is a short trip to Spain any great catastrophe? You are upsetting yourself for nothing. Why, think of the benefits of having holdings in such a place. Once you and Perry are married, you can pass your winters there instead of here in cold, wet England."

"How do I know he'll even want to come back to England? With me nagging him about marriage, and that harridan of a mother who won't leave him alone, coming back is the last thing he'll want to do! We parted on terrible terms. . . ."

"Ah, Nerissa. Have you never heard the old adage, 'Absence makes the heart grow fonder'? Think. If Perry goes away for a while, it is only natural that he'll start missing you. Let him go. Let him miss you; it is good for him. Perhaps, when he returns, he will suddenly decide he can't live without you, and you'll get him to commit to a wedding date."

"Oh, Lucien . . . do you really think so?"

"I am optimistic."

Nerissa flung her arms around his neck, reminding him of the little girl she had once been, running to him for comfort after falling and scraping a knee, reminding him of all the times he'd stood at that same window behind him and watched Charles and Gareth racing their ponies down the drive. How he had longed to be out there with them, enjoying a childhood that had ended the moment he'd found his father dead on the tower stairs; how he'd resented being forced to stay indoors and compose himself with the maturity and dignity his new role as duke had demanded—

"Oh, Lucien . . . sometimes I just want to strangle you . . . other times, I love you beyond reason because you always say the right thing at the right time." She pulled back, hastily wiping at her tears and smiling bravely. "I will be patient, then. I will wait here in England, and when he returns . . ."

"Perhaps he'll have an offer for you," Lucien finished, with an encouraging lift of one brow.

Nerissa left the room in higher spirits than she had

entered it, never seeing the satisfied triumph in her brother's eyes.

Absence makes the heart grow fonder.

"Indeed," he murmured—and smiled.

Chapter 4

The Duke of Blackheath wasn't the only one tormented by what might have been.

With the real aphrodisiac safe in her possession, Eva de la Mouriére had reached the coast of England early the next morning, caught the packet to France, and was in Paris by late that afternoon.

She was in excellent spirits as she called at Dr. Benjamin Franklin's residence, only to find the famous statesman, scientist, and politician looking as old as his years.

"What is it?" she asked.

Franklin gave her a bleak look. "Twelve months I have been here, trying to convince the French to officially ally themselves with us in our fight for freedom. Twelve months of negotiations, of hope, of playing one side off the other. And still, no change. We cannot penetrate the British blockade of our coast. Their spies are everywhere, watching our every move. None of the munitions we sent home reached Washington's troops." He removed his spectacles and rubbed at his eyes. "Without French alliance—and a colossal loan—I fear that independence will soon be a lost cause."

He looked so weary and hopeless that Eva couldn't resist reaching into her satchel. "I got the aphrodisiac," she said with sly triumph.

"The aphrodisiac?"

Poor Franklin—he had so much on his mind these days, it was no wonder he had forgotten all about the elusive love potion. His eyes brightened as Eva handed him the bottle.

"So, this is the magical elixir that is supposed to aid young Marie Antoinette. . . ."

"It is indeed. The *correct* one, this time." Eva watched in satisfaction as Franklin examined the purple-garnet liquid that would set everything to right in the royal bedchamber and, he hoped, banish all rumors that the king was impotent. If it succeeded in bringing about a royal heir, then surely France would officially align herself with America and help them win the war against Britain!

He handed the bottle back to her. "Well, Eva, let's just hope it works. In the meantime"—he smiled, looking much more like his old self—"well done. Very well done, indeed."

"Well, it wasn't difficult," she boasted, wrapping the bottle back in its cloth as she told him how she had procured the substance. "The Duke of Blackheath may think he's the most cunning person on earth, but even his wiles cannot compare to a woman's."

Franklin's old eyes twinkled. "What I can't understand, Eva, is why you didn't take advantage of the situation. Any other woman would have, you know."

Eva started, then gave a snort of contempt to hide her momentary loss of composure.

"I mean, there you were, in his chambers, in his bed, the potion right there. Any other woman in your position would have just tapped a few drops of it into his port to ensure it was the genuine article, and perhaps snared herself a duke as well."

Eva forced a careless peal of laughter. "Now, why on earth would I have wanted to do that?"

"I'm told that the current duke is a very handsome—and wealthy—man."

"Yes, well, I have sworn off men. You know that."

"Ah, Eva." His eyes were kind behind the spectacles. "You're too young to be so jaded . . . too lovely to harbor such anger . . . too beautiful to spend the rest of your life loathing the opposite sex." He smiled. "We're not all bad, you know. One of these days, I think, you will meet your match."

This time, Eva's laughter was genuine. "My match does not exist," she scoffed, and got to her feet.

Franklin only shook his head and saw her to the door. Moments later, she was in a cab and on her way home to the fashionable apartments where she had lived ever since Jacques—may he rot in hell—had died and left her with a fortune won largely through bribery, embezzlement, and greed. Directing a servant to fetch her trunk, Eva let herself in and, with a sigh, settled down on the divan, a glass of wine in her hand, as she contemplated the events of the past two days.

"Lucien de Montforte."

There, she'd said it.

And he had not materialized from out of the shadows like some phantom mist.

Another swallow of wine gave her the courage to follow her imagination—and yes, the memory, so fresh in her mind, of their recent encounter. Here, in the privacy of her apartments, she could let her mind's eye wander over that splendid body once more, remembering how magnificent he had looked when he'd entered his apartments—only to find her waiting in his bed like some poisonous scorpion. Even now, a thrill seized her blood and she shuddered, wishing it away, fearing its implications.

But it did not go away.

Just the thought of Blackheath was enough to make her nipples tingle and her blood to flush with heat.

"Damnation." She should be able to flick Blackheath from her mind as easily as she might a fly from her horse's neck. What was the problem here? Impossible that any man could hold her thoughts, let alone her interest, when she thought so little of the entire lot of them. Ridiculous that she now regretted not taking Blackheath up on his heady invitation.

His compelling command . . .

Seduce me.

Without warning, her skin went hot. Her mouth, dry. Again she saw that ruthless face with its watchful, magnetic eyes. Again she felt that hard body against hers, skin to skin, hearts pounding against each other in a silent, angry battle of wills. Eva shut her eyes, trying to control her sudden trembling. Perhaps Franklin

was right. Maybe she *should* have seduced Blackheath . . . after all, when was the last time she'd had a
man such as he? The last time she'd had a man at all?

Not since I found Jacques in bed with my maid.

Her blood ran cold. Her fingers clenched and the
wine went to acid in her mouth. Men. Why even let
herself think that Blackheath was any different from
the rest? They were all alike, every last damned one of
them. She had learned *that* lesson at her mother's
knee, all those years ago. . . .

Her mother, cold and moldering in her grave.

She was stronger than that.

She always had been.

Her face hard, Eva hurled the half-finished glass
into the fireplace and sat back, staring out into the
darkness beyond the window.

Lady Nerissa de Montforte was at her desk answering her correspondence when she heard the sound of
an approaching horse.

She put the quill down, rose, and hurried to the
window. It was a gray morning, the sky so low she felt
she could reach up and stir those heavy gray clouds
with her finger. Sure enough, a rider was just galloping
up to the castle. She watched as, his face grave and his
boots spattered with mud, he leaped off his sturdy
black cob and strode toward the doors.

A chill pervaded Nerissa's bones. Shuddering, she
hugged herself and went to stand before the fire, trying to banish a sudden, inexplicable sense of dread.
Something has happened to one of my brothers. Her heart
began to pound. *Oh, dear God, something had happened.*

Picking up her skirts, she left the salon and made her way toward Lucien's domain, trying not to break into a dead run.

The library doors were shut. Behind them, she could hear voices, and then the doors opened and a footman was showing the messenger out.

Nerissa cast a momentary glance toward her brother. Lucien was seated at his desk, his face totally without expression, his eyes as black, as bleak as she had ever seen them. And then he shifted his gaze and saw her, and that moment of naked horror she had glimpsed in his eyes was gone, to be replaced by his habitual mask of unflappable calm.

She hurried forward as he rose.

"Oh, Lucien . . . what is it?"

He looked at her for a moment, and then took a deep breath. "Sit down, my dear."

But Nerissa did not want to sit down. Not if something had happened to someone she loved, not if she was about to hear news that might forever alter the course of her life. *Oh, please God, let time stop here, in this very moment, when everyone I know and love is still alive and well; do not let time march on because I simply cannot bear to see what the next moment will bring.*

But no. She was a de Montforte, brave and strong. She shook her head and met his direct stare, noticing for the first time that his face was unnaturally pale. Almost haunted.

He offered her a glass of brandy. "It's Perry," he said quietly.

Nerissa's hand froze in the act of accepting the glass, and it fell from her nerveless fingers, crashing to the floor. She stared numbly at her brother, her body going cold all over.

"The ship on which he took passage to Spain was attacked by an American privateer just off the coast of France," the duke continued in an odd, toneless voice. "The captain gave a good account of himself, but he was outgunned. The ship went down and what survivors remained were picked up by the Americans and brought into a French port."

"Dear God," Nerissa choked, her steepled hands going to her mouth. "Perry—is he—is he—"

"We don't know. His name was not listed amongst the survivors."

Nerissa stepped back, her knees trembling. She looked at her brother and shook her head, unable to speak, unable to think, unable to accept what he had just told her.

"I am sorry, my dear. I will do all in my power to learn his fate. If he is alive, rest assured that I will find him and bring him back to England for you. If he is not . . ."

Nerissa felt the blood draining from her cheeks, and now a myriad of black spots danced before her eyes as the full impact of Lucien's words slammed into her heart. Perry. Her dear Perry with whom she had quarreled, cut to pieces by a cannonball, shot to death by a musket . . . drowned—

Lucien caught her as she collapsed. He stood for a long moment, holding his little sister close to his heart and staring into the flickering orange flames. He heard the messenger galloping off. Heard the rain, now beginning to fleck the window outside.

And heard Fox's words echoing in his head:

For the love of God, Lucien, one of these days you'll go too far and your scheming machinations will come back to haunt you. . . .

He took a deep breath, unable to admit that this time he had, indeed, gone too far.

One thing was certain. Nerissa must never learn that he had engineered Perry's departure, had bought the estate in Spain that Perry had supposedly inherited. He shut his eyes. *God and the devil, she must never know what I have done or she will loath me forever.*

There was no time to waste. His sister in his arms, he strode from the room, already calling for his servants. "Phelps, lay out traveling clothes and send word to the stables to prepare my coach. I am going to Paris."

Chapter 5

"A toast, ladies and gentlemen! To the brave General Washington!"

"To the brave General Washington!"

All around the glittering Parisian ballroom, glasses were raised. Eva de la Mouriére, standing beside Dr. Franklin and several of the American dignitaries, smiled, tipped her own glass, and downed the champagne.

"Now the French will have no choice but to sit up and take notice," Franklin predicted. "Burgoyne's surrender, Washington's attack on the British army at Germantown ... Pray God, it won't be long now before we've got France into this war, my friends!"

He turned to Eva. "Here comes General Lavisson; bend his ear, if you will, about our victory ... he is close to the king, so turn all of your charm on him." He watched the general approaching from across the crowded floor. "Have you given the potion into the queen's keeping?"

"I will see her on Saturday."

"Good. Now here's Lavisson. Every man in this room is chomping at the bit to dance with you, my dear. . . . Go, make them all envious of our hopelessly besotted general."

Lavisson bowed low over Eva's hand. "*Madame*," he murmured, letting his gaze sweep her face, "you are a vision. Will you honor a poor soldier with a dance?"

"It would be my pleasure," Eva purred, offering her gloved hand.

He drew her out onto the floor. Lavisson was a stocky man, packed with muscle, possessing a raptor's pale blue eyes and a hooked nose. He looked very French.

"I must congratulate you Americans on your capture of Burgoyne," he said gallantly. "Such feats are enough to warrant a second look at ze fighting prowess of your countrymen."

"Ah, well, we are used to dealing with the frontier, with Indians, with all sorts of dangers," Eva said airily. "I'm sure we can handle a few pompous Britons." She smiled, aware that he was trying hard to unglue his gaze from her bosom, swelling in high, creamy glory just inches from his nose.

"I hate ze British. Zey are vain and arrogant, boastful and proud. Why God put zem across the Channel from us is a joke only He must enjoy—"

He broke off as a low murmur swept through the room. A sudden chill snaked up Eva's back and, instinctively sensing danger, she stiffened and looked up, missing a step and nearly tripping over Lavisson's shoe. He caught her in time to keep her from falling, but Eva, eyes narrowing, was already scanning the ballroom. All around, others had also gone quiet, and heads were turning toward the great double doors of the entrance. The music stopped. A hushed murmur rippled like a current through the swell as people craned their necks, trying to see who had elicited such a widespread and universal reaction.

A man stood by the door, exquisite in fitted indigo velvet, a good head taller than those who surrounded him. And then Eva saw his face.

Stark cheekbones. Penetrating black eyes. A cold stare that was focused entirely on *her.*

"Le Duc de Blackheath!"

Eva's heart stopped. Her mouth sagged open, involuntary ripples of excitement quickened her blood, and she stared in disbelief. What was *he* doing here? Why was he in France? Had he purposely sought her out, come to take his vengeance for destroying the potion?

Had he learned that she'd stolen the genuine one after all?

Dear God.

Her heart started up again. And began to beat too fast.

"Well, *madame*, as I was saying, ze British are an arrogant race. . . . Why, only an Englishman would have ze audacity to come to a ball celebrating a victory against his own people. Only an Englishman would dare show himself at a party given by ze enemy. Only an Englishman . . ."

But Eva had forgotten Lavisson. The room was suddenly stifling, the oppressive heat and odors of too many bodies, too much perfume, too many candles—

and now, not enough air—suddenly making her feel faint. And there was Blackheath, coming through the stunned crowd, nodding to an acquaintance here, bowing to a lady there, ignoring the stares and whispers that followed in his wake as he headed straight across the ballroom with a single-minded, unerring purpose.

Toward *her.*

Eva's pulse began to hammer against the string of diamonds that now choked her throat. She pulled away from Lavisson and glanced about for the most expedient means of escape.

But there *was* no escape. She was trapped. All she could do was raise her head, adopt the haughtiest expression she could muster, and try to retain the upper hand she had won the last time they had met.

"Eva de la Mouriére," the duke murmured in that smooth-as-cognac voice she remembered so well. Up close, his eyes were bottomless pits of black fire. There was no feeling in them, just an icy, deadly heat that both chilled and burned her. He gave Lavisson an imperious look that made the Frenchman's nostrils quiver with indignation, took Eva's hand, and bowing deeply over it, forced her away from the general and back onto the dance floor as the musicians struck up a waltz.

"In case you didn't notice, I was *occupied* with General Lavisson," Eva gritted, strangely excited by Blackheath's brazen display of courage—and infuriated by his single-minded display of possession. She was keenly aware of the hard, honed body against which she was pressed. Held. Trapped. God help her, what would Franklin think? What would the other Americans think? What would the *French* think, seeing her consorting with the enemy? "Are all the English as rude as you?"

"On the contrary. I am singularly ruder than most."

"And you've just proved it. I do not recall granting you a dance."

"And I do not recall asking you for one." He smiled down at her, his gaze moving over the white column of her neck, the burgeoning swell of her breasts, in a seductive visual caress that left her flushed and twitchy. "But then, there are some things I simply take without asking."

"Oh, so you think to take me, do you?"

"Madam, I have just done precisely that. Now close your mouth and stop glaring at me. Do you want people to think you're not . . . enjoying our little dance?"

Eva's eyes narrowed and it was all she could do not to slap that severe, perfectly composed face as Blackheath's hand, its elegance emphasized by the expensive lace that draped it, snugged more firmly about her waist. There was no escaping it. No escaping *him*, as he whirled her about the dance floor with dizzying prowess. He held her close. Too close. So close she could feel the heat of his body, feel that smoldering stare burning every inch of skin it touched, feel the raw, barely contained lust emanating from him like fire from the sun. She wanted to get away from it; she wanted to get closer to it. She took deep breaths, devoting all her concentration to keeping up with the steps—and resisting, with everything she had, this strange, terrible effect he had on her.

"You are a most elusive creature, my dear. I spent the better part of that night searching for you. My compliments on such a daring escape." He raked her with a mocking look. "I trust your knees aren't too bruised?"

She gave him her most poisonous smile. "I am sure they're in better health than your thigh. By the way, did you need stitches, Your Grace?"

"I am afraid I did, though as wounds go, it was not exactly life-threatening. Were you deliberately trying to kill me, or merely destroy the aphrodisiac so neither of us could have it?"

"Really, now, Blackheath. Had I been trying to kill you, I can assure you I would have succeeded."

"Ah. So you simply wanted to destroy the potion, then."

Eva's eyes glowed. *Tell him. Oh, tell him, if only to see his shock and fury at being so cleverly outwitted!* And why not? This would be her moment of triumph, the one she would have had to otherwise only imagine after sending him a taunting letter. *Tell him!*

"On the contrary, Your Grace. You see, I didn't destroy the aphrodisiac at all."

"My dear madam, I can assure you, I saw the bottle explode with my own eyes."

"And so did I"—she grinned, buoyed by savage triumph—"but that wasn't the real aphrodisiac."

His smile faded abruptly. "I beg your pardon?"

"Well, I really *did* want you to know that whatever you can do, I can do better. You were so good at fooling us all with that substitute potion, I thought it only fitting that you become reacquainted with it. The substitute, that is. After all, you went through *such* trouble to create it, I thought you might like to have it back."

He impaled her with an icy stare, his eyes glittering

like jet. "Are you trying to tell me that the bottle you shot to pieces contained my original substitute?"

"Dear me, for a man, you certainly *do* show flashes of limited intelligence! That is exactly what I'm saying. After I broke into your chamber—and your safe, I might add—I took the real article, put it in my canvas sack, and offered you the substitute in its place. What a pity that you refused to sample some. It would have forged an intimate liaison between yourself and the chamberpot, you know." His expression went absolutely still. Thunderously black. "And now, if you'll excuse me, the dance is over and I have business to conduct. Good day, Your Grace."

His hand shot out and snared her wrist. "I beg your pardon. I also have business to conduct." His eyes were black as nightshade. "With *you*."

"Unhand me this instant," she commanded, her smile fading.

"Or what? You'll produce a pistol and shoot out my heart? Denounce me as a cad? Oh, no, madam. You look a little . . . pale." He gave a chilling smile. "Some fresh air, I think."

A hand beneath her elbow, he propelled her through the crowd, still smiling at people he knew, inclining his head to his French peers. Everyone was staring. Fans were fluttering wildly, ladies twittering, mouths gaping open at the English duke's outrageous display of possessiveness and insolence. Rage flooded Eva, but she would not satisfy Blackheath by making a scene. Oh, no, she would walk civilly beside him, this frigid smile pasted on her face while every fiber of her being itched to do him serious bodily harm. Itched to humiliate him in a way he would never forget.

Itched to find out what it would be like to bed him.
Stop it!

He was heading straight for the doors. Still gripping her elbow, he steered her past the fringes of the crowd and outside. The night was frosty. Clear, cold moonlight shone through a velvet sky. He let go of her long enough to take off his coat and place it around her shoulders, then, raising a brow, he offered his arm.

As though she had any choice! Trembling with fury, Eva took it.

Silently, he escorted her past a frozen fountain, where icicles dripped from the arms of a stone cherub. Their shoes crunched on frozen gravel, their breaths plumed the air. Tension crackled between them. Tension—and a raw, sexual awareness that Eva was trying her best to ignore.

Trying—and failing.

Blackheath led her some distance from the house, then, to her surprise, he released her.

"Do not leave me until you hear me out."

Confused, Eva stepped back to put some distance between them, drawing his heavy velvet coat about her shoulders. It was warm with the heat of his body. Rich and lusciously expensive against her skin, emanating his own uniquely male scent. She resisted the urge to bury her nose in it.

"I'm listening," she said warily, trying to ignore the pounding of her heart, the feverish tingles of anticipation that were racing across her skin. "What do you want?"

He leveled his flat stare on her. "Your help."

Of all the reasons a virile, dangerous man such as himself might drag a woman out into the night, this was the last one that Eva might have expected. His answer threw her totally off balance. Brought a rush of unexpected disappointment. For a moment, she couldn't respond to such a bald plea, and had to quell a burst of laughter. Why, the idea of this arrogant, manipulative monster asking for *help* of all things was almost ludicrous.

"My help," she scoffed, with an arch, pitying look. "Well, Blackheath, you've certainly found the last person on earth willing to give it to you."

"I am sure that for a price, you will give me anything."

"Some things cannot be bought."

"No, some things can only be given," he said coldly. "I know you would have me believe you're a hard-hearted witch, but, as tempting as the thought is, I am not totally convinced of it."

She smiled sweetly. "No? After what I did to your brothers? After what I nearly did to you? How much more convincing must I be?"

"Help me and I will consider your offenses against my family forgiven. It is for their sake, not mine, that I have sought you out."

Eva raised a brow.

He moved a little distance away, no doubt trying to rein in the natural enmity he must certainly feel for her. She could almost see him collecting himself. Retreating behind that impeccably aristocratic mask that would remain in place no matter what emotions, what thoughts, boiled behind it. But no. She was mistaken. In the silent majesty of the night, his eyes were darker than the deepest water of the ocean, and for a moment, just a moment, he allowed her to see the haunting anguish in their depths, the pain she didn't think he was capable of feeling.

Something in her softened, responding to that naked revelation; he was human, then, after all.

Imagine.

"I have a sister," he continued, gazing out into the night. His back was toward her, rising in splendid magnificence from his lean torso, crowned with powerful shoulders of a breadth that was nothing short of . . . mesmerizing. She feasted her eyes on that back, on those shoulders, even as she cursed herself for taking such a liberty. "Her name is Nerissa. She means more to me than anything on God's earth."

Eva said nothing, merely watched him.

"She is young and romantic, and hopelessly in love with a fellow who has no wish to settle down and get on with the responsibilities of his birthright." He turned and, offering his arm once more, began to walk. *You must be freezing*, Eva thought. He had only a sleeveless waistcoat to ward off the cold. But the Duke of Blackheath's iron control was such that he would never shiver, let his teeth chatter, or even allow a tremor to mar his urbane voice. "A fortnight ago, this beau of hers—the Earl of Brookhampton—was . . . sent to Spain aboard the English ship, *Sarah Rose*. Just off the coast of France, the vessel was attacked and sunk by an American privateer."

Eva felt herself softening, a dangerous thing. It scared her—so she reacted as she always did when threatened.

With sarcastic hostility.

"Ah, yes," she drawled. "I do recall hearing of that particular triumph on my country's part."

A muscle tightened in the duke's jaw, but he would not allow himself to be goaded. "Lord Brookhampton was amongst those feared lost when the ship went down. My sister is inconsolable."

"Why was Brookhampton sent to Spain?"

Blackheath's face closed up. "That is of no importance. The only thing that matters is finding him and bringing him safely back to England."

"Well, I'll ask the fish and crabs off Calais, then, if they happen to remember eating him."

This time, the duke could not rein in his anger. He turned on her, his eyes so dark and savage that Eva involuntarily took a step back. "That was crass and uncalled-for. We are talking about a human life here."

"We are talking about an Englishman who'd just as soon see Americans slaughtered, starved, and beaten into submission."

"If you believe that, then you are a fool," he said coldly. "There are those in Parliament, and throughout England, who are friends of America. Men like Pitt and Burke, who wish to see this war at an end, who oppose George's American policy, who are willing to meet your countrymens' demands."

"And are you one of them?" she asked, her tone poisonously sweet.

His eyes had never seemed so black. "Two of my sisters-in-law are American. My brother Charles—the one *you* struck down—served with the army in Boston, where he gained both an understanding of the American people and sympathy for their plight. He owes his life to their benevolence. Yes, madam, I can assure you that I am *one of them*, and the sooner there's an end to this damnable conflict, the happier I shall be."

Eva looked away, suddenly regretting her caustic words. Humility was a bitter pill to swallow. "So what do you want from me?"

"Your help in finding out what happened to Lord Brookhampton."

She shrugged. "I don't know how much help I can be. If the reports say he went down with the ship, that's probably exactly what happened."

"Reports can be falsified. Perry might have used a different name to escape detection. He might have been injured, taken in as a hostage. . . . Any number of things might have occurred. I will not be satisfied until I have the truth."

"Isn't that something you can find yourself?"

"As you so quickly reminded me, madam, I am English—not exactly a friend of the French, and soon to be an enemy, if you Yankees get your way." Inwardly Eva winced, though she was aware the English, thanks to their own spies, knew exactly what the Americans had been up to. "You, on the other hand, can move quite comfortably within the higher echelons of French society. I want you to find out if Perry survived. If he did, I want you to learn where he is imprisoned." His jaw tightened and he looked away, his voice harsh. "I want you to help me give my sister her life back."

I want you to help me give my sister her life back.

Nothing he might have said could have swayed her more. Blackheath had said she was young, romantic, and in love. Eva remembered what it had been like to be young, romantic, and in love. She remembered it with a bitter pang that still hurt after all these years, causing the back of her throat to ache with the pain of betrayal, the loss of innocence, the death of dreams. She had no desire whatsoever to help the duke, of course. But his sister . . .

She gave a deep sigh. "I will do what I can, Blackheath. But not for you. For your sister."

"Despite the fact you've never met her?"

"It doesn't matter. She's a woman. She hurts. I sympathize with her pain."

"You think men do not hurt?"

"I *know* men do not hurt. How can they? They do not have hearts, which is why they take such delight in breaking ours."

He studied her for a long moment, and Eva had the uncanny sensation he could see right into her soul and all its long-buried, deeply guarded secrets. She shivered. With awe. With nervousness.

And with unspoken longing.

"Are you cold?"

"Yes," she lied.

"I will remedy that," he said.

And, pulling her into his arms, he kissed her.

Chapter 6

The night was frigid, the air as brittle as glass, but when Blackheath's lips came down on hers, Eva felt nothing but a searing, sweeping warmth.

His hands slipped beneath the velvet coat and down, cupping her figure, the thumbs grazing her silk-clad breasts, the palms following her rib cage, snugging into the curve of her waist and out over her hips, her bottom. He pulled her close, right up against the unforgivably hard wall of his body, trapping her there even as his mouth covered hers. Eva had no desire to reclaim the space he had stolen. She spread her palms against his chest, feeling the taut, coiled muscle just beneath, the steady beat of his heart. How delicious it was to be in such powerful arms! How dangerously heady, this unexpected abandonment of her senses, her convictions! She forgot her anger; forgot regret, indignation, outrage. There was only his mouth against hers, demanding and impatient, cool and hard and wonderful.

And now his tongue, tracing the swell of her lower lip, painting it with warm, tingling heat. With a sigh of defeat, she opened to him. Clung to him. Let him touch and taste and explore even as she returned the intimate caress. Her blood caught on fire, engulfing her in flames, a heretic burning at the stake.

There was no denying it. She wanted him. God help her, she wanted him, and if she was any sort of a woman she would have him—on her terms, of course, not his, never his—and she would have him tonight. It was a seductive thought. A delicious thought. One that flared to life on the kindling of her own rising desire. . . .

His hands pressed against the small of her back now, molding her, holding her, drawing her right up against the rock-hard length of him, pelvis to pelvis, until her head tipped back under the onslaught of his kiss. Her arms came up to encircle his neck, the heavy velvet coat now sliding from her shoulders, tumbling off her back, and landing in a crumpled heap at her feet. But she never felt the cold. There was only his lips against hers, his breath mingling with her own, her hands roving across his shirt and tracing the fascinating interplay of muscle, ribs, and hard, flat abdomen just beneath the fine lawn.

Eva pulled back, resting her hot forehead against his chest and breathing hard.

"If you do that again I shall have to kill you," she said without conviction, trying to catch her breath as she stared somewhat dazedly down at their feet.

"And you think that threat will deter me?"

"You know I feel nothing for you."

"Then you are a magnificent actress."

"I loath you. I've loathed you ever since I found that you were the one who was sabotaging our spying efforts here in France. . . . The matter of the aphrodisiac was just the icing on the cake."

"Hmm, yes . . ." His hand, so warm despite the night air, stroked her nape, his thumb caressing the sensitive skin just behind her ear. "I wish I could make the same denial, but I fear I've been fascinated with you from the moment I first saw you, when your cousin brought you to my brother's wedding."

"Lust, nothing more. Ignore it and it will go away."

"I have tried to ignore it. It has not gone away."

"Find another woman, then."

"I don't want another woman." His voice dropped to a husky murmur, and she felt his breath against the side of her neck. His lips. The whisper of a kiss—dark, forbidden, dangerous. "I want *you*."

Hot tremors shook her body. He could break her heart. Take it apart, stomp on it, and walk away without a backward glance. Fear almost paralyzed her—but Eva had no use for fear. If this was frightening her, it was all the more reason to confront it head-on.

"What do you say, my lady? You are an adult, a widow, no blushing innocent who's ignorant of what she'll find in a man's bed. And unless I'm mistaken, you're as eager as I am to finish what we already started in mine. But I'm not usually mistaken, Eva. Let me prove to you that men can be very . . . *interesting*, indeed."

Her knees began to weaken. "I have . . . work to do at the ball."

"You have work to do for me. But pleasure before business, no?"

He took her arm. Fear and wanting warred within her. The night pressed in around her, icing her skin, trying to freeze her blood, but Blackheath had ignited something that was burning her from the inside out and could only be satisfied in one way, and one way only.

And then a sudden idea occurred to her. A wicked idea, so totally perfect for the occasion, so totally in line with her own plans, that she could barely contain her triumph.

Her relief.

"Very well, then, Blackheath," she murmured, looking up into his shadowy face. "I'm no champion of the male gender, but I'm willing to give you a chance to change my mind about it. You and I will return to my rooms, but"—she narrowed her eyes—"it will be on *my* terms."

"And they are?"

"Complete domination."

Up went one black, arching brow. "Dear me, this night promises more excitement than I'd originally thought. . . ."

"And I'm telling you right now that if you disappoint me in any way, I swear I'll kill you."

"In that case, I promise to do all in my power to leave you completely . . ."—his lips curved in a slow, dangerous smile—"satisfied."

They returned—individually—to the ball and, pleading a headache, Eva excused herself and left the great noisy chamber.

She had seen Franklin eyeing her with raised brows, obviously not fooled by her excuse. He had seen her with Blackheath. He was certainly wondering why she was consorting with the enemy. But Eva had a plan, and Blackheath would be the perfect man on whom to carry it out.

He was waiting for her, as promised, at the foot of the great stairway that led to the guest rooms on the mansion's upper floors. It was quiet here; not even a servant was about.

"Last chance to change your mind," he murmured, with a challenging little smile that said he knew she would not.

Eva took his offered arm. "I am not such a coward as all that. Though you'd like everyone to think you're the devil incarnate, I am most assuredly not afraid of the big bad wolf."

"Really, now? Then why, might I ask, are you trembling?"

She gave a flippant little laugh to cover her nervousness. "Anticipation."

He only smiled, a thin, knowing smile that made her insides twist in a knot. So, she'd lied. A bit. She *was* afraid of the big bad wolf, because wolves were perfectly capable of tearing out your heart and eating it. And Eva was all too aware that her heart, which had been feasted on before, was dangerously close to finding itself on an offered platter.

Stay calm! YOU are in control. He has consented that you will be in control! You have nothing to fear, as long as you don't start imagining he's something he's not, as long as you don't start dreaming little-girl dreams about him, as long

as you don't start deluding yourself that he's any different
from the rest of his abhorrent gender. . . .

She raised her head, haughty, flirtatious, in command once more. Yes, she was in control. She just had to convince herself of the fact. They reached the top of the stairs, and, her heart pounding, Eva led the way to her room. The closed door looked ominous. And exciting. What would lay beyond that door tonight?

She turned then and faced her companion with a hard stare. "Let me remind you, Blackheath. This is on *my* terms."

"Ah, yes." His smile gleamed. "Complete domination."

"And remember, I am perfectly capable of killing you if you deceive me in any way."

"I know you are, my dear. It is one of many reasons why I find myself so fascinated by you." He reached out and placed his palm against the door just behind her ear, effectively trapping her between his arm and dark, ruthless face. His voice dropped to a seductive whisper. "You see, I *adore* dangerous women."

Eva tensed, her heart beginning to race. "You may not adore them so much if one decides to kill you."

"Ah, yes. Kill me. That is a threat you seem to revisit quite often, madam. Perhaps, before this night is over, you will convince me of how . . ."—he smiled—"dangerous you really are."

She gave him a level stare. "I would be most happy to."

He merely laughed, and Eva felt a brief stab of fury that he would dismiss her so lightly. But then, he had done much the same when she'd broken into his apartments back at the castle, blatantly turning his back on her when she held a gun on him, as if to prove that he did not take her as seriously as she did herself.

But then, that's one of the reasons you're so fascinated by him, isn't it? Because he respects but not fears you, as so many other men do. Because he is totally unfazed by the fact that you could so easily kill him. You enjoy his courage. You have met your match, Eva.

And she would best her match. She would.

She merely smiled at him and glanced pointedly at his arm. It was still blocking her way. After a deliberate pause, he finally removed it. Eva pushed open the door. A fire burned in the hearth, and a candle stood on a lowboy with curved, spindly legs in the French fashion, its light casting a warm orange glow over the lacquered wood, across the fine Turkish carpet on the floor, and bringing out the lights and shadows from the heavy drapes at the windows and around the bed.

"Have you no maid?" Blackheath asked, raising a brow.

"I gave her the night off. It took her hours to prepare me for the evening. She deserved no less."

He was standing just behind her. She could feel his heat. His hunger. He was very close, and though Eva was a tall woman, he somehow managed to make her feel quite diminutive indeed. She resisted the urge to shudder. She must be mad to be doing this. Mad to let the Duke of Blackheath into her bedroom. Into her life. But she was doing this for her country. And there were far less agreeable things she could do than inviting one of the deadliest men in England into her bed.

Detachment. It was the only way to both enjoy Blackheath's body and keep her own heart safely locked up where he could never reach it. Detachment. It was the only way that she'd be able to keep from fantasizing that he was something he was not, to keep from imagining things that could never be, to keep from dreaming of something that would never happen.

Detachment.

And then he was kissing her, and she knew she was fighting a losing battle, for there was no way anyone could detach from *this*.

His hands, so broad, skillful, and warm, cradled her jaw, her cheeks, tilting her head up to his. She lost herself to the kiss. Her senses began to swim, and from some distant part of herself, she felt pressure behind her legs. A moment later he had swept her up in his arms, her feet dangling, as he carried her effortlessly toward the bed.

Somewhat breathless, Eva struggled to reclaim control. "*My* terms, Blackheath."

"But of course."

"So put me down."

He smiled.

"Put me down, *now*."

With a sigh, he did so, then stood eyeing her with a lazy, confident smile that made no promises whatsoever.

And yet, made all the promises in the world.

"Undress me," she said.

He raised a brow, clearly fascinated, despite himself.

"You men are always the ones to indulge us in your sexual fantasies. Well, tonight you will be indulged in mine."

"I *do* like the sound of that," he murmured, deeply amused. "I daresay I will enjoy your little . . . indulgences, Eva."

"I can assure you, you will."

She stood quite still, barely daring to breathe as he approached. He came right up to her, until he stood so close that she could feel the heat radiating from his body, hear the breath moving through his lungs, feel it stirring the tendrils of hair at her temples. He let his fingers graze her cheek; unflinchingly, she met his gaze. He pulled a pin from her hair. Another. And yet another. A thick, powdered tress tumbled to Eva's shoulder, then down her back.

Another.

She shut her eyes, her nerves on fire, her knees so weak she feared they would give out beneath her. She heard the thin tinkle of pins hitting the floor. Shivered as Blackheath's fingers brushed the delicate shell of her ear, the nape of her neck . . . the line of her jaw. More hair tumbled down. The horsehair pads atop which her coiffure had been piled fell out. Eva stood before him, heavy masses of hair, stiff with powder, spilling down her back.

He reached for her—

But no, not yet. She mustered a coy smile, then walked a little distance away; there, she shook the powder from her hair until it was its natural, vibrant red once more, glowing like claret in the light of the fire.

And then she faced him.

Assessed him.

Made a brief circle around him, letting her fingertips trail around his waist as she moved behind him.

He was smiling now. Eyeing her like some lethal, barely restrained predator.

"Are you hard for me yet, Blackheath?" she purred, lifting her lips to his ear.

"I have been hard for you for the past two weeks."

"And what if I disappoint *you*, Your Grace?" Deftly, she unbuckled his dress sword and let it drop to the carpet. "Will you kill *me*?"

"I do not think you will disappoint."

She smiled. He didn't move. Her hand drifted back up, unbuttoning his velvet waistcoat, peeling it away from his chest until she could feel the muscles just beneath his shirt. A blood-red ruby was pinned to his stock. Eva removed it and placed it on the lowboy. She pinched one end of the silky cravat between thumb and fingertip and pulled, slowly, until the knot collapsed and the long strip of fabric was in her hand.

"I thought you wanted *me* to undress *you*," he murmured, an amused smile dancing about his lips.

"I do. But I am the one in control here—and right now, I prefer to undress you."

She pulled off his waistcoat, let it fall to the floor. He stood before her in shirt and breeches now, the rich lace of the former tumbling over the backs of the finest, most beautifully male hands she had ever had the pleasure of looking upon. There was breadth across the palms, and a lengthy elegance to the fingers that proclaimed the finest breeding in England, generations of bluest blood—perfection. They were a gentleman's hands, though there was nothing soft about them, nothing foppish, and certainly nothing benign. Eva knew those hands had killed; most recently, they had taken the life of her odious stepcousin, Gerald, when Gerald had tried to kill the duke's brother, Andrew. She was not fooled into thinking they were anything less than dangerous. . . .

And she wanted those hands on her. All over her. But not just yet. For now, she wanted to be the one doing the touching.

And so she walked another circle around him, this time her fingers tracing his ribs beneath the fine shirt, trailing around his hip, and finally coming to rest in the faint curve of his lower back, just above the waistband of his breeches. She stood just behind him, admiring the lean, beautifully inverted triangle of that proud, splendid back—then she grasped his shirt at the waist, pulled it free of his waistband, and let it drop, its hem coming down, as was the fashion, almost to his knees.

"Will you not take it off?"

She smiled. "I wouldn't want you to be cold. It might have a disastrous effect on your . . . condition."

"I can assure you, madam, that my condition is quite a *hard*y one. And I am far from cold."

"Then step out of your shoes."

He inclined his head and, giving her a sidelong glance from over his shoulder, did as she asked.

"Unbutton your cuffs."

He did.

"And stand still."

She came around in front of him, never removing her hand from his body, letting it draw a slow, seductive line from hip to the front of his hard, muscled thigh. He gazed down at her, a watchful predator, his eyes very, very black beneath heavy lids. Eva met that heated stare, letting her hand rest right where it was. He gave a slow smile of invitation—and moving her hand, Eva let her fingernail graze his thigh through the thin veneer of his breeches, exulting in the control he had granted her. She wondered what he would ask in return. Or better yet, what he would *give* in return. . . .

Her fingers found the buttons of his drop front, and one by one, she slid them through the holes.

She looked up into his face. The lazy smile had faded, and in its place was something darker, something more intense; something far, far more dangerous.

Eva undid the last button, and the breeches slid down his thighs and around his knees. Immediately the long hem of the shirt floated down to preserve his maleness from her triumphant gaze; Eva looked up, stared into those black, black eyes for a long moment, and then ran her hand over the rigid bulge beneath the shirt.

She was unprepared. For the fierceness of his arousal, for the size of it, for the shock waves that simple touch flung through her own body. Prickly heat suffused her. It was all she could do not to throw him to the carpet and have her way with him right then and there; but no, she was surely more civilized than that.

He smiled, noting her momentary confusion. "If you are trying to torture me, madam, you are doing a damned fine job of it."

Big, bad wolf, indeed, she thought shakily—but managed to muster her most feline smile. "Perhaps some wine will take the edge off your impatience?" She palmed him through the shirt, seeing his nostrils flare, his eyes growing fixed and dark and deadly. "After all, you still have to undress me."

"I am within inches of taking you right here, right now."

"Do so and I'll—"

"Kill me?" he murmured, lips twitching.

"Something like that." She let her fingers fall away from him. Then, casting an inviting smile over her shoulder, she went to her dressing table, where bottles of perfume, jars of cosmetics, pots, brushes, and boxes were arranged around a vase of flowers. A bottle of champagne stood nearby, nestled in a bucket of ice. Eva uncorked it, poured two glasses, and brought them both back to the duke.

She kicked off one slipper and handed him a glass. She hooked a toe around the other, kicked it off as well, and raised her own glass to her lips.

"A toast," she murmured, eyeing him from over the rim. "To . . . peace."

His dark gaze held hers. "To peace," he echoed, leaving her wondering whether they drank to peace between the two of them—or to his country and hers.

She put the glass down. "And now you may undress me."

For answer, he merely gave a dangerous smile, set down his half-finished champagne, and with a skill that unnerved her, went to work on her own clothes.

She shivered as he unclasped the choker of diamonds, his warm fingers grazing her neck, caressing the sensitive flesh as the heavy metal setting dropped away. It was soon apparent—more than apparent—that he knew his way around a lady's gown better than her own maid did, deftly unhooking an eye there, untying a tape there, his fingers making short work of buttons, ties, and fastenings. Off came her beautiful gown of dark raspberry velvet, off came the stomacher of rich rose satin, the lightly laced stays, the petticoats belling out over her hoops, until she stood before him, her skin pocked with gooseflesh, in just her chemise, garters, and stockings.

She was burning up inside.

Absolutely on fire.

And then he reached out and pulled her close, his hands molding her waist, pressing firmly against the small of her back, holding her hard against him. She felt his arousal driving against her hips, her pelvis, protected by nothing more than the flimsy lawn of his shirt . . . and the even flimsier fabric of her chemise.

Two layers of cloth. It was all that separated them.

Eva moaned as his mouth slanted down atop hers. She fought wildly for balance—between her heart, which demanded absolute abandonment, and her head, which demanded absolute detachment so she could do what must be done. She was quickly losing control of this situation . . . and that frightened her.

She pulled back, holding on to the threads of sanity. "I—I'm nervous. I need more champagne. Can I offer you more, Blackheath?"

"By all means."

He handed her his glass. Eva set them both down, then, regaining her poise, eyed him speculatively. "I think I need you to lie down on the bed."

"We'll get there eventually."

"I need you to get there now."

"Ah." He gave her that slow, spreading smile. "Let me guess. This is where the . . . domination comes in?"

"How astute you are."

"Very well, then." He moved to the bed and sat upon it, removing his own stockings and revealing the handsomest, most powerful calves she had ever seen. Dark hair peppered his legs in a sparse mat; muscles stood out in wondrous relief, inviting the touch of a finger. A tongue. Ohhhh, Lord help her!

"And now, my dear?"

"Lie back. I need to tie you up."

He laughed. "Tie me up? What, do you think I plan to go anywhere?"

"It is part of my fantasy. You know me to be a dominant woman. I know you to be a dominant man. My fantasy demands that I master you, and master you completely. So therefore, I must tie you up."

"I suppose it will be nothing short of interesting," he murmured, amused.

"Perhaps you will even find it exciting."

"I would very much like to touch you, Eva."

"Oh, I'll set you free after the first round." She smiled. "And I wouldn't tie you up so tightly that you couldn't have *some* movement."

He lay back on the pillows, raised his arms over his head, and regarded her with dark, watchful eyes that glowed with amusement. Was he intrigued? Probably. Was he apprehensive? Probably not, for he was arrogant enough to assume he could overpower her at any moment, escape no matter what binds held him. He was indulging her, nothing more. Finding some sort of strange satisfaction of his own, thinking that he was allowing a woman to be in control. *Allowing.* Oh, what a surprise she had for him!

Remembering the champagne, she carried the glasses back to her dressing table, opened one of her perfume bottles, and dabbed a bit of scent behind her ears. As she replaced the stopper, she clandestinely tapped the few drops still poised there into one of the two glasses; then she refilled them both with champagne, brought them back to the curtained bed, and set them down on the night table. The duke lay on his back watching her, his knees bent; the shirt had slid down his thighs, rumpling atop his abdomen. She could see just the barest hint of dark hair and male flesh beneath the hem. It was just enough to tease. To tantalize.

Her mouth went dry.

"If you're afraid, Blackheath, we don't have to do this," she taunted, her voice a little shaky.

"Perhaps I am not the one who's afraid."

"You think *I* am?"

"You tell me."

She tossed her head. "Ha, if I *was* afraid, I would most assuredly not tell you. Besides, you'll be tied up. Perfectly harmless."

He smiled, a slow, chilling smile that caused her insides to seize. "Perfectly harmless."

"Totally incapable of doing anything I don't want you to do."

"Whatever you say, my dear."

She handed him the glass into which she'd tapped

the few drops of perfume. She raised her own. They faced each other, two wary adversaries, over the crystal rims.

Enigmatic black eyes met glittering ones of green.

"To an enjoyable evening, then."

"An enjoyable evening. . . ."

Chapter 7

Crystal clinked, and she allowed him to drain his glass before picking up the cravat she had discarded. Loosely looping it around his wrists, she tied them in a figure eight before securing them to the bedpost above his head.

He smiled up at her, a chained wolf.

A chained wolf who was very much looking forward to eating her after she was through stroking him.

Eva's stomach was in knots. She didn't know how long she had before the aphrodisiac took effect. She shuddered inside, sitting down on the edge of the bed and affecting a satisfied, amused smile as she gazed down at her willingly helpless captive. God help her, she wasn't even sure she could go through with the act; she wanted only to see how effective the potion really was, before passing it on to Marie Antoinette, wanted only to restrain Blackheath so he couldn't leap up and ravish her, wanted only to test it on this cunning devil while minimizing the dangers to her own heart—and body. How long would he suffer before its effects finally wore off? Or would he suffer until whatever savage lust he experienced was finally slaked?

"You do not drink much," he murmured, noting her half-full glass. "Champagne not to your liking?"

"Oh, no, that's not it at all, Blackheath. I want to be totally alert, totally aware, so that I can experience whatever is about to transpire with none of my senses dulled."

"I see," he said, pushing himself upward a little, so that he was more comfortable against the stack of pillows behind him. Furtively, Eva glanced down. Though the shirt preserved his modesty, she had no doubt that he was fully aroused; but was he even *more* aroused?

"I also have a family intolerance to alcohol," she added, jumping as a spark exploded in the hearth. "My mother died from overindulgence."

Well, that wasn't completely true; she had died of a broken heart, and only used the alcohol as a spiritual anesthetic on the way to killing herself with it.

"I am sorry to hear that," he murmured, his eyes taking on a strange gleam and fixating on her with the unwavering concentration of a predator. She saw muscles beginning to bulge in his arms; rigid triceps, taut biceps, strained, defined tendons in the forearms. "My own mother died in childbirth. It is difficult to lose someone you love."

"You never forget, do you?"

His jaw was tensing up. She could see the very controlled way he was breathing, as though each inhalation might shatter him. "No. You do not." He had his teeth clenched now. "Especially when you lose two parents within the same week."

"Then I am sorry for *you*," she said. "What happened?"

"Mother was in childbirth with Nerissa and having a damned hard time of it. . . . Papa couldn't bear to hear her screams of agony. . . ." He shut his eyes, tiny beads of sweat breaking out on his forehead now, his great chest rising and falling laboriously. "He ran up to the tower to get away from the sounds . . . fell, and broke his neck."

"Dear God," Eva said, fingertips touching her mouth.

Blackheath was now straining against the bonds that held him. The cravat was stretched tight; too tight—in danger of tearing. Fear drove through Eva—fear that it would tear, fear that she had poisoned him. That he was in some sort of agony, she did not doubt. "I was the one who . . . found him," he said hoarsely, clenching his fists. "As you say, you . . . never forget."

"Are you all right, Blackheath?"

Black eyes shot open, burning her with their intensity. "I'm in bloody agony for wanting you," he exploded. "Christ, woman, have mercy."

It would be so easy to just leave him here, tied to the bed as she had planned; so easy to just put her clothes back on and return to the ball as though nothing had ever happened, as though everything inside her weren't aching with a reciprocal need. She would have the last laugh; she would deal the final humiliation. But though Eva prided herself on her calculated hardheartedness where men were concerned, even she had more compassion than that . . . and with her enemy safely tied up and on his back, able to pleasure but never to dominate her . . . well, was there really any harm in having her way with him?

She reached out, running her hand down the side of his cheek. His breath was hot and ragged against her fingers, and then she felt his lips, his tongue, against her palm as he turned his face into her hand and began kissing it. Sensation exploded between her legs. Moaning softly, she eased herself up and onto him, straddling his torso just above his arousal, her knees sinking into the mattress on either side of his hips. She drove her hands beneath the hem of his shirt, dragged it up his chest, and allowed herself to feel the muscles, so hard, so powerful, so beautifully, splendidly *male*, bunching and writhing beneath her small white hands.

"Lower," he rasped. "Don't tease—not now."

No question about that aphrodisiac, Eva thought in triumph. She had definitely stolen the right substance this time, and she—and America—would be well rewarded for her efforts.

"I'm not teasing, I . . . have to get ready myself," she said, trying to prolong the inevitable.

"Move up, then, and I'll get you ready."

"Sorry?"

"I said, move up, damn it." His eyes opened, impaling her with their black ferocity. "*Near my face.*"

Had Eva been a maid, she would have blushed as red as her hair. But Blackheath was clearly moving past restraint, past the trappings of a gentleman; he was past the point of caring *what* her reaction was, wanting only relief from whatever agony the potion had put him in. Gingerly, Eva rose to her knees and moved her way up his chest, her thighs spread wide to accommodate its significant breadth, every nerve quivering, every bit of skin shivering, her heart doing a furious *boom-boom-boom* against her sternum and ready to explode any minute.

"I will hurt you," she protested, her knees beneath his armpits now, the cords in his neck standing out in high relief and glistening with sweat in the candlelight.

"You are hurting me more by hesitating. Get up, then, and balance on your knees. I want to taste you, Eva." His eyes blazed into hers; any moment now, his bonds were going to snap and he would be on her like an enraged beast of prey. "I want to possess you. By God, I want *all of you.*"

Eva, washing hot and cold, braced herself against the headboard, raised herself to her knees once more, and thrust her pelvis forward.

Blackheath buried his face in her moist red curls.

Found the top of her hidden slit with his tongue.

"Higher," he ordered, his voice harsh.

She heard herself whimpering in her throat as she complied, arching her back and angling herself toward his seeking mouth—and then his face was totally buried against her, and she felt his hot ragged breath there, his lips, and oh—oh, *God*—the stab of his tongue, expertly priming her before he settled into a controlled, ruthless stroke against her wide-open cleft, her moist folds, that sent her senses careening toward the ceiling.

"Dear God," she gasped, her fingernails gouging into the headboard, her thighs trembling from holding up her weakening body. "Dear God, Blackheath, I never dreamed it could be like this—"

"Dream harder," he snarled, and then his lips, his tongue closed around that engorged but hidden bud, manipulating it, licking it, suckling it—

Eva let out a scream of surprise. Her legs gave out from beneath her as she climaxed, her senses exploding in a million pieces. She all but collapsed atop the very mouth that had brought her to such a shamelessly wanton state, pushing herself back at the last moment so that she landed on his chest. His breath came out with a loud *oomph* and he stared up at her, a man past the point of sanity, his eyes so savage, so intense, that she knew their image would be forever branded in her memory.

She knew what he wanted.

Knew what he craved.

Give it to him.

And then that wounded, perpetually suffering part of her that would never stop demanding vengeance: *Dominate him.*

She moved back, raised herself, and impaled herself on his shaft, gasping as his size stretched and filled her, stretched and filled her past the point that she could painlessly tolerate, pleasurably bear—

She had no time to rethink her decision. His hips were already moving, the hard muscles of his chest and abdomen bunching and glistening with fine sweat. His eyes were savage. Harder and harder he drove, his breath coming fast and harsh now as he drove himself farther and farther inside her with every ruthless thrust. The pain went away and Eva felt only swimming pleasure, a desperate need to take and be taken, to dominate and be dominated, and yes, oh, yes, that wonderful, splinter-apart climax that she could feel rushing down on her once more—

His black gaze impaling hers, he gave a final lunge and sent them both careening out of control. Eva cried out and fell, sobbing with the sweet agony of the experience, against his damp chest, her body still convulsing all around him.

There she lay, her lungs heaving, her hot breath dampening her hair. She had just made love to the Duke of Blackheath.

Had just bedded her enemy.

And at the moment, she damn well didn't care.

Rap rap rap.

Eva, her lips still buried in the hollow of Blackheath's neck, drifted lazily in her dream state. She was a little girl again. Her papa was home from the sea; he had candy for her, a box of spices from Morocco, and tales of grand adventure—

Rap rap rap, harder this time, more persistent.

"Answer the door."

But the voice wasn't Papa's. Eva, confused, moved toward wakefulness. "Madam, answer the door," said the voice again, and with a start, Eva realized that the clipped command had come from just under her ear, and that her ear was resting at the hot junction of a man's neck and collarbone.

Blackheath's.

Remembrance hit her, hard. Her head jerked up in alarm. Wild-eyed, she stared toward the door, knowing that if she was caught in this position she would never be able to face any of her male peers ever again.

"Who is it?"

"Henri, *madame*. I have ze message for you, from Dr. Franklin."

Eva froze.

"Dear me, but your assignations never cease, do they?" murmured the man beneath her.

"Quiet, Blackheath!" She leaped from the bed, grabbed her dressing gown, and, pulling it on as she moved, stalked quickly to the door. She opened it the barest crack, filling it with her body.

"*Je regret, madame,* but Dr. Franklin sent me to fetch you. Said that ze Count de Vergennes eez about to make a speech concerning your American victory, and zat eet would be poor form if *madame* does not make an appearance." The lad bowed, looking sheepish. "*Le monsieur's* words, *madame*. Not mine."

"Of course. Tell Dr. Franklin I will be down in a moment."

Eva slammed the door shut and leaned against it, breathing hard. De Vergennes was the French foreign minister, a man whose support for the Americans' cause was one that Franklin had been trying to gain for months! To stay up here would be an insult—oh, God, *now* what?

Blackheath, still securely tied and reposing on the bed, smiled insolently up at her. " 'Twould be a pity if the good doctor is forced to come up and get you, no?"

"I don't want to hear it."

"*Tsk, tsk,* Eva. I'm sure you can get yourself back into a presentable state by the time the speech is, oh, at least half finished. Release me, on the other hand, and I'll get you there in time for the whole thing."

"I can't release you, not now!"

"Whyever not?"

"I don't trust you!" she all but howled, knowing, from the gleam in his eye, that her intuition was entirely correct. From the totally relaxed look about him, she guessed that the effects of the aphrodisiac had worn off, but Eva wasn't about to take any chances; she dared not leave Blackheath alone in her bedchamber, where he would be free to search her room and, inevitably, find the love potion.

"I'll release you, but you have to leave," she said, frantically grabbing her clothes.

"*Au contraire, madame.* I very much prefer to stay."

"You *have* to leave, Blackheath!"

He gave an urbane smile. "What, and miss the rest of the evening's . . . entertainment? I wouldn't dream of it." His smile turned cunning. "Especially with the *real* aphrodisiac so near at hand. Time to see if it works as well on you as it did on me, my dear."

He knew then. Knew that she had drugged him. *Damn!* Eva, her blood starting to boil at this unforseen complication, turned and glared at him. At that magnificent chest, most of which was still prominently displayed beneath the rucked-up shirt. At the broad shoulders, the upper arms that rippled with muscle. At the handsome neck—

The neck.

God forgive her. But it wouldn't hurt, and if he wouldn't leave, there was only one thing she could do to contain him. She had to do it.

She also had to get downstairs, and get downstairs *now.*

"Very well, then, Blackheath," she spat, hastily untying him and throwing her clothes at him as she hopped into her hoops and tied them on, as she yanked the petticoats over her head and let them float down over the hoops, as she turned her back so her smug lover could obligingly lace her back into her corset. She glanced at the shelf clock in rising panic, resisting the urge to swear at him for each sharp yank, resisting the urge to curse him for not being quicker, though she could see that he was faster, even, than her own maid.

She tied on her stomacher, crammed her hair beneath a smart hat, grabbed her gown, and donned it. Downstairs, she could hear a rising commotion. Applause. Oh, God, any moment now—she had to get down there!

"Thank you, Blackheath," she cried, turning in his arms and pretending to throw herself at him with such gratitude that he had to step backward, his legs coming up against the side of the bed. "You are a godsend."

She hooked her arms around his neck and kissed him.

Hard.

He never suspected, of course. That was the magic about what she was about to do. She let her hands slide back down, so that one fitted against the side of his waist, and the heel of the other rested just below the base of his throat, the thumb and first two fingers splayed in an innocuous V on either side of his neck as she pretended to caress him.

He'll never know. Just do it.

It felt vile. Treacherous. Underhanded.

Your country needs you.

She pretended to lose herself in the kiss, pressing up against him, using desire as an excuse to get closer to him and increase the pressure against the sides of his neck. *Come on, come on!* she urged, keeping the pressure steady, even though she regretted that this kiss was going to end as quickly as it had begun. And then suddenly it did.

His mouth went slack upon hers, his legs buckled, and he slumped, unconscious, only the bed behind his legs and her arm around his waist keeping him upright. Even so, Eva could not hold him up; he fell against her, his chin slamming the top of her shoulder, his dead weight nearly toppling her backward. With all her strength, she shoved him away from her, sending him sprawling on his back across the bed. She leaped up beside him, telling herself this was necessary, that it was kinder than a blow, that she had only moments before he came back to his senses and was on her in full fury. She did not want to have to put him out again.

But as she fumbled to tie his wrists together, he began to stir, and she feared she would have to do just that. His limbs began to spasm, and mighty shudders convulsed his body as he fought to regain consciousness. Hating herself, Eva reached down and pressed her fingers to either side of his neck once more. He opened his eyes, dazedly impaling her with a look of stunned accusation, fighting her with the strength of will alone; but will alone was not enough. His eyes rolled back and with a sigh, he passed out once more.

She kept her fingers against him for a few more perilous seconds, biting her lip, finally releasing him and hoping she'd bought the additional time she needed. She flew into action. On all fours, she crawled to the head of the bed, seized his newly bound wrists, and with all her strength, tried to move him. To no avail. Sweat broke out on her forehead. A seam popped somewhere in her gown. She heaved and jerked and swore, and finally managed to slide him an inch . . . several inches . . . several more, until his lax wrists were just shy of the headboard.

Not close enough—

Rap rap rap!

"I'm coming!" she yelled frantically.

"Eva, it's me," came Franklin's worried voice from the other side of the door. "Are you all right? May I come in?"

"I'm on my way," she gasped, hauling tightly on the knot that bound the unconscious duke and leaping back off the bed. He would not be going anywhere anytime soon. She'd be back just as soon as the speech was over.

She glanced at his still face. Guilt and shame filled her, and she hurriedly turned away before they could be her undoing.

Funny, but when she had held up the coach and struck down this man's brother—who, granted, had never done a single thing in his life to offend or hurt her—with a blow to the back of the neck, guilt and shame had been the last thing she'd felt.

No. Just a contemptuous delight in her mastery over men, and the ease with which she could overpower them.

Not this time.

She fled.

Chapter 8

Lucien came slowly back to his senses.

He opened his eyes to an empty room with only the flickering glow of the candle for company. For a moment he lay there, disoriented, groggy, and dazed, trying to discern what had happened to him. He was tied once more to the bedpost. His head throbbed with pain, yet he had no idea why. Certainly she had not struck him a blow; the pain was not localized, but a general ache quite unlike anything he had ever felt before.

He blinked and lifted his head, fighting dizziness. He supposed he ought to be furious, and yes, humiliated, by being done in by a woman—but no. Instead, he was fascinated. Totally intrigued. He gave a disbelieving little laugh. What the devil had she done to him?

A dangerous woman indeed. . . .

He racked his brain for answers. He remembered her riding him furiously, and the splintering climax that had claimed them both. He remembered her falling asleep for a few moments atop his chest, and the way her hair had felt beneath his hand as he'd stroked it, like heavy silk. He remembered someone at the door, her desperate attempts to get away, her untying his wrists—and there his memories stopped.

Yet here he was, tied up once more. And she—along with her clothes—was gone. How had she managed to get them all back on by herself? If he'd helped her, he damn well couldn't remember doing so. . . .

He'd find out the answers, but not now. Tensing his arms, Lucien hauled himself upward on his back, toward the post to which his wrists were bound. His cravat strained with the force. He smiled. As he suspected, she had left his inert body far enough down the bed that, just by moving himself toward the headboard, he had enough slack to work himself loose. She must have been in one hell of a hurry to be so careless.

It would have been just as easy, but much less satisfying when she discovered he was gone, to simply use his own strength to tear through his sacrificed cravat. But that wouldn't make for such a complete victory. Oh, no. Far better to simply untie himself and leave the article folded mockingly across her pillows. . . .

It was not hard to free himself.

But it was *very* hard to stand up.

He nearly fell as his feet took his weight, and, grabbing a bedpost, he cursed his brain for its inability to control the rest of his body. But it was functioning quite soundly in the one way that mattered. Having personally witnessed the effects of the aphrodisiac on others, Lucien was in no doubt about what Eva had put in his champagne to get such a reaction from him. Releasing the bedpost, he staggered to the dressing table, remembering that she had dabbed perfume on herself just before handing him his drink.

Ah, yes. There was no mistaking the aphrodisiac's seductive purple-garnet color, though she had tried to disguise it by storing it in a perfume bottle. Grinning wryly, Lucien shook his head. He couldn't help but admire her wiliness. Well, she might think she could outsmart him, but she had a thing or two to learn about just whom she was dealing with. Calmly donning the rest of his clothes, Lucien checked himself in the mirror. Pity about the cravat. Otherwise . . . perfect. Totally unruffled. As if nothing had even happened.

He picked up his sword, pocketed the perfume bottle, and was just about to leave when he spied a stack of writing paper on a nearby desk. A dry smile twisted his lips.

Oh, he couldn't resist.

He just couldn't.

He picked up a quill pen, uncapped the nearby ink, and sat down, purposely waiting for the last of his vertigo to clear so it would not show in his writing and give his beautiful adversary something to gloat about.

His grin spreading, he began to write:

My dearest Eva,

*The next time you plan to tie up an unconscious pris-
oner, do allow me to show you the proper way it is
done. In the meantime, my compliments on your
ingenuity, my hopes for immediate news concerning
Lord Brookhampton, and my gratitude for a most
rewarding and pleasurable evening . . . as well as for
the aphrodisiac, which, I am happy to report, is back
with its rightful owner. If you have any wish to
reclaim it, do come to England. I would dearly love
to . . . have you.*

Blackheath

He underscored that last *have* three times to ensure
that the innuendo was clear; then, with a triumphant
smile, he calmly exited the room.

Another round played, another match won.

A fortnight after the Duke of Blackheath's escape,
Eva awoke with a headache and a roiling stomach that
threatened to divulge itself of its contents when the
smell of toast came drifting up from the kitchens
downstairs.

She pulled the drapes and lay back down on the
bed, massaging her temples, willing her jumpy stomach to be still. She had been furious when she'd
returned to her room and found not only Blackheath,
but the aphrodisiac, gone. Cursing, she had collapsed
on the window seat, ruefully eyed the bed where
Blackheath had brought her to such dizzying heights,
and given way to moroseness. Then, grudging respect.

And finally, peals of laughter. How could she be furious with the man? Yes, he had outsmarted her once
again. He had won the latest battle. But there would
be another round between them. She was sure of it. In
the meantime, she could not help but admire his ingenuity in escaping . . . the devious way he had turned
the tables on her. Her blood ran hot just thinking
about him.

Eva wasn't laughing, however, when Marie Antoinette demanded the potion several days later. She
wasn't laughing when she had to confess that she
didn't have it. The French queen's fury was such that
she banished Eva from the royal chambers. Not long
afterward, Eva was summoned to Franklin's residence, where she was soberly informed that her presence in Paris was a threat to the American's careful
negotiations. "I'm sorry, Eva, but you cannot stay here.
Her Majesty is most upset with you . . . first the false
aphrodisiac that so sickened the king, and now an
empty promise about the real one. You must leave
Paris for a while . . . at least, until we have secured an
alliance with France."

Simmering with fury, wondering if Blackheath
knew to what extent he was ruining her life—let alone
her reputation—Eva retreated behind a haughty
facade and left the capital. She would just as soon have
abandoned her search for the missing Lord Brookhampton as well, but she considered herself a woman
of honor and had given her word that she would do all
in her power to find the young earl. Besides, her efforts
on Lord Brookhampton's behalf would give her a perfect excuse to return to England and go for another
round with that devil Blackheath.

Oh, yes. She was very much looking forward to *that*.

Before leaving France, she visited the port where *Sarah Rose* had been taken, and then the prison where the survivors from the British ship were being held. There were no civilians among the lot; just the crew, still wearing their nankeen trousers, pea coats, and checked shirts. Eva eyed them critically; they were a motley, hostile lot, ill-kempt, bearded, one or two wounded and in need of medical attention. Yet another lay all but dead in a corner, his head pillowed on a filthy, matted tangle of blond hair encrusted with old blood. Eva's sympathy for their plight warred with her own delight at finding them; the very fact that Britons were being held in a French jail was cause enough for protest from the English government.

Her eyes gleamed. She studied the prisoners from beneath the brim of her broad hat, a little smile twisting her lips. Franklin didn't care whether France declared war on England or England declared war on France, as long as war came about. Hmm. She tapped her lips with one long fingernail. All the more reason to go to Britain and stir up some trouble. . . .

After all, it didn't matter who fired the first broadside now, did it?

And she would enjoy continuing her own private battle with the infuriating Duke of Blackheath.

That very duke's sister-in-law, Celsiana Blake de Montforte, was in the midst of directing the preparations for her first annual New Year's Eve ball when a footman approached, bearing a card on a silver platter.

"My lady?" He bowed. "You have a visitor in the parlor."

"Thank you, Mulligan. I'll be right down." Watching a maid climb up on a chair to hang silver tissue above the door, Celsie shoved a strand of tawny hair out of her face and took the card. She was just about to read it when a deafening explosion shook Rosebriar's very foundation and the maid, shrieking, grabbed for the door frame to keep from tumbling from her precarious perch.

But Celsie never even blinked. "It's all right, Freckles," she said, tucking the card in her pocket and kneeling down to reassure the elderly gundog at her feet. "It's only Andrew, testing that new explosive he's working on. Shall we go make sure he didn't blow himself up?"

The dog, with some effort, hauled himself to his feet and on weak, age-achy legs, followed his mistress from the ballroom.

In a far pasture outside, Celsie found her handsome inventor-husband examining a blackened pit in the ground and making notes on a pad of paper. His wavy auburn hair was pulled back in a careless queue, and he looked very distracted. Impatient. Hearing her approach, he raised his head—and Celsie bit back a peal of laughter.

"Oh, Andrew," she said, with a giggle. "Whatever happened to your eyebrows?"

Scowling, he touched his fingers to what remained of them—nothing but stubby bristle singed to the roots. "To hell with my eyebrows; how many more attempts must I make before I get this damned mixture correct?"

"Listen, Andrew, don't you think it's safer to stick to inventing, um . . . less dangerous things?"

"What, like aphrodisiacs?" He snorted with laughter and, straightening, brushed the ash from his clothes and mopped his sooty face with a handkerchief. "No, Celsie. This new explosive I'm working on will be far more useful to society. If I can get it stabilized, that is. Imagine it instead of gunpowder in a pistol! Imagine it in a controlled environment, perhaps powering a machine, a boat, my double-compartmented stage-coach—"

"Yes, Andrew." She smiled, touched her tongue to her fingertips, and smoothed what remained of his russet brows. "I'm sure it will be a valuable contribution indeed, if you survive the experimentation stage." She took his arm. "Do you fancy some tea? It has just gone five o'clock."

He looked up at the sky, thick and gray and swollen with cloud, and shivered, suddenly realizing how cold and raw the day was. "Tea sounds wonderful."

"And an early bedtime?" she murmured, suggestively running her hand up his chest.

His eyes gave her all the answer she needed.

Walking slowly so that Freckles could keep up, they made their way back to the house. The smell of damp earth and vegetation hung over the heath and Freckles even managed to flush a pheasant from a tangle of twisted brambles. It was only as they entered the house that Celsie remembered she had a visitor. Horrified by her lapse of manners, she reached into her pocket to withdraw her guest's card . . .

Just as her cousin came around the corner.

Both women stopped in their tracks, Celsie in shock, Eva with a pleasant smile, as though their last meeting had not been violent, upsetting . . . memorable in the most unfortunate sort of way. Beneath her fingers, Celsie felt Andrew's arm stiffen as his greenish amber eyes hardened and went cold.

"E-Eva!" Celsie managed, with a nervous smile. "It is a—"

"Pleasure to see me?" her cousin finished with a rueful smile, gazing out at them from beneath the brim of an oversized hat that only emphasized the extraordinary beauty of her features, the mysteriousness of her bearing. "No need to pretend, my dear cousin." She glanced at Andrew, who had turned away, refusing to look at her, refusing, even, to honor her with a bow. "And you, my lord. Has marriage robbed you of your civility?"

"You are the last female on earth deserving of civility," he ground out, and then, bowing to Celsie and not even sparing a nod for Eva, he stalked from the room.

"My, my," breathed Eva, raising her brows. "Not exactly the forgiving sort, is he?"

Celsie, noting Eva's pallor, her brittle demeanor, and the haunted shadows beneath her slanting green eyes, decided to ignore that remark. Something was wrong here. "Come, Eva. Let me offer you some refreshment. Surely you have traveled some distance. . . ."

"From France. I arrived just this morning and"—her voice went flat and hard—"thanks to your diabolical *brother-in-law*, will not be returning anytime soon."

"Oh, dear, what has Lucien done now?"

"I would rather not discuss it in front of the servants." Eva drew her cloak more tightly around herself, hoping Celsie would not see beneath her casual facade, her mask of uncaring aloofness, to the hurt and fear she was hiding just beneath. Andrew's reaction had made her feel awkward and uncomfortable, though she knew it was justified. But what was her cousin feeling? Why, she and Celsie had all but grown up together. She had taught Celsie how to fence. How to shoot. How to make her way in a man's world. Celsie had idolized her. Once.

But that was before the robbery.

Eva doubted Celsie idolized her now. She doubted she even *liked* her.

"Come, then. Let us take tea in the parlor."

There, the younger woman quickly poured hot, steaming brew for them both. Eva lifted her cup, her stomach roiling as Celsie offered her a plate of cheese biscuits. She shook her head and, paling, bit back a shudder of nausea.

"Eva, forgive me for prying, but are you in some sort of trouble?"

Eva gave a sharp bark of laughter. It was a brittle sound, even to her own ears. She set down her cup in its saucer before she could spill it. "Me? Trouble?" She was in more trouble than she knew what to do with. "Oh, no, Celsie. I am here to make some for the man who has all but ruined my life."

"Lucien? He all but ruins everyone's lives, but I can assure you, everything usually works out in the end."

"I cannot see how my being tricked, humiliated, and banished from the French court, let alone Paris, can be 'worked out' in the end. But never mind. I will have my revenge."

"Oh, good."

"*Good?*" Eva eyed her as though she'd lost her mind. "We're speaking about your brother-in-law here."

"I know." Celsie smiled and sipped her tea. "So what has he done?"

Eva had not intended to confide in her cousin, but there was something so genuine in Celsie's silvery green gaze, something so compassionate and forgiving in her manner, that Eva succumbed to temptation. Sparing only the details that would sabotage her own pride, namely, that she'd bedded the notorious Duke of Blackheath and had the very best lovemaking of her life, Eva told all. She explained why she'd held up the de Montforte coach and stolen the supposed aphrodisiac. She told how she'd broken into Lucien's bedchamber and stolen the real potion upon discovering the first was a substitute. She related how Lucien had come to France seeking her help in locating Lord Brookhampton, and how she had left him tied up and helpless in her room, only to find him—and the aphrodisiac—gone upon her return.

"Tied up and *helpless?*" Celsie cried, choking on her tea. "*Lucien?*"

"It is not such a difficult thing, if one knows the proper methods," Eva admitted with a little smile.

At that, Celsie began to laugh so hard that she had to set down her teacup so as not to spill the hot beverage all over herself.

Eva said wryly, "I take it the Duke of Blackheath has made his own enemies, even within his own family."

"I'm not sure *enemies* is the right word, but let me just say this—he had it coming to him. He thrives on control. It is all that matters to him. It is good to see him taken down a peg or two. I just wish I had been there to see it."

Eva smiled, rather glad that Celsie had not.

"But you need my help, don't you?" Celsie asked, sobering. She touched Eva's hand, showing more kindness than Eva, given her recent behavior, felt she deserved. "What can I do for you, Eva?"

Eva gave a rueful smile. "I'm not sure there is anything you can do for me, Celsie. But I do need a place to stay, at least until things settle down in Paris." She looked away, trying to retain her pride, her dignity. "I hesitate to ask, knowing the trouble I've caused you and your new husband, but would you put me up for a short time, Celsie?"

"*No.*"

Both women looked up. Lord Andrew stood in the doorway, eyeing Eva with flat dislike.

"But Andrew—"

"No, Celsie. I will not have this woman under my roof."

"Andrew, you don't understand. She stole the aphrodisiac for a reason that was very important to her. A—a patriotic one."

"She threatened to kill me, knocked Charles senseless, and would have had no qualms about killing any of us, yourself included."

"Oh, no, I would never harm a woman," Eva said, smiling. "Celsie and Lady Charles were really quite safe."

Andrew stalked into the room, six feet of angry male fire. He came right up to Eva and glared down at her. "What is your big complaint against men, then?"

Eva eyed him calmly "The way they treat women."

Getting to her feet, Celsie laid a hand on her husband's arm.

"Andrew, my cousin needs refuge for a few days. I'm sure that once the two of you get to know each other, you might even learn to be civil to one another. Besides, she came here for a reason that even you will approve of." Celsie, grinning, stood on tiptoe to loudly whisper into her husband's ear. "To take Lucien down a peg or two."

"What?"

"Oh, yes, your brother has ruined my life," Eva said, picking up her teacup once more. "I really couldn't leave Europe without coming back for a final round with him."

Andrew turned away, paced toward the door, turned, and came back. Though his jaw was still set, the blazing coldness in his eyes was gone, to be replaced with something speculative . . . almost cunning.

Celsie took advantage of his momentary indecision, the lowering of his defenses. "Andrew, in case you doubt Eva's ability to do exactly what she says, it was she who scaled the tower of Blackheath Castle, broke into Lucien's chambers, and stole the real aphrodisiac."

"You?"

Eva merely smiled and shrugged.

Andrew looked at Celsie. Celsie returned the look with a scheming grin of her own.

"Very well, then," the young lord finally consented. "But, you realize I'm only doing this for Celsie's sake. If you cause me any grief whatsoever, you're out of here on your ear, do you understand?"

"Perfectly," said Eva. "And thank you." She rose to her feet, determined to show civility to her host even if he was too stubborn, and still too angry, to reciprocate. He merely gave her a black look and turned to go.

But Eva couldn't resist.

"Do tell me one thing, my lord. . . ."

He turned and shot her a quelling glare.

"Whatever has happened to your eyebrows?"

Chapter 9

Lady Nerissa de Montforte had no desire to leave her bed.

She had no desire to leave Blackheath Castle.

And she had absolutely no desire to go to Celsie's New Year's Eve ball, but Lucien was insistent.

"My dear girl, I cannot bear to see you languishing in that bed another instant. I suggest you get up, break your fast, and prepare yourself for travel." He pulled open the drapes, a dark angel in immaculate burgundy velvet come to drag her from her refuge from pain. "The preparations have already been made."

"I'm not going."

"You *are* going." He yanked open another drape. "I can think of no better way to restore you to proper health and spirits than spending some time with your family."

"Having Perry back is the only thing that will

restore me to proper health and spirits." She blinked back the tears that always lingered near the surface. "I cannot go to Rosebriar, Lucien. Do not ask me."

"I'm not asking, I'm ordering. It will do you good." He raised his voice and called, "Martha? Prepare a bath for Her Ladyship, and lay out warm clothes suitable for travel. We leave this afternoon for Rosebriar Park."

"*I—am—NOT—going,*" Nerissa ground out, sitting up in bed.

"Really, my dear, you should know after all these years that it is pointless to argue with me. I have decided that you need to get away from the castle for a while. And since I must go to France to follow up on a lead about Perry, I don't want you here languishing all alone."

"France?" she asked anxiously. "When are you departing?"

"Immediately after I make sure you attend tomorrow night's ball."

"I'm going with you."

"No, you're not."

"But Lucien—"

"I do believe I have made up my mind on the matter," he murmured, and, bowing, left the room.

Damn him! Nerissa lay there in bed, seething. How could he be so heartless? So insensitive? She was fed up with his high-handedness! She yanked the covers over her head, shut her eyes, and stared into the close darkness.

Lucien could go to hell. He really could.

"I'm not going to Rosebriar," she vowed.

But in the end, of course, she did go, because her

brother always got his way— no matter what the expense to others. Several hours later, Nerissa was bundled into the ducal coach and heading east toward Rosebriar Park, the duke astride Armageddon just outside.

She blinked back tears as they passed Perry's lands. There was the house of mellow stone where he had lived. Where they both would have lived. Raised their children. Grown old together.

Oh, God help me, this hurts so very much. . . .

She squeezed her eyes shut, trying not to let the tears fall. She didn't want to go to Rosebriar and pretend to be happy. She didn't want to mix with others, paste a smile on her face, when all she wanted to do was cry, fend off the attentions of men who were not Perry, and try to fool her family into thinking she was coping just fine. She wasn't coping just fine. She wanted only to bury herself in a hole, go to sleep, and let the world go by without her.

And now the coach was carrying her farther and farther away from the Brookhampton lands. Away from her memories. Away from the home of the only beau she had ever loved.

She leaned her face against the squab and finally fell asleep, a single tear tracking down her pale cheek.

Eva, her stomach heavy with nausea, was late for the evening meal.

Resplendent in an open sacque gown of shimmering copper satin trimmed in green, she entered a dining room aglow with candlelight. Several of Celsie's dogs had already claimed spots beneath the table, forcing their mistress and Andrew to contort their legs in impossible positions in order to accommodate them. As Eva took her seat, Andrew pointedly ignored her, refusing, even, to rise. He was a surly creature, she decided, even though she knew she deserved his contempt. Still, she was unable to forget his earlier words: For his wife's sake, he would allow her to stay here at Rosebriar . . . and for that, she couldn't help but be just a little bit impressed.

Imagine, doing something for your wife's sake.

The concept was alien to her.

She cast a furtive glance at the young lord as he piled Celsie's plate high, attentive to her every need, his gaze softening whenever their eyes met. Right, so maybe Lord Andrew was a cut above other men. Maybe he, unlike the rest of his kind, actually considered and cared about a woman's feelings. A rarity, that. She didn't think men like that existed in real life, only fairy tales.

Eva shook her head and picked up her fork. Well, *that* certainly wouldn't last long.

But as she turned her attention to her meal, the sight—and smell—of the fowl drenched in currant sauce brought on a sudden wave of nausea. Cold sweat washed over her and she put down her napkin, trying to decide how to leave without appearing rude . . .

Or raising Celsie's suspicions.

But Celsie saw her starting to get up. "Eva, Andrew was just telling me about his plans to revise his new explosive," she explained, mistaking Eva's tense expression for awkwardness about being excluded from their banter. "He's going to try it out again on the morrow."

"Then I should dearly like to watch," Eva said faintly,

thinking to make peace with the sullen young lord by showing an interest in his pursuits.

"No doubt because she hopes to see me blow myself up."

"Now, Andrew," Celsie chastised, shaking her head. "Why don't you tell Eva about your explosive?"

Eva crunched her napkin in a damp fist. *Dear Lord, I have to get out of here.*

"Why should I? A woman as dangerous to England as *she* is doesn't need to know about my new explosive." He stabbed his fork into a potato and added sarcastically, "Next thing you know, she'll be trying to abduct *me* so she can get the formula and use it to help her beloved America."

Eva smiled through her worsening nausea. "Oh, no. I couldn't bear to separate you two lovebirds. But really, that is the nature of men, isn't it, Celsie? What women build, men want only to blow up."

"That isn't true of *all* men, Eva. Why, Andrew is always building something—flying machines, double-compartmented coaches, automatic roasting machines. . . . He's *far* more interested in creating than destroying."

"Well, imagine that," Eva drawled, trying to maintain her air of polished cool. "A man with brains. Who would have thought?"

Andrew, glowering, slammed his napkin down.

And Eva, despite the fact she was growing perilously near to disgracing herself, turned all the charm of her smile on him. "Do relax, my lord. I just gave you a compliment, in case you didn't realize." Her hands were beginning to tremble. She was sweating fiercely. "And now I fear I must excuse myself—"

"Eva, are you all right?" Celsie rose to her feet. "You look quite pale—"

"I am fine. Just"—she smiled at Andrew, hoping to fool him and Celsie into believing her excuse—"finding it difficult to share a table with an 'intelligent' man. Such a singular prospect quite overwhelms me, I fear."

She rose and hurried from the room, leaving Andrew staring after her.

"What was that all about?"

"I don't know. But she's behaving in a most peculiar manner, and I suspect there's more here than meets the eye." Celsie put down her napkin. "I'll be right back."

She ran out into the hall, but Eva, her hand pressed to her mouth, was already rushing up the stairs. Celsie paused, frowning. She was just debating whether or not to follow her when a servant approached, bowing.

"My lady. Their Lordships Charles and Gareth have arrived with their families and await you in the parlor."

Celsie quickly took control. "Show them in and see that additional places are set at the table."

Oh, God help her! Charles and Eva under the same roof?

Sure enough, her worst fears were realized.

"She's *here*?" thundered Major Lord Charles de Montforte as the newly arrived entourage filed into the dining room and was seated. The tall, crisply impeccable officer lunged to his feet, his eyes glittering like aquamarine as he turned his wrath on his brother Andrew. "What are you, *mad*? That woman is a menace! You'd have her here in this house after what she did to us on the road that night?"

Celsie tried to placate him. "But Charles, she needs

help—Lucien turned her life upside down." She proceeded to tell everyone about how Eva had scaled the tower at Blackheath, broken into Lucien's bedchamber, and stolen the real aphrodisiac. "He went to France to get it back, and Eva overpowered him and tied him up and then he got free and stole it back from her. It's all quite amusing, really. Wait until you hear the whole tale. . . ."

Charles turned away, stiff and angry. The last time he'd seen Eva de la Mouriére, she'd been masquerading as a peasant woman on a lonely road, her carriage disabled, her wits at an end. He had stopped to offer his help—only to wake up facedown in the dirt, his family shaken up, and the aphrodisiac—not the confounded, wretched aphrodisiac that had wreaked such havoc on so many lives, but what had turned out to be a false substitute—stolen.

He could not bear to face her again. He could not bear to even look at her.

"Come, Amy, we're leaving. I will not allow you and our daughter to remain under the same roof as that treacherous witch."

"Treacherous witch?"

Everyone stilled at the sound of the faintly amused voice. There in the doorway, the light from a wall sconce glowing upon thick, pinned-up hair of a red so striking, so brilliant, it nearly pained the eye to look at it, stood Eva—as tall as a willow, as regal as a queen. She was smiling.

Everyone gasped as Charles's hand went for his sword.

"Please, Major. There is no need for bloodshed," she murmured as Andrew and Gareth leaped forward to stay their brother's hand. "For the sake of your family, and especially poor Celsie, let us forget our past grievances and at least try to pretend a measure of civility."

Charles's pale blue eyes chilled as they met Eva's slanting ones of cut green glass. For a moment he didn't move, merely surveying her with dislike, distaste, distrust; then, seizing Amy's arm, he bowed to Celsie and Gareth's wife Juliet, and all but dragged his protesting wife from the dining room.

Eva bit her lip.

Celsie and Andrew exchanged glances, and Juliet glanced at Eva, frowning.

Gareth was the first to react. "Don't worry, he won't take his family back out on a night like this," he said, trying to smooth the awkward silence. "He won't leave."

But the others were still staring at the woman who had so unnerved the taciturn, normally unflappable Lord Charles—and hadn't even batted an eyelash at his rude reaction. Now she looked around and met their gazes, her smile rueful.

"Dear me. I had forgotten how slow male pride is to heal once it has been wounded. I really *should* have started out by apologizing to him, shouldn't I?"

Just then, a footman bearing a missive on a silver plate entered the room. He paused in front of Andrew, bowing. "For you, my lord."

Andrew took the folded vellum, dismissed the servant, and broke the seal. As he read, he began to smile. And then to grin. His eyes gleaming, he refolded the note.

"Well, well. It seems that our autocratic eldest brother has deigned to attend our ball tomorrow night and expects to arrive with Nerissa sometime early tomorrow evening." His gaze lifted to Eva. "So, madam. Here's your chance."

"Chance?" echoed Gareth, looking from Andrew to Eva. "Chance for what?"

But Eva, her heart suddenly pounding, had just lost her appetite for the second time this night. And now, her composure. Blackheath. He was coming *here*.

God help her nerves.

"Revenge," she said sweetly, and, excusing herself, left the room.

Chapter 10

Sleep that night was all but nonexistent.

She lay awake thinking of Blackheath. Of their last encounter together, of the heights of passion to which he had brought her, of his threat—promise—at the end of that infuriating note he had left for her back in France:

Do come to England. I would dearly love to . . . have you.

Well, here she was, in England. He would be here tomorrow. And she knew in her bones that he would have her. It was inevitable.

The clock in the hall outside struck one. Two. Three. Eva, hot and flushed, threw off the coverlet. Got up and went to the window. She gazed out over the darkened heath, at the cold stars winking down at her from behind high, scattered clouds that veiled and unveiled the moon.

Blackheath.

He would be here in a matter of hours. Tomorrow night.

She poured herself a glass of water and returned to bed. Tried to sleep. And finally fell into fitful slumber . . .

Where she dreamed of making love to the Duke of Blackheath.

The ball started promptly at nine and *he* hadn't arrived.

Eva danced with more men than she could count, glanced toward the doors more times than she would acknowledge, and spent the early part of the evening battling a rising case of both nerves and anticipation. Damn Blackheath to perdition for unsettling her so! Damn him for what he was doing to her!

And then, just as the clock struck ten, something like a charged current rippled through the room and she knew that *he* had arrived.

And he had.

He was glorious, virile, dangerously masculine despite the elegant lace at throat and wrists, the fitted waistcoat of dark gray satin, the powdered hair, the ruby pinned in his cravat, the fancy buckled shoes.

And he had seen her.

His hand beneath the elbow of a stunning blonde who looked as ethereal as mist in a gown of pale blue tissue, he moved nonchalantly through the crowd. Women were gazing hungrily at him; men were eyeing him with respect, with wariness.

And all three of the younger de Montforte brothers were watching him—and Eva—most closely indeed.

Too closely.

Celsie, her eyes gleaming, leaned close to Andrew and whispered something in his ear, but Eva was still staring at the duke, trying to summon her composure. Perdition, it was hot in here. She was unable to think. Unable to breathe. Fixated.

On him.

Who the devil was that blonde?

"Eva. We meet again." He drew the vacant-eyed beauty forward. "Allow me to present you to my sister, Lady Nerissa de Montforte."

His sister. Relief—unwarranted as it was—flooded her. She and Nerissa exchanged greetings, and out of the corner of her eye, Eva saw Lord Gareth eyeing the situation with high interest, subtly maneuvering himself and his wife Juliet closer so as to be within earshot of any volleys that might soon be flying. As for Blackheath, if he was surprised to see her, he showed no sign of it. Not a flicker of emotion gave him away as his gaze moved over Eva's face and down her gown of emerald green satin—and remained on her for a long, uncomfortable moment.

She raised her head and eyed him steadily. Could he know what those penetrating black eyes, that faint, self-contained smile, were doing to her? Could he hear the way her heart had fisted in her chest and was now beginning to thunder out of control? Thank God she'd worn the brilliant emerald gown, for it set off her coloring, her hair, her eyes to best advantage. Not, of course, that she wanted to impress him. Oh, far from that. She just wanted to throw him off balance. Gain the upper hand. Distract him so she would emerge the victor in whatever battle of wills lay before them.

That was all.

"My dear Lady Nerissa! Would you care for a dance?"

A young swain was there, bowing, his brown eyes merry, his powdered hair caught in a bag wig and tied with blue velvet. Nerissa opened her mouth to refuse, but immediately the duke intervened.

"She would love a dance, Trombley. And a glass of punch, I think."

"Lucien—"

"No, no, my dear, go, enjoy yourself. I wish to hear no more about it."

For the first time, Eva saw emotion in the other woman's pale blue eyes: anger. And then Trombley was drawing her away, out onto the floor.

"That was incredibly insensitive of you," Eva snapped. "It's plain as day that she had no wish to dance with him!"

"I know, but she has been languishing in bed ever since she heard news of Lord Brookhampton, and it is high time she returned to the land of the living. Dancing will do her good."

"You're a monster."

"So I've been told." He took her hand, raising it to his lips, those fascinating black eyes holding hers from over the tops of her knuckles. She set her jaw even as her pulse quickened. "So, tell me, madam. Did you come for the ball"—his smile grew positively wicked—"or in response to that little note I left for you?"

Do come to England. I would dearly love to . . . have you.

Eva eyed him flatly. "I came for revenge."

"Ah. How delightful. I had hoped you would, you know. Life gets so boring, up here in the country."

"I can promise you, Blackheath, that I intend to make your life anything but boring."

"Oh, I have no doubt of that. Why, I would be most disappointed if you had not taken me up on my . . . invitation to come to England. I have been waiting for you, you know."

"Waiting for me, or to get me back into bed?"

"Both, of course."

"Well, then, Blackheath, you can wait until hell freezes over, because the latter is not going to happen."

"Care to wager on it?"

"I think not."

He smiled, his eyes suddenly crinkling with humor. "Coward."

"No, just wise."

"A dance, then?"

"Better that than stand here and give your siblings the satisfaction of seeing us sparring with each other."

"My sentiments exactly." Guiding her out onto the floor with a hand beneath the elbow, he swept her up into a waltz. "So, tell me, madam, what means did you employ to render me insensible back in Paris?"

"If you think I'm about to tell you, you've got another think coming."

"Ah, well. I shall find out in good time. Though I must confess, your actions did nothing but fuel my fascination with you all the more." His hand fitted to her waist, he swung her out and away from a hard-eyed Charles and his wife Amy, the latter of whom was watching them most curiously. "So when do you plan to exact this revenge that I cannot wait to taste?"

"You think I'm in jest?"

"I most certainly hope not." He spun her again, making her dizzy, making her fixate on his hard mouth, those enigmatic black eyes, in order to center herself. "In fact, I do hope you'll start this little crusade of yours soon, as I leave for France in about fifteen minutes."

"So soon?" she asked, too quickly, too anxiously.

Too late.

He noted her disappointment, try as she might to conceal it. She saw the wicked, self-satisfied smile that came over those same hard lips, though he was gallant enough not to rub salt into the wound. "Alas, I have contacts to meet in Paris first thing in the morning. I only came to the ball to make sure my sister attended."

"What is so important in Paris?"

His fingers stroked the middle of her back as he pressed her close, too close, so close that her body felt as though it were going up in flames. "You are too curious for your own good, my little spy. But I go to France to follow up on a piece of information about Lord Brookhampton. As I told you earlier, I cannot bear to see my sister so unhappy."

"Then you should stop forcing her to do things she has no wish to do."

"It is for her own good."

"Her own *good*?"

"But of course."

"You are truly a wicked man to interfere in others' lives so!"

He inclined his head as the dance ended, then guided her to the refreshment table, where he pressed a glass of punch into her hand. "That is why I'm called the Wicked One."

"A fitting moniker. No doubt you courted such a label yourself."

"On the contrary." His smile was positively maddening. "The people of Ravenscombe gave nicknames to all the de Montforte males. Charles is the Beloved One, Gareth is the Wild One, and Andrew, the Defiant One. Now drink up, my dear, as I must be on my way now. And do use the next few days perfecting your plans for revenge, for I look forward to whatever"—he smiled—"punishment you have in mind."

He took her hand, his long, elegant fingers sending tremors of excitement through her as he pressed his thumb gently into her gloved flesh and raised the hand to his lips. Eva felt them even through the soft kid. Saw the sultry promise in those black-fire eyes as he held her gaze for a long, telling moment. And then, all too soon, he released her and straightened, the elegant, unaffected duke once more.

And just in time, too. Celsie was approaching, her eyes gleaming.

Blackheath made his excuses, bowed, and melted back off through the crowd.

"Well? What did he say?" Celsie asked eagerly.

But Eva was still staring after that broad and tapered back, wondering why she felt such an empty ache where she knew her heart to otherwise be. Wondering why a lump rose in her throat as the doors swung open and he was gone.

She smiled faintly. "Only that he will be back."

Nerissa was miserable.

As the evening wore on, more and more coaches

had pulled up outside, discharging powdered and perfumed guests in expensive silks, satins, and velvets. Laughter and music filled the ballroom, made her head ache, emphasized her own anguish all the more. Andrew, looking perpetually annoyed—but then, he hated social gatherings—caught her eye and ordered her to cheer up. The Honourable George Dartingford wanted to dance with her. Lord Islington wanted to dance with her. Everyone wanted to dance with her . . .

Everyone, that is, who wasn't lining up for a dance with the mysterious Eva de la Mouriére.

So this was the woman who had stolen the aphrodisiac, sent Lucien into a black rage, had turned her brother's life upside down. Nerissa eyed her closely. The American was beautiful, confident, aloof. And every man in the ballroom, with the exception of her brothers and especially of Charles, watched her like dogs with heatstroke, eyes glazed with fascination—and lust. Eva de la Mouriére appeared to be in her element, expertly handling the excessive flattery, flirtation, and dogfights between her slavering swains—but Nerissa, unlike the smitten men, could see that it was all an act. The other woman was merely enduring the attention; her comments bordered on cruel, on taunting, and it was obvious that she just didn't like men.

Obvious that she, like Nerissa, wanted to be anywhere but here.

Obvious that a certain spark had gone out of her the instant Lucien had left.

And now she looked tired as well as irritated—and painfully alone. Maybe even vulnerable. The men continued to swarm around her. Nerissa was not surprised when Eva finally excused herself and stepped outside for a breath of fresh air.

It was at that moment that Lord Islington, smelling strongly of spirits, approached, bowed, and asked Nerissa for a dance. She didn't want to dance, of course; she didn't have the heart to make merry, but perhaps if she closed her eyes she could pretend . . . pretend that this short, rotund man was someone else. Someone who was a good head taller than she was, someone with cool gray eyes, someone with bright gold hair and a suave, inborn elegance. Nerissa's throat closed up. Tears stung the back of her eyes and she bravely blinked them back.

Perry. Oh, Perry. . . .

Taking a deep breath, she allowed Islington to escort her out onto the floor.

"You are very beautiful tonight, my lady."

Nerissa heard herself making the obligatory sounds of acknowledgment, of gratitude. Islington was either lying or blind. She had seen herself in the mirror as her maid had dressed her hair. The bluish shadows under her dulled, vacant eyes, the sad curve of her mouth, the lackluster tone to her once-shining mass of golden hair . . . looking in that mirror had been like looking into the face of a stranger.

". . . I was most aggrieved to hear about the *Sarah Rose*," Islington was saying. "Please accept my condolences on the loss of Lord Brookhampton."

Nerissa looked away. "He has not yet been declared dead," she snapped. "He will be found. Lucien will find him."

"I suppose that if anyone can, it is the duke. Still, I

feel as though it's all my fault. Silly of me, perhaps, but if I hadn't sold that Spanish estate to His Grace, you'd be sweeping around this dance floor with the one you love, not a poor substitute—"

Nerissa stopped in her tracks; Islington nearly went sprawling over her stalled feet. *But if I hadn't sold that Spanish estate to His Grace—*

Her blood went cold. "What Spanish estate?" she asked sharply.

"Dear me, I didn't realize the very mention of it would so distress you—"

"*What* estate?" Nerissa demanded once again, pure, hot color flooding back into her cheeks. She was suddenly sweating. People were staring at her, beginning to whisper.

Islington was a bright radish red. "My dear lady, I—I don't wish to upset you, but your brother bought an estate from me, a rather neglected one that I never paid much attention to, as it was so far away—" Islington began to flush and stammer, knowing he'd said too much, that his words were the cause of Nerissa's speechless horror. "I couldn't understand why His Grace would want some Spanish estate when he has so many perfectly fine English ones, unless, of course, he was interested in it for the grapes—I beg your pardon, my lady, I fear I have upset you. Please, let me get you some refreshment—"

Upset? *Upset?* Nerissa, shaking violently, was more than upset. Suddenly everything was clear. She remembered the conversation she'd had with Lucien the night before she and Perry had quarreled. She remembered Lucien promising to do something drastic if Perry didn't soon propose, remembered the way she had gone to him in tears when Perry had gone off to Spain to claim this *estate,* remembered how Lucien had been so brotherly and compassionate when word had come back that the *Sarah Rose* had gone down and Perry wasn't among the survivors. Nerissa fought for breath. Nausea rose in her gut, and for a moment she thought she was going to black out with the realization of what her brother had done.

"I must have some fresh air, sir. If you'll please excuse me . . ."

She hurried away before he could offer to escort her outside. The reality of the situation was growing more horrific with every moment. Lucien had sent Perry away in an attempt to engineer a fast union between them. What was it he had said to try to calm her that night she'd received Perry's letter?

Absence makes the heart grow fonder.

Oh, God help her! Through a blinding haze of tears, Nerissa ran through the crowd, through the great doors, and outside. How could her brother, who claimed to love her, have done this to her? To Perry? Not only had he separated them, he'd been responsible for the probable death of an innocent man!

Outside, the damp winter air hit her with a shocking chill, but by now the tears were flowing, and flowing hard. Nerissa ran through the garden. Rosebushes tore at her ankles. Mud soaked her slippers, shrubbery ripped at her gown. Sobbing so hard she could barely see, she kept running, wanting only to escape the rising agony that obliterated everything else—

And collided hard with someone heading back toward the house.

Nerissa reeled backward, aware of only a mysteriously exotic perfume before her feet went out from under her and she landed hard on her bottom. Gulping back sobs, she looked up into the face of Eva de la Mouriére.

The other woman reached down to help her up. "Let me guess," she said wryly, steadying Nerissa when she would have slipped in the mud and gone down once more. "It was a man, wasn't it? But of course it was, it always is. Trust me, sweetie, they're not worth it."

The simple words tore open the floodgate of Nerissa's anguish.

"It's all his fault Perry's dead!" she howled, her hair tumbling from its pins and falling about eyes gone wild with pain and rage. "He sent Perry away! There was never any estate in Spain, never any reason for Perry to go, he just made that all up so he could get us separated and make Perry miss me enough to want to marry me when he got back! He planned it all, and now Perry's dead and it's all his fault! I will never forgive him for this! *I swear, I will never forgive him for what he has done!*"

Eva tried to fold the younger woman against her and offer what comfort she could, but Nerissa pushed away, too distraught to allow another to console her. Protectiveness—and a cold anger—rose in Eva's breast. Men. They were always the cause of a woman's pain, weren't they?

Awkwardly, she draped her own shawl around the thin, shaking shoulders. "Cheer up, sweetie," she said, reverting to the flippant sarcasm she always sought when her own heart needed protecting. As she moved silently away, she muttered, "At least *you're* not carrying some man's bastard child."

* * *

For a moment, Nerissa wasn't sure she'd heard the softly spoken words.

At least you're *not carrying some man's bastard child.*

Nerissa lifted her head and watched the other woman, as haughty and dignified as a goddess, make her way back toward the house. Had she heard her correctly? Was Eva just telling her her situation could be worse, or was she telling her her *own* situation was worse?

Nerissa was just about to go after her when Celsie came hurrying out, her face grave with concern.

"Nerissa! Whatever is the matter? Did Islington say something to upset you?" Her eyes widened as she took in Nerissa's mud-stained gown, her red-rimmed eyes and wet cheeks. She squeezed her sister-in-law's hands. "Tell me what happened!"

Nerissa took a deep breath and met Celsie's alarmed eyes. "Lucien. He—he killed Perry."

Celsie reeled back. And as she stared at her in horror, Nerissa told her what Lucien had done. She told her how he had bought a Spanish estate. How he had apparently sent Perry off on a false mission just to engineer yet another de Montforte union. How it was *his* fault Perry was probably dead. Her voice broke, and she couldn't stop the tears from flowing down her face.

Celsie pulled her into her arms.

"And to make this night even more wretched, Eva just said the strangest thing to me. I don't think I was meant to hear it, but I could swear I heard her say, 'At least *you're* not carrying some man's bastard child.' " Nerissa looked up. "Here I am, so wrapped up in my own misery that I failed to notice someone else's. She's . . . she's not in the family way, is she, Celsie?"

But Celsie was staring at her. "Oh, my God."

"What is it?"

"That explains it, then. Good heavens, why didn't I *see*? No wonder she's so pale . . . no wonder she's been complaining of a stomach disorder . . . no wonder she came here to me, and *no wonder she's so determined to get her revenge on your brother for ruining her life!*" She grabbed Nerissa's shoulders. "Dear God, Nerissa, do you know what this means?"

Nerissa just gazed in confusion at her sister-in-law, whose face was glowing with barely constrained excitement.

"I'd bet everything I own that Eva is carrying Lucien's child!"

Chapter 11

Celsie hurried into the ballroom and, not seeing Eva among the crowd, dashed up to her apartments.

"Eva?"

She knocked, then pushed open the door. Her cousin stood at the window, her hair glowing like wine in the light of the candle just behind her.

"Good evening, Celsie. I trust your ball was a success," she murmured without turning around.

"Why didn't you tell me?"

The other woman remained staring out into the night. "Because I can barely acknowledge the fact even to myself."

"But—it's a baby!"

"It is Blackheath's baby."

"Does he know?"

"Of course not. No one does—except you, now."

"And Nerissa."

"Yes. . . . That poor child. She has been cruelly used, I think. I ran into her—literally—out in the garden, sobbing her heart out." Eva turned around then, her eyes flat and hard. "Over a man, of course."

"She was sobbing because she'd just learned her own *brother* was the one to send Perry away, and under false pretenses, too! Damn him! Damn him, Eva! It is bad enough that he manipulates people for what he thinks is their own *good*, but the fact that he takes such a malicious delight in doing so makes it utterly unconscionable, totally unforgivable."

Eva raised a brow. "Blackheath did this?"

"Yes, and this time he has gone too far!" Celsie stamped her foot in rage. "Mark me, this is not the end of this. Not by any stretch of the imagination. I swear, Eva, this is the last—the *last*—time he'll ever go interfering in anyone's life, ever again!"

Celsie called a family conference to be held in the dining room immediately after the ball.

It was late, and everyone was tired, but they were a family, and they were there. Charles, still in his dress regimentals, looked coolly composed but concerned as he sat next to Amy. Gareth came in with his arm around Juliet, his ever-present grin changing to a look of worry when he saw his sister already seated, a fire in her pale blue eyes that proclaimed banked fury. Andrew was the last to arrive, rubbing at the bristle that remained of his singed eyebrows as he took a seat next to the tight-lipped Nerissa. He cast a questioning glance at Celsie, apprehension clouding his face when he saw her look of bristling fury. Savage glee. That, coupled with the explosive expression on Nerissa's otherwise gentle face, boded ill.

Celsie waited for everyone to be seated. Her foot tapped impatiently as footmen served port to the men and tea to the ladies. She dismissed them, and began to speak.

"I know you're all wondering why Nerissa and I have called you together tonight, and at such a late hour besides, but what I have to say is of utmost importance. I'd let Nerissa tell you what your brother has done *this* time, but as you can see, she's not exactly in any mood to talk."

"I can't even bear to mention that—that *bastard's* name," Nerissa burst out, her eyes flashing.

Charles nearly choked on his port. Gareth's eyebrows shot up. They were not used to hearing such coarse language from their sister.

Andrew leaned back in his chair. "So what has he done this time?"

Her own voice sharpening with anger, Celsie told them what Nerissa had learned from Islington, and what she and her sister-in-law had puzzled together in the wake of such a damning revelation. "Spanish estate!" she fumed. "Obviously he was just trying to separate Perry from Nerissa so he'd miss her so much he'd come back and propose marriage!"

"Really, now," Charles began, shaking his head. "I can't believe Lucien would go to such lengths."

"Well, believe it! This time, his machinations have gone tragically awry," Celsie spat. "This time, he has not only made another of his siblings miserable, he's ended up killing someone as well!"

Charles, always one to approach a situation from a

variety of angles, was toying with his glass. "Who's to say that Perry's death isn't a fabrication, too?"

"It's not," Gareth said. "The son of one of my constituents was a crew member on the ship. It *did* go down."

Nerissa held herself erect, her throat moving as she bravely held back fresh tears.

"We have all been manipulated by Lucien into doing his will," Celsie continued. "We have all been unwitting puppets in his diabolical plans to get each of his brothers—and now his sister—married off. He truly is the Wicked One! Look what he did to you, Gareth, and Juliet. And Charles! The way he schemed to get you and Amy together was totally inexcusable."

"But he wasn't as heavy-handed with us as he was the rest of you," Amy protested. She was a gentle soul, and had taken a liking to Lucien when others had only barely forgiven him his transgressions into their lives.

"Regardless, he still schemed, and he still got what he wanted," Celsie continued. "And he went completely over the top with how he manipulated Andrew and I into marriage with that aphrodisiac! Well, it's time he got a taste of his own medicine."

Suddenly every eye in the room was on Celsie.

She began to pace back and forth before the fire, her skirts whispering with her movements. "I'm sure all of you have noticed that Eva is here to wreak some sort of revenge on Lucien. Did any of you ever wonder just what he *really* did to ruin her life so? Well, I have, and she is the other reason I've called you all together. You see, the most opportune situation has, with Eva's arrival, fallen right into our laps. *She* is how we're going to give Lucien his long-deserved comeuppance."

"I can't stand the woman," Charles said coldly.

Andrew tipped his chair back on its legs. "Neither can I, but I want to hear this one out."

"Yes, do tell all, Celsie," urged Gareth, raising a brow.

Celsie looked at all of them in turn, and poor Nerissa, still sitting at the table and staring into space.

"He got her pregnant," she announced, folding her arms on a note of triumph.

"What?" cried Gareth, Charles, and Andrew in unison.

"He got her pregnant," Celsie repeated. "I have just spoken with her, and she confirmed it."

"Good God!"

"Pregnant?"

"Does he even know?"

"No, he does not. Which is how *we're* going to turn the tables on him." Celsie began to pace once more, her eyes gleaming. "Eva came here looking for refuge. She told me that he'd ruined her life, but I never did catch on to just what she *really* meant. But think about it. Andrew, you remember last night, when she ran out of the room feeling sick? Well, why do you think she was feeling sick? Why do you think she's so unnaturally pale? At the ball this evening, I caught her holding on to the edge of the table and taking deep breaths. She told me she felt a little faint from the heat and number of people in the room, but as Juliet and Amy will tell you, that, too, is a sign that she's in the family way."

"I can't believe this," Charles said, shaking his head. "Lucien would never be so careless."

"Well, let me tell you something else," Celsie continued. "When Eva came here, she told me she 'overpowered' Lucien and rendered him quite helpless. I suppose that if she's capable of doing *that*, she's capable of having her way with him."

"Come, now, Celsie," said Gareth, not unkindly. "We know she's some sort of spy and a woman of extraordinary prowess, but I hardly think she's the sort to prey on men in *that* sort of way."

"Yes, especially as any fool could tell she was doing her best to get away from them all tonight," Juliet put in.

Amy was shaking her head. "She may have been doing her best to get away from the men at the ball, but that doesn't mean she was doing her best to get away from *Lucien*." She looked around the room at the others. "No matter what you all think of Lucien, and of Eva, there's one thing that none of us here can deny: They're a perfect match for each other."

"Exactly!" cried Celsie, clapping her hands once in triumph.

Charles was staring at them. "You don't mean to try and force Lucien to marry the woman—"

"Oh, that's exactly what I'm planning," Celsie returned, eyes gleaming. "Think about it. For years, we've been wanting to give Lucien a taste of his own medicine. Well, Eva herself is the absolute best comeuppance we can give him."

"I suppose he *did* ruin her life," Gareth said, thoughtfully rubbing his chin.

Andrew added, "He also got her thrown out of France, cost her the trust of her American compatriots, and robbed her of her dignity."

"Charles?"

"I'm listening."

"I think we're all in agreement about one thing," Celsie said. "Lucien has it coming to him—"

"And Eva de la Mouriére will make a matchless duchess," finished Gareth.

Juliet was beaming. "Oh, I *do* like this plan! Go on, Celsie."

"Well, if we want to bring them together, we'll need to resort to a bit of scheming as diabolical as anything that Lucien has come up with regarding us. Eva will never consent to marry Lucien on her own, of course. And Lucien will not be so easily forced into matrimony. This is what we must do." She stopped before the fire, tapping her chin. "Gareth, as a member of Parliament, you can convince your peers that Eva is dangerous and must be neutralized by the only person capable of controlling her: Lucien."

Gareth inclined his head. "My pleasure."

"Meanwhile, Nerissa and I will petition the king to the same effect, painting Eva as a misguided woman who deserves better than what she's received at Lucien's hands. If we're successful, we'll be able to convince His Majesty to order Lucien to marry this poor woman he has ruined, not only so she can't make any further mischief with France—but to finally beget an heir for the dukedom of Blackheath."

She paused, looking at each face in turn. "So, what do you all think?"

"I think it's a brilliant plan," said Andrew.

"Diabolically wonderful," added Juliet, nodding.

"Yes, it's about time Lucien gets a taste of his own medicine," said Gareth, warming to the idea.

"Charles?"

The major glanced at his sister. "I detest the woman

and am in no mood to forgive her, but if Lucien truly is responsible, even indirectly, for Perry's death, then the two damn well deserve each other."

Celsie smiled and waited for Andrew to pass around a bottle of port. When everyone had filled their glass, she raised her own. "A toast, then!" she said. "To Lucien's comeuppance!"

"To Lucien's comeuppance!"

Chapter 12

L ucien returned from France after an unsuccessful quest to locate Perry, only to find that in his absence, his life had been totally taken over by others and was now fully out of his control.

He was livid.

"How *dare* anyone tell me what to do?" he seethed as Charles handed him the decree, signed by the king himself, insisting upon an immediate marriage between His Grace the Duke of Blackheath and Eva de la Mouriére.

"Well, really, Luce, the king of England isn't just *anyone*," Andrew said cheerfully as Lucien, his face like a thundercloud, stared numbly down at the decree as though it were a warrant for his own execution. "I do think you've got to listen to him."

"Yes, it would be very unwise to deny His Majesty's wishes," Gareth added, idly lounging on the library settee.

"Disastrous," Charles put in.

Getting up, Gareth splashed a generous shot of whiskey into a glass. "It appears you don't have any choice but to marry the lady, especially since she's carrying the Blackheath heir." He handed the glass to Andrew.

Andrew handed the glass to Charles. "And we all know how seriously you take family responsibility. Must carry on the line, you know."

"Absolutely," said Charles, carrying the glass of whiskey toward his stricken brother. "And best of all, Luce, your bride-to-be is right here at Rosebriar."

"Which is most convenient," said Gareth.

"Yes, no chasing after her back in France," Andrew added.

"We even took the trouble of procuring you a special license so you can get married right away."

Lucien lowered the decree and stood staring into space.

Charles plucked it from his hands and replaced it with the glass of whiskey. "She'll make a splendid duchess, Luce. Absolutely magnificent."

Lucien managed to keep his face perfectly still, though inside, it was a different story indeed. A towering rage such as he'd never known was rising like mercury on a thermometer suddenly plunged into boiling oil. For a moment, his vision was obliterated by red haze. For a moment, he feared his very head was going to explode. His fists clenched at his sides—but no. Breeding prevailed. Tight-lipped, his eyes murderous and the untouched whiskey still in his hand, he turned his back on his brothers and walked a little distance away, unable to look at those three benignly innocent faces, all of which looked just a little too happy, a little too satisfied, a little too . . . triumphant.

Were they somehow behind this appalling mess? Were they scheming to manipulate *his* life, as he had schemed to manipulate theirs?

They wouldn't.

They wouldn't dare.

But he knew that they had . . . and that he had it coming to him.

He heard Andrew say as much from somewhere behind him. "Really, Luce, it's not so bad. Just think of all the underhanded things you did to get us married, when that was the last thing any of *us* wanted. But you knew best, didn't you? Well, in this case, *we* know best. You need a duchess. Blackheath needs an heir. Hell, with Eva, you have both, all ready and waiting for you."

Lucien set the untouched glass down, keeping his back to his brothers as he used every ounce of control to hold his temper in check. He would not let them know how very, very angry they had made him. So angry, in fact, that he could hear his pulse pounding in his ears. So angry that he dared not speak for fear of losing control of his words and the volume of his voice. So angry that he was ready to do something totally crass and vulgar, such as pummel each of those smirking faces with his fist.

Better to leave before he could do just that.

Back stiffly erect, his face darker than an incoming storm, he left them without another word.

He walked blindly out of the house and outside, into the bracingly raw winter wind. He welcomed the discomfort. He needed to think. To plan. Revenge was the furthest thing from his mind; he wanted only a solution. Alternatives. Escape. He strode to the stables and, summoning a groom, ordered Armageddon saddled. The servant took one look at his thunderous face and paled, then hurried to do his bidding.

Lucien paced back and forth, his blood boiling as he waited for the stallion to be tacked up. He heard the great beast's savage kicks ringing against its stall, and then the commotion as the jet-black Arabian, a gift from a Bedouin sheik during one of Lucien's many travels, was brought out of the stall, shaking his head, striking out with his lethal forelegs, and nearly yanking the two grooms who were trying to restrain him straight off their feet.

Moments later, Lucien was astride the foaming, fractious animal and cantering away from the manor.

Once out of sight of any watching eyes, he let the horse have his head. Armageddon's body leveled out as he thundered across a pasture, his hooves cutting up the flinty turf, flushing a pheasant, and sending two rabbits diving for cover as he pounded past a thicket of brambles. The winter wind was exhilarating, heavy with the scent of damp earth, but Lucien's fury was inescapable; even a headlong gallop across the cold winter heath could not dispel it.

Suddenly Armageddon's head went up, his ears flicked back, and Lucien knew he was no longer alone.

He glanced over his shoulder. Another rider, mounted on a lathered chestnut, was coming up just behind him, approaching fast.

It was Eva.

For a moment, the sight of her—face flushed with

wind, skirts flying, her slender, curvy form beautifully erect in the saddle—made desire swell his loins and the breath catch in his lungs. But only for a moment. He was too angry with her to indulge himself by admiring her superior horsemanship, her flawless seat and balance, the picture she made—that glorious red hair swept up beneath a hat, eyes glowing with the exhilaration of the ride—atop her mount. He shortened rein so she could catch up.

"You shouldn't be pounding across the heath in your condition," he said coldly as she drew up alongside him.

"You are aware of it, then."

"Of course I'm aware of it. My gloating siblings couldn't wait to inform me." He turned and fixed her with his blackest glare as Armageddon, furious at being held back, pranced forward. "You'll be happy to know, madam, that for the sake of both our prides I neglected to tell them the real story."

"What, that I had my way with you?"

He directed his cold stare forward. "Precisely."

"Well, Blackheath, be that as it may, if my memory serves me correctly you were as equally determined to have me as I was to have you. You consented. It was a game. I thought you understood that, as did I. Just because I initiated it on my terms is no reason to put all the blame for this unfortunate consequence on me."

"You were careless."

"*I* was careless? May I remind you, Blackheath, it takes *two* to conceive a child."

"Do not condescend to lecture me, madam. I am not in a fit temper at the moment."

"And don't *you* condescend to lecture me about fit

tempers," she returned sourly. "It's bad enough to find myself in the family way, but to know that you, of all people, are the father causes me no end of grief."

He turned and regarded her levelly for a moment, expertly controlling the prancing, blowing stallion. "And do we know, madam, that I am indeed the father?"

Her eyes narrowed beneath the brim of her plumed riding hat. "I loathe men," she said frostily. "You were the first since my wretched husband died and, I can assure you, will be the last." She turned to face straight ahead, letting her horse keep pace with Lucien's. "The only reason I allowed you into my bed at all was because I needed to ensure that I had the real aphrodisiac."

"Which, may I remind you, is now safely out of your treacherous clutches, and shall remain so."

"As it's twice been my undoing, I no longer have need of it, so try not to revel in your triumph."

"Ah, yes, your *need* of it. For what nefarious purpose was it intended, madam, that you were willing to inflict bodily harm on my brothers and break into my bedchamber in order to get it?"

"That is absolutely none of your concern."

"Perhaps not." His smile was chilling. "But I can assure you, I will find out. In the meantime, I am still waiting for you to tell me how you managed to render me insensible back in Paris without even a blow."

"I am not about to share my secrets."

"Ah, so you intend to remain a woman of mystery, do you?"

"I intend to remain a woman of independence. Now do stop talking to me, Blackheath. I—I must think."

They continued on side by side, the horses blowing great plumes of steam from their reddened nostrils, their hooves sinking into creamy white mud as the track took them uphill between a copse of maple and beech; overhead, leafless branches scraped against the low pewter sky. Lucien shot his companion a sidelong glance. Her color was high, her eyes bright, and there were cracks in her otherwise composed bearing. A thin smile stole over his lips. He knew enough—more than enough—about women to know what those signs met. He had rattled her. Shaken her. Thrown her off balance.

She wanted him as much as he wanted her.

And God help him, he certainly wanted her—despite his fury with her, with his brothers, with fate. And how could he not? He let his gaze slide over her bosom, admiring the way it filled out the rich plum velvet of her riding habit. He suspected the nipples beneath were taut and hard, the coral flesh aching for his touch. Well, they wouldn't be aching for long. And neither would he—for there was no pretending the pressure in his loins was anything but what it was: lust. He wanted nothing more than to reach out, snare her reins, and kiss that proud, unhappy expression from her beautiful face.

Wanted nothing more than to slide his hand between the tightly buttoned closure of her smart-fitting jacket and let those perfect breasts fill his hand.

Wanted nothing more than to yank her off that horse, tumble her to the ground, and take her right here in the damp grass, over and over again, until he'd had his fill of her.

He tore his gaze away. "So here we are, neatly maneuvered into a situation that neither of us wants.

Tell me, madam, how do you propose we settle this matter?"

"I should let you figure that out, since it's all your fault that we're even in this predicament."

"*My* fault?"

"Yes, yours. If your sister hadn't found out that you—not some fictitious Spanish relative—machinated Lord Brookhampton's departure from England, your brothers wouldn't have gone to the lengths they did to give you a taste of your own medicine. They are all very upset with you, you know. And now *I'm* expected to pay the price for your diabolical schemes."

Lucien felt the blood drain from his face at this added disclosure. "My sister—knows?"

"Of course she knows! And don't think she's going to forgive you for it anytime soon, you monster."

Lucien took a deep breath, trying to calm his suddenly pounding heart. *Hell and damnation!* Nerissa knew. *She knew.* Oh, dear God. . . .

He set his jaw. "My brothers have good reason to turn the tables on me, but I can assure you it has nothing to do with Nerissa or Lord Brookhampton."

"Ah, yes. I've heard all about how you *arranged* their lives, too. You're despicable, Blackheath."

"Yes, so I've been told. But this senseless bickering about my character will not resolve our own situation. Let us get to the heart of the matter. I assume it's marriage you're after?"

"Marriage? Ha! Marriage, especially to an odious monster such as yourself, would be a burden, not a blessing." She jerked her head up, her gaze distant. "Besides, I know far too much about men to ever regard matrimony as a state worth repeating."

"My dear Eva," he murmured sarcastically, "surely you must have had marriage in mind, otherwise you never would have sought me out in England, let alone remained here after learning of my brothers' plans for us."

"I came to England because I was asked to leave Paris and had nowhere else to go—another disruption to my life for which I can place all blame directly on you."

"An eye for an eye."

"This isn't funny, Blackheath."

"Indeed, madam, I am not laughing. In fact, this is a serious matter we are discussing."

"I don't see as if we have anything to talk about."

"A child is something to talk about. Regardless of the circumstances of its conception, regardless of our feelings toward each other, regardless of our mutual aversion to the idea of marriage, the truth is, you are in the family way. I will not pay you off and send you away like some unwanted baggage. I will not allow you to manage this complication on your own."

She gave him a sidelong glance. "What are you saying, Blackheath?"

"That I see no alternative but to make you my duchess."

She paled and abruptly reined up her mount. "Oh, no, Blackheath, don't even *think* it. I will not—I repeat, not—even consider your proposal."

"You have no choice." He brought Armageddon in front of her horse and down its opposite side so that the stallion faced the direction from which they'd come. Eva was riding sidesaddle; her legs, hidden beneath generous folds of lush aubergine velvet, were all but crushed beneath his own hard thigh as he pressed his own mount close. He snared her horse's reins and stared into Eva's defiant green eyes. "And neither, I might add, do I."

"Of course you have a choice; men always do. And you, being a duke, have more choices than most."

"Not when the king himself decrees that said duke must marry."

"Your king—not mine. I need not abide by his wishes, and won't."

"I am not asking you to abide by his wishes. I am asking you to abide by the needs of this child."

Eva stared out over the heath for another long moment, fighting the urge to yank her mount—and her legs—safely away from Blackheath's thigh, fighting her rising panic, fighting the maelstrom of emotions that were making her heart spin like a top in her chest. God help her, if she wed him and he were to learn the real reason she'd stolen the aphrodisiac, that same English king who wanted a marriage between them would have her head for treason. Eva's mouth went dry. She felt suddenly trapped. Scared. Desperate—

Something in her face must have alerted him to what she was thinking. He leaned close—so close that she could see straight down into the empty black well of his eyes, straight down into the demise of her own freedom. He reached out and grasped her chin, forcing her to look right at him. "I warn you, Eva, that if you think to flee me, I will find you. Always. I will hunt you down as a wolf hunts a rabbit. And I will not give up until I find you." He released her. "Do I make myself clear?"

She stared off over the heath, head high, refusing to

look at him and hoping he wouldn't see her shaking hands or hear her suddenly pounding heart.

"Remember, it is not your wishes we are discussing here—but the needs of an unborn child. I will give you until the end of the week to accept my suit, Eva. No more." He moved the stallion into her line of vision, forcing her to look at him, and into those black, black eyes that held no pity, and even less compassion. "Good day, madam."

He sketched a bow from the saddle, and it was only as he sent the hellish beast galloping off that Eva allowed herself to take a great shaky breath . . . and the very real freedom to feel exactly what she was.

Terrified.

Chapter 13

Lucien galloped back to Rosebriar, handed Arma-geddon to a groom, and immediately sought out Nerissa. She was closeted in her apartments, unwilling to receive anyone.

He knocked on the door. "Nerissa," he called gently.

"Go away, Lucien. I have no wish to see or speak to you ever again."

If she had taken a carving knife to his heart, Lucien could not have felt more pain. He bent his head and rested his brow on two fingers for a moment. She was his sister. His only sister, his littlest sibling, the only woman he would gladly give his life for, if only to see her happy. And now he had destroyed her—and any chance she might have had for finding that happiness. He took a deep breath, let his hand fall to his side, and tried again. "Nerissa, please. We have much to discuss."

Silence. Then the dull patter of feet across a floor, the latch lifting, and there—Nerissa.

The sight of her shocked him. She had lost weight. Her once-sparkling blue eyes were sunken and lifeless in cheeks that had gone hollow; her hair had lost its shine and her mouth looked as though it would never smile again. She looked at him flatly, her face mirroring hurt, betrayal, and loathing.

"Why?" she whispered. Her lower lip began to tremble. "Why couldn't you have just left us alone, Lucien?"

For once in his life, Lucien didn't know what to say. He moved into the room and shut the door behind him.

"You weren't content to all but ruin our brothers' lives," she continued in that awful, fragile whisper. "Oh, no. You had to play God again, didn't you?"

"How did you find out?" he asked hoarsely, his voice sounding distant even to his own ears.

"Oh, one of your friends had a bit too much to drink at Celsie's and Andrew's ball and got rather loose of tongue. He told me about the Spanish estate. I guessed the rest. You just wanted to get Perry out of England, didn't you?"

Lucien could not face the accusation in those tragic blue eyes. He looked down and then away, his jaw hard.

"I hate you," she murmured. "I hate you so much that it hurts to even look at you."

The words cut him to the marrow, but not as much as the revulsion in that once-trusting, once-loving face. Nothing—not even death—could strike such a blow as that. His stomach tightened, and pain seared his chest until it hurt just to breathe. He deserved this, he could not deny that; but he could not stand here and face what had become of his little sister, could not stand here and know that he—and he alone—had done this to her.

He did not trust himself to speak. He would talk to her later, when he'd had time to gather his thoughts, time to brace himself for her disgust and revulsion. He bowed, turned, and somehow found himself at the door. He had just lifted the latch when her voice cut through his stupor of grief, a tiny, pathetic sound that was little more than a choked whisper.

"Why?" She paused. "Why do you do the things you do, Lucien?"

He remained where he was, staring hopelessly down at his boot. "Does it matter?"

"You knew that Perry and I were as good as affianced, but you weren't content to wait, to give him the time he needed to make it official."

Lucien went very still. He shut his eyes, his chest throbbing with agony. How could he explain such a complicated thing to her, when he barely understood it himself? He thought of his own childhood. A childhood that had been sacrificed for the dukedom and the responsibilities that went with it, to this sibling and her brothers so that they could be young and care-free—a childhood that had ended the moment he'd found his father lying dead on the tower stairs, his neck broken. Lucien had thought he was invincible, that the world would obey his every command. But he had been unable to keep his father from falling down those stairs. And he had been unable to save his mother when she'd followed him to the grave so soon afterward.

Was it any wonder that he'd been obsessed with

control ever since? Obsessed with ensuring that his world and those that inhabited it all went and behaved exactly to plan?

He turned away, his eyes bleak with pain. He understood why he did the things he did . . . but his sister never would. And the explanation, in light of the fact that he had—in seeking to exert control once again—probably killed the man she loved, sounded trite and pathetic, even to his own reasoning.

He had nothing to say to her. Absolutely nothing.

He turned and left.

Supper was a grim and silent affair. Nerissa took her meal in her room. Eva picked at her food, then pushed it around on her plate and stared miserably into her untouched wine. Juliet, Amy, and Celsie tried to get conversation going, and eventually gave up when they saw their husbands exchanging looks of concern. Lucien, though he ate in silence, noticed all that went on about him. He was keenly aware of his sister's absence. Of Eva's despondency. But as for his brothers—he couldn't even bear to look at them.

He could not get Nerissa's face out of his mind. Those empty blue eyes, that naked revulsion in her face, still haunted him.

Movement from across the table disturbed his morose reverie. He looked up; Eva had pushed her plate away and was mumbling her apologies, her excuses. The men rose respectfully as she stood and left the room.

With sullen eyes, Lucien watched her retreating back, then returned his attention to his plate. He ate in silence, waiting until the meal was finished and his sisters-in-law had left before finally glaring up at his brothers.

"What ails her?" he demanded harshly of Charles, who sat nearby, pondering his own glass of sherry.

His brother lifted his pale blue gaze and regarded him levelly. "She's pregnant, Lucien."

"Juliet didn't eat much when she was carrying, either," Gareth added helpfully.

Lucien said nothing, though this reminder of Eva's condition did nothing to soothe his mounting frustration. Frustration that he had no choice but to make her his duchess. Frustration that she was determined to refuse him. Frustration that the entire bloody earth had fallen off its axis. He slammed his napkin down on the table. By God, when had the world stopped obeying his command?

"She is thinner than when I last saw her," he said abruptly. "I thought pregnancy makes women increase, not decrease."

Andrew shrugged. "Not in the early stages."

"How would you know?" Lucien impaled Andrew with his blackest look. "You're not a father."

"Not yet. But I will be by summer's end."

Lucien stared at him, momentarily taken aback. He had thought Andrew far too immersed in his science, and Celsie far too involved with her efforts to improve the lots of dogs and cats, to ever hope for a niece or nephew where they were concerned. Despite his anger with his three brothers, he rose to shake Andrew's hand. "Congratulations. When is the big day?"

"Late summer," Andrew said, beaming.

Lucien stood back as Gareth and Charles also rose

and congratulated Andrew, slapping him on the back and proposing toasts to the unborn child. Andrew's face glowed with pride. Lucien smiled and looked away, fighting envy. He thought of Eva, carrying his own child in her womb. The fact that she cared more for her precious freedom than his heir's welfare burned at his insides. It was all he could do to adopt his normal mask of indifference as talk centered around the newest generation of de Montfortes, all he could do to pretend a certain aloofness from this conversation he so desperately wished he could partake in.

Presently, though, the tall case clock in the corner struck midnight. One by one, his brothers, yawning, took their leave and sought their beds—and their loving wives.

Lucien was left alone.

He pulled his chair up to the fire and sat there in the vast, drafty room, feet thrust out before him as he stared sullenly into the dying flames. He sipped his sherry. Watched a shower of sparks tumble from the coal-red embers in a little hiss, sending up a puff of smoke that quickly dispersed into the chilly air. He set the sherry down, listening to the howl and whine of the wind outside. Thinking. . . .

All this talk about babies brought back memories. Of Nerissa as an infant, so tiny, deprived of her mother—and her father—at birth. He thought of Andrew, so small at the time, of Charles and Gareth, brave little lads trying to accept the loss of their mama and papa and failing miserably. Lucien had stepped into the role of parent as naturally as he had stepped into that of new duke. He had taken responsibility for them all—

just as he would take responsibility for this new little one that Eva was determined to keep from him.

He leaned his head back against the chair. Eva. Nerissa. The nightmares. The world had spun out of his control. Never had he felt more powerless; never had he felt so adrift. There was nothing more he could do for Nerissa, save for continue his quest to find out Perry's true fate.

As for Eva . . . And marriage . . .

He dragged a hand down his face. He wanted her in his bed, yes, but he didn't want her in his house, and he certainly didn't want her in his life. Pride had been the catalyst for his demand that they marry. Pride— and responsibility. She was carrying his child—and by God, no child of a Duke of Blackheath would be born a bastard, no matter what its mother had in mind!

Damn her!

She would marry him, no matter how vehemently she might refuse, because that was his will, and he would have his way. She was going to be the next Duchess of Blackheath whether she wanted the title or not. He had no illusions that his would be the sort of marriage his brothers had. Oh, far from that. His duchess would be nothing more than a vessel meant to bear the next Duke of Blackheath. Not a wife. Not a lover. A vessel. He would be civil to her, resist the lust she aroused in him, and ensure that she and the child would lack for nothing after he was gone. Once that happened, she would be restored to the independent lifestyle she so treasured—this time, with all the power and resources of the duchy of Blackheath at her disposal.

After he was gone.

Lucien took another sip of sherry, set the glass down, and stared unblinkingly into the dying flames. He must see his solicitor about adding a clause in his will. A clause that would ensure she never took his heir out of England. That much, at least, was within his control.

Even from beyond the grave.

He stretched his feet toward the fire, leaned his head back, and let the dimming flames play against his closed eyelids. His anger had exhausted itself. He felt back in control now. Set upon a course of action. Relaxed. In the corner, the clock ticked softly. At his feet, the fire crackled and hissed as it retreated farther into the glowing embers. His chin fell to his chest, and from out of the flickering orange glow against his eyelids came the cloaked figure he had come to dread.

The dream was the same as it had been last night, and the night before that, and every night before that for the past two months. There was his opponent, all in black, his equal in skill, strength, and cunning. Ten paces, the drop of a handkerchief, and then steel ringing against steel as Lucien battled the one, the only opponent he knew he could never best. It was a duel to the end . . . and then Death came, riding the blade of his opponent's sword, riding it straight through the wall of his chest and impaling his heart in one agonizing burst of fire. Lucien went down. He was on his back, staring up at his opponent's form, dimming now, as it stood triumphantly over him. He could feel the blood bubbling from his chest, his life ebbing away with the dying flow from his mortally injured heart—

He jerked awake with a start.

His heart was thundering in his ears, his skin damp with sweat. He blinked and straightened up. Nothing but the glowing embers, the creaking of the house as it settled for the night, the steady ticking of the clock.

But *she* was here.

He knew it as surely as he drew breath.

Slowly, he turned his head to the right . . . and there she was, sitting quietly in a chair not five feet away, the firelight glowing upon her beautiful, treacherous face.

"Bad dream?" She leaned forward to retrieve what remained of his sherry and pressed it into his hand.

He said nothing, only taking the glass and downing its contents before his still-shaky hand could spill it.

"I gathered as much." She leaned back as he set the glass aside and dragged a hand down his face, trying to banish the terrifying images. "Shall I light some candles? Stoke up the fire, to chase away your demons?"

"No. There is no need."

Stay with me, though. I would like that very much indeed.

She refilled his glass, poured one for herself, and sat beside him, saying nothing, as though she understood his need for companionship, for the time to steady his nerves. He was surprised, and strangely touched, by her compassion. He hadn't thought her to be in possession of such tender emotions.

"I have bad dreams, too," she murmured at length, "but I suppose they're more the product of memory than unconscious imagination."

"Do they keep you awake at night?"

"No." She gazed into the fire, smiling ruefully. "They torment me so much during the day that I suppose they need their own rest come darkness." She leaned her head back against her chair. Her hair was loose around her shoulders, thick, sensual, luxurious, a dark contrast to the stark paleness of her face, her delicately arched throat, the creamy swells of her breasts. Lucien felt desire swell his loins, ignite his blood. Oh, how he ached to pull her into his arms and banish the nightmarish specter his life had become, to bury himself in her womanly warmth and let her heal him. A foolish thought, that. He knew she had her own share of demons. Perhaps too many to ever completely exorcise.

"I have been observing your family," she said at length. "Your brothers seem to cherish their wives."

"They worship the ground they walk on."

"So it appears. I do not quite know what to make of it."

"What is there to make of it?"

She lifted one shoulder in a negligent gesture. "I'm not accustomed to seeing husbands treat their wives with such respect and affection." As he raised his brows, she flushed and looked away, unable to meet his penetrating gaze. "Oh, I know men do, of course, during the courtship stage, but once that ring is on the finger, their interest wanes, and off they go toward other pursuits. Neglect replaces what was once fascinated attention. Cruelty replaces kindness. But your brothers"—she shook her head—"they perplex me. Did you know that Andrew only allowed me to stay here because Celsie wished it? Because *she* wished it." She gave an incredulous little laugh. "Why, any other man would have stomped her wishes beneath his feet and asserted his will over hers. I must confess, such unusual behavior on the part of Lord Andrew quite astonishes me."

"Then I must assume you are equally astonished by that same behavior as exhibited by his brothers."

"Yes." Her mysterious little smile faded, to be replaced by something hopeless. Something tragic. "One can only hope that when they revert to true type, they don't shatter their wives' hearts."

"What makes you think that what you have witnessed is not their true type?"

She snorted and gave a dismissive wave of her hand, then looked at him as though he lacked the sense of a grasshopper. "Oh, Blackheath, really. Don't be so idealistic. I know they're your brothers, but they're still men, and as I told you earlier, I know men. Trust me, once the newness of their marriages wears off, they'll be as vile as the rest of their gender. It's only a matter of time."

He smiled, intrigued by her odd notions. "And if they prove you wrong?"

"They won't."

He looked at her contemplatively. "I suspect you were not the recipient of such devotion during your own marriage, then."

"My husband was a wretched excuse for a human. A weak and disgustingly pathetic worm who, I can assure you, did indeed run true to type."

"Why did you marry him, then?"

She took a sip of her sherry. "I was young. Naive. Foolishly enamored of the idea of leaving constrictive, Puritan-minded Salem and living in France with a dashing *comte*. I looked forward to having adventures, to becoming a woman of power and importance, to enjoying the love and devotion of my husband. But he did not love me. He only married me because he knew he could depend on me to perform the majority of his political duties . . . leaving him free to chase every skirt that swished across his path." She set the sherry down, her eyes distant. Hard. "One day I caught him rutting with my maid. I had long since stopped allowing him into my own bed, you see, because I had discerned his true nature shortly after we exchanged vows. It was just as well, really. She had my husband's babe and died of syphilis shortly thereafter. The baby perished with her." Her face was white and still. "It"—she swallowed and briefly closed her eyes, remembering—"was born a monster."

Lucien was appalled. He eyed her narrowly, certain mysteries about her behavior, her beliefs, beginning to make sense. No wonder she had such a cynical view of marriage. No wonder she despised and distrusted men. He ached to reach out to her, but pride was evident in the set of her chin, the glitter in her eyes, the way she held her mouth—firm, flat, unforgiving. Instead, he topped up her glass and said gently, "My dear Eva, not all men are like your husband."

"All the men of my experience have been."

"Even your father?"

She stiffened, and a shadow came over her face like a cloud shutting out the sun. "*Especially* my father," she said in a low, tremulous voice. She raised her eyes to his, those mysterious, slanting eyes that so fascinated him, and he saw that she was no longer contemplative, no longer amenable to conversation, but savage and angry once more. "Why am I telling you this, Blackheath? There is nothing you or anyone else can do to change my mind about your gender. Nothing you or anyone else can do to make me respect them, trust them, like them." She rose to her feet. "I was wrong to come in here, wrong to confide in you. Good night."

"Eva."

She paused, her back to him, a proud figure in glittering amber silk.

"What did your father do to you?"

"It is in my past, Blackheath. Leave it there."

"Then consider your future. You cannot deny the child that is in your belly," he said softly.

She remained where she was, unmoving.

"You cannot deny the attraction that lies between us."

He saw her shoulders stiffen, heard the measured intake of her breath.

"And you cannot deny that the only sensible course of action is to accept my proposal and become the next Duchess of Blackheath."

She turned then, her eyes flashing green fire. "And that is *exactly* the sort of arrogance that I so detest about your gender, Your Grace."

She dropped in a stiff, mocking curtsy, and was gone.

Chapter 14

Once Eva was safely away from the library, she found herself running from Blackheath. Not just running.

Fleeing.

Her heart was pounding by the time she reached the safety of her apartments. Shutting the door, she collapsed back against it, breathing hard, her eyes wild and frightened as she stared across the dimly lit chamber.

She raked her hands down her face, trembling. It was happening all over again, this time with a man so dangerous he made her dead husband seem positively benign. "Oh, damn you, Blackheath," she whispered as she stood there shaking and trying to ground herself in the strength of her own fortitude, the safety of her own cynicism. It was no use. She let herself slide down the door until she was sitting on the rug, legs bent to her chest, her hair spilling over her arms and shutting out the world. She felt cold all over, as though ice ran in veins that had once held blood as warm as any other woman's, pumped from a heart that had once been as capable of love, of dreams as any other starry-eyed female. It was a long time before her breathing steadied and she could think once more.

What had happened, tonight?

She relived the past half hour. So unsettled by her earlier encounter with Blackheath that she'd been unable to sleep, she had gone down to the library intending to get a book. She had never reached her destination. As she'd passed through the apparently deserted dining room, she'd seen a chair pulled close to the fire and, filling it, her nemesis's commanding, splendidly handsome form.

For a moment, wild elation had chased through her—*he* was here. Her heart had leaped. Her body had flushed with heat. She should have bolted right then and there, but no, she had stayed, when every instinct of survival, of self-preservation had screamed at her to run. She had stayed because he, mighty duke and god of arrogance, was having a nightmare, laid low by something that mere mortals such as the rest of the world battled all the time. She had stayed, because she had wanted to see the man she both feared and despised, respected and admired, rendered as human as anyone else, instead of the unreachable, inscrutable being she had come to know. She had stayed—for reasons she did not fully understand, did not *want* to understand . . . reasons that had nothing to do with wanting to see him suffer, and everything to do with the softer, more tender aspects of womanhood that sought only to comfort; softer, more tender feelings she had long denied existed in her own empty breast.

The very thought that those soft, tender feelings might lurk there like some encroaching cancer was enough to start Eva trembling all over again. They were feminine feelings. Protective feelings. Dangerous feelings.

The sort of feelings that led to broken dreams and shattered hearts.

Memories flooded her. She saw her mother's face, twisted, bitter, poisonous, ravaged by fifteen years of heartbreak and betrayal. . . .

"Men! They're all alike, Eva!"

"But Papa's different—"

"Your father is no better than the rest! Just because he comes home from sea with candy and trinkets, Eva, don't think he loves you! He wanted a boy! He wanted an heir! But he got a girl, he got you, and he's never forgiven me for it!"

"But Mama—"

"I don't want to hear it! Men, they're all alike, every last damned one of them, and don't you ever forget it!"

But she had forgotten it. She had married Jacques. She would not forget it again.

"I cannot marry the duke . . . he will destroy me," she said to the darkness. To the ghost of her long-dead mother.

To herself.

Of its own accord, her hand strayed to her still-flat belly, beneath which lay Blackheath's growing child. No, she could not marry him. She could not sacrifice what was left of her pride, her freedom, and yes, her heart. She could not let her child suffer the heartbreak she had endured, by saddling it with a father.

She gazed out into the cold and misty English night.

Perhaps it was time to leave. Time to go back home to America— where she and her child belonged.

When Eva came downstairs the next morning, determined to eat something despite the nausea the sight—and smell—of breakfast lately produced, she found the de Montforte family already gathered around the table, surrounded by begging dogs, servants, and children running to and fro. Laughter and chaos filled the room. For a moment, she hesitated just outside the door, feeling like an unwelcome intruder and reluctant to impose upon this merry scene of domestic bliss.

Especially if it meant confronting Blackheath.

"Oh, I don't know, I think it's going to be a girl," Juliet was saying as she buttered a piece of toast. "Girls always make you more sick, don't you think, Amy?"

Eva froze.

"Well, I really can't say," answered Amy, whose high cheekbones, straight dark hair, and bronzy skin proclaimed Indian blood. Like Juliet's, her accent reminded Eva of home . . . that humble New England twang that always brought back memories of Salem, shipbuilding, Yankee frugality, and good old common sense. "After all, I've only had Mary, so I don't know how it feels to be carrying a boy."

"I was much sicker with Charlotte," Juliet proclaimed, putting the toast in front of the blond, blue-eyed little girl who climbed up into the chair beside her. "Now, Gabriel, on the other hand . . ."

They're talking about me, Eva thought, horrified. *Talking about my unborn child, making guesses about its gen-*

der. She felt suddenly self-conscious; as eager to leave this happily chaotic scene to which she could never belong as she was to join it.

"Well, you can all speculate as much as you want," Celsie said as she reached for a large helping of cold beef, "but since I haven't had one moment of sickness, I'm going to guess it's a boy."

She happened to glance up at the same time that Eva realized this conversation wasn't about her unborn baby at all—but Celsie's.

Celsie was pregnant?

"Why, Eva! No need to stand there. Come, have some breakfast."

"Yes, Celsie and Andrew have some wonderful news to share!"

The three brothers rose as Eva, feeling somewhat shamefaced for her premature judgment, and very ill at ease, entered the room. Gareth, as usual, was grinning; he was as hard to dislike as he was to take seriously, and she knew his smile was meant to make her feel comfortable. She was grateful for his efforts. Andrew, on the other hand, appeared resigned and uncaring; only Charles looked displeased to see her.

Where was Blackheath?

She felt a stab of disappointment. He was not here.

Eva took her seat as conversation resumed, wondering how an aristocratic family such as this could talk about unborn babies, of all things, in not only mixed company but with children about. She would have thought such a well-bred lot would have considered the subject inappropriate, if not vulgar. And how could Celsie stomach the sight of food, let alone look eager to put away vast quantities of it? Why was her face glowing with health, her eyes bright and her smile quick, when Eva felt positively wretched?

Irritation built. *And where the devil is Bluckheath?*

She smiled at her cousin. "It appears that I owe you and Andrew my congratulations," she said, trying not to feel envious of Celsie's obvious delight at her condition and radiant health. "How long have you known?"

"Oh, for about a fortnight, now," Celsie answered, snaring another slice of toast. "We were going to wait awhile before we announced the news, but we couldn't—we're just too excited!"

Gareth was still grinning. "Everyone's trying to guess whether it will be a boy or a girl, but *I'm* wondering whether it will be an inventor or a crusader for the plight of animals!"

"Perhaps it will be both," Amy put in, picking up her own little daughter and bouncing her on her knee. "Celsie and Andrew are both people of great accomplishment."

"And how are *you* feeling, Eva?" Celsie asked, crunching her toast.

"Sick," she replied with a wan smile. She looked ruefully down at her plate, empty still, despite her resolve to eat something. "I had no wish to intrude upon this happy scene, but I thought I'd let you all know that I'm leaving this afternoon. I have imposed upon your and Andrew's hospitality for long enough."

"Leaving?" Celsie dropped her toast. "You can't do that, you have to marry Lucien!"

"I'm not marrying Lucien."

Immediately there was a buzz of voices around the table, worried frowns and hasty protests, people getting to their feet and the women trying to change her mind.

"But you have to marry Lucien!"

"You must think of your unborn child, Eva!"

"The king has decreed that the two of you marry!"

Eva shook her head. "As much as you all love your brother, and as much as you'd like to see me shackled to him as punishment for my crimes against you"— her gaze went briefly, pointedly to Charles—"I cannot marry him. I have no wish to subject myself to the abhorrent fate of matrimony. No wish to relinquish what remains of my freedom to a man who would surely abuse it. Yes, there is the baby to think of, but I can assure you that it will be well provided for. My father left me a considerable estate upon his death. My child will have everything it needs back home in America—the protection, the comfort, and the love of its mother."

Nerissa, who had been subdued and no doubt brooding over Perry, spoke up. "But what about the protection, the comfort, and the love of its father?"

Abruptly Eva's smile vanished. "Fathers do not matter," she said bitterly. "It will have no need of its father, and neither do I."

There was a horrified gasp from someone, probably gentle Amy, and then a hush as all eyes went to the door.

Blackheath. There he stood, impassive and silent, his gaze impaling Eva where she sat, quite stunned by his sudden appearance, in her chair. Involuntarily, her gut tightened, and tingles of warning tracked up her spine. He had obviously just returned from a long walk; he was still in his country clothes, dark gray broadcloth and mud-spattered boots, his cheeks flushed with cold. Or anger. His face was so still, so guarded, that it was impossible to tell which.

The room went dead silent as everyone waited for something perfectly horrible to issue from his lips.

"Why, hello, Luce," Gareth said uncertainly, trying to alleviate the sudden tension.

"Here, have some breakfast," Charles said, motioning to the expanse of food.

But the duke only gave an icy smile, came around the table toward Eva, and, as she stiffened, bent to drop a kiss against her suddenly hot cheek. His clothes smelled like winter wind, morning air. His lips were as cold as the outdoors from which he'd just come. Nevertheless, they burned her where they touched. Made her nether regions stir. She swallowed, hard.

"You must forgive Eva," he said magnanimously. "Unlike the rest of you, she has yet to realize how . . . satisfying matrimony can be."

"Past experiences have dictated otherwise," Eva ground out.

"Future ones will change your mind."

"My mind is made up, *sir*."

"Your mind merely needs an . . . adjustment."

"So, my dear duke"—she smiled poisonously—"does your arrogance."

Someone snickered. Blackheath just looked at her, his eyes inscrutable.

Eva gazed calmly back, unwilling to back down.

And Blackheath smiled. Chillingly. *We will continue this discussion later,* that smile—those eyes—seemed to say. She knew him well enough by now to know that he would not give his siblings the satisfaction of seeing him argue with her. Not, that is, when they were probably all gloating over engineering what was surely destined to be a disastrous marriage.

His warning sent, the duke plucked young Charlotte from her seat, perched her on his knee, and, holding the little girl securely, whispered something in her ear.

Charlotte's tiny hand plunged into her uncle's pocket. "Sweets!" she squealed, brandishing a wrapped peppermint with triumph.

"Oh, Lucien, not before breakfast!" wailed Juliet.

Gareth started laughing. Tiny Mary Elizabeth and Charlotte's little brother Gabriel immediately began screaming for their share.

The duke only chuckled. "See if you can't find some more where that came from, Charlotte," he murmured, smiling as her hand plunged back into his pocket. "Mary's too young, but I think your little brother would quite enjoy some, don't you?"

Charlotte, two treats clutched in her fist, jumped from her uncle's lap and raced around the table toward Gabriel.

"Lucien!" howled Juliet.

Even Amy looked distressed.

But Eva noticed that Blackheath was quite enjoying the commotion he had caused. Was this how he behaved when the real focus of his frustration—herself—remained out of reach? He was still chuckling, and out of the corner of her eye, Eva could see his lips twitching as he watched Charlotte unwrapping the sweet. Little Gabriel was screaming impatiently for it, Juliet was trying frantically to calm him, and now even Amy looked as though she were about to tear her hair out when Mary started shrieking as well. Eva tightened her lips. How like Blackheath to revel in causing a stir. She was just about to excuse herself and retreat to the safety of her rooms when he reached back into his pocket, produced a last piece of candy, and, quite unobtrusively, placed it on Eva's empty plate.

She gave a snort of laughter. "Really, Blackheath, if you cannot buy me with the offer of making me a duchess, don't think a piece of candy will do it."

"Suck on it," he said simply, ignoring her waspishness as a footman stepped forward and poured coffee into his cup. "It will calm your stomach."

"But how did you know—"

He merely looked at her empty plate and lifted a brow.

Slanting him a look of distrust, she unwrapped the peppermint, placed the wadded-up paper beside her glass, and put the candy in her mouth. For the briefest instant, her stomach recoiled, the nausea rising in the back of her throat. She paled and almost bolted—and then, just like that, the queasiness was gone—and a ravenous hunger was in its place.

Stunned, Eva lifted her gaze and stared suspiciously at her erstwhile tormenter.

He merely smiled. "Better?"

"How did you know that would help when none of the women here knew of such a remedy?" she hissed for his ears alone.

He took her plate and placed two slices of lightly buttered toast on it. "Like you, my mother was also sick whenever she was carrying a little de Montforte," he said affably. "My father would give her peppermints to make her feel better. They worked every time."

"It was a remedy your *father* came up with?"

"He was a very clever man. He loved my mother, and it upset him to see her so ill." He smiled, but there was something significant behind that smile. Something meaningful. "You see, Eva, fathers really *do* matter."

She flushed, embarrassed that he would recall her earlier remark. "Now, here, have some toast. And eat heartily, as I should like to go riding after breakfast and would enjoy the pleasure of your company."

Eva gave him a last, lingering look, and then bit into the toast. It tasted wonderful. Hot and buttery and crunchy on the edges, just as she liked it. She ate the whole slice, then another, and then attacked a slab of cold ham.

It was the first breakfast she'd eaten in over two weeks.

Chapter 15

For Eva, getting through the rest of breakfast was a nearly impossible ordeal.

With the nausea gone, her mind was free to wander, and presently, she became aware of other things: the satisfaction of filling her hungry belly, the joy of being amid the cavorting children and dogs, the laughter of this extraordinary family—and Blackheath's thigh. Oh, yes, his thigh. She kept glimpsing it just beneath the edge of the tablecloth, a mere two inches from her own, close enough to touch, close enough to rob her of the ability to think of anything else. She could feel the heat emanating from it, could remember the naked look of it from their one encounter back in Paris; could even remember how it felt beneath her fingers, the muscles like rock beneath the sparsely haired skin.

Eva tried to concentrate on her ham and toast. On the antics of the three children. On joining the conversation around her—and failed. It wasn't long before the world began to close in, everything fading into the background, leaving nothing but Blackheath's presence beside her—and that thigh. As he leaned toward her and offered another slice of toast, it brushed her own. As she bit into the toast, the reality of his nearness was enough to dry out her mouth and cause her to nearly choke on the crumbs. And by the time she finally got the hapless slice of bread down, she was obsessed with that tantalizing expanse of Blackheath's leg, all but hidden beneath the tablecloth.

Prickly heat suffused her blood. It warmed her cheeks, changed the measure of her breathing. She resisted the urge to peel off her jacket. Fan her face. God, it was hot in here. Again, she glanced at Blackheath's thigh. If they were on better terms she might have reached out beneath the cloth and playfully run her nails, the pads of her fingers, over it, savoring the feel of hard muscle sheathed by butter-soft leather breeches. She would have liked to see if she could arouse him with just a touch, would have enjoyed the anticipation that later they might have sought a bed together.

But they weren't on better terms.

And they never would be.

She pulled her leg closer to its twin and with a somewhat shaky hand picked up her teacup. Thoughts of going to bed with Blackheath, enjoyable as they were, would only get her nowhere. Still, there was no harm in fantasizing over the idea—as long as she didn't forget that fantasy and reality were two different things. Fantasizing over having his hands on her flesh, stroking her body to arousal as he lay her down on that giant medieval bed, was all well and good as long as she reminded herself that it was not going to happen. Therefore, it was a fairly safe activity. Strip Blackheath of his compelling personality, his ability to make her heart grow too hot and heavy for her chest, the glimpses he allowed her of a compassionate man beneath that ruthless, arrogant surface—and render him nothing more than a perfect specimen of a masculine body—and she would be all right. But once she started adding character, feelings, personality, and passion . . .

Well, at that point fantasizing started getting dangerous indeed.

Too dangerous.

Her palms were sweating. Furtively, she wiped them on her skirts, wishing she could calm her thumping heart. Wishing she hadn't started fantasizing, after all. Really, she ought to know better. She glanced around the table—but what she saw, as she allowed the present to overtake her once again, only added to her confusion.

There was Lord Andrew smiling into Celsie's eyes in a way that had his wife blushing; Eva suspected that *their* thighs were certainly touching, if not pressed against each other's. Her face heated, and she jerked her gaze back to her plate. Right, so Andrew was devoted to Celsie, but that was only because they were newlyweds; things would soon change. She glanced at Lord Charles, who was spreading marmalade on a piece of toast for Amy. A display of love and devotion? No, nothing but an act, a gentleman living up to his name. His sweet, doe-eyed wife really shouldn't be looking at him as though he were some earthbound god . . . but then, she was young and impressionable, and there was no denying that Lord Charles *was* an unusually handsome man, in or out of uniform. Eva smiled thinly, satisfied with her conclusions. But what of Lord Gareth, making his wife laugh with the way he was making foolish faces at their little son? Well, his seeming affection for Juliet was easy to explain. Men of Gareth's temperament—men who were gregarious, fun-loving, charming—were that way with *all* women, which is why they all kept mistresses. Eva, feeling quite smug, returned her attention to her plate. Gareth, of course, was no different. She would bet money on it.

And then there was Blackheath. What would he be like as a husband? She could not see him behaving as his brothers did. She could not see him exhibiting such softness, could not see him cherishing her as if she were the most precious thing in the world, could not see him displaying such love and affection. He was different from his brothers. He would certainly be a monster.

No, she wasn't missing a damned thing by refusing his offer. She wasn't missing a thing by deciding not to join this family, by raising her child alone, by taking it back to America. No, the three de Montforte wives, so happy and in love with their handsome husbands, did not deserve her envy; only her pity. Oh, if only they knew what heartache lay before them.

"Uncle Lucien! Will you take me to see the dungeon afterward? Will you?"

Little Charlotte had leaped off her father's knee, raced around the table, and thrown herself into the

duke's lap. His thigh, that damnable thigh, was
shoved sideways, bumping hard into Eva's leg.

Blackheath did not remove it.

Eva, startled, shot him a poisonous look of warning,
but he only smiled and kept it there as the child settled
herself on his lap and, giggling, began pulling at his
stock. Eva moved her leg away from Blackheath's,
clamping her thighs together, swinging the both of
them off to the side; Blackheath's followed, its considerable length pressing against her own, the child still
giggling in his lap as she happily began to undo his
necktie.

"I'm going to be your valet for the rest of the day,"
she announced importantly, then laughed as she set to
retying the once-impeccable length of silk.

"What, not my groom?"

"Oh, no, that was yesterday. Today I am your valet.
You have made quite the mess of this cravat, Uncle
Lucien!"

He chuckled, the very picture of innocence, but only
he and Eva knew that beneath the tablecloth, quite a
different drama was being played out. His thigh still
pressed against her own. She was almost angled in
half trying to escape it. She directed her gaze, now a
glare, straight across the table into the fireplace, determined not to let him know how much he was unsettling her. And unsettling her, he was. Her stays were
suddenly too tight. Her clothes were too warm. Her
pulse was starting to pound.

Damn him!

"All right, Charlotte, that's enough for now," the
duke finally said, grinning as he removed the child's
hands from his hopelessly spoiled stock. "I will take

you to the dungeon this afternoon. First, the comtesse and I are going for a ride around the estate."

"Can I go, too, Uncle Lucien? Can I?"

"Next time, sweeting. The lady and I have matters to discuss. Now off with you!" He rose, tossed the little girl high, and handed her, squealing with delight, back to her mother. And then he extended a hand to Eva . . . who, with everyone in the room observing her closely, had no choice but to accept it and rise.

Bowing to the ladies, Blackheath led Eva from the dining room, hailed a groom, and called for their horses to be saddled.

"Really, Blackheath, I am not in the mood to go riding with you," Eva snapped, damning her body for responding in a most carnal way to his nearness.

"Then what *are* you in the mood for, hmm?"

"Don't use that suggestive tone with me. What happened between us in Paris is most assuredly not going to happen again."

"What a pity. And here I had such high hopes. . . ."

"Quell them, then, and put yourself out of your misery."

He laughed. "Misery? Oh, no, madam. I am quite enjoying the thought of future . . . encounters." He walked along beside her, tall, arrogant, and amused, totally in control of the world that surrounded him. "Surely you will agree that anticipation of the dessert always makes it sweeter."

She could feel that black, simmering gaze upon her. Could feel it warming every inch of her body from head to toe. "Really, Blackheath, you are the most pompous man I have ever met. Just when I start to think that maybe I could like you, you have to say something stupidly, totally . . . *male*. Let me tell you something. I have no interest in going to bed with you, not now, not ever, so you might as well put the thought right out of your mind."

"You sound very sure of yourself, madam."

She slanted him a look of amusement. "Having lived with myself for nearly three decades, I am more than sure of myself. Besides, you're nothing but a typical man, Blackheath, thinking of one thing, and one thing only."

"Ah, so you would have me believe that you're not thinking of the same thing?"

"I am most assuredly *not* thinking of the same thing," she scoffed, but her color was high and she dared not meet his eyes. She could feel that knowing gaze of his searching her face, then moving downward, lingering on the column of her neck, the swell of her bosom. Her blood flushed with answering heat. Desire tingled in her breasts, between her thighs, and she felt a sense of rising panic at her inability to control her body's response to him. "Oh, no, that is the last thing on my mind."

"So what *are* you thinking of, madam?"

"Leaving," she said abruptly. "In fact, this is my last morning at Rosebriar. My maid is packing my trunk as we speak. By this afternoon, I will be on my way south to the coast, and then back to America."

"I will escort you, then."

"What?"

"As far as the coast, at least. I assume you wish to leave from Southampton or Plymouth?"

She eyed him suspiciously. "Yes. . . ."

"Ah, good. I have an estate in Dorset that I would

like to show you before you depart. I had thought to give it to you, but—"

"*Give* it to me?"

They were almost out to the stables. Lucien kept his expression perfectly affable, his manner inscrutable as he waited for her to take the bait. "Well, yes. You see, I have been thinking about our . . . impasse. You have no wish to marry for fear of losing your freedom. And to be quite truthful, I am not inclined to take a wife, though circumstances now necessitate a reappraisal of our mutual wishes. In any case, I think the best solution to our dilemma is to marry but live separate lives. I thought you might like to make Gingermere your permanent residence."

She narrowed her eyes. "You would *give* it to me?"

"Yes. I have been in contact with my solicitor, who went through hell and high water to find a way to deed it to you. It is yours, if you want it. Yours to run as you see fit."

She was staring at him, blinking—but he could see the excitement building in her eyes, could tell that he had hooked her, and hooked her soundly.

"You'll never have to worry about your independence again," he added, reeling her in further. "All you'll have to do is collect and live off the rents, which will be yours to keep, to spend, to invest. Raise cattle, grow corn, do whatever you wish to do with the place—it will be your nest egg for the future, your means of independence."

"And you would not interfere?"

I won't be alive to interfere. "No."

"What are the terms, Blackheath?"

"Marriage, of course. As well as unlimited access to

the child, a promise that you will cease your political activities—which, after we are wed, could get you hanged for treason—and"—he smiled—"an agreement to share a bed."

She flushed. "Is that all?"

"Yes."

But even as he uttered the word, he knew he owed her the full truth. She deserved to know the one stipulation of his will that would sour her on the idea: that in return for Gingermere, she could never take the child out of England, or she would lose everything. But surely that issue would never even come up. After all, why would she want to leave, once he was gone? The condition to keep the child here in Britain, where he could protect it even from beyond the grave, where his family would ensure that it would never lack for anything, was a mere formality. He was simply protecting his heir—and the duchy.

Simply carrying out the responsibilities of his birthright.

She looked at him flatly. "In exchange for marrying you, you'll give me Gingermere and my freedom."

"Yes."

She took a deep, bracing breath, and slowly let it out. Her gaze was fastened on a distant hill. "In that case, Blackheath, I'll be your wife."

Chapter 16

T hey left for Dorset several days later.

Lucien had used that time wisely. He had sent for Fox and ensured that his will—and the transfer of Gingermere's ownership upon his death—was in order. He had taken pains to ensure that his siblings didn't learn of Eva's acceptance of his hand, for he was not yet willing to concede that particular victory to them.

And he had sent more queries off to France regarding Perry.

For Eva, the days had passed in a mixture of excitement and nervousness. Was she doing the right thing? She looked forward to seeing Gingermere. To investigating its possibilities. How ironic it was that in marrying Blackheath, she would obtain the very freedom she'd feared she would lose.

As for the stipulation that she must share his bed—

No. She would not think about how she would deal with that. Not yet, anyhow.

Now Rosebriar was far behind them, the night pressing in as they headed steadily south. Blackheath rode just outside, Armageddon's head appearing occasionally at the window. The coach was well sprung, its gentle rocking motion so comfortable that Eva was having trouble keeping her eyes open. But sleep wouldn't come. Every so often, she parted the curtain and stared out into the frosty night, searching the darkness until she saw the duke out there on Armageddon, his black greatcoat and round hat making him and the stallion as one with the night that surrounded them. She was glad that he was out there and she was in here, because the distance between them guaranteed a certain amount of safety.

And the way she was feeling these days, she knew she would not refuse him when he came seeking her bed.

Funny, what pregnancy does to a woman, she thought.

They stopped for supper at a coaching inn some miles from the coast, where the owner, upon learning from the servants who had traveled ahead that the mighty Duke of Blackheath was to be his overnight guest, fell all over himself to make them comfortable. When they arrived, ostlers were already stationed to take the horses, a meal was being laid on the table in a private room, the finest port in the cellars was being brought up for His Grace's inspection, and Eva thought rather wryly that the king himself would not have received better treatment. Despite all, she could not help but be impressed. In fact, as she and the duke settled down to a hearty meal of gammon, roast potatoes, and boiled vegetables, she began to think that maybe traveling with him had its advantages, after all.

"Shall we stay the night or press on?" he asked as they finished their meal.

"Press on. I'm eager to see Gingermere."

Besides, if we stay the night, you will seek my bed—and I have not the will nor the wish to resist you.

He nodded. But her relief was cut short when he announced that he would leave Armageddon overnight at the coaching inn in the care of one of his own grooms, who would continue on his way with the horse on the morrow.

"So—how will you travel, then?" Dread and anticipation filled her, for she already knew the answer.

"Why, I shall join you inside the coach, my dear." He smiled at the look on her face. "After all, it must get rather lonely in there, with no one to talk to."

"Really, Blackheath, I don't know why you must persist in irritating me so," she muttered, trying to cover her sudden nervousness. And excitement. Just the idea of being so near to him made her flushed, hot, and prickly—feelings that were amplified as his gloved hand took hers and he handed her up into the waiting coach. "But I suppose I shall have to put up with it, since you take such obvious delight in vexing me."

"On the contrary, madam. There are other things we could do that would bring me far more delight than vexing you."

"I am not in the mood to thwart your innuendos, Blackheath. Join me if you will, but for your own health and well-being, you'd best keep your distance."

"Ah, but you agreed that we would share a bed."

"*After* we're married."

He merely smiled. It was obvious he had other ideas.

He climbed up into the coach after her. His presence filled it, made it seem smaller than it really was. Eva felt suffocated, trapped, fretful, wary. Blackheath, of course, seemed indifferent to the effect he was having on her. He pulled the shade partway down, and moments later they were on their way, Eva wrapped in a wool blanket, a hot brick at her feet.

And now what? Blackheath was in the opposite seat, but he was still so close she could smell his shaving soap, the damp wool of his greatcoat, the mingled scents of leather and horse and cold outside air. His long, booted legs were thrust toward her. In the gloom, she could just make out his face, the inscrutable eyes that idly watched her.

Her skin prickled. That scrutiny was more than idle. She moved her feet farther away from his, yanked the blanket up to her chin, and turned her cheek against the leather squab so she wouldn't have to look at him. So he could see as little of her as possible. So she could, with any luck, lose herself in sleep, where she wouldn't feel the weight of that heavy-lidded stare.

"I am going to take a nap," she announced, her voice muffled by the blanket. "Why don't you do the same, Blackheath?"

"It is not my bedtime."

"Surely you must be fatigued."

"I rarely sleep more than four hours per night, madam. I can assure you I'd prefer to remain awake."

"So you can stare at me while I sleep, is that it?"

"I must confess, you make a most delectable sight. You will forgive me if I indulge myself by looking."

"You are despicable and rude, Blackheath."

He chuckled. "So I am. Let's not argue the point. I want you to rest, Eva. After all, you're sleeping for two now."

She merely shot him an irritated glare and shut her eyes. Of course, sleeping with *him* only inches away would be impossible—especially since her traitorous body was sending all sorts of thoughts to her tired brain about how the darkened privacy of the coach would make the perfect setting for a bit of lovemaking. Wouldn't it be nice to just throw off all barriers for once and give in to animal instinct? Wouldn't it be nice to be curled up on Blackheath's lap instead of this lonely seat, while his hand sought her breast and lazily pleasured her until all anger, all inhibitions were pushed aside?

No!

Inwardly cursing, Eva tried to make herself more comfortable against the squab. Blackheath's leg was still too close to her own—he must have moved it, damn him, probably just to annoy her. Peeved, she drew her legs up beneath herself and the blanket, and tried not to think about those enigmatic black eyes silently watching her. Tried not to hear the measured sound of his breathing, tried not to examine the sudden, out-of-nowhere wish that he'd get up, join her, and provide a better pillow than her own folded hands . . . and more warmth, *far* more warmth, than this scratchy wool blanket. . . .

She must have fallen asleep, because only his hand

prevented her from tumbling to the floor when the coach jerked to a sudden stop.

"Stand and deliver!"

Eva was instantly awake and sitting up, even as Blackheath opened the shade and, with a sigh, gazed out into the darkness.

"Highwaymen. How damnably inconvenient," he murmured, reaching calmly into his pocket for a small pistol.

"Yes, and just when I finally got comfortable enough to sleep," muttered Eva as she, too, reached calmly into her pocket for her own gun.

They both happened to look up at the same time, each seeing the other's weapon. Eva raised a brow, waiting for Blackheath to do something unforgivably, insultingly male—such as demand that she put the pistol away so he could deal with this nuisance himself.

But he didn't.

He only cocked the gun and settled back, casually laying the weapon across his knee so that it was pointed out the window. His gaze met her own. "So, madam. It appears we must make a decision."

"Shall I deal with this, or would you prefer to?"

"Though I would very much like to deal with it, I must confess that my curiosity is aroused. Therefore, I should be most intrigued to see how *you* deal with it."

Nothing he could have said might have surprised her more. Eva narrowed her eyes. "Are you serious, Blackheath, or merely indulging me?"

"My dear Eva, I am more than serious."

"Even though I'm a woman?"

"You are a clever, capable, dangerous woman." He

smiled. "I have utter faith in you. Just mind you have a care for the child as well as yourself."

Eva, stunned by this show of respect, could only blink in surprise. Shaking her head, she cleared the hair from her eyes and let a helpless smile curve her lips. She felt more like a partner than his enemy, and her blood was already beginning to race at the prospect of danger—and yes, of impressing the man who sat across from her.

"Ah, yes," she murmured, checking her pistol. "I'd almost forgotten. You love dangerous women."

Footsteps were now approaching from out of the darkness, headed toward the open window. "I love them as long as they manage to stay alive. If you wish to handle it, my dear, you are fast running out of time. Now go to it—as long as you do so without minding the fact that I will be, shall we say, *monitoring*"—he raised his pistol—"events most closely indeed."

"Suit yourself."

He inclined his head. "Then I relinquish control of this situation to you."

"*Relinquish* control of it?" Eva lifted a brow in high amusement. "Careful, Blackheath. Don't go ruining things just when I'm starting to like you."

A pistol appeared at the window; without even glancing at it, Eva yanked the shade down on the robber. "Right. I'll deal with these slugs, and you can cover me."

He put the shade back up and, also without even looking, shoved his own pistol in the robber's face, holding the surprised highwayman at bay as he gazed calmly at Eva. "Consider it done."

Throwing off the rug, Eva got up, opened the coach

door, and, keeping her gun concealed in a fold of her cloak, stepped outside. The rutted ground was partly frozen, and her heel sank through a crust of ice and into the mud; in the frigid night air, her breath was white and ghostly. She could see the first robber still standing beside the window, too terrified of Blackheath's pistol to challenge its owner's temper by moving; his unsuspecting partner, on the other hand, was busy relieving the driver of his watch and coins. Smiling, Eva walked up to the man even as the driver, seeing her, went white as the moon above.

"I beg your pardon," she said sweetly, as the robber whipped around only to find himself staring into the apparently guileless face of a beautiful but harmless noblewoman, "but I really wish you'd leave poor Roberts alone. He has a wife and family to support, and I'm sure they need the money more than you do."

The robber stared at her in amazement.

Eva smiled prettily and jerked her head toward the stricken Roberts. "Don't just stand there like an imbecile, give my poor driver back his watch and money."

The thief grinned; and then his face seemed to change as he took in Eva's priceless emerald choker, her rings, her emerald-tipped hairpins—and her wickedly curvaceous body.

"The hell with Roberts," he muttered, eyeing Eva with undisguised menace. He pointed the pistol at her face. "I'll have those pretty baubles round your neck, ma'am, as well as that pocket at your waist—and then I'll have *you*."

Still smiling, Eva untied the pocket and pretended to let it drop. She bent to retrieve it—and came up with a savage jerk, her elbow slamming into the robber's nose. There was a satisfying crack of bone, his pistol went flying, and he stumbled backward with a scream of agony, his nose gushing blood.

"I *am* sorry," Eva said prettily, picking up his pistol and returning Roberts' possessions. She eyed the thief with false pity. "Perhaps if you stick that ugly face of yours in a puddle, the bleeding will stop."

And then, smiling, she sauntered back to the other robber, still held captive by Blackheath's pistol. Seeing her predatory approach, the man tensed with nervousness.

"You may release him to me now, Blackheath," Eva said sweetly.

Blackheath did. And Eva, armed with two pistols now, walked calmly up to the robber, brought the butt of one of the weapons up hard underneath his chin, and watched in satisfaction as he crumpled, unconscious, into the half-frozen puddle at her feet.

Smiling, she stepped gingerly over his inert body and got back into the coach, where she sat down, pulled the shade, and rapped sharply on the roof. "Drive on, Roberts."

And then she looked at Blackheath—who was staring at her with such raw hunger in those black and dangerously still eyes that the smile all but froze on Eva's face.

Unnerved, she tossed her head. "So, Blackheath. What do you think?"

"Very"—his gaze remained fixed on hers—"impressive."

But Lucien was more than impressed. In fact, he was so thoroughly aroused by what he'd just witnessed that he dared not move for fear he would lose control and hurl her straight to the floor of the coach. He stared into those slanting green eyes, that full, smiling mouth, and tried to slow his pounding pulse. To quell his escalating desire. Never—aside from when she'd given him the aphrodisiac—had he been this close to losing control of his restraint. Never had he been reduced to the mentality and potential impulses of an animal. And never—*never*—had he wanted a woman as much as he wanted this one.

His throat went dry and he shut his eyes, concentrating on breathing in, breathing out—

"Is that all you have to say, Blackheath?" came his companion's amused, lightly chastising voice. "That you're very impressed?"

Lucien raised his gaze and impaled her with all the hunger in his stare. "No, madam—I have a lot more to say than that."

And then he leaned forward, pulled her into his arms—and kissed her.

Eva had been prepared for it; with her senses honed by the danger she'd just faced, with her whole body thrilling to the knowledge of what she'd provoked in Blackheath, she could even admit she'd wanted it. She didn't fight as his lips came down on hers, rocking her head back into the iron bar of his arm. She made a faint noise of token protest, but she was helpless against the onslaught, drunk with the knowledge that she had brought him to this. Her arms wrapped around his neck, her hand threaded up through his hair, and the next thing she knew, she was giving herself up to the kiss, her mouth opening to admit his tongue, little breathy sounds coming from the back of her throat. She felt his fingers at the buttons of her jacket, and then his hand, plunging between the closure and finding her breast. Fondling it. Squeezing, kneading, caressing it.

She was breathing as hard as he. Drowning in sensation. And then his fingers found her nipple and she arced upward—even as she realized what she was doing.

And who she was doing it with.

Aghast, she shoved him back, yanked her jacket shut, and snatched up one of the pistols. With a shaking hand, she thrust it against his chest, her pulse banging like gunshot. "Don't," she said hoarsely. "Just—don't."

Blackheath stared at her. His eyes were dangerously still. Bottomless wells. The cobra's again. He looked at her for a long, silent moment—then, very deliberately, he reached up, pushed the gun away from his chest, and returned to the other seat.

There he sat, watching her. Just watching her.

Eva didn't know what to say, what to do, what to feel, where to go. Her emotions were so tangled, her nerves so shattered, that she could only revert to her customary flippant bluster—especially in the face of that cold black stare.

She gave a shaky little laugh and shoved her hair off her face, finally daring to put the gun down. "Look, Blackheath, there's no damage done, all right? People often lose control of themselves and do incredibly stupid things in the wake of a scare, and certainly, seeing your precious heir in potential danger was enough to frighten even you. I'm sure we can both forgive and forget your temporary lapse in restraint."

His eyes went even blacker. Frighteningly so. Eva

tensed, knowing he had seen beneath her lie, for neither of them had lost control of themselves because of fear. They had lost control because of raw, unbridled desire, and that desire went both ways.

"You just don't understand, do you?" he said softly, his voice so still that it sent shivers up her spine.

She shrugged and drew the blanket about her. "Oh, I understand perfectly. You're angry because you desperately want to ravish me, but can't do so in good conscience. Really, Blackheath, don't be obtuse. I know men. I know how they think. Of course I understand."

He didn't say a word. Not one word. And as Eva sank farther down into the blanket's protection and stared into the gloom, she could only wonder why she suddenly felt so empty and alone. Why her whole body felt as primed as a gun that had never been fired. Waiting. Wanting.

Yes, she knew men.

But maybe she didn't know herself as well as she'd thought she did.

Chapter 17

Though the air inside the coach was still and cold, Lucien had no need of a blanket. Unrequited lust still pounded in his veins, swelled his loins; he was so damned hot he couldn't breathe.

Not just hot, but angry.

Not just angry, but downright furious.

Savagely, dangerously *furious*.

He looked at the woman curled up on the seat opposite and didn't know what he wanted more: to throttle her or take her like some conquering sultan. He shut his eyes and relived the scene that had prompted his lamentable lack of control. Eva, calmly confronting the highwaymen. Eva, dispatching them with cunning and skill. Eva, never wavering, never unsure, brimming with rare and beautiful courage . . . and returning to the coach as though she'd done nothing more than step outside for a breath of fresh air, her wicked green eyes glowing with unspoken invitation, her very words demanding the admiration he was so very willing to give her.

She was a tease.

A heartless, dangerous tease.

And in that moment he hated her almost as much as he wanted her.

The miles passed beneath them, and he remained silent and still, imprisoned by his own torment. Sleep was out of the question. And there was nowhere to direct his gaze but on her, curled up beneath the blanket, one long tendril of hair falling from the hood she'd made of its folds and teasingly draping, lovingly curling around, one breast. Damn her. She was a beautiful, treacherous creature, Salome, Aphrodite, and Diana all wrapped in one. And looking at her in sleep, it was almost possible to imagine her as something she wasn't—an innocent, trusting soul, untarnished by life and open to all the wondrous experiences it had to offer.

If only, he thought bitterly.

What had happened to make her the way she was? Was it something that could be mended? Something that could be overcome? He looked at her, sleeping like the innocent child she must once have been, and felt his anger fading . . . only to be replaced by such fierce protectiveness, it was nearly too much for his heart to contain. He wished she could be like this always, instead of guarded, distrustful, and sarcastic; wished the barriers that separated them when she was awake could be banished, as they now were in sleep.

Wished he could wake her with gentle kisses and caresses, and slake the desire that even now made his blood pound, his nerves raw, his skin damp and hot.

Her last words came back to him:

Really, Blackheath, don't be obtuse. I know men. I know how they think.

A wry smile twisted his lips.

You think you know men, do you Eva? Well, you do not know me. You do not know the lengths to which I will go to get what I want, the single-minded passion I give my every pursuit, the fact that every ounce of that passion, that pursuit, is centered on you. I will have you, you know. You cannot win. You will not win. Try as you might, you cannot reduce me to the repugnant creature you think me to be, will not taunt me into behaving like the unprincipled beast you think all men really are. Make me furious, make me insane, but there is one thing you will never take from me—and that is my determination to have you. You are magnificent . . . the equal of any man, the superior of any woman. But oh, you can never know the rage that makes my temples pound even now. . . .

Rage that she had been hurt so badly that she refused to trust a person simply because he was a male. Rage that she had the courage to face a pair of highwaymen, but not to let go of her own bitterly twisted notions about men. Rage that she painted all men with the same black brush . . . when his restraint, let alone her own observations about the way his brothers treated their wives, should have changed her mind.

He looked at her sleeping there, and felt cold, ruthless determination.

He would rout her devils before that innocent babe was born, and he would do all he could to heal her.

Not only for her sake, not only for his own—

But for his child's.

*   *   *

Eva spent the night dreaming about sex.

Or, more specifically, dreaming about sex with the Duke of Blackheath.

When she awoke, hot and empty and full of a restless longing, dawn was bright behind the pulled shades of the still-moving coach.

She lay there for a moment, trying not to think of the vivid dreams, trying, instead, to concentrate on the present. She was in Blackheath's arms. She had no idea how she'd ended up there, though a dim memory of being cold sometime during the night, and seeking the heat of her companion's larger, stronger body, pervaded her conscious thoughts and flooded her with embarrassment. To think that she'd sought him out after shoving him away at gunpoint! What a hypocritical fool he must think her. Now his arms banded her like iron strapping a wooden cask, making her feel snug, safe, and warm despite the fact that those were the last feelings she sought to gain from him, banishing the chill air inside the coach to something she felt only against her cheeks and face.

How nice it was to just lie here. Her head rested against his chest. His heart beat steadily beneath her ear. She wished she could stay like this for a few moments longer, wished she trusted him enough to let down her guard around him, wished she were a different woman—one who didn't carry a legacy of pain and betrayal, one who could enjoy men for what they were, one who would follow the path of her own wicked desires. . . . Oh, *that* woman would bring this dangerously virile creature to arousal and spend the next five or ten miles enjoying the fruits of her efforts. The hot throbbing between her legs returned, and her nipples peaked with longing. *Damnation.*

"Good morning," he murmured.

"Good morning, Blackheath." With forced nonchalance, she moved away from him, reestablishing the distance that kept her safe and hoping he wouldn't mention what had transpired between them last night. "Thank you for providing both bed, pillow, and blanket all in one."

"My pleasure. I trust you were able to sleep?"

"A little," she lied, wary of his polite formality when she had expected chilling rage. Already she missed the close contact with his strong, hard body, the feel of his arms around her—being held so had almost made her feel loved. Cherished. Too bad such illusions weren't for real, and never would be.

Banishing the fanciful longings, she opened the shade and peered out, blinking as sunlight shone down through high clouds and impaled her face. Outside, she could see the knobby crests of endless green downs, valleys cloaked in frost, and, in the distance, a thin blue line that marked the sea.

Blackheath was watching her with a lazy but unnerving intensity. Eva could not tell what was going on behind that inscrutable stare, and dared not ask. He had wanted her last night, and she suspected he wanted her this morning. Thank heavens he could not know she wanted him, too.

Or could he?

Oh, God. She redirected her gaze out the window. Her nipples tingled against her chemise. Her skin was hot beneath her clothes. And she was wet down there—very wet.

She clamped her arms around herself.

"So, how is your mood this morning, Blackheath? Suitably improved over last night, I should hope?"

"Suitably improved. But I daresay a meal will improve it further. There is a coaching inn in the next village. We will break our fast there."

"I shan't join you, I think. I cannot stomach the thought of food at the moment." Eva placed a hand on her suddenly queasy belly and watched some sheep grazing on a distant down.

"Would you like a peppermint, then?"

"Do you have any?"

"I always come prepared." He dug into his pocket and produced one.

"You know, Blackheath, I've been thinking."

He quirked a brow.

"About this estate of yours, Gingermere. I'm looking forward to seeing it."

"I think you will like it."

"I like the idea of complete freedom even more. An independent income. You will, of course, continue to work with American sympathizers such as Pitt and Burke, pleading on behalf of America in Parliament?"

"I give you my word."

"And thwart those who would see America oppressed?"

"Most assuredly."

Eva swallowed. He was still eyeing her with that fixed, lazy gaze. She had the distinct feeling that though he was engaging in conversation, his mind was occupied with other pursuits. Carnal ones. In fact, she could feel the heat of that black stare caressing the swell of her bosom, the still-tiny curve of her waist, the flare of her hips.

Her lower regions ached in response.

She clamped her legs together.

"I'm, um—not sure about some of the other, er, conditions of our bargain, though."

"Such as?"

"Sharing a bed when we're together."

He smiled. "I daresay you won't find it to be the trial you anticipate."

"Maybe not for you."

He stretched his legs out, his feet touching hers. "Come, now, Eva. Do not play games with me. I want you. You—though you're loath to admit it—want me. Why do you fight something so natural?"

She raised her chin and turned away. "I have my pride. You know that, Blackheath. And these . . . these *feelings* I have for you—and yes, I will admit, I *do* have them—they come from out of nowhere. It must be because of the pregnancy. It has to be. I mean, there's no other explanation. . . ."

His smile turned into a lazy, knowing grin. "I think you simply can't resist me."

"Can't resist you? Codswallop, Blackheath. I can resist you. Easily."

"Ah. And do you think you could resist me should I put my mind to seducing you?"

"I *know* I could resist you."

"And I think that upon arrival at Gingermere, I shall put your convictions to the test."

Eva's head snapped up. She stared into that smiling

face, those dark and fathomless eyes, and knew she was trapped. That he had won. If she refused his challenge, he would think her a coward. If she accepted it, he'd win the wager so quickly she would have to clamp her hands over her ears to stop her head from spinning. Oh, *how* had she let herself be so neatly manipulated?

"Damn you, Blackheath, you don't play fair," she snapped.

"No. I like to win. Hence, I play by my own rules, fair or not."

"And when do you intend to carry out this absurd little test?"

"When we arrive at Gingermere. Not before. You see, I would like to savor the idea as I would a good wine . . . and besides, madam"—he smiled indulgently—"here in the coach would be most inappropriate."

"*Anywhere* would be most inappropriate."

He tickled her ankle with the toe of his boot. "We shall see, my dear. We shall see."

Chapter 18

Gingermere was beautiful.

But Eva, thinking of the impending challenge with Blackheath, was so tense she could not revel in her first sight of the manor house perched high atop the edge of a distant sea cliff.

Freedom, she told herself. *This is your ticket to freedom. Your future. Don't think about what Blackheath intends to prove within its walls.*

Instead, she tried to focus on the house's stark, sea-swept beauty as the coach moved steadily up the winding track that led to it. On the gently sloping fields that surrounded it, some newly planted with wheat, others dotted with sheep and cows. Beyond the house, she could see a sliver of blue sea. The house was isolated. Windswept.

She loved it.

"What do you think, my dear? Will it suit?"

"It will suit," she said simply.

But despite her calm demeanor, Eva was in a state of near-panic. This was reality, then. This was the beginning of another marriage, doomed, she was sure, to failure. And inside that house of weathered gray stone, she would be forced to match her will against Blackheath's in a contest she could never win.

Not that *he* seemed to have given the matter a second thought, and this after she had spent the last hour both dreading and anticipating the idea of losing to him. She imagined soldiers going into battle against a vastly superior force must feel much the same way. All her efforts had been spent on trying to make her behavior appear as normal as her companion's had been, though whether Blackheath, confident of victory, had truly dismissed the impending contest from his mind, or had such iron control over his facade that he could make her believe anything he chose, was something Eva could not fathom.

There was no way out of this.

No graceful, dignified, soul-saving way at all.

As the coach moved up the drive and finally stopped before the house, the duke roused her from her panicky reverie.

"We will be married this weekend," he announced, handing Eva down. "My brothers took the trouble to procure a special license, so we might as well put it to immediate use."

"You don't waste time, do you, Blackheath?"

He smiled. "Never."

Together they walked toward the house. "But surely you must want your family to witness our nuptials?" she asked, hoping her voice didn't sound as shaky as she felt inside.

"After the way they engineered this union, I am not inclined to give them that particular triumph. Besides, we can have a grand ceremony at Blackheath for the benefit of my tenants and staff. In the meantime, we will say our vows here so that the child will not suffer any undue speculation as to its date of conception, and then we will go to France and continue our search for Lord Brookhampton."

"Perhaps Lord Brookhampton is dead and will never be found."

"Perhaps he isn't."

"And perhaps you ought to think twice about going to France, especially as war between it and Britain is imminent and you will be in danger there."

"My dear Eva," he murmured, gazing down at her with a half smile curving his lips. "Don't give me the mistaken impression that you actually care."

She flushed and looked away. "Don't be absurd, Blackheath, of course I don't care," she said flippantly. "But I do care about the child, so in that respect, I think it best if you endeavor to keep yourself alive, at least until it's born and, if a male, can inherit the title."

"My survival is irrelevant. Should I meet my demise before its birth, I can assure you that Charles, who is heir-presumptive, will see to its welfare."

"Charles despises me."

"But he will not despise the child. Now let us go inside; the wind is raw, and I won't have you catching a chill."

A crew of servants, all of them shivering in the raw and blustery sea wind, were waiting to greet them on the outside stairs; their own staff, which had been sent on ahead, were presumably inside, preparing rooms, laying out clothes, making the house ready for their comfort. Taking Eva's arm, the duke escorted her up the stairs and inside, where they were greeted by an aging butler named Jackson who bowed so deeply that Eva thought a block and tackle would be needed to haul him back upright.

Introductions were made, and then Blackheath was leading her down a corridor flooded with sun. He called for tea, and shortly thereafter Eva found herself in a parlor hung with curtains of blue damask and papered in cobalt silk that matched the sea just outside.

She could see it beyond the window's salt-flecked glass, thrashing far below against the cliffs, stretching as far as the eye could see in a marching parade of foamy whitecaps before becoming as one with a horizon hung with cloud.

And she could hear Blackheath, murmuring instructions to a servant who had entered the room just behind them.

Blackheath. Her palms went suddenly damp. Was this bright and sunny room to be the scene of her seduction? Or would he delay it all the more, winding her nerves tighter and tighter until she felt she would snap like the strings of a viola tuned too tight?

Blackheath seated her on a small divan, where she pretended to be at ease while the tea was brought. She tried to distance herself from the present—and what she suspected was the immediate future —by watching the silver being laid out, the little wisp of steam rising from the teapot's spout, the servants bustling about with trays of cakes. From above, she could hear small bangs and thuds as servants aired long-unused rooms and Blackheath's valet, who had traveled on ahead, unpacked his master's clothes and readied his chamber. Would *that* be where Blackheath took her? Or would it be here, in this sunny, thickly carpeted parlor?

She glanced at the maid, who was busy stoking up the fire, attempting to ward off the damp chill that drove through the very walls and even now slid its icy fingers up Eva's ankles, her calves.

And then she, too, was gone—and Eva was alone with Blackheath.

He took his seat, pushing his long legs toward the fire, his chair half angled to face her. Eva poured the tea, thankful for an excuse not to have to look into those enigmatic black eyes. Suddenly her decision to marry him seemed hasty, even foolhardy. Was she making the biggest mistake of her life by agreeing to become his duchess?

She picked up her cup with a shaky hand.

"Don't look so troubled, my dear. I promise not to seduce you until after we've had tea."

"And then?"

He merely smiled.

Eva's hand jerked and a few drops of the hot brew splashed into her lap. She hastily set the cup down, trying to summon protective fury, trying to intimidate her tormenter into backing off—or even changing his mind. "I just want you to know, Blackheath, that if you think I'm going to be an easy conquest, you're sadly mistaken."

"If you were an easy conquest, my dear, I wouldn't even bother trying."

"And don't think for one moment that you're in

total control of this situation. I'm in equal control of it—maybe superior control—and I'm not above rendering you helpless should things progress in a way that I dislike."

"My dear Eva—I can assure you that things will progress in a way that causes you anything *but* dislike." He smiled, a man totally at ease with the situation—and in total, indisputable control of it. "As I have told you countless times before, I love dangerous women. If you were some simpering pansy, I would not be interested in following through with this little game."

"Is that all it is to you, then? A game?"

"No—it is much more than that." He sipped his tea and regarded her from over the edge of the cup for a long, uncomfortable moment, a wolf sizing up its prey, deciding upon the best angle of attack. "And what is it to you, madam?"

"A mistake."

He put down the cup. There was no emotion in those black eyes, no expression on that severe and uncompromising face.

"Would you like to call it off, then?"

"Oh, really, Blackheath, as though I could! I'm sure I can put up with sharing your bed in return for a far greater prize, that is, my freedom." She saw a flicker of something move across his face. Annoyance? Determination? Regret? "Besides, to back out now would only make me a coward in your eyes."

"And is my opinion of your character so very important to you?"

Eva snorted with feigned amusement. "Of course not."

"Then why, I ask you, does it matter whether or not I deem you a coward?"

She gave a flippant laugh, growing more and more uneasy with that steady, fixated stare. "Really, Blackheath, do try using what little brains your gender has bestowed upon you—because of pride, why do you think?"

"Eva."

She froze, trying to muster anger and feeling hot and panicky when she could not summon it. She tried instead for droll amusement; anything to keep him from getting too close, anything that maintained self-preservation.

"Yes?"

He looked at her flatly. "I want to know why you despise men so."

Nothing he might have said could have caught her more off guard. Fear drove through her; if he learned the reasons for her contempt of his gender, he would ruthlessly address them, not stopping until he'd stripped away the armor it had taken her all these years to build up, armor that had, up until she'd met this dark and omniscient being, kept her safe.

She tossed her head and all but grabbed for her teacup. "I've already told you, Blackheath, my first husband was a miserable, cowardly worm who—"

"No, Eva. I don't think this is about your first husband. I think it goes deeper than that. *Much* deeper." He impaled her with that stare, so still, so black, so uncompromisingly ruthless, that fear slid up her spine and her palms began to sweat. "Doesn't it?"

"You have no right to pry into my life, Blackheath."

"If you're to be my duchess, I have every right. And you owe it to me to confess the truth."

"The truth doesn't matter. Besides, it's all in the past, and happened so long ago that I don't care to bring it up now and relive memories I'd just as soon forget."

He pulled his chair up to hers and, setting down his cup, leaned forward—so close that she found herself pressed against the back of her chair in order to maintain distance between them. "If you don't tell me, I can assure you I have my ways of finding the truth. But I would rather you tell me. It would make it easier on us both."

"Don't threaten me, Blackheath, or you'll regret it."

He merely smiled and leaned back. It was a chilling gesture, one that made her very bones feel cold. Dear God, he was one man she never wanted to make an enemy of. One man who was able to inspire fear and respect in her when every other male had aroused only contempt. She'd best be careful. She didn't like the look in his eye, she didn't like this unfathomable, dangerous side of him that always seemed to be one step ahead of her, didn't like this feeling of being so off balance.

"Did you hear me, Blackheath? I said don't threaten me."

"I heard you, my dear."

His lack of response was making mincemeat of her nerves, a twisted mess of her control. Her hand shaking, she set down the tea and got to her feet. "I find myself exhausted from the journey and your company. I am going to bed."

"Good. I shall join you."

"I prefer to sleep alone, thank you."

"You have no intention of sleeping, and neither do I."

She *was* angry now, seriously angry, and there was no pretense about it. "How dare you presume to tell me what I feel! I have had it up to my neck with you and your arrogance, Blackheath, and I'm starting to regret ever coming here with you. And furthermore, our little *contest* is off!"

He smiled. "That is indeed a pity," he murmured, and, snaring her arm as she whirled to leave, he yanked her back against his chest—and kissed her.

His lips came down so hard against Eva's that she nearly tumbled backward over his elbow. In the next heartbeat, she knew that was his intent, for she felt his other arm go behind her knees and a second later she was up in the air and weightless in his arms, her legs swinging, his body all but crushing hers as his tongue swept into her mouth and her world tilted dizzily.

She was suffocating, starved for breath, panicked, furious. She fought him to no avail, making helpless noises of fury against his mouth, trying to kick legs that were crushed against his hard abdomen, trying to free an arm so she could land a stunning blow against the side of his head. He only deepened the kiss. His chin's faint stubble ground into the soft skin around her mouth, the heat from his body seared, burned, consumed her, finally bringing the raw ache of arousal flooding the space between her thighs—a space that had been crying for fulfillment ever since she'd woken in his arms this morning, ever since she'd gone to

Rosebriar in search of him, ever since she'd left him back in that bed in Paris.

She managed to tear her head away. *"Put me down, Blackheath!"*

"Gladly."

He sank to his knees, but did not let her go—instead, he laid her out on the rug and did not let her up. And Eva knew then that she was lost. That there was no going back, no place for pride when it came to feelings such as he was stoking to life within her. For here he was, kissing her again, driving her head down into the rug, one masterful hand skimming down her neck, unbuttoning her wool riding habit, impatiently parting it . . . and finding her breast. She moaned as his fingers circled the sensitive dome of flesh, hefting it, caressing it, teasing the nipple just beneath her shift until it burst into bloom like a spring rosebud.

He broke the kiss as his hand went to her other breast, thumbing and stroking this one, too, through the thin fabric. Her resistance was melting fast. Fear and anger were just a distant memory and she was swimming in a haze of sensation. Eva arched back against the rug, her breath coming hard now, her pulse fluttering in her throat as Blackheath's mouth covered it, kissing the fragile beat before moving lower. *Oh, yes. Oh, yes, please kiss me —*

There. His mouth fastened around her nipple, drawing it, and the delicate fabric that sheathed it, up and into his mouth. He began to suckle it, increasing the pressure until Eva was writhing on the carpet and making whimpering noises of assent. She couldn't get enough air; couldn't think beyond the sensation of his tongue sweeping the taut, aching bud, stroking it through the now-wet lawn, suckling, sucking. She was too close to the fire; she needed to move away from it, needed to move closer to the source of this agonizing pleasure-pain, needed . . . needed . . . oh, just *needed.* Her arm wrapped around Blackheath's neck, drawing him down; her fingers impatiently untied his queue and thrust through the thick and lustrous waves of his hair even as another part of her, long relegated to some distant background, would have used the opportunity to hurt him . . . to free herself.

But no, she had no desire to escape the sensation of his tongue rasping over her fabric-clad nipple, no desire to escape the hot mouth into which the sensitive peak was being drawn, no desire but to melt even farther down into the carpet as he hauled up her petticoats. His hand slid up her bare leg, higher and higher, until his fingers hooked the garter. He pulled the silken band down her thigh, her knee, her calf, peeling the stocking off with it, causing her to sigh at the delicious feel of his palm moving over her skin. She felt that same hand stroking her calf, and drew up her leg so he could touch and warm her ankle, her foot.

"Eva."

He had broken the kiss; dazedly, she looked up into his face. His eyes were like the midnight sky, velvety, black, and almost mystical, their depths continuing on into forever. "Eva. Shall we stop?"

"Oh, hell, Blackheath, you've already proved your point."

"I asked you, shall we stop?"

"Eventually . . . not now."

His eyelids lowered, thick black lashes veiling any triumph he might have revealed, and he began kissing her once more. He pulled her shirt free of the waistband tapes of her petticoats and removed it and her jacket, then turned her onto her stomach and unlaced her stays, parting them, peeling them away, baring her body like some ripe, exotic fruit. Her petticoats followed; there was only her shift left. He pushed it up, revealing every inch of her legs. She was nearly naked now, and his fingertips were running down her spine . . . his palm smoothing the dip in her lower back and caressing the upward curve of her bottom. The carpet prickled her cheek; her hair lay tangled beneath her eye, her temple. And now he gently turned her over once more, and Eva's eyes slipped shut in defeat as his head dipped again to her breast . . . kissing, suckling, loving. She felt his hand bracing her hip; felt his fingers searing the soft inner flesh of her naked thigh . . . now moving toward the junction of her legs. She was hot for him. Wet. She sighed and let her legs fall open as his fingers parted her soft, moisture-slicked curls and slowly, skillfully, slipped inside.

"Ohhhhh," she breathed, arching upward as he sucked and pulled at her stiffly peaked nipple, still sheathed in soaking-wet fabric. "Oh, Blackheath . . . I don't know how I can allow you to do this . . . how you manage to strip me of control, of resolve. . . ."

His hand was cupping her mound, his fingers sliding deeper within her hot folds, the thumb stroking her nub, his fingers moving up and into her until her blood was buzzing with frenzied heat, her senses stifled in fog. "The feeling, my dear, is mutual."

"Thank God. . . . I could not bear the idea that our effects on each other are one-sided."

With his free hand, he took her hand and guided it to the front of his breeches, where his arousal swelled so hot, so huge, that she wondered why the fabric that fought to contain it hadn't split beneath the pressure. "There, my dear Eva, is your proof that we are fairly matched. You are my undoing, as you have been from the moment I met you. Now be still. Lie back and close your eyes, for I want to make love to you . . . to taste you with my tongue, to make you realize that sharing the bed of a Duke of Blackheath is not the odious tenure you believe it to be."

If his fingers, buried within her warm silken cleft, hadn't sent her careening toward the edge, his words certainly would have. Eva, flushed with heat, lay back on the carpet . . . or tried to. It was hard, when Blackheath's fingers had replaced his mouth on her nipple . . . hard, when his other hand was stroking and readying her for his mouth, his tongue, that straining arousal that swelled against his breeches. Hard . . . when he lowered himself fully down beside her, his body heat searing her, his hand now splaying against her pelvis, covering the lowest part of her abdomen, while his thumb parted her . . . readied her . . . stroked her.

His mouth brushed the underside of her breast.

The apex of her ribs, the hollow of her belly just beneath.

The outer fringes of her silken red curls.

Eva tensed, relaxed, fought for control. She felt his unshaven jaw there against the soft white skin . . . felt his lips moving through her mound, his breath against her flesh . . . and then the first gentle touch of his tongue, pressing warmly against that part of her that his thumb and finger held open, held exposed.

Eva's world began to swell and tumble upon itself, every ounce of blood in her body gathering in that one spot of assault. But she held herself back, determined to hold out for as long as she could, her fingernails ripping into the carpet beneath her, the sweat rolling down her temples as the pressure of Blackheath's tongue became stronger, more insistent . . . more invasive.

She heard the tormented whimpers, the agonized moans coming from her own throat as he slowly dragged his tongue up and down that pebble-hard bud he held pinched and captive between thumb and forefinger; heard her own keening cries as if from a distance as he pressed the heel of his hand against the pit of her belly, spread her even wider, and lightly licked and nibbled the quivering bud. She felt her womb contracting, her body going taut, all the muscles of her abdomen constricting . . . but still she resisted, feeling only the relentless, ruthless stroke of that tongue, the savage hunger that drove him as he pushed her legs even farther apart and, with a growl of defeat, buried his face within her honeyed warmth.

It was too much. Eva lost all control over her body and arched upward, crying out in sweet agony as climax seized her in great wracking waves of intensity. Later she would remember how much she had resisted this idea; later she would rub at her rug-chafed bottom; now she could do no more than fasten her arms, and her legs, around Blackheath's magnificent body as he unfastened his breeches and lowered himself down atop her in the classic posture of male domination.

And Eva, for once, did not care.

She welcomed the sweet invasion pushing between her slick thighs, driving farther and farther into her until the root of him pressed against her still-throbbing womanhood, demanding more space, demanding more spread, when she had none left to give. The sensation was exquisite. All-consuming. And then Blackheath, his fingers buried in her hair and anchoring her head, began to move within her, and Eva felt her body gathering itself for that rapid plunge into ecstasy once again.

He took her higher and higher, never losing control, setting the pace. And then, just when Eva thought she would die of pleasure, he found his own release, driving into her with a final, savage thrust and sending her own body jerking and convulsing against the rug.

Hot, panting, and spent, she lay on her back beneath him, all but crushed by his weight, enjoying the lingering aftereffects of their coupling while his ragged breath stirred the damp hair that draped the side of her neck and lay fanned out and tangled on the rug beneath her.

It was a long time before she spoke.

"I ought to hate you, Blackheath."

He lifted her just enough to slide an arm beneath her neck and draw her up against his still-pounding heart. "I daresay, madam, I would much prefer your charity."

And a long time before she realized that she had

allowed a man to dominate her by being the one on top.

She fell asleep, still curious about this disturbing fact, too tired, too depleted, and yes, too splendidly satisfied to lend it the examination it deserved.

Chapter 19

Exhaustion also claimed Lucien.

For a long time he fought it, unwilling to give up these rare and precious moments with the woman who was damned determined to give him as few of them as she could. He delighted in his seduction of her, but would not gloat about it. Triumphed in the fact that she had not demanded to ride him in a skewed display of female domination, though that, too, was something he wouldn't mind doing whenever the mood might strike them. Reveled in the sensations that engulfed him . . . the sweet lemon-lavender scent of her hair; the feel of her in his arms; the gloriously curving, endlessly exciting length of her body lying alongside and beneath his own on the thick carpet. What more could a man want in life?

He nestled his face deeper within her hair, pressing his lips to the side of her neck, kissing, nibbling her skin. He loved its creamy whiteness; loved the silken feel of it, its slightly salty taste. She purred with contentment. He wrapped his arm around her and let himself relax, feeling his body's first involuntary twitches as sleep claimed him. He did not fight it.

Down through the depths he sank, like a swimmer that has run out of air and given up the fight to stay afloat in a bottomless sea. Images flickered through his mind along the journey down into nothingness. Nerissa's accusing eyes . . . his brothers smugly informing him of the king's decree that he marry Eva de la Mouriére . . . and Eva herself, neatly dispatching the two highwaymen, crawling into his arms in the coach, denying her own attraction for him in a magnificent lie that hurt no one as much as it hurt herself.

He hit bottom.

The nightmare.

The dueling field. Eva was there, engulfed in morning mist, the grass wet with dew. She held the handkerchief as the paces were counted off. Lucien tensed; his gut tightened and he spun on the final count, already leaping forward with his sword, hoping to change an ending that was as fixed as the path of the sun across the sky. Over and over again he rehearsed this dance of death, as he had done every night all these weeks, knowing it was a dream, knowing the outcome would be the same no matter what he did—terrifying, merciless, and brutally final.

And there was his opponent, dressed all in black, masked, hooded, dreadful. It was an apparition; it had to be, for no earthly being could fight with such unrivaled skill. No mortal man could toy with him so, drawing out the impending agony of death. And no human combatant could so easily get past his guard, only to send the rapier piercing shirt and skin and bone, impaling his heart with one thrust, and twisting it into a butchered ball of pulsing, dying flesh.

He fell to his knees in agony, the tinny-metallic taste of blood bubbling up in his throat, filling his mouth, leaking out between his clenched teeth. The ground came up to meet him. He lay there gasping on the wet grass. Choking. Dying. And as he dragged open his eyes for the last time, he saw Death, triumphant, standing over him—reaching up now to finally draw back the hood—

"Lucien!"

And yanking it off that terrifying face.

Lucien's own scream jerked him awake. His heart was pounding. Sweat rolled down his back. Inches away, a pair of anxious green eyes stared into his own.

Eva. Gingermere. The drawing room.

He flung an arm across his brow. No dream.

She was there beside him on the warm, sunlit carpet, her hair down around her shoulders, her face white as paste. He sat up, driving the heels of his hands into his eyes, trying to banish the terrifying images. There was movement beside him, and then he felt Eva's strong, slim arms go tentatively around his shoulders. He dropped his hot forehead against her breast.

"My God, do you always have such horrible nightmares?" she asked, her voice shaky. "I've been trying to rouse you for the last several minutes. You really know how to scare a person, Blackheath!"

He could say nothing; his heart was still pounding, and he was breathing too hard to gather enough air to speak. Instead, he just sat there, the pulse booming in his ears, his brow resting against her chest as her arms lost their frightened stiffness and instead wrapped comfortingly around him in a way that made him wish this moment would never end.

"Look, Blackheath—I'm sorry. I didn't realize that even the big bad wolf has nightmares, too. It's all right. I'm here now. There's nothing to be afraid of."

"Don't leave me."

She pulled him closer. "I'm not going anywhere. Relax. Just take a few deep breaths and everything will be fine."

He did just that, though the nightmare was fast receding into the inky depths from which it had come, taking the terror with it. It would stay there until he sought sleep again; would stay there until the death these dreams foretold finally caught up with him. Gradually, his body calmed, leaving him with an over-whelming sense of exhaustion. But he didn't want to move. Not just yet. He had not been held like this, had not been so comforted, shown such tenderness, since his long-dead mother had last held him in her own loving arms, all those years ago. . . .

It was a sensation he wanted to drown in. One that he could easily come to crave, if he was foolish enough to imagine it would ever be repeated.

"Do you want to talk about your nightmare?" she asked gently, pulling back a little and searching his face with what appeared to be genuine concern.

"Yes, but first . . . first I have a need to affirm life, the continuation of my own existence." He pulled away just enough to rest his hand atop her abdomen. "It comforts me, knowing our child lives."

Her face filled with horror. "Oh, Blackheath, surely you didn't dream that it died—"

"No. No, nothing like that."

She eyed him with confusion, then leaned back on her elbows and let him rest his hand there on her still-flat belly. Lucien closed his eyes. At least the baby beneath his palm would be here when he was gone, carrying on his name, carrying on his own flesh and blood. The knowledge soothed him, brought a raw ache to the back of his throat. Slowly, he removed his hand, closing the fingers around his palm to try to hold the sensation in.

"I will tell you about my dream now, Eva. But do you really care so much?"

She shrugged, but even the negligent gesture could not mask the concern and compassion in her slanting green eyes, and for once she didn't try overly hard to fool him into thinking she felt something she did not—though she did give it a token effort. "Care? Of course not. But really, Blackheath, you can't wake a woman from a sound sleep with such frightened ramblings of the unconscious mind, and allow her to go about her day with no explanation whatsoever."

"You do care, then," he said with a weary smile.

"Of course I do, you cretin. Go ahead, then. Tell me about your demons, and maybe, one of these days, I'll tell you about mine."

"Let us move closer to the fire, then. I am cold."

The hearth was blazing, its leaping flames banishing even the winter drafts that snaked across the floor. Their tea had gone chilly, so Lucien poured two glasses of wine from a nearby decanter, pressing hers into her hand before lowering himself to the rug once more. She hesitated, then sat down beside him, cross-legged, stiff-backed, farther away than he would have liked, closer than he would have expected.

He ached to move up next to her.

Wanted nothing more than to lay on his back beside her, pillow his head on her thigh, and enjoy her nearness.

But no. He would not take advantage of her like that. He would not use this thread of caring compassion she had offered him in a way that would make her feel uncomfortable.

Instead, he drew up his knee and draped his wrist over it, the glass dangling from his fingers as he began to tell her about the dream.

She sat listening, never interrupting, never commenting, never mocking, never scoffing. He told her everything—something he had not been able to do with his siblings, for he was the big brother, the leader of the family, and he had a place to uphold in the family hierarchy. But he had no place to uphold with Eva. He had nothing to hide, nothing to prove, no reason to hold anything back, because she was his equal, and he knew it.

At last he finished and, draining the last of the wine, held the empty glass in his fingers as he gazed unseeingly into the crackling flames before them. "It's the same dream every night," he murmured. "The first time I had it, I passed it off as nothing but a meaningless but unpleasant nightmare and promptly put it out of my mind. But then it happened again. And again. I started having it every night, and soon sleep became something I began to dread.

"It wasn't long before I realized the dream would

likely become reality. I could not die knowing two of my siblings were still unmarried. Given the love and happiness my parents shared within their marriage, I wanted the same things for my siblings. Yes, I did orchestrate matters so Gareth, and then Charles, ended up in wedlock. Then the dreams started. Andrew had just met Celsie, and I took advantage of the situation. I was abominable to them. Beastly. But I was desperate. I succeeded, manipulating Andrew into wedlock as I had done with his brothers, until only my dear Nerissa remained." He dragged a hand over his face. "Everything you've heard about the whole Spanish estate affair is true, I'm afraid. My motives were good; my methods were unforgivable. I had hoped that absence would indeed make Perry's heart grow fonder . . . fond enough that he'd come back to England with an offer for my little sister. I knew I was overstepping the bounds, knew that I was tempting fate, but I had beaten fate before and was determined to do so again. I had a vow to fulfill; I had no choice but to get them together."

Eva felt his pain as though it were her own. She looked at him, the noble profile painted in firelight, the stark face gazing unseeingly into the flames. "A vow? What vow?"

He turned his head and looked at her, and she saw past the arrogant, omniscient duke, past the Machiavellian monster, and into the man behind those silent black eyes . . . a man who was very different from what he would have others believe he was, a man with a soul so deep, a heart so worthy and true, she feared it was only an illusion, for men surely didn't possess such depth of character, such naked, vulnerable emotions as Blackheath was allowing her to see.

He turned his head and gazed into the flames once more, his face very still.

"A long time ago, when I was just a boy, my mother went into labor with her last child." He stared unblinking into the fire. "She had safely delivered the rest of us, but with Nerissa, something was wrong. Her struggles, her pain, her strength . . . they were to no avail. The midwife could do nothing. My father was frantic. He sent for the doctor, but even he could not help her, nor, in the end, could he save her." Blackheath set the glass down beside his knee. "Sometimes, when I am alone and companion to only my memories, I can still hear her screams."

Eva sat unmoving. The duke was still gazing into the flames. His face showed such raw, naked pain that Eva instinctively reached out and took his hand, cold despite their proximity to the fire.

"You scoff at the love a man may feel for his wife, Eva, but my brothers are not so unlike their father. He loved my mother more than life itself. He loved her so much that every cry that issued from her poor, tortured body might have been his own, every tear that streamed down her cheeks might have been his. He grew frantic in his inability to help her. Frenzied. He tried to escape, to flee the cries of pain that only emphasized his own helplessness, and so ran upstairs to the ducal apartments, high in the tower. . . ."

Here, Blackheath stopped. And Eva tensed, gripping his hand, dreading what he was about to tell her.

"I found him some time later." Blackheath shut his eyes. "Found him lying there on the cold stone stairs that led up to what are now my own apartments, his neck broken and the tears still wet upon his cheeks."

"Dear God."

"He must have tripped and fallen in his haste. I knelt beside him and gathered him up in my arms, wiping the tears from my eyes with the inside of my elbow, telling myself that he was just sleeping—yet knowing by the angle of his neck, the blank stare in his eyes, that he was not. I held him until he grew cold, held him until my nanny found me hours later, because I thought that as heir-apparent to a duke, I had all the power in the world . . . including that of holding the life within him. But, of course, I could not do that." He shook his head. "Just as I could not hold the life within my mother when she, too, died, shortly after Papa." He gave a faint, distant smile. "I was ten years old."

Ten years old.

Eva's heart constricted, and it was all she could do not to gather him—this man who had never finished being a little boy, this man who had been thrust into adulthood, into a dukedom, in the cruelest way imaginable—into her arms and comfort him like the mother that had been wrenched from him. No wonder he was so controlling. As a child, he had been unable to save his beloved father. His mother. No wonder he had tried to address the imbalance by imposing his will on everything else that surrounded him. Dear God, could she blame him?

He was still staring into the flames, his eyes empty of expression, empty of everything but the memories that still haunted him. She had not thought that he could own such terrible demons, could feel such anguish, could bring himself to share it with another person—let alone someone like herself. But he had, and the knowledge humbled her, filled her with compassion and a strange sense of protectiveness toward him, toward what he had told her. He was braver than she. He was made of a stronger substance. Tears filled her own eyes and she looked away, blinking, to hide them.

"Hell, Blackheath, you're making me want to hold you and cry my heart out for the little boy you were, the suffering you must have endured," she said shakily, trying to find firm ground beneath her suddenly tangled emotions.

"I will not stop you, should you wish to do so."

"You want me to hold you?"

He looked at her, unafraid to admit to such a humble need. "I would like it very much."

She moved closer to him, closing the distance, and slowly, tentatively, put her arms around his shoulders. They were so wide she could not contain them within the circle of her arms. It broke her heart to think how small they must have been when he'd found himself with the weight of a dukedom, and the care of four little siblings, upon them. She lay her cheek against his back, her heart aching in a way she could not understand.

"We laid them both to rest on the same day," he continued in that same flat, quiet tone. "And as I looked at those coffins being lowered into the vault, I promised my father and mother that I would be the parent my siblings would never have. I vowed that I would see to their welfare at all costs, that I would always take care of them, that I would put their happiness above all else—even the dukedom, if need be, because I loved them, and they were all I had left."

"But you went too far."

"Yes. I was overzealous. Arrogant. I took my vow, and my responsibility, too seriously. I may have triumphed where my brothers were concerned, but with my little sister . . . I failed." He took a deep breath, let it slowly out. "Instead of happiness, I have brought her only grief. Instead of love, I have brought her only agony. I have . . . destroyed her."

Eva held him within the circle of her arms. "I wish I could take away your pain, Blackheath. I wish that the little boy you were could have had his childhood."

"I do not suffer so much anymore, Eva. It was all a long time ago . . . though it is still, after all these years, difficult to get past that spot on the stairs where I found my father. Old memories never die, I guess."

"No," she said, remembering her own. "They don't."

For a long moment, they sat there together, two souls who had come together in pain and sharing, her arms around his shoulders, the fire snapping with melancholy quiet in the hearth.

"I will help you find the truth about Lord Brookhampton," Eva said at length. "But please, don't go to France. It is too dangerous for an Englishman now."

"I must."

"Your life may be imperiled."

"What does that matter, when my days are counted anyhow? No, Eva, best that I use whatever time I have left to undo the damage that I have wrought. I cannot live with the knowledge of what I have done to my sister . . . what I have done to the man she loved."

"Oh, Blackheath . . . do not be so noble, it will be the death of you."

"My sister's grief will be the death of me. I must do what I must do, Eva."

She shook her head. "Listen to you. Listen to us, sitting here like . . . like friends, instead of adversaries. And look at me, actually grieving for the little boy you were."

"My dear Eva, it is not such a bad thing, to be in possession of a heart."

"Hearts are good for nothing; they only get broken. Yet you—you don't seem to have any qualms about baring your own to me, when you know very well that I might happily crush it beneath my heel. Why do you tell me these things, Blackheath? I do not feel worthy of such confidences; I do not feel deserving of your trust. I—I am confused and beset by guilt."

He unhooked her arms from around him just enough to turn and look at her. His eyes were so deep and black, she felt she would never find her way out of those fathomless depths. "And why is that? Despite what you feel for mine, I have no illusions about the nature of your gender."

"I don't understand why you trust me so."

"I do not need your trust in order to give you my own. That is not how life works, Eva. It is only when one has the courage to give that he—or she—will be in a position to receive. I have given you my confidences, my trust. I have received your compassion in return, perhaps even sown the seeds of friendship. I ask nothing from you, save that you do not judge me based on your ill-conceived notions about my gender. I ask nothing, except that you see me as an individual, and not just another male who deserves only your distrust, loathing, and contempt." He smiled, and ran his finger down her chin. "Despite all, I am not really the monster I would sometimes have others believe."

She looked away, tormented.

Oh, Blackheath . . . I so desperately want to trust you. I want the same relationship with you as your sisters-in-law have with their husbands . . . I want your love, your admiration, your devotion—and the certainty that you will never betray me with another woman, tire of me when someone else catches your eye, cast me aside when I no longer amuse you. But please—don't expect something I cannot yet give you. And please . . . prove me wrong when it comes to men.

A lump rose in her throat, and she hugged him fiercely.

I beg of you, Blackheath, prove me wrong.

She looked into the flames, her eyes stinging. And it was only when she felt his thumb on her cheek, gently wiping the tear away, that she realized she was doing something she'd never thought she'd do.

Crying.

In front of a man.

For some absurd reason, she began to laugh through her tears. The world had been turned upside down.

Chapter 20

Many miles away, in her rooms at Rosebriar Park, Lady Nerissa de Montforte sat curled on a window seat.

She was alone. From downstairs came the sounds of her family at dinner, laughing children, the distant strains of music. How happy their lives were in comparison to her own. She had no wish to join them. Outside her closed door, she knew a dinner tray waited, growing cold as she sat here looking out over the darkening fields. But she had no desire to eat.

Perry. A choking sob lodged in her throat.

She had never before thought of ending her life, but she was in such misery that the idea had crossed her mind several times since Lucien had left for the coast with Eva. Life had been marginally more bearable with him here to hate—it had given focus to the heartache that had nowhere to go. Rage was preferable to desolation. Anything, in fact, was better than this mind-numbing limbo of anguish, this imprisonment in time and space and mood, this endless mental lethargy that provided her with only enough energy to summon her memories . . . to think of what might have been . . . and to weep.

Lucien. Her brothers thought they had triumphed in forcing him to marry the beautiful American, but Nerissa had no illusions that the two of them weren't holed up in some cozy bed, doing the things lovers do. She had noted the sensual tension, the heated looks that had passed between them. She had noted Lucien's single-minded fascination with this woman he could not have. Oh, he and Eva would not be looking for her dear Perry. They would not even be thinking about him. They would be too wrapped up in each other to pay Perry a second thought.

So much for promises, then. So much for Lucien's vow to find Perry, and this after *his* manipulations were what had caused Perry's disappearance—if not his death.

And what use were her other brothers? Charles had his army career, an estate to manage, a wife and daughter to love—he would not have the time to go chasing phantoms. Gareth was busy with his duties as a Member of Parliament, his own holdings, and his family. And Andrew was not exactly suited to matters of diplomacy and would be loath to leave his beloved Celsie, especially since she'd announced her own delicate condition. Besides, he was totally obsessed with the new explosive he was trying to perfect. Eyebrows aside, he'd be lucky if he had any hair, let alone a head, left, when all was said and done.

Which meant there was only one option.

She would have to go in search of Perry herself.

She pulled herself up on the window seat, the idea filling her with a resolve she hadn't felt in weeks. *Go find Perry myself.* And why not? She was young, clever, determined, and resourceful. She was passionate in her commitment to find him. And she was a de Montforte.

Nerissa rose, opened her wardrobe, and began to select the clothes she would take with her. She put on her wool riding habit. Her thick cloak, trimmed with ermine, that she had worn during her last day with Perry. Her gloves, her riding boots, her heaviest, warmest petticoats. . . .

By the time she had finished packing, it was nearly dark outside. Clouds had moved in, and spots of rain dashed against the window. She hated the wet, but counted her blessings—with no moon, her departure from Rosebriar would go unnoticed, and it would be morning before her brothers even noticed she had gone.

Her brothers.

Dear Charles, Gareth, Andrew—

A moment later, her thoughts were words on a sheet of vellum:

Dearest brothers,

I have gone to find my Perry. God bless you all.

Love,
Nerissa

She folded the note, propped it against the candle holder, and blew out the single flame. She picked up her small satchel. Nobody saw her creep downstairs, slip outside, and hurry out to the stables.

As she led her mare out to the mounting block, it began to rain in earnest.

Nerissa swung up in the saddle and never looked back.

A day after, Nerissa's three brothers discovered her absence and left Rosebriar in pursuit, hoping to catch her before she could leave England, the fifth Duke of Blackheath married Eva Noring de la Mouriére.

It was a wedding that should have counted royalty, statesmen, and the bluest of English blood among the honored guests—but instead was witnessed by only the vicar who presided over it, staff, servants, and villagers, and the few sparrows that managed to find their way into the ancient church, their wings fluttering silently as they wheeled, chirped, and flitted through the rafters high above.

It was growing dark. Evening was rushing in like a racehorse tonight. Outside, the wind whistled around the old stone walls, promising a storm off the sea; inside, the chill was enough to make the teeth of even the dead who slept in the surrounding tombs chatter. Lucien, standing stoically beside Eva, listened to the timeless words, repeated the age-old vows, with a sense of otherworldly detachment. This was his wedding day. It should have been the happiest one of his life, the triumph of his heritage, the celebration of the continuation of his line. Instead, he felt only a curious absence of feeling, a sterility of emotion. This was not a marriage, it was a business arrangement. This was not a lifelong commitment, but a short-term affair whose tenure would be dictated by however long he had left on this earth. This was not a love match, but a sort of life insurance for his unborn heir, an official guarantee that the child would carry its proper name, be raised with all the pomp and privilege its birthright deserved.

His gaze passed over the guests: villagers, tenants, the staff of Gingermere, a few servants from Blackheath. Most were smiling, excited, their faces glowing in the candlelight. How privileged they must feel, sole witnesses to the wedding of a Duke of Blackheath. But Lucien felt only a pang of loneliness. Emptiness. Someone was missing. His brothers. His little sister. It was not the same without them. But they were ignorant of the fact that he was finally getting married. They were absent because he, Lucien, had refused to allow them the triumph of seeing him felled to their plan of getting him wedded at last. But he had planned it this way, hadn't he? He had planned it, and thus should have reveled in having the last word on the matter. Instead, he felt only a sense of guilt for his underhanded, and self-depriving, method of revenge.

Guilt, and loss.

Finally, it was over; the ring was on her finger, the final vows were said, the deed was done.

He had a duchess.

A wife.

A partner till death did them part—which, surely, would come sooner rather than later.

He shook off the sudden prickle of dread and offered his arm to the woman who stood, white with cold, by his side. In the soft glow of the candlelight, dressed in a polonese gown of green and gold Italian silk, she had never looked more beautiful. He tore his mind from his own bleak regrets, his sadness about his missing siblings, by envisioning how he would make love to her when they got back to Gingermere. How he would peel that shimmering gown from her body, make her moan and thrash with passion.

"Well, that wasn't so difficult, was it?" he quipped, for his own sake as much as hers, as he led the procession out of the church. Outside, they were instantly buffeted by the wind off the darkening sea, which stretched into forever just beyond the cliffs.

She looked over the parade of incoming waves, the wind sending her voluminous skirts twisting and whipping against her long, lethal legs. Lucien's throat went dry. Ah, yes. Definitely better to think of what awaited back at Gingermere. . . .

"As my mother always said, getting married is the easy part. The hard part is *enduring* marriage."

"Ah, but with any luck, you shan't have to endure me for long, my dear."

"Really, Blackheath. You make it sound as though I look forward to becoming your widow."

"Well, I daresay the idea seems to hold more appeal for you than that of being my duchess. Shall I be on my guard tonight, lest you have aspirations of achieving that widowed state earlier than expected?"

"Oh, I think you are quite safe, Duke." She flashed him a wicked look from beneath lowered lashes. "For now."

The coach was brought around and servants and villagers hustled about, laughing, congratulating them, some already carrying torches to hold back the gathering darkness. The smell of burning pitch mingled with the salty tang of the sea. Leaping flames glowed orange against excited faces. Lucien cast a glance at his bride, standing silently beside him. Though she wore a smile, he could sense her nervousness, her doubts, her fears. She reminded him of a porcelain figurine left out in the cold: brittle, beautiful, and about to crack.

"Your cloak, m'lady."

Lucien took the heavy garment from Eva's maid, put it over his bride's shoulders, and, removing her hat, pulled the hood up over her vivid red hair, already loosened from the pins that were no match against the brisk wind off the sea. She was trembling.

"Really, Blackheath, I am not a child—"

"Shh."

She made a noise of helpless impatience, but let him finish the task. Her cheeks were flushed with cold; her eyes sparkled like jewels in a face of porcelain beauty, but whether it was regret or desire that fired them, Lucien could not tell. As he tied the hood under her chin, his fingers brushed her jaw in a gentle caress. Her eyes flashed up to his, briefly, and in them he saw guardedness, the desperate need for reassurance that they had done the right thing. He smiled, trying to bolster her courage by his own example.

"Really, my dear— it won't be so bad. Remember, you will have all the independence you require, both while I live and after I die. The child will be provided for. You will be provided for. There is no need for worry."

She offered him a wan smile in return. "Then I will be happy at Gingermere, I think." She raised her chin and eyed him with her normal, haughty amusement.

"As long as you keep to your side of the bargain and never threaten my freedom, we might actually make a go of this . . . marriage."

Lucien handed her up into the waiting coach, his eyes dark with hunger as she adjusted her hoops and skirts and took her seat.

"And what about you, Blackheath? Not once have you confided *your* feelings regarding this union. Will it be a trial for you, having found yourself wedded at last?"

"I do not intend it to be, my dear."

She raised a brow and slipped her hands into her fur muff. "I'm sure you don't. After all, men always have the loftiest aspirations for marital bliss when the union is young, but those aspirations never hold up to reality, nor to time, nor to their own lust for variety. Marriages spoil and go rotten the older they get, just like old meat, bad cheese."

He climbed up into the coach behind her. "My dear Eva, I *do* wish I could do something to change such a wretched attitude."

"Pah, Blackheath. How could you? Besides, what do you know about marriage? She jabbed a finger at her heart and raised her chin. "Trust me, I know what I'm talking about. After all, I've been down this road before. You haven't."

"I am determined to ensure that our marriage will far exceed your dismal expectations of it."

She gave him a pitying look and shook her head. She had taken her muff off and was now twisting the wedding band around and around her finger, as though it agitated her, as though she could not accustom herself to the feel of it. "Oh, Blackheath. For such a worldly man, you are sometimes so . . . naive. But never mind. I shan't spoil your illusions. You'll learn soon enough."

"No, madam. *You* will."

She merely arched a brow at him and gave him a faintly amused smile, obviously convinced of her own wretched predictions.

"I'm not joking, my dear. I intend to prove that marriage to me will not be the penance you anticipate."

"Oh? And how do you intend to do that, Blackheath?"

"I shall start by keeping you very satisfied in bed."

Even the gathering gloom could not hide the sudden blush, nor conceal the way she squirmed on her seat and began fidgeting. "And I suppose you intend to start . . . *satisfying* me tonight?"

He eyed her from beneath hooded lids. "I could start now, if you wish."

"After supper, I think."

"No, before. A little bedsport will cause us to . . . work up an appetite."

She glanced away, but not before he saw the desire reciprocated in her own veiled gaze. She took a deep breath, faced him once more, and eyed him from down the short length of her nose. "There's a man for you," she said, affecting an air of superior knowledge. "Always thinking of one thing, and one thing only. At least you're honest about it, Blackheath."

"It is not something I could lie about, even if I wished to."

"So you *are* thinking about it."

He smiled slowly. "Do you think to convince me you're not?"

She was toying with the ring again. "Of course I'm thinking about it. But I can't help what I think. Pregnancy does strange things to a woman. I'm sure that my increased . . . appetite for that which I would normally find repulsive—that is, sharing a bed with you, Blackheath—is due only to the fact that my body is no longer my own."

"Hmm, yes. But it was certainly your own when I planted that seed within you, was it not?"

She shot him a look of mock outrage. "Really, must you bring that up?"

"My apologies," he murmured, but he was grinning. "Shall we depart?"

"The sooner, the better."

The coach moved off, the wheels crunching through ice-rimmed puddles before picking up speed. Lucien sat back, absorbing what warmth he could from his heavy woolen greatcoat as he glanced out the window. He could see the downs filing away to the north, great, brooding sentinels against the darkening sky; to the south there was only the cliffs, and beyond them, the sea. In the close confines of the coach, his breath frosted the air.

He glanced at his bride. "Are you warm enough, my dear?"

"Tolerably so."

She would not look at him; instead, her pensive gaze was directed out the window toward the sea, where, in the deepening dusk, miles of charging whitecaps could be seen marching toward shore as though fleeing the oncoming storm.

"Feels like rain," she said.

"Snow, I'll wager."

"Snow and cold on our wedding night. Hmph. How fitting."

"Stop it, Eva," he said quietly.

She flashed him a defensive look. "Stop what?"

"You are doing your best to sabotage this marriage and I won't have it."

"I beg your pardon?"

"You heard me. You are determined to fulfill this prophecy of misery to which you cling. Determined to prove that marriage will be an insufferable penance. Very well, but I tell you, should this marriage fail, it will be because *you* wish it to—not me."

Her eyes narrowed to angry slits. "Are you accusing me of poisoning this union before it even starts?"

"As a matter of fact, yes, I am." He smiled and draped an arm across the back of the seat. "Tell me, madam, what do you intend to do about it?"

She stared at him, temporarily at a loss for words. Again, he had trapped her, and they both knew it. If she carried on with her waspish attitude, he was more than justified in his thoughts; if she capitulated and tried to make amends by honestly working on this marriage, she would be letting her guard down, laying her heart open to hurt and betrayal.

"You're a monster, Blackheath," she muttered, reaching for her muff once more.

"Yes. I know." He smiled. "But even monsters don't like to spend all of their time in battle armor. Now, shall we call a truce and try to make the best of it?"

She sighed and offered him a wary smile. "Yes. Yes, let's try." She looked down. "I'm sorry, Blackheath. Perhaps you're right."

"Of course, my dear." He gave her his most maddening, self-assured grin. "After all, I always am."

She tore off her muff and, laughing, flung it at his smugly smiling face.

Chapter 21

They returned home to a feast.

Lobster in an elegant sauce of cream and sherry. Lamb, still sizzling in its fat, bathed in mint sauce and garnished with sprigs of fresh parsley. Baked fish drizzled with lemon; rolls, still hot from the oven, into which creamy pats of butter immediately melted. Carrots in a sugary wine glaze, parsnips, and a host of winter vegetables. All were beautifully prepared, set on gleaming platters of finest silver that, together with the crystal glasses and fine china plates, threw off the light of dozens of candles.

The staff and servants had proposed a toast to the new Duchess of Blackheath, a gesture that warmed the ice Eva was trying quite hard to maintain around her heart. But Blackheath, with his refusal to anger despite her baiting, with his long, simmering looks of promised passion, seemed as determined to breach her defenses as a general laying siege to a city.

His earlier words echoed in her head. *You are doing your best to sabotage this marriage and I won't have it.*

Eva, troubled, took another sip of her wine.

You are determined to fulfill this prophecy of misery to which you cling. . . . I tell you, should this marriage fail, it will be because you wish it to—not me.

Guilt suddenly assailed her, beating down the anger she could no longer sustain. Was Blackheath right? Was *she* the saboteur of her own happiness?

But I don't dare trust him. I don't dare trust any man! How can I, after what Jacques did to me? After what Papa did to Mama?

Dessert arrived, a fabulous cheese board with wedges of Stilton, Cheddar, and Cheshire, garnished with celery and accompanied by a small bowl of nuts. Servants brought out two more gleaming silver bowls, one containing Spanish oranges, the other, shiny red cherries. Blackheath dismissed the servants, picked up a small knife, and began peeling an orange.

Despite herself, Eva couldn't help but be transfixed by his hands, framed by elegant white lace. She watched them deftly peeling the orange, pulling away the tough outer skin, exposing the sweet, fleshy ball of fruit inside. They were beautiful hands. Skilled hands. Dangerous, powerful, sensual hands. Her hunger for Blackheath must have shown in her eyes, for he looked up, caught her staring, and with a lazy smile, placed a delicate segment of orange on her plate.

She put a hand to her stomach. "Oh, please, Blackheath, I cannot eat any more."

"My dear wife, you've barely eaten a thing all night. Are you ill?"

"No. Just—"

She couldn't finish the sentence, but the heat in her cheeks, and her inability to meet his eyes, must have told him all he needed to know.

His lips twitching, he popped the sweet wedge of fruit into his own mouth.

"—not myself," she finished lamely.

"I see." He picked up a cherry by its stem and, eyeing her, twirled it between his fingertips. "Perhaps you need to be in bed."

She met his dark, simmering gaze. "Perhaps you're right. After all"—she gave him an arch look—"you always are."

"Hmm. I'm glad you've finally acknowledged that fact."

She laughed nervously. He put the cherry down. Then he rose, tall, powerful, elegant in indigo velvet, dangerous in every way. Eva's blood warmed. Shivers climbed her spine. *What are you doing?* her mind screamed. But she knew what she was doing, and at the moment, she had no desire to try and reclaim the anger that Blackheath's ruthless kindness had stolen from her.

Not to mention his alarmingly close-to-the-bone words.

You are doing your best to sabotage this marriage, and I won't have it.

Had she been trying to do just that? Well, then, she would be brave. She would put her anger aside, and let come what may. She would ignore this feeling of vulnerability, ignore experience, ignore, even, her pride, which was lodging an angry protest against this strange capitulation on the part of not only her body this time, but her mind. Yes, she would ignore all of that, and just . . . *feel.*

And feel she did. A gathering ache between her legs . . . a sensitivity in her nipples . . . a tautness in her belly . . . a yawning emptiness in her hard, hard heart that demanded one thing, and one thing only.

Fulfillment.

Blackheath had come up behind her chair.

He was standing just above her. Eva sensed the heat emanating from his body, felt it searing her through her clothes. She tensed, waiting—

And then he laid a hand on her shoulder.

That dangerously beautiful hand that had so transfixed her just a moment ago.

Eva sat spellbound, not daring to move, her breath coming slow and feathery through her lungs.

She felt the spreading warmth of that strong, possessive hand as it rested there on her shoulder. Felt the crisp tickle of frothy white lace against the exposed skin at the base of her neck. Felt the brush of velvet there, and the heady, teasing touch of his fingers, now stroking her skin, the thumb rounding her collarbone, pushing into the faint indentations from which it rose. She swallowed hard, trying to draw air into lungs that had forgotten how to breathe.

I want this. I want him. Why fight it? Why fight something that feels so right, that does neither of us any harm, that will not hurt me as long as I don't lose my heart to him?

Yes.

Don't lose your heart to him—that was the fatal mistake you made in the past. Give him your body . . . he cannot hurt that. But never give him your heart.

She leaned her cheek against the soft velvet, the lace at his wrist, and her hand came up over his, pressing it down into her warmed flesh.

And now those long, skillful fingers were dipping lower, idly teasing the edge of her bodice, back and forth, back and forth.

Eva didn't move. Her breathing was the only sound. Keeping perfectly still, she glanced down, watching his hand . . . the thumb, drawing a little circle against her milky skin; the fingertips just roving over the top of her bodice. He moved his hand ever so slightly, and his fore and middle fingers dipped into the warm valley of cleavage, the thumb now caressing the swell of her left breast.

Eva shut her eyes on a sigh. She was melting into her chair, filled with a sluggish languor, a rising need to give herself to this man who was now her husband. And now that hand came gently up beneath her chin, cupping her jaw and tipping her head up and back until she was looking up into black, black eyes that were burning with unmistakable hunger.

She gave a breathy sigh and offered her lips to him.

He claimed them immediately, his tongue sweeping between her teeth and into her mouth, his hand still cupping her jaw, cradling the back of her head. She felt his thumb stroking her cheek. Felt his breath warming the side of her face. Tasted sweet, tangy oranges on his tongue.

Slowly, he pulled away, his hand still beneath her jaw so that she, opening glazed eyes, had no choice but to stare up at him.

"Bedtime, I think," he murmured.

She could not find the breath to answer. He drew his hand away, stepping back from the chair so that she might get up.

Dazed with sensation, Eva took his offered hand and began to rise—but her legs were too heavy, her feet shod in lead. A moment later, she was swept up in Blackheath's arms, held close to his chest, his heart pounding just beneath her ear.

She hooked an arm around his neck.

He paused only long enough to retrieve the silver bowl of cherries, and, carrying her as though she weighed no more than the air that surrounded them, headed from the dining room.

Eva looked at that bowl and felt her insides melting as she considered what he might plan to do with the fruit. She felt totally helpless, powerless in his arms. She shut her eyes, treasuring, enjoying, fearing this maelstrom of sensation.

Up two flights of stairs he carried her, a strong, silent victor waiting to savor the prize of battle. His steps never wavered. His arms were bars of steel from which she had no desire to escape. He reached the top of the stairs and unhesitatingly swung right, moving soundlessly down a long hall lit by flickering sconces whose light gilded his skin and set her hair aflame.

I want him. God help me, I want him.

He pushed open a door, shut it behind him, and carried her past a blazing hearth, past furniture that glowed a rich mahogany in the light of the candelabra set atop a highboy—and toward the large bed curtained in blue and gold damask that dominated the room.

He laid her down upon it. He put the bowl of cherries on a bedside table, retrieved the candelabra, and set it on the opposite one. Eva gazed up into his dark face and, unable to speak, to even muster the strength to move her sluggish limbs, felt as though she were going to melt right down into the mattress.

She watched him with naked hunger as he slowly, methodically untied his cravat and unbuttoned his velvet waistcoat, his inscrutable black gaze roving heatedly over her body, burning her everywhere it touched. Eva shivered. Outside, she could hear the wind gusting, the distant roar of the ocean, and the occasional hiss of something, probably snow or sleet, flinging itself against the window behind the drawn drapes. But she felt cozy, safe, protected. She was here in a secluded bedroom, all alone with Blackheath, her enemy, her lover—her husband—and she was right where she wanted to be.

And he was still watching her, a wolf sizing up its prey, the candlelight throwing his face into flickering planes and shadows, deepening his eyes, glowing upon the queued waves of his midnight-black hair. Off came the waistcoat, only to be tossed carelessly over a chair. Eva's tongue traced her suddenly dry lips. He was splendid. Matchless. Her gaze locked on his, she reached up and pulled a pin from her hair, pulled out another, and another, until the thick red waves, glowing like wine in the candlelight, tumbled down around her shoulders, her breasts.

Blackheath was watching her.

She smiled and, arranging her hair beneath her, lay back against the pillows—watching him.

He was unbuttoning his cuffs now, their rich, expensive lace frothing over his long fingers as he

worked. The shirt was loose and billowing, cut gener-
ously through the shoulders, the soft white lawn rip-
pling as he moved. Eva's gaze grew hooded, her
mouth dry, as his hands moved to his throat, loosening
the button at the base of his neck, opening up the slitted keyhole to reveal a wedge of skin that contrasted
with the whiteness of the shirt. Absently stroking a
thick tress of her own hair that lay on the pillow beside
her cheek, she watched with undisguised hunger as
Blackheath removed his shoes, unbuttoning his
breeches at the knees as he straightened up.

He stood there for a long moment in the light of the
candelabra, watching her. Then he came toward the
bed.

Eva's hand left her hair and drifted to her heart,
beating like a drum beneath her suddenly too-tight
stays. It was an effort just to draw breath. An effort
not to spring from the bed and tumble him down to
the floor like a leaping tigress as he approached. Her
body quivered with the effort of lying still; her lips
parted as he unbuttoned his breeches, hooked his
thumbs around the waistband, and slid them down
his legs and off, taking his stockings with them.
Finally, he stood barefoot on the thick Turkish rug.
Only the shirt still covered him, its hem reaching partway to his knees, teasing her with the knowledge of
the arousal it veiled, revealing long, straight, well-
muscled thighs and calves of athletic power . . . of
aristocratic grace.

Eva smiled her appreciation of such masculine perfection, and Blackheath, his own gaze moving to her
prone body there on the bed, pulled the shirt up and
over his head.

There he stood, just watching her, naked ...
proud ...

Magnificent.

Eva swallowed hard, trying to banish the sudden
dryness of her throat. Every inch of her skin was afire,
every shard of feeling in her body was centered in her
breasts and between her thighs, damp with wanting
him. Her gaze drifted from his face, framed in thick
waves of glossy black hair that swept back from his
brow and now hung loosely about his shoulders,
emphasizing their breadth, their beauty ... down the
strong column of his neck, down the splendid length
of his body, its gilded planes and hollows a study in
candlelit perfection ... down the flat, tapering abdomen, laddered with muscle, the lean hips, and there,
yes, the evidence of his desire.

He was glorious.

And he was waiting for her invitation to join her
there on the bed.

She smiled and, spreading her hand on the coverlet
beside her, gazed up at him with a hunger she didn't
even bother to conceal.

"Well, don't just stand there, Blackheath—you'll
catch cold."

A faint smile touched his mouth and he took the last
steps toward the bed. The mattress sagged as it took
his weight, and a moment later he was lying alongside
her, searing her with the heat of his body, so much
longer, bigger, stronger than her own. Propping his
weight on an elbow, he gazed down into her eyes, just
watching her ... and smiling.

"I'm sorry," she whispered as he caressed her
breast, half of which was pushed up by her stays and

bare to his gaze, half of which still lay concealed beneath shimmering silk. "It did not occur to me that I was sabotaging our marriage. . . . I was simply trying to protect myself from further hurt."

"I know."

"I may never be able to give you my love, Blackheath, but I promise that I will give you my loyalty, my strength, my—best efforts to make a go of this."

"I am in no doubt of that. And for now, that is enough."

"For now. But what about later, Blackheath?"

"Hmm, yes . . . later. If we have a later, Duchess."

"And if we do?"

He smiled, and in that moment she saw his soul, deep as the universe, in his eyes. "Then I would like the sort of marriage my brothers have." His hand moved over her partly concealed breast, teasing the nipple, bringing it to a hard peak beneath the thin silk. "I would like to have a marriage based on trust and friendship. A wife who is never afraid to tell me when I am wrong . . . and children. Many children." His smile spread. "Lots of children."

"Girl-children?"

"Girls, boys . . . their gender matters naught to me." He caught a length of her hair, dragging his fingers down and through it, letting them just touch her pebble-hard nipple as he came to the end of each gentle pull.

"I could grow to like this, Blackheath."

"My dear madam, I daresay you already do." He cupped her jaw with his hand, making her feel tiny, fragile—cherished. "Now . . . let us get you out of these hopeless confines of fabric and hoop, yes?"

Off came jewels, accessories, shoes, and hoops. The beautiful Polonese gown followed. Then, wearing only stays, shift, and stockings, she rolled onto her stomach, arms crossed beneath her on the pillow, back arched and her cheek resting on the backs of her wrists. "Oh, yes. . . ."

She felt his fingers caressing her nape beneath the heavy mass of her hair. Her blood thickened with sensuous languor, her body ached with desire. She craved his touch. Sighed as his fingers combed through her hair, gently pulling it up and away from the top of her chemise, gathering the weighty, silken mass up in his hand before laying it alongside her neck and out across the pillow. Cool air kissed her exposed nape . . . then the gentle, all-consuming warmth of his hand.

She closed her eyes in bliss as he slowly caressed her, his knuckles lingering in the hollow between her shoulder blades; there they remained for a long, dragged-out moment, skating over the thin chemise that separated her skin from his, massaging out a knot before continuing downward, unlacing her stays, freeing her from their constraints, traveling ever lower until his fingertips met the dip where spine met hips. There they lingered in a warm caress.

"If I were a cat, I'd be purring," she mumbled, as he lifted her slightly and pulled the stays out from under her.

His hand was roving down her lower back, stoking the fire within her, now rounding the high curve of her bottom. "Ah, but you are a cat, my dear, sleek and lustrous, one moment purring, the next hissing and clawing."

"Mmmm . . . purring versus hissing and clawing. . . . Do you have a preference, Duke?"

"No, as long as I have variety."

"Then make me do more than purr, Blackheath."

"With pleasure, madam."

And with those husky words, the bed sagged a bit more as he leaned down over her, and she felt the press of his lips there in the dip of her spine, grazing the sensitized skin through her thin chemise, making her sigh and flex her fingers beneath her in pleasure.

"Mmmm, Blackheath . . . I'm definitely purring now."

He pulled the long, loose garment up over her legs, lifted her, and dragged it up her back. She felt his hand tracing the curve of her bottom, his mouth teasing the small of her back; then, slowly, his lips, his tongue, his teeth all working in a heady caress, he moved up her spine, going to work on each vertebra, making her every nerve tighten and tingle.

She raised her head from the pillow, breathing hard.

"Oh, Blackheath—"

Still he dragged his mouth up and over each vertebra, his hand still caressing her bare bottom; beneath her, pressed against the sheet, her nipples were on fire, and the restless ache between her legs was growing unbearable.

"Purr for me, Duchess."

His tongue was stroking into each dip of her backbone now, drawing little circles on her skin that the air instantly chilled, and she began to moan and squirm, fast reaching the end of her tolerance. In a moment she wasn't going to be purring; she was going to be yowling. And then he pulled the loose chemise back down and his hand, which had been caressing the high, rounded curve of her bottom, moved lower, finding her cleft through the thin fabric.

"Oh, *damn* you, Blackheath!"

He only laughed, and continued stroking her through the fine lawn, and Eva, beginning to perspire now against the pillow, felt a spreading slick of moisture between her thighs, soaking into her chemise as he pressed it against her aching center, slowly moving the fabric up and down, the rough pressure bringing her nearer and nearer to climax.

"Oh . . . oh, you are a merciless *beast*. Please—stop!"

"But my dear lady, I haven't fully . . . prepared you."

"Any more preparation and the sheets are going to catch on fire beneath me."

He laughed, and his hand left her hot, aching nether regions, pulling the chemise up once more. He lay the fine fabric across her bottom, her back, the bed on which she still lay facedown and trembling. Cool air assaulted her exposed legs, whispered up her inner thighs. His knuckles roved up her calves, grazing her skin through her thin silk stockings. It was nearly her undoing—but no, she had control, she did, she *did*. She would not let herself go over the edge just yet, even though she wanted nothing more than those knuckles, those hands, that warm, knowing touch, higher . . . wanted it where it had been a moment ago, wanted him, and that hard, pressing arousal she could feel stabbing into her hip, inside her. Penetrating her.

But no.

No, he was kissing, caressing, the sensitive backs of her knees . . . turning her over now, his hands warm and guiding, peeling the chemise from her hot body as he had earlier peeled the orange from its protective flesh. His fingers were at her throat, untying the neck of her chemise, sliding it down her shoulders, baring them, baring her, to his simmering gaze, his skillful hands. She lay there for a moment, wrapped in only the thin lawn, now damp with her own excited perspiration. Finally, he removed this last barrier and she lay beneath him, skin to skin, as naked as he.

He gazed down at her, smiling as he took in her lush curves, her flushed skin, his eyes lingering at the junction of her long white thighs.

"Now I think"—his finger traced the valley between her breasts, drew a light, agonizing line down her abdomen—"that I will make you hiss and scratch."

Anticipation pulsed through Eva; she was so primed and ready for him that she feared one more touch would make her splinter like crystal.

But he did not touch her, except with that enigmatic black gaze; he did not lay a finger on her, even, only allowing her to simmer in her own steam, smiling as she gazed up at him through the tangled, damp skeins of her hair.

"And how do you plan to do that, Blackheath?"

For answer, he only let that grin widen—and reached for the bowl of cherries.

Eva's eyes widened; she stared mutely at him. Fascinated, she watched as he plucked a cherry from the bowl, holding it by the stem and slanting her a wicked sidelong glance; then, his eyes hooded, he lowered it to her mouth, dragging it lightly over her lower lip, and then the arched contour of her upper one.

His command was an unspoken one. Eva opened

her mouth and bit off the bottom edge of the sweet fruit. She boldly met Blackheath's gaze; his eyes went even darker.

He bent down and kissed the thin trickle of red juice from her lower lip; then, still holding the partly eaten fruit by its stem, he dragged it down the damp white arch of throat.

Along the base of one breast.

Around the flushed areola, circling it once, twice, until the nipple tingled and ached; still twirling the cherry by its stem, he let its soft wet flesh, the slick raspy roughness of the exposed pit, graze the edges of her nipple until Eva felt the tension coiling between her legs once more, building, until she could not contain her tortured moans of desire.

Breathing hard, her hot body filmed with dampness, she opened her eyes just in time to see Blackheath's mouth fasten upon the fruit-stained nipple, sucking and licking the sweet red juice.

Eva gasped and arched upward, using every bit of her will to keep climax at bay, her hands shoving at Blackheath's shoulders, her nails scoring the skin stretched over the hard, bulging muscle as his tongue flicked and rasped the engorged bud.

"Ah . . . my cat shows her claws," he murmured, pulling back and smiling.

She stared up at him, breathing hard, her nipples so tight she thought she would explode. He was still holding the half-eaten cherry; still twirling it lazily between thumb and forefinger, his gaze dark, promising, and very, very wicked.

And then, as she watched, he brought it to his mouth, and, his eyes never leaving hers, took a tiny bite, exposing that much more of the fleshy red fruit, the paler pit.

His gaze still holding hers, he held the cherry out, just over her stomach . . . and began to lower it.

"No—oh, Blackheath, no, you wouldn't dare—"

"Oh, but I would," he murmured, and she gasped as he touched the cool wet fruit to her abdomen.

He dragged it around her navel, leaving a thin trail of fruity red juice . . . and just skirted the top edge of her silken curls, teasing her, making her writhe with wanting.

"Blackheath—"

But he only bent down and began to follow the trail of juice with his tongue.

Eva shut her eyes as his mouth grazed her midriff, as his lips teased her skin into prickles of exquisite agony, as his tongue ran over the sweet red juice. She knew what he was going to do . . . oh, God, she knew what was coming—

And then, yes, he pulled back, took another bite of the cherry, and, still holding the fruit by the stem— now nothing more than a pit and a wedge of dark red flesh—he dragged it around the triangle of soft red curls, coaxing her legs apart with his other hand.

"Oh, dear heavens, Blackheath—"

He merely smiled, pulled the fruit through the thatch of silken hair, and then drew it up, then down, between the parted lips of her femininity.

"Black*heath*—"

She writhed on the pillow, drowning in sensation, fighting the inevitable, her hair spilling across her face and twisting beneath her.

But he was relentless. Ruthless. She felt the tiny ball

of fruit touching her most intimate folds, felt him pulling it between the petals of her womanhood, held open by his thumb and forefinger, and then—

Oh, God—

And then he was holding her fully, tautly open . . . and touching the sweet fruit to her engorged bud, fully exposed to his gaze, the air, the wet pit of the cherry.

Eva began to sob. To thrash. To whimper and make strangled noises of desire. Desperately, she clawed at his hands, but he only caught her flailing wrists, lowered himself down, and with his mouth and tongue began to follow the sweet red juice from where he'd left off at her navel.

Down through her hot, moist curls.

And there—*there,* right at the peaked, burning center of her last kissed by the fruit, as he held her thighs wide apart with both hands.

Eva felt a climax rushing down upon her. She screamed and tore free, pushing at his head as his tongue flicked and rasped over the hardened bud, mercilessly bringing her higher and higher until she was raking at his shoulders, twisting helplessly beneath him, crying out his name. She forgot to breathe, and for a moment she nearly blacked out . . . and when she came back to herself, he was atop her, covering her with his body, his hands anchoring her head, his mouth covering her own cries of passion as he slipped, oh-so-deeply, inside her. . . .

Filling her.

Stretching her.

Causing her to arch upward to meet his slow, driving thrusts until they came faster and faster, carrying her right along with him, little cries ripping from her throat as she soared with him toward climax yet again. And then his body went taut. He hung poised above her before giving one last thrust, and she buried her scream against his damp shoulder as she convulsed with passion once more.

Exhausted, they lay together, breathing hard, their bodies separated by only a film of perspiration.

Outside, the sleet hissed against the window. The storm gathered force, and Eva felt sleep pulling the curtain down around her eyes.

And as she faded toward oblivion, her arms wrapped loosely around her husband's broad shoulders, she was smiling.

Chapter 22

Lucien did not go to sleep.

He lay there, his arms and shoulders taking most of his weight, his body half covering the woman beside him. Outside, in the darkness beyond the heavy drapes, wind and sleet hissed against the windows, rattling the casements, bringing to his ears the distant roar of the sea. He had no wish to give in to his body's demand for rest, no wish to revisit the nightmares. No, better to just lie here with her, enjoying the feel of her in his arms, the scent of her in his nostrils, the sight of her curving, long-legged body in the light of the flickering candelabra.

She was beautiful. And this had been the first time she had given herself to him with no coercion and little seduction; the first time she had let down her guard enough to tentatively trust him. The first time the aloof, contemptuous Eva had allowed a softer, sweeter side to take its place.

Lucien smiled. He quite liked this sweeter side.

Now that their passion was spent, their bodies cooling, he realized how chilly it was in the room. Carefully, so as not to wake his bride, he rolled off her, seized the thick coverlet, and pulled it up over them both.

She opened her eyes.

"Lucien."

He froze. *Lucien*—she had called him by his given name. Not Blackheath, not Duke, not Your Grace—but Lucien. His heart swelled almost painfully. He swallowed hard against the sudden tightness in his throat and managed a little smile.

"You called me Lucien."

She rolled over, using his arm as a pillow, and gazed up into his face. Her eyes were glowing, her lips curved in a soft, teasing smile. "Is that not your name?"

"I do not recall your ever having used it before."

"No."

She didn't need to tell him that she'd never before used it because to do so would be to discard yet another barrier she'd insisted on keeping between them; to use it would be to embrace an intimacy she was not ready to allow; to use it would be to imply friendship and trust when there was none—

But she had used it now.

He reached out and ran his fingers over the line of her jaw. "Say it again, Eva. I like the sound of my name on your lips."

"Lucien."

He couldn't help his spreading grin, couldn't help

the sweet, all-consuming ache that threatened to overwhelm him. Just the sound of his Christian name on her soft, sultry voice was enough to stir him back to arousal. He stretched out beside her, his arm still under her head, and ran his fingers through a thick skein of her hair. "You are making a mess of my heart," he murmured.

"Well, Duke, if that's all it takes, maybe you'll be easier to handle than I'd previously thought."

"You think so, do you?"

"Don't forget, I, too, like challenges."

They lay together, mutually enjoying this newfound peace, this lack of enmity and distrust. For once, the beautiful slanting eyes that gazed up into Lucien's were not narrowed or flashing fire, but glowing with something that looked like hope. The sensuous mouth was not twisted with contempt, but smiling almost girlishly. He sighed as her small white hand—a hand that could fell a man twice her size with one blow, a hand that was as strong as it was feminine—came up to trace the bones of his face, the point of his cheek, the noble, sloping, nearly unbroken line of his profile.

"You still haven't told me," he murmured, still thinking about that hand as he enjoyed its gentle caress.

"Told you what?"

"How you rendered me senseless back in Paris."

She merely smiled.

He lifted a brow, waiting.

"Oh, very well," she said, and let her fingers drift to the sides of his neck. "There are arteries here. If you can find just the right spot and press gently, it produces a brief loss of consciousness."

"Ah, then. Something you learned during your tenure in the Orient?"

Again, that slow, mysterious smile.

She traced his lips with one finger. "I suppose I should apologize for what I did to you that night, but I really didn't dare to leave you, unguarded, with the aphrodisiac so near at hand."

"And I suppose *I* should apologize for making such a mess of your life back in France. It was not very gentlemanly of me, though I do not regret the end result."

She ran her fingertip down the bridge of his nose. "Yes—the end result. I never knew that you were baiting me with all your talk about 'the colonies.' Never realized that your sentiments toward America are benevolent, and that you empathize with the struggles of my homeland. All I knew was that because of you, I had to leave Paris, my ability to bring an end to the war between our two lands compromised. But sometimes fate deals us a hand that's every bit as good. I will welcome your intercession in Parliament, Lucien, to bring about independence and peace."

"And I promise you that peace between our two lands is something I will work most diligently for, my dear."

"Yes—yes, I think I believe you."

"You must trust me implicitly."

"I'm not very good at trusting people."

"It is a skill that will take practice, then."

"But I'm working on it, don't you think? I mean, look at us, here and now, interacting as if we actually like each other, as if we're friends instead of wary enemies."

He smiled as her fingers traced the roughness of his

jaw. "My dear Eva. I have never thought of you as my enemy."

She, too, smiled, and then looked away—but not before he saw the sudden troubled confusion in her eyes.

"What is it?"

"Do you think your brothers—well, Charles in particular—will ever forgive me for what I did to him the night of the robbery?"

"I am sure that if you ask his forgiveness, he will give it." He smoothed her hair back from her face. "Is it so very important?"

"Yes, it is." She gazed up into his eyes. "Because, you see, Lucien, I, too, want what my sisters-in-law have. A happy marriage. Cheerful, bouncing children. A husband who lo—" She flushed. "Cherishes and respects me."

He knew what she'd almost said. "It is conceivable that love, given time and half a chance, may blossom between us, Eva. But the trust must come first."

"Do you trust me?"

He smiled, his eyes very dark and deep. "With my life."

She looked away, assailed by guilt. How brave he was, willing to risk everything: his heart, his pride, his dignity. Was he that much stronger, that much more courageous than she? Why could she not reciprocate?

I can reciprocate. And I can start right now.

"Lucien," she said haltingly. "Do you remember how you once asked me about my father, and about what he . . . did?"

"I do."

Eva swallowed. Fear began to speed up her heartbeat, cause her palms to grow damp. Trusting him—trusting anyone—was hard. More difficult, even, than agreeing to marry him. She wasn't sure if she could do it.

"Is there something you wish to tell me, Eva?

She took a deep, bracing breath. "Yes."

His face lost its smile, became grave; he said nothing, just waited, allowing her the time she needed. Finally, Eva shut her eyes and let her mind travel back over the years.

"I was the only child of a sea captain turned merchant," she began. "We lived in Salem, Massachusetts"—she gave a nervous little laugh—"the witch town."

She waited for him to make a comment about *that*, but he did not. He merely lay there beside her, watching her face, letting her tell this tale that had shaped her into the woman she had become.

"My mother was the youngest daughter of an English baronet whose seat is near Bristol . . . a thriving port, as I'm sure you know. It was there that she met my father. He was tall, charming, adventurous—and altogether off limits for a woman of my mother's noble blood. Her family forbade her to see him, but of course, she did so anyhow . . . and soon found herself pregnant. With me. My father married her, her family cut all ties with her, and he took her back to America with him, where he became one of the richest men in Salem.

"My earliest memories are of my mother weeping as my father prepared for a sea voyage. It was the same thing, every time. The house would grow silent and still, the air almost brittle. I would not dare to speak,

but would stay out of their way, watching my father as
he silently packed his trunk, watching my mother as
she sat crying noisily, a handkerchief in one hand and a
bottle of spirits in the other . . . looking for attention
and never getting it.

"It was a grand performance, but he would ignore
it. Always. And when it came time for him to leave, he
would kiss her on the cheek— always formally, with no
more feeling than if he were saying farewell to a dog—
ruffle my hair in a pretense of affection, and that
would be it. Off he would go, plying the Orient or the
Indies, returning weeks, months later with wondrous
cargoes of spices, china, and other exotic treasures that
made me ache for wanting to see and visit those same
places."

She smiled sadly and, pulling a thick tendril of
glossy red hair over her shoulder, began to plait it,
needful of something to do with her fingers, her con-
flicting emotions. "Oh, how I used to beg him to take
Mama and me with him on his voyages! But he never
did, of course. He'd just shake his head and say that the
sea was no place for women. Looking back, I suppose it
was as good an excuse as any; Mama would not have
gone with him even if he'd wanted us to be there."

She came to the end of the braid, combed it out with
her fingers, began plaiting the skein of hair once more,
tighter this time, neater, her movements growing more
agitated. "My father was favored with youthful good
looks, wealth, and charm. Too much charm. The sort of
charm that women usually find impossible to resist."
Her face grew shadowed. "He was gone to sea a lot,
but when he came back from a voyage, smelling of
wind and sun and salt, he always had a trinket for me,

a shawl of silk, a bag of fruit from some faraway port. I loved it when my papa came home." She swallowed, hard, staring at the three ends of the little braid. "I loved my papa."

Lucien smiled gently; he could feel her pain as keenly as if it were in his own heart. "Loved him, or worshiped him?"

"A little of both." She looked at him then, chin high, making a vain attempt to maintain her pride— but he could see the suffering in her eyes, suffering that she was unable to hide. "I loved him . . . but I never knew, until one horrible day, that he did not love me."

Outside, the wind flung sleet against the windows, the draft moving the heavy drapes. Lucien pulled the blanket up and tucked it around his wife's bare shoulders.

"I could never understand why Mama was always so bitter and unhappy, her eyes full of poison, when she spoke of my dear papa. I could never understand why she grew furious when I extolled his virtues, could never understand why she said the things she did about men, and always in a venomous tone, the words forced out between clenched teeth, her hatred so forceful it was often enough to drive me from the room."

"What things?"

"Oh, the truth . . . things such as, 'You can't trust any of them, not a damned one of them,' and 'Never fall in love, Eva, it will only break your heart,' and other such advice that I did, of course, fail to heed until it was too late for me as well. But I will get to that. What was I saying? Oh, yes. I was saying how I never

understood why Mama hated men so, why she was
never kind to my father, why she loathed the idea of
him coming home as much as she loathed the idea
of him leaving . . . why she would invite the women of
Salem over for tea, shutting the door so that I could not
eavesdrop, even though I knew that behind that closed
door she was maligning him in front of those harpies,
playing the martyr with a vicious intensity that, at the
time, I thought was largely undeserved. Unfair." She
gave a bitter little laugh and wiped at her eye. Wiped
at the other. "Oh, if only I'd known. And on the day I
turned nine, I found out."

Hot tears were spilling from her eyes, racing each
other down her cheeks; wordlessly, Lucien touched his
thumb to the damp tracks and gently wiped them
away. "You don't have to tell me if this is too painful,
my dear—"

She shook her head, her eyes suddenly fierce.
"No—I have started this, I will finish it."

He leaned back, watching helplessly as she ripped
the hapless little braid apart with trembling fingers
and once more set to work on plaiting it.

"I could not bear to be in the house with Mama,
could not bear to see her drinking, raging against my
father, her fate, and men in general. It was no more difficult for me to slip out of the house and, disguised as
one of them, join the boys who used to gather around
the docks, waiting for ships to come in, trying to absorb
some of the sea's excitement, than it was for me to
adopt the guise of a man some years later, fabricate ref-
erences, and gain entrance into Harvard. Though the
lads of Salem knew me to be a girl and accepted me as
such, at Harvard I had everyone fooled. I was tall, ath-

letic, quick—and, being something of a late bloomer, I looked the part in breeches and coat. But those boys at the docks—they taught me how to fight dirty. And those at Harvard"—she gave a contemptuous laugh—"they taught me how to fight like a gentleman. Fools . . . for all their brains at that revered institution, nobody ever caught on that I was a woman."

She came to the end of the braid and began twisting it around her fingertip. "But I digress. One day, when I was at the docks with my young friends, a ship came in—I immediately recognized it as my father's. I grew excited, as I always did when he returned from a long voyage, and ran down to greet him after the ship dropped anchor. I came up short before reaching him. Before he saw me." She paused, her face very still. "There—there was a woman there."

Lucien tensed, seeing the stricken look on Eva's face that must have echoed the one she had worn all those years ago.

"I had never believed my mother when she raged about men, had always defended my papa because I thought he was . . . different. But there, all dressed in fancy silks and jewels that he, no doubt, had paid for, stood proof of my mother's convictions. She was the most beautiful woman I had ever seen, a painted woman, and there she was, smiling a slow, seductive smile as she watched my father being rowed toward shore. He—he got out of the little boat. His face became animated and loving, the way it never did when he was with my mother, and he offered that . . . that woman his arm and led her off . . . while my world closed up around me."

Lucien ached for her. Lamented the fact that he

could do nothing to ease the misery in her eyes. "He betrayed you," he said quietly.

"Yes. He did. And there I stood, humiliated, stricken dumb by the realization that my papa was unfaithful, not only to my mama—but to my belief in him. It was too much. I began to cry. The boys who I thought were my friends laughed at me, told me my papa was 'acting just as he should,' and that it was time I faced reality. I ran home in tears. I burst into the house, found my mother with a bottle, and blurted out what I had seen . . . and it was then that she told me the truth. That when she gave birth to me, the experience nearly killed her, and as a result the doctor advised her to never have any more children."

"Dear God," said Lucien, understanding making him want to gather this poor, still-hurting child up in his arms and comfort her.

"You're no dull blade, Blackheath. I'm sure you can figure out the rest. After I was born, my father was so resentful that my mother could not give him the boy-child he'd wanted, the heir to not only his name but his fortune, that he sought only to punish her for her failings. He did it by taking mistress after mistress, flaunting them in front of her, sating the appetites that she could no longer satisfy. And that's how I spent the rest of my childhood: watching my father come home from sea to be claimed by a different woman every time, and listening to my weak, self-pitying mother's endless diatribes about the baseness and untrustworthiness of men while she drank herself closer and closer to an early grave." She flung the braid aside, her eyes tragic, sullen. "Eventually she got there, and put herself out of her own misery."

Lucien felt his heart constricting. Now it all made sense. From childhood on, his wife had been molded to resent men—and her father's betrayal had crystallized the seeds of her distrust. He wanted to strangle this sire of hers who had so betrayed her; felt a desperate desire to prove that *he* was different, that he would never, ever betray her with another woman, even under pain of death.

"And this . . . father, of yours," he murmured. "Is he still alive?"

"No. He died at sea, somewhere off the coast of Madagascar, and good riddance to him."

"Eva."

She buried her face in her hands, the white fingers splaying up through thick, curling ropes of vibrant red hair. "I am sorry, Blackheath. I am sorry that it is nearly impossible for me to trust you, to trust any of you, that I am so . . . damaged. I am doomed to the same unhappiness as my mother; doomed to repeat her own dire and vicious warnings, doomed to relive her own miserable existence—"

"Eva."

"All those years she warned me, but I had not listened . . . I wanted what I would never find, I hated her for murdering my fairy-tale dream of love happily ever after with a handsome, loving husband. I hated her for being right about my father, for making me resent men, for making me distrust them as thoroughly as she did. We became allies, of sorts. Enemies, as she always envied my strength. I grew up. Grew breasts and hips and a caustic tongue. And wherever I went, I was surrounded by men. My head swelled. I enjoyed the attention, the power I had over their pathetic hearts and ungoverned lusts . . . the power I had to break their hearts, as my father had broken mine so many years before.

"Flattery was my undoing. I grew weak. Soft. Stupid. I began to think that maybe, just maybe, my father was one in a million. That what happened to my mother would never happen to me, because I . . ."—she gave a bitter laugh—"I was *strong*. And so, when I met Jacques and he joined my circle of admirers, I accepted his hand and married him. He was dashing, just like Papa. Aristocratic, like my mama had been. And attentive—at first. But he soon grew cool. Distant. One day, Blackheath, I caught him in bed with my maid. I never let him near me again. And from that day on, I vowed that I would never again allow a man to control my destiny. That I would never again tie myself to a man, set myself up for heartbreak."

Lucien shook his head. "And yet you married me," he said softly, overwhelmed by what she had sacrificed—or what she thought she had sacrificed—for her unborn child.

"You have promised me my freedom. If there is nothing else I trust about you, it is that you are a man of your word."

"I want you to be happy, Eva. Not only for your own sake, but for that of the child."

"As long as you keep your word about my independence, Blackheath, I will be happy."

"And if fate should separate us?"

"Do you refer to your nightmares?"

"I do."

"Then I shall take the child back to America. There is nothing to keep me here in England."

Lucien felt the blood drain from his face. A chill settled in his spine, spreading out into his limbs, numbing, even, his fingers and toes. *Oh, no. Oh, dear God, no. The will.*

She looked up, frowning in concern. "Lucien, what is it?"

He got to his feet, raking a hand through his hair before bending to pull on his breeches. "I am afraid that is impossible."

She laughed. "Of course it's possible. I simply take the child, get on a ship, and go."

"No," he said, shaking his head and buttoning the breeches, "you cannot."

She stilled. Gamely, she tried to muster that flippant, amused laugh she'd mastered so well, the one that was designed to mask the hurt that lived perpetually in her heart. "Really, now, Blackheath, what are you trying to tell me?"

He straightened and faced her, already regretting the visit to his solicitor, already fearing the impact of what he was about to tell her. *Oh, hell. Oh, bloody, thundering, hell.* Taking a deep, bracing breath, he murmured, "I am trying to tell you that I made an adjustment to my will. That you cannot leave England with the child, Eva, whether or not I am dead."

She just stared at him, unmoving.

"The child, should it be a male, is heir to the dukedom of Blackheath," he explained. "And if it's a girl, it is still my flesh and blood. My responsibility. I cannot allow it to be brought out of England until it reaches its majority and makes that decision for itself." Her face was growing pale. Almost opaque. "Please, Eva, I beg you to understand; I did not do this to curtail your freedom—I did it to protect my son or daughter."

She climbed down from the bed, her nostrils flaring, her eyes cold, hard jewels of fury. "You did it because you wanted full control over both me and the child, even from beyond the grave!"

"No. That is not true. I acted only out of concern for both the child's welfare and its responsibilities toward its birthright."

"You *deceived* me!" she cried, shaking her head in denial, as though unable to fathom what he had done. "I trusted you, Blackheath!"

"Eva—"

"You deceived me, created the illusion that I would have my freedom, but you had it all planned, didn't you? You wanted me to think I had my independence, but no, it's all meaningless, isn't it, meaningless by virtue of a simple clause in your damned will!"

Lucien set his jaw. "Eva, you must listen to me, try to understand—"

"Oh, no, Blackheath, there is nothing to understand. I see you now for what you are—the diabolical monster your siblings claim you to be, an arrogant, manipulative bastard who isn't happy unless he's in control of everyone and everything around him!" She yanked on her clothes, abandoning the corset and hoops, jerking the tapes and ties with vicious fury, her eyes on fire beneath angry red brows. "Well, this time you've gone too far, Blackheath. You can have your precious pile of stones, your precious title, your precious birthright, but I'm telling you right now, you've just lost your precious *wife*!"

He slammed his fist into the wall in a rare display of temper. "Damnation, Eva, *listen to me!*"

"No, Blackheath, you listen to *me*." She hauled on her bodice, stabbing her arms through the sleeves, jerking the garment down over her hips. "You listen to me, because I'm leaving."

And with that, she spun on her heel and did just that.

Chapter 23

He came after her, just as she knew he would, authoritative, autocratic, demanding.

"*Eva.*"

She kept walking, head high, fists clenched, her fury blazing behind eyes squeezed shut. Oh, this was just what she deserved for trusting a man, just what she had expected all along, wasn't it? Wasn't it? What a damned *fool* she'd been!

"Eva!"

His terse command echoed from just behind her as she swept into the hall. She stopped only long enough to grab her cloak and face him, her eyes narrowed. "Get away from me, Blackheath," she snarled, her voice quivering with wrath, self-loathing, and the pain of betrayal. Her fingers trembled as she fumbled with her buttons, cinched her hood around her hair. "I need time to think. The least you can grant me is a few

273

moments to do just that, unless you plan to deprive me of my freedom to think as well as to leave."

He moved to block the door from which she planned to make her escape, arms crossed, eyes blacker than Hades, his body an impenetrable wall of solid male flesh. "You are not going anywhere until we have a talk, madam."

She yanked on her gloves, bristling at his autocratic tone, his domineering manner. "No, Blackheath, *you* need to have a talk, preferably with yourself. You need to consider the consequences of governing other people's lives, making their choices for them, imposing yourself upon their free will. You may have succeeded in ordering the lives of your siblings, but I swear you will never order mine, not now, not tomorrow, and certainly not from beyond the grave." She walked up to him, skirts dragging, feeling as though she were made of crystal and needed only the slightest tap to shatter; only strength of will enabled her to maintain her composure. "Now, I am asking you, Blackheath, to stand aside and allow me a few moments to myself."

"I will gladly allow you a few moments to yourself, madam, a few hours, even"—his face was set, his eyes glacial, his mouth hard—"but not if you plan to spend them outside."

"Ah, so you're my gaoler now, are you?"

"I am your husband."

"You are the bane of my existence, and I am *asking* you to stand aside."

"No." He remained where he was, arms crossed, barring the door. "You are not going outside in this sort of weather."

"Damn you to hell, Blackheath, I am not a child, and if you have any shred of respect for my feelings, you will *let—me—pass*."

"At the moment, I have far more respect for your health and well-being than I do for your feelings, madam. You will turn around, find a bedroom, a parlor, a sitting room in which to nurse your bruised temper, and when you have reached a state of calm, we will discuss this matter further."

They faced each other, neither willing to give an inch, neither willing to back down. Eva's face was white with fury, her hand curled into a fist and buried within a fold of her cloak. Lucien didn't move.

"So—is that your verdict, then?" she asked, her voice dripping acid.

"It is."

She turned her back, as though she could not bear to look at him. Lucien set his jaw, keeping his own temper under a tight rein. How the devil had things come to such a state? All he'd done was try to protect his child by keeping it in England where it would be safe. He had not wanted to make Eva feel like a prisoner within her own marriage, had not wanted to make her miserable, had fully intended to spend his life with her, proving that he was different from all the other men she had ever known.

And now he'd done just the opposite.

Inadvertently, of course, but he'd done it just the same.

Bloody *hell*.

Guilt assailed him. And self-loathing. He should have known that a simple thing like protecting his child from beyond the grave would lead to such an impasse. Why hadn't he foreseen the consequences of what he'd thought was a completely natural and appropriate act? Ah, but of course. She was American. A rebel. An advocate of *freedom*, and a woman who—despite all—did not understand the critical importance of preserving an aristocratic line, a powerful family. He had misjudged her; he had thought she would understand, even support his actions. He had thought she'd be happy to stay in England, rich, pampered, powerful, after his death . . . but he had been wrong.

Wrong.

Deliberately, he softened his voice, trying to find a way to compromise, to reason with her, as he addressed her back. "Is it so very important that you leave, Eva?"

"Important? Ha! It is imperative. You see, Blackheath, I cannot stand the sight of you another moment. You make me ill. You disgust me. And I can assure you that unless you intend to confine me under lock and key, I *will* find a way to leave you and this wretched marriage I was foolish enough to enter."

Her words cut to the marrow. Punched a hole in his heart. Wordlessly, he stepped aside, his jaw clenched with fury, his lips a thin, severe line of suppressed pain. For once, he was at a loss what to do.

She turned then, and just as silently jerked up her chin, walked past him, and out into the night.

Lucien kicked the door shut behind her.

And stood there all alone in the room, his temples throbbing, his hands balled into fists as, outside, the wind whistled around the house, and sleet hissed against the windows.

Rage boiled up inside him. He could feel it leaching out of every pore, burning through his veins, making his heart pound and pulse and throb until his whole chest felt as though it were on fire. If he didn't leave, he feared he would lose control of his temper, do something vulgar and totally animalistic, such as . . . break something. Hurt someone. The idea of losing control was something he dared not even contemplate.

She left me.

His body began to quiver, to shake.

She bloody left me.

Cursing, he stalked back to the study and threw himself into a chair, willing his mind, his body, to calmness—and failing miserably. Desperate for control, he reached for a glass and a bottle of brandy, his hand shaking so badly that he could barely bring the spirits to his lips. He downed the liquor, felt it burning a path down his throat. He got to his feet and began to prowl. To pace. He caught a glimpse of his face as he passed a looking glass on the wall; it was a thundercloud of fury.

She must be in the stables by now. Probably choosing the fastest horse upon which to make her escape.

I'll never see her again.

He raked a hand over his face and refilled his glass. *I'll never see her again.*

And look at him, sitting here like a fool, just allowing her to leave and making no move to stop her. The depths to which he'd sunk! What the blazing devil had she done to his brain, to his self-control, to everything he prided himself on being? How had she managed to reduce him to this impotent fury, this raging self-doubt that was consuming him from within?

He slammed the glass down, shattering it. Damn

her. She wasn't going anywhere, not tonight, not tomorrow, not ever. They were going to resolve this matter, and they were going to do it whether she wanted to or not. His jaw like steel, Lucien stormed back out into the corridor, through the hall, and, without even pausing to grab a coat, outside into the night.

Sleet stung his face, wind lashed his cheeks, and the cold was a thousand needles driving through his thin shirt as he stalked across the courtyard and headed for the stables. He could see lantern light glowing at the windows, and shapes moving behind them. Savage satisfaction filled him. She was still here, then. He had caught her. He would not let her leave.

He had just reached the door when out she came, stiff, erect, a riding crop in her hand and a worried groom trailing behind her, leading a saddled mare and protesting that it was no night for Her Grace to be traveling.

"Her Grace *isn't* traveling," Lucien bit out through clenched teeth.

Her head jerked up and she saw him standing there in the sleet. Something passed over her face, settled in her beautiful slanting eyes—and in that moment Lucien knew he'd made a grave mistake.

Her mouth curved in a poisonous little smile. "I should have known you'd interfere," she murmured, her voice colder than the sleet that beat down against their faces. She no longer radiated the furious temper he had left her in; now there was nothing but resentment. Loathing. "Even now you try to control my destiny. My fate. You despicable wretch."

"You are not going out on a night like this."

"Ah, listen to you, Blackheath . . . ever the dictator,

aren't you?" She shook her head. "You just can't let a person control their own destiny, can't allow them their God-given freedom of will. How can you, when you think you rank right up there with the Creator himself?" She took the mare's reins from the groom. "You just don't learn. I suspect you never will." She led the mare to the mounting block, gathered the reins, and swung neatly up onto the horse's back, where she sat staring down at him in disdain, the sleet beating down around her face. "I am well rid of you, Blackheath. Just remember, things *could* have been different . . . if only you'd been able to relinquish some of that precious control you value so highly."

She put her heel to the horse's flank; the mare began to move.

Lucien stepped in front of the animal. "Eva, I beg of you, don't go."

"You *beg* of me? You, the mighty Blackheath, reduced to begging?" She gave a high, mocking laugh, though he saw the pain in her eyes, the wounds that he had torn in her soul. "Oh, you can beg all you like, but it's not going to get you anything but humiliation. I think I would like to see you humiliated, though. It's nothing less than you deserve. Now out of my way. I am through with you."

Lucien caught the mare's reins as Eva tried to get past. The sleet was pelting his face now, running through his hair and down the back of his neck, the wind knifing through the thin shirt that was all he had against the elements. "For God's sake, woman, if you insist on leaving in this weather, at least let Rothwell drive you into the village. I don't want—that is, you can't be out riding in this sort of storm. Let Rothwell take you in the coach—if not for your own sake, then for that of the child."

She glanced down at him, weighing his words against her own fierce pride. Then she jerked her gaze up and away, glaring out into the silent darkness. Around them, the sleet hissed down, caking the mare's neck with ice, tracking down her thick winter coat in dark rivulets, making her lay her ears flat against her head. The cobbles upon which they stood were growing slick. The wind was picking up. A short distance away, a worried Rothwell stood shivering.

"Eva—*please.*"

She swung back to face him, her eyes burning with something like hatred as her gaze met his. Wordlessly, she stared down at him through the stinging sleet; then she kicked free of the stirrups, swung down from the saddle before he could step forward to assist her, and stalked back into the stable.

Rothwell looked toward Lucien for instruction.

But he was still staring into the black rectangle of darkness into which Eva had disappeared.

"Hitch up a team and see her safely into the village," he bit out. "There's an inn on the High Street. Deliver her safely to the door, and do not leave until you have the landlord's assurance that she will have a room for the night and all the comforts she desires."

And with that, Lucien turned on his heel and stalked back through the worsening weather toward the house, his last words still stinging his tongue, his heart sitting like a ball of lead in his chest.

They were the hardest words he'd ever had to utter in his life.

Chapter 24

He slammed into the house, ice melting from his hair and sliding down the back of his neck as he stalked toward the study.

He was so angry he couldn't even think. Never—not since he'd found his father all those years ago, lying dead on those cold stone stairs with a broken neck—had he felt so out of control, so near to . . . tears. He seized the bottle of brandy, got another glass, and immediately tossed it back, uncaring that he was soaked through to the skin and shaking with cold. He was too distraught to seek the warmth of the hearth. Instead, his gaze, of its own accord, jerked up and found the window, hidden from his blazing eyes by thick, pulled-shut drapes.

Only supreme force of will kept him from getting to his feet, yanking the drapes aside, and getting a last glimpse of her as she came back out of the stable and entered the coach. In fact, he could envision it now: Eva, his wife, his duchess, pacing back and forth as she waited for it to be readied, her eyes like two chips of emerald, the riding crop still in her hand, no doubt, and impatiently slapping her thigh. It was all he could do not to go to her—again—and infuriate her all the more with his bungled attempts at stopping this nonsense, at trying to reach an understanding, a reconciliation. But he had tried that once and failed; all he'd succeeded in doing was making her hate him all the more.

To hell with her, then. He'd lived without her for nearly thirty years, he could live without her now. He could. Damn it, he was the Duke of Blackheath and he didn't need to be chasing after a woman's skirts, making a fool of himself and losing his own self-respect in the bargain! God above, if his friends could see him now . . . how they would be laughing!

He downed the brandy, turning his back on the window so he could not be tempted to observe her departure. But the brandy would not dull the churning, writhing torment that made him unable to sit still, unable to rein his thoughts into some semblance of order, unable to do anything but pace back and forth and curse her for her stubbornness and inability to see reason.

He was just reaching for the bottle once more when he heard hoofbeats and the jangle of harnesses just outside the window. His insides tensed; he froze, jaw clenched, shutting his eyes against the emotions that threatened to consume him, willing himself to stand right where he was until the vehicle was long past the window. The noise peaked, then diminished, soon lost to the howl of the wind. Lucien finished the glass of brandy, and then, his face set and cold, stalked to the window and finally ripped open the drapes.

There, fresh tracks through the crusted ice that covered the ground, leading off toward the road. He swallowed the sudden lump in his throat. Heard his heartbeat echoing in his ears.

There was nothing out there now but beating-down sleet, and vast, empty darkness.

She was gone.

It was freezing cold in the coach.

Inside, Eva sat as stiff as a corpse, willing her body not to shiver, staring straight ahead as she tried to banish that last sight of Lucien stalking back toward the house like a sullen, angry wolf.

She wanted to cry. To give lease to the tears that stung her eyelids, rose up in the back of her throat, threatened to reduce her to contemptible, pathetic weakness. It was her own fault, of course; she had trusted him, a man. As soon as she'd begun to trust, he had betrayed her. *She* didn't seem to learn, either.

She was no better than he was.

She settled back against the seat, burying her hands within the heavy folds of her cloak, watching the needles of sleet streaking the dark window. She could hear the wheels crunching through the icy crust that now covered the ground. They had left the drive now, were on the road that led to the village. Was Blackheath giving chase? She resisted the urge to look out the back window. She rather hoped that he was . . . she needed him as the target for her fury, needed her fury to chase away the niggling thought that maybe, just maybe, he had come back outside not in order to control her, but because he truly did care about her safety.

About their marriage.

About her.

Codswallop! He didn't care, didn't care one jot; all he cared about was his precious dukedom and the power he wore about him like a mantle, power that he, in all his aristocratic arrogance, expected to exert upon everyone whose lives touched his. Control. It was all about control, wasn't it?

The bastard! She was well rid of him!

She heard Rothwell shout a command to the horses, and then the vehicle veered left, the wheels sliding for a heart-stopping moment as they crossed the bridge, frozen now, that spanned the inlet. A moment later they were turning south, following the coastal road. The wind began to pick up as they neared the sea. Already Eva could feel it rocking the coach, could sense the difficulty the horses were having in keeping their footing on sleet-covered ice. A prickle of unease chased up her spine, and she hastily banished it. She was safe and dry in the coach; she could, at least, thank Blackheath for insisting she take it.

She settled back against the seat, staring into the darkness. *Go back.* She shut her eyes, pushing her fingertips against them and trying to ignore the persistent little voice. *Go back, talk to him, try to see things from his side. . . .*

No! She would not humiliate herself so, she would not give him another opportunity—not one!—to have the upper hand, the mocking triumph, the victory that would be his if she went slinking back to him with her tail between her legs. She would go to the inn, sleep on her troubles, and maybe in the morning, when her head was cooler, when she could think instead of just feel, she would consider what to do next. For now, she only wanted to escape—

Again the wheels slid on ice, and Eva's hand shot out, her heart banging as she steadied herself against the door handle. She looked out the window. They were very near the sea; she could see its dark, almost frightening expanse out there beyond the edge of the land, could feel the wind that drove ruthlessly off the long, endless waves, buffeting the coach, rocking it on its axles.

Her uneasiness built. Her hands were sweating now, despite the chill inside the vehicle. Perhaps she ought to tell Rothwell to turn around and take the longer road into the village.

Perhaps she ought to consider going back to Blackheath.

Perhaps she ought to—

She screamed as the coach skidded hard to the left, then the right. She heard Rothwell's desperate shouts, the frightened whinny of a horse, and then, in slow, sickening motion, her world went awry as the vehicle, still moving, careened over. Eva was hurled against the side. Glass broke all around her and there was a horrible screech of metal. Her knees shaking, she got to her feet— and, reaching up, found the door where the roof had been just a moment before.

The coach was on its side.

Her knees gone to jelly, she pushed the door open. Immediately the wind caught it, ripping it back on its hinges, nearly crushing her fingers and sending sleet driving into her face. Rothwell, who must have been flung from the box, was trying to calm the horses, one of which was down, the other wild-eyed with fright and ready to bolt at any minute. Eva's relief turned to angry frustration. This was just what she should have expected would happen. Just what she should have predicted, given that she'd taken Blackheath's advice and allowed Rothwell to drive her when she would have fared much better on horseback. Men. Stupid, impossible *men*!

The hell with this. She'd *walk* to the village before she suffered another minute in the company of a male. Hooking her hands around the sill, she pulled herself up through the door. Instantly the wind blew her hood back, slinging sleet and salt spray into her face and knifing through her cloak. She balanced herself on the edge, her legs dangling within the coach—and what she saw filled her with horror. Not ten feet to her left was the edge of the cliffs, and beyond them, several thousand miles of ocean. And there was Rothwell, who'd just freed the standing horse and was now trying to calm the downed one, still tangled in its harness and thrashing wildly as it tried to get to its feet.

He looked up and saw Eva poised atop the coach, ready to leap down—and flung his palm out, trying to stay her.

"Your Grace, please don't move! I'll help you down as soon as I free the horse!"

But Eva had had enough. More than enough. She drew her legs up and prepared to jump down—just as the horse, still writhing on the ice, managed to gain its feet—and bolted. The overturned vehicle jerked forward. Eva's feet went out from under her, and she was pitched over its side.

Straight toward the cliff.

She careened through space, only to hit the ground with a bone-jarring crash, feet scrabbling for purchase, hands flailing as she tried to slow her fall. But it was no use. Her fall had momentum. And it was taking her straight down the cliff.

She screamed. Her fingernails ripped out as, sliding feet first on her belly, she clawed at icy outcroppings. Rocks broke loose, charging past her on her downward slide, bump, bump, bumping around her, racing her toward the sea that boiled and thrashed so far below. She groped frantically for a handhold; kicked her feet, raked furrows in the ice with what remained of her nails. Rubble tore open her legs, bruised her knees, sent her skirts riding up around her waist as she belted down the slope on a toboggan of loose stone and ice, falling ever faster, ever downward—

Bang.

She slammed against a rocky outcropping in a brilliant explosion of agony. Agony that burst from her pelvis, from her midriff, from the lowest region of her belly. The pain tore at her consciousness, at her ability to even draw breath. Far below, the ocean boiled. A few last pebbles skittered past. She lay there, the sleet stinging the back of her bare legs, feeling herself bleeding in a hundred tiny places . . .

In one frighteningly vital one.

"Help me. . . ." She raised her face to the wind, the sleet that was now turning to sifting, whirling snow. "Oh, dear God . . . help me. . . ."

But she knew, even as she clung to the ledge of rock, even as the pain became a thousand knives impaling her belly, that it was too late.

Too late for her.

Too late for the baby.

And too late—far too late—to go back.

She tipped her forehead against the icy stone and, as the tears came, surrendered to the darkness.

Chapter 25

By the time Lucien finished the bottle of brandy, the sleet had stopped. Now only snow whispered against the windows.

He sat sprawled in a chair, damp shirt clinging to his back, his eyelids heavy, his brain refusing to shut down as he had tried so hard to get it to do. Another bottle, then. Yes, that was what he needed. Setting his glass aside, he pulled himself to his feet. Immediately his legs folded beneath him, and he narrowly missed clipping his chin on the edge of a table as he went down. He lay there on the carpet for a moment, fighting dizziness, realizing, with a sense of stupefied wonder, that he was drunk.

Drunk. He had never been drunk in his life. He had never been willing to relinquish control of his mind, his body, to something outside of his own will, and the sensation of finally having done so filled him with horrified amazement, curious self-disgust. *Drunk.* And why?

Because of a woman.

A woman who had stripped him of all control, all sense of self, all identity . . . and left him lying here on the floor, helplessly afloat on a sea of brandy.

At least he was warm. Comfortable. Filled with a sense of lassitude that managed—only just—to blanket the emotions that still churned his heart. He pulled himself up and, careening off a table, managed to retrieve another bottle from the cabinet. With a curiously unsteady hand, he splashed some into his glass and sank back down into the chair, contemplating its color, its clarity, with flat, unseeing eyes.

Yes, he was warm. Comfortable. He took a sip of the liquor. But what about her? Was *she* warm and comfortable out there in the winter darkness? How could she be?

She—out there in the winter darkness.

Lucien frowned. Something wasn't right here. She was his wife. His duchess. She shouldn't be out there in the sleet and snow while he sat here in a sleepy, stuporous fog.

Look at what she has reduced you to.

Indeed.

Look at you, lying here in your own misery. Why don't you go after her? Bring her home where she belongs? It is your duty.

Duty, duty, duty. Always duty. But damn it all, that was his first obligation. Duty. And his wife.

He got to his feet, feeling as though he were swimming, clawing through fumes of brandy. The house was silent. Not a servant was in sight. Thank God for furniture, which aided his precarious balance. Thank

God for brandy. He staggered out into the hall, remembering how *she* had confronted him here an hour ... two? ... three? ... before. Agony sliced through him. He might still be able to catch her. She would be at the inn. He would go get her, bring her back home.

He pulled open the door, using it for balance, and tottered down the stairs out into the night. It was only as he slipped and fell just outside, ice cutting his hand, that he realized he had forgotten his greatcoat. The devil, it was snowing. *Snowing.* He looked back up at the steps down which he had all but fallen, decided they were too much for him to negotiate, and, pulling himself back to his feet, headed down the drive, slipping and sliding all the way, a lonely figure in the snowy darkness.

From some distant part of himself, he felt the cold against his skin, scarcely protected by his thin wet shirt. Dampness came up through the soles of his shoes. Snow melted against his face. But the brandy kept the sensations at bay. He bent his head and, mustering all his concentration, focused on putting one foot in front of the other, one step, another, one step, another, as he lurched with a strange, disjointed purpose down the dark, lonely road toward the village.

Eva, Eva. Didn't she know, didn't she care, how besotted he was over her, how wretched she had made him? One step, another, one step, another. Steadier steps now; the air, the exercise, the cold, the concentration ... the fog that obliterated his mind was parting, and through it, patches of clarity were showing.

Patches of clarity that brought only pain.

One step, another, one step, another. Damnation, it

was cold. Should have brought the greatcoat after all. Why hadn't he? Ah, yes, the steps. Steps. One step, another. One step, another. He watched his shoes scuffing through the falling snow. Felt the terrain beneath the crusted ground changing, and realized he was no longer on the road. Ah, yes. The bridge that spanned the little inlet. He reached out, grabbed the handrail for support, and skidded back down the other side.

A strange sound was coming from his mouth. His teeth, chattering with cold. He wrapped his arms about himself and continued on, following the road toward the sea. The wind had stilled, though he could hear the distant roar of the ocean now, the eerie silence of the vast and lonely night.

He trudged on. From far behind him, back along the road, he heard hoofbeats, and men shouting to each other. Oddly familiar, those voices. Ah, hell. Keep going. He couldn't go back to the house and play host until he had his wife back.

And then silence, deep, brooding, still, closed about him once more, the only sound that of his feet crunching along the frozen ground.

Time lost all meaning. He pressed on, head bent against the snow, his breath frosting the air. He was near the sea now. He could smell it. Taste it. Hear it. Ah, yes. There it was, cold and black, stretching into forever beyond the cliffs.

He kept going, and then something made him stop and look up. There, melting out of the darkness far ahead, was a figure, leading a pair of horses.

Lucien stood there, frowning. A sense of anxiety pressed down upon him, but he could not identify its source; desperately, he tried to gather his wits, but they eluded him.

"Your Grace!"

The voice was all but obliterated by distance and lingering gusts of wind, but Lucien recognized it.

Rothwell.

Inebriation beat a retreat behind alarm.

Panic.

"Your Grace!" The figure was running toward him now, slipping and sliding on snow-glazed ice, the horses trotting to keep up. Lucien shook the cobwebs from his head and hurried forward to meet the solitary figure. Rothwell. The coach. Eva. It was all becoming clear to him now—

"Your Grace, there's been an accident. . . . I tried to help her, but I couldn't—"

Immediately Lucien was sober. More sober than he had ever been in his life. Dread paralyzed him—then he was running toward the groom, his heart pounding, a thousand awful thoughts racing through his suddenly alert mind.

"Where is she? What happened?"

"Coach overturned," the groom panted. "She tried to jump out . . . fell . . . down the cliff—"

"Down the cliff?"

Lucien staggered back, unable, for a moment, to see past the sudden blackness that nearly wiped out his vision.

"I was just coming to get you, Your Grace . . . figured you'd know what to do. . . . She's lying partway down the slope just after Taverton Bend—I tried to reach her, but she—" The man's voice choked on a sob. "She wasn't answering."

Lucien gripped the servant's shoulders. "Listen to me. The duchess's life may well depend upon it! Return to the house at once and call out the staff. Bring as many as you can find back with you, along with blankets, additional horses, and the other coach. Send someone into the village for the doctor, and be quick about it. Move, man!"

Oh, dear God. *Dear God!* Lucien broke into a run, heading down the path from which Rothwell had just come. Taverton Bend. Oh, dear God, if she'd fallen there—

He refused to think about it. Refused to think about the sifting snow, the low whine of the wind, his own rising panic. He pounded on across the treacherous terrain, every cold breath searing his lungs, every thought that entered his mind causing him to find more speed, more stamina, as he charged across the frozen landscape. Eva. Oh, dear Lord, he must reach Eva. . . .

There, just ahead, was the bend, meandering dangerously close to the cliffs. From out of the darkness, Lucien saw the coach, still on its side, the snow already collecting atop its still-open door, the harnesses lying in a twisted, broken heap nearby. He ran to the edge of the cliff—

And stopped.

There she was. She lay some twenty feet down, a small, broken doll pinned against a wedge of rock, the snow already covering her body like the first earth thrown onto a new grave.

The blood rushed to his head and he tipped it back, fists clenched, eyes squeezed shut, feeling such agony rising up from his soul that it was all he could do not to give way to the howl of pure animal anguish that threatened to consume him.

"Eva! Eva, answer me!"

The snow swirled around her; she did not move, did not raise her head, did not make a sound. She was dead. She had to be.

His heart constricted. The back of his throat closed up. Lucien set his jaw and mustered every shred of his formidable self-control. He turned back toward the overturned coach, the mangled harnesses, and it was only as he bent down and began working with the automatic motions of the driven that he realized the dampness running down his cheeks was tears.

I've killed her. His raw, frozen fingers worked to unfasten a buckle, another. *I've killed her, and the child with her. She was right. I did not learn my lesson; in seeking to control others I have lost the love of my sister, and now the life of my wife.* He fastened two strips of leather together, unbuckled another section, fastened it to the first, the frozen line growing as fast as the tears that leaked, uncontrollably, from his eyes. *I've killed her. . . . Oh, Eva, you are free of me at last. Free, forever.*

He furiously wiped a hand across his eyes, but the tears would not stop. The harnesses lay in pieces now, stiff beneath his numb fingers; one by one, he shook them out, buckled them together, and at last had a sizable length of leather. He carried it back toward the cliff's edge, steeling himself for the grim task he must perform, this last husbandly duty to his duchess—to bring her body home.

He looped one end of the line around the base of a rock, wrapped the other around his wrist, and began the treacherous descent.

He allowed no feeling to penetrate his wall of icy resolve. No thought, beyond reaching the snow-covered figure wedged down there against the rocks, to penetrate his brain. He had no fear, though he knew that one slip, one misstep, would mean his own death. He had killed her. Life was not worth living without her. He had nothing to fear.

Slowly, he picked his way down the slope, testing each outcropping to be sure it was solid, checking each tentatively placed step to be sure his footing was secure. The wind howled around him; far below, the sea thrashed, boiling and breaking white against the rocks.

He was almost there. Stones and chunks of ice, loosened by his progress, skittered down the slope, some of them bouncing off the still, cloaked figure crumpled beneath him before arcing out into space on their journey toward the sea. Lucien winced with each one that struck her, though he knew she was beyond feeling.

Eight more feet and he would have her.

Six more—

And then his foot slipped, pain blazed up his leg, and for a moment he hung suspended by the leather line, heart hammering; then the wind slammed him back against the cliffside.

He looked down and saw what the fall had cost him. His calf was ripped open, his stocking awash in blood. Lucien deadened his mind against the pain. It was only physical. Nothing like the wound that had torn apart his heart.

He continued down, cursing, for his ankle would no longer support him. He must have twisted it.

Maybe broken it. He no longer cared. All that mattered was reaching his Eva.

On one leg now, he descended the last few feet, gingerly testing the ledge upon which she rested to be sure it would take his weight. Then, and only then, did he take a deep, bracing breath and, his face expressionless, reach for the cold, stiff body of his dead wife.

His free arm slid beneath her body, so frail, so tiny in death—and pulled it up against him. Her head fell against his shoulder. The wind blew her hair against his face, twisting the wet strands around his neck, wrapping him in its sweet smell. *Eva. Oh, Eva. . . .* For a long moment he held her against him, squeezing his eyes shut against the pain, the tears that threatened to overwhelm him, the urge to just let go of the leather line and give up, for he had nothing left to lose; he had lost it already.

Lost it because of his own arrogance.

He took a deep, bracing breath and raised his face to the falling snow, willing strength back into his will. He could not take the easy way out. He had to bring her home. She was a duchess of Blackheath. She deserved more—he swallowed the ache in his throat—so much more. . . .

Buckling the end of the harness around her body to secure her to himself, Lucien began the slow, dangerous climb back to the road. Wind pummelled his back. His fingers went numb, snow and ice hindered his progress, and his injured leg would not take his weight. He used his knee instead, pressing it against rock in place of his useless foot, letting his good leg do most of the work. Snow sifted against his neck, his face; his frozen hands were raw and bleeding. He paused to catch his breath, letting his cheek rest against ice. Continued on. Stopped to rest once more. At last he reached the top of the cliff and hauled himself and his precious burden over its edge.

He collapsed and lay there in the thin snow, cradling his dead wife to his chest and finally allowing the tears to come. Tears that, once started, would not stop, but only gathered force like a river that has broken its dam. Great, hitching sobs locked up his chest and convulsed his body with grief. He crushed her in his arms, buried his face in her hair, and unbuckling her, let the wracking sobs consume him.

Blackheath.

At first he thought it was only a product of his tortured mind, his bitter, crushing guilt, that brought the word into his head. He tightened his arms around her. She was dead.

"Blackheath."

A ghost.

"Lucien . . . you—you came for me. . . ."

No ghost. He raised his head, shoved his fingers into her hair to anchor her head, and looked down at her white, white face. At the eyes, half closed and glazed with shock, that stared up into his. She wasn't dead. She ought to be, but she was not.

"Eva—"

"Lucien . . . I hurt. Hurt all over." Her voice was thin, thready. Dear God, he had to get her warm. Had to get her to safety. Had to get her to a doctor.

He gathered her up in his arms and, slipping on ice, carried her to the lee of the overturned coach, settling her against the undercarriage. He wished he had his coat to cover her. Wished he had a horse. Wished to

God he'd set out in search of her earlier, instead of drowning himself in self-pity and despair.

"Where do you hurt, sweeting?"

She tipped her head back against the coach, closing her eyes. "It's gone, Lucien . . . gone."

Immediately, he knew what she meant. His hands shaking, he tried to warm them on his own freezing body, to no avail. Fearing the worst, he carefully lifted her skirts—and felt everything inside him still. She was covered in blood. Her legs were streaked with it, her thighs soaked with it. And it was still coming out of her.

She began to cry.

Wordlessly, Lucien gathered her close as her body lurched with great, hitching sobs of pain and grief. He set his jaw and squeezed his eyes shut and rocked her, his own pain so intense he thought he might die from it. Her arms came around him, clinging like a child. She tried to bury herself against him, her tears scalding his neck. Lucien's throat closed with agony. This was all his fault. He had done this to her. To their unborn baby. In seeking to keep his child here in England, he had killed it.

Killed it.

"Eva."

He held her against him, feeling the wind rocking the overturned vehicle against which they rested. Rothwell should have returned by now. Where was he? "Eva, I must go get help."

"Don't leave me, Lucien—oh, please, don't leave me."

She was crying again, unable to think, only feel. Gone was her hatred of him; gone was her stubborn, willful pride, her beautiful fire; in its place was only this broken shell to which he had reduced her, this pitiful, sobbing little girl-woman who would die if he did not get her to safety soon.

"Eva, listen to me," he said, peeling her from his chest and setting her back. He looked into her eyes, but her soul was gone, along with all reason, comprehension, and understanding, and only two empty orbs of pain looked back at him. "Eva—I am going for help. You must stay here, do you understand me?"

"Don't leave me. Please, don't leave me."

"Darling, I have to. I will be back for you. You must promise me to hold on, to stay awake, to muster every reason you can think of to hate me, if only to keep fighting, do you understand? Do not fall asleep—do not leave *me*, Eva. I cannot go on without you." He pulled her close, dropping a long, trembling kiss upon her icy brow. "Don't leave me, because I love you."

"Don't leave me," she repeated, her words a whisper.

He loved her. He had said it, but she had not comprehended, for the only thing she knew was pain and shock and grief. Lucien stood up on his one good leg, knowing, even as he surveyed the coach that he had not the strength to push it back over. Oh, hell. Oh, bloody, ripping hell. Snow sifted down around him, coating his eyelashes, and his body was shivering uncontrollably. Desperately, he wondered what he could do to shelter her . . . and then realized there might be a rug in the boot.

On one leg, he hobbled around the overturned coach, managed to get the boot open, and yes—oh, thank God—found a blanket.

He carried it back to her. Her eyes were closed. Panicking, he grabbed her shoulders and shook her until they opened once more.

"Don't leave me, Lucien. . . ."

He could not answer her. If he did not leave her, she would die here, in his arms. He pulled her closer to the coach, trying to wedge her between the axle and undercarriage, and tucked the blanket around her to keep out the cold. Then, gently taking her hands, he kissed each palm and tucked them beneath the blanket.

He got to his feet, resolved on a course of action, cursing Rothwell, who should have returned long before now. Around them, the snow whispered down . . . slow, deadly, silent.

She looked at him, a flicker of comprehension in her eyes, of panic—before her lids lowered once more.

Lucien turned on his heel. He tucked his raw, reddened hands beneath his armpits to try and warm them, and, dragging his useless foot, shivering in the cold, began the long trek back to the house.

Chapter 26

The riders that Lucien had heard galloping through the night had been no mere drunken hallucination. His brothers, who had set off in immediate pursuit of Nerissa, had found her in Southampton, waiting for a ship to take her to France; now she was safe in the coach that accompanied them, and her brothers had decided to spend a few days at Gingermere before returning their angry sister to Blackheath Castle.

Covered in snow and frozen to the bone, they entered the house, only to find the place in an uproar. His and Her Graces had argued. *His and HER Graces?* Charles had expostulated, when his siblings could only stare in shock.

"He married her last night," explained the housekeeper.

"They had a blazing row and she left him an hour

ago," added the butler. "In the storm."

And then an extremely distraught young man whose face was blistered with cold had burst in, babbling that the duchess was dead, fallen down the cliff, and that he had met His Grace—who'd appeared to be quite under the weather with drink—out on the cliffs, wearing no coat, no greatcoat, nothing but a thin shirt to protect him from the elements, and that His Grace had gone to retrieve the duchess's body and that everyone in the house was supposed to turn out to help—

Thank God for Lord Charles, whose military training and competent, reassuring manner were enough to bring order out of chaos. "Everybody *quiet*," he ordered in a sharp voice that instantly quelled all clamor. He faced them all, snow and ice still dripping from his blond queue and down his broad, commanding back. "Now listen to me."

He was not wearing his army uniform, but he might as well have been. He was the officer his men knew and respected—and as one, the panicky household quieted and gave him their full attention.

Charles faced the shivering groom who had just arrived. "Someone fetch this man a hot drink. What is your name?"

"Rothwell, my lord."

"Rothwell, tell me exactly what happened, where you left the duchess, and where you last saw my brother."

Teeth chattering, Rothwell croaked out the tale, repeating His Grace's orders, wringing his reddened hands, and saying over and over again that if only the duchess had stayed put she wouldn't have died. "She's at Taverton Bend, my lord . . . partway down the cliff."

Grim-faced, Charles listened to this tale and then immediately began to bark out orders.

"You there"—he beckoned to a footman—"what is your name? Peterson? Well, Peterson, listen closely. I want you to ride into the village and fetch the doctor. You will detain him here until my brothers and I return with the duke and duchess. Go now."

"And you." He summoned the housekeeper. "You are?"

"Mrs. Cantwell, my lord."

"Mrs. Cantwell, I want you and your staff to ready the bedrooms, build up the fires, gather all the blankets you can find, and have something hot and nourishing waiting when we all get back. My sister will help you."

"Yes, my lord."

"And you. Johnson, yes? Run to the stables, find twenty yards of rope, and get the saddles back on our horses as fast as you can move. I'll need blankets and a lantern as well. Now hurry."

One by one, Charles took the trouble to learn the names—and earn the loyalty—of those he would entrust with each task, and then, satisfied that all was running as smoothly as he could make it, he sent for his own wet greatcoat, called for a spare, and, with Gareth and Andrew hot on his heels, hurried back into the night.

He had a feeling there was no time to lose.

Lucien had long since given up trying to walk.

Where his ankle had been, there was only agony. Had he the time, he might have torn a strip from his breeches and bound up the gaping wound, but he

dared not waste even a single moment. All that mattered was reaching the house . . . and bringing help
back for Eva.

But his leg, damn it, would not support him. He
found a stick, frozen to the ground, and managed to
pry it loose, only to have it break when he tried to use
it as a crutch. He flung it aside and continued on, hob-
bling on one foot, dragging the other, until ice cost him
his balance and he went sprawling, landing hard on
his chin and sending his teeth through the tip of his
tongue. He hauled himself to his feet, spitting out
blood, the cold making him dizzy now, light-headed.
Still he pressed on. And fell again.

He began to crawl, ignoring the pain in his frozen
hands as he pulled himself through the thin, crusted
snow. How far had he come? How far back had he left
Eva? He wasn't sure. Nothing existed now except cold.
Pain. And the only thing that continued to drive him:

The knowledge that if he did not reach the house,
his wife would die.

The ache in his hands became unbearable. He got to
his knees and then, using his injured ankle for balance,
back to his feet. He put weight upon that ankle, forcing
it to do work it could not do, hating it for its incompetence, punishing it with pain for giving out on him. He
would not let it stop him. Would not let it keep him
from saving his duchess's life.

He was getting ever so cold. His wet shirt had
frozen now, chafing his skin raw. And still the snow
fell, whispering down all around him. He paused,
panting, and gazed out into the night. Nothing but
darkness. The persistent hiss of falling snow. And far
off to his right, the sea.

Keep moving.

It was anguish just to move his legs. Agony just to draw breath. To stay awake.

Don't fall asleep, he had told her.

Don't fall asleep, he ordered himself.

But he was fast losing the ability to think. His mind was no longer obeying his will, and neither was his body. He shook with cold, with exhaustion—with shock. It became an effort just to keep his eyes open. Again he fell. Again he managed to get to his feet, rods of agony shooting up his injured leg, the snow behind him bloody where he had fallen. But the agony kept him awake. Alive. In sleep lay death. He knew that. He pressed on, forcing weight onto the leg, welcoming the pain because pain meant survival.

He concentrated on each step. Welcomed each burst of pain. Thought only of Eva, lying back there alone, helpless, probably dying, maybe already dead. She was depending on him. He could not fail her. Where the hell was Rothwell? Why hadn't he returned? Where was everyone?

Where, for that matter, was he?

Keep moving.

He did—and then his leg gave out from under him. He tumbled down an incline, his body crashing through ice, salt water stinging his eyes, filling his nose, choking him.

Recoiling with cold, he clawed to the surface and, gasping hoarsely, blinked the salt from his eyes.

The inlet. The damned inlet. He was nearly home, then. Nearly to safety. Warmth. And most importantly of all, help for Eva.

But he was too cold. All strength had deserted him.

Flocs of ice were drifting down on him, hitting his face, the arm he raised to try and deflect them. He went under. Clawed back to the surface just as another chunk of ice smashed into his back. He willed strength into his exhausted arms, his legs, but there was nothing left. Nothing. With one last, desperate kick, he propelled himself to shore, dragged himself partway up the frozen bank, and shut his eyes, ice water still flowing over his legs.

Keep moving.

He tried.

Keep moving, damn it!

His face fell against the frozen bank. His body would no longer obey him. And then Lucien whispered the two words he had never before uttered, only his lips moving against the ice that pillowed his face.

"I . . . cannot."

And let himself go.

Charles, mounted on his faithful Contender, a lantern in his hand, led his brothers toward the bridge. He refused to think of what they might find out there in the darkness. Refused to think they might be too late. Refused to think at all, except of finding his brother and sister-in-law.

"Charles, hold up!"

It was Gareth, just behind him on Crusader, pulling the horse up as they crested the bridge; behind him, Andrew's gray thoroughbred, Newton, nearly plowed into Contender's haunches. "Look, there's someone in the water down there!"

Charles stared in the direction that Gareth indicated

and felt his heart still. "It's Lucien," he said, already swinging off Contender and running across the bridge.

He charged down the bank, seizing his brother's hands and hauling him out of the water. Instantly Gareth and Andrew were there, helping him, until they had Lucien safely up on the sandy, ice-strewn bank.

"Oh, God," Andrew choked out, seeing the duke's still, pale face. "Is he—"

"Dead?" Gareth whispered.

Charles refused to speak; he merely ripped open Lucien's drenched shirt and put an ear to his chest. In the darkness, his brothers knelt in stricken horror, watching the snow sifting down upon Charles's pale lashes, Lucien's still face. Neither spoke. Neither dared to breathe.

Charles straightened. "No. Not dead. Hurry, let's get him wrapped in a blanket and onto Newton's back. You two bring him back to the house and get him warmed up. Don't let him try to come to Eva's rescue when he wakes up. *If* he wakes up," he added darkly. "Christ, he reeks of brandy."

Gareth and Andrew exchanged glances; Lucien had never been one to overindulge. But there was no time for speculation. They all knew that something horrible indeed must have happened to bring their brother to such a state, and they all knew that in all likelihood, the duchess was dead.

"Come on, Luce," Gareth said, trying for bolstering cheer as together they rolled their unconscious brother in the thick wool blanket and carried him back toward the waiting horses. "You're going to be all right."

Lucien stirred just as they managed to get him across Newton's back. "Eva . . ."

Charles, grim-faced, leaned close. "Lucien, where is she?"

"Taverton Bend . . . left her with the coach. You must save her, Charles. I . . . am depending on you."

Charles was used to people depending on him—indeed, he thrived on it—but he had no more power over life and death than anyone else. Still, for his brother's sake, he would give it his best effort. He squeezed Lucien's hand. "I will bring her back to you, Lucien. I promise."

And then, his face grim and his heart full of dread, he ordered Gareth and Andrew to take Lucien back to the house and, swinging up onto Contender's back, sent the big horse galloping off into the snowy darkness.

Hoofbeats.

She heard them above the wind, the thundering roar of the sea, which had tried, ever since Lucien had left her, to lull her into the sleep of death. But she had made a promise to him. She had not gone to sleep, and now she could hear a horse, coming up fast from out of the night, ever closer, ever louder. Someone was coming for her. Her eyes stung with tears. *Oh, Lucien.*

Eva, shivering, huddled deeper into the blanket. It took all her strength just to turn her head. Sure enough, a rider was approaching, heading her way with relentless purpose; he held a lantern high, a beacon of light that shone like the star of Bethlehem over his head. Eva began to shake; help had come. *He* had come.

Except it wasn't him. Something was familiar but not right about the rider in the sweeping greatcoat, and as he pulled the horse up before her and swung down in the same motion, the lantern shone full in his face and she saw who her rescuer was.

Saw it, at the same time she remembered that same face in the light of another lantern when she had ruthlessly struck him down as he had tried, then as now, to help her.

Eva began to cry.

"Your Grace." He was there before her, all kindness, all concern, all stern, trustworthy competence. "I have come to take you home."

"Lucien—"

"He is unwell. He needs you." He knelt before her, brusque, efficient, and yes, worried. Worried, when he should feel nothing but hatred for her. "Will you allow me to take you?"

She heard the benevolence in his voice even as she reached out and placed her icy hand within his own. "You mean you will not order me, then?"

He smiled gently. "No, Your Grace. You outrank me now."

His kindness overwhelmed her. Kindness, when she had treated him so despicably. When she had hurt him. Fresh tears tracked down her cheeks. She was so unworthy. Unworthy of his kindness, unworthy of anyone's love, unworthy of anything but death.

He was gentleman enough to allow her the dignity of her tears without calling attention to them. She tried to get up. Couldn't. She had no strength left. He saw it and, reaching down, gathered her up in his arms and, keeping her wrapped in her cloak and blanket, carried her to the waiting horse.

She didn't know how he did it, but somehow he managed to get her up into the saddle, bracing her there while he swung up behind her; then, holding her against his chest, he turned the big horse's head for home.

He was warm and solid beneath her ear. She could smell the dampness of his wool greatcoat, the hard strength of his arm holding her safely close. His nearness did not fill her with lust, but with comfort—the sort of comfort she might seek from a brother. And he was a brother now, wasn't he?

A brother. She did not deserve this; oh, God, she didn't deserve it. As he sent the horse moving slowly across the icy terrain so as not to jar her pain-wracked body, great, gulping sobs claimed her and she cried like a baby in his arms, no longer caring what he might think, no longer trying to maintain an illusion of femininely superior strength.

He didn't say a word.

"I'm so sorry, Charles," she choked out. "How can you be so kind to me after what I did to you?"

"I believe in giving everyone a second chance."

"But I hurt you . . . I struck you down and humiliated you and this is how you repay me, by saving my life. Oh, God . . . I'm sorry." She started crying again. "I'm so sorry. . . ."

"It is all right, Eva. I have forgiven you. Now hush. Save your strength. My brother needs you. We all need you."

She spoke no more, and as her brother-in-law held

her tight and safe, she shut her eyes, realizing, as the fog of oblivion began to close around her, that she had been wrong all along. Wrong about men. Wrong about Lucien.

Wrong about everything.

If she survived this, she had a lot of catching up to do.

A lot of amends to make.

Her head fell back against the strong arm that held her, the tears still wet upon her cheeks.

Chapter 27

hey were a family, and they rallied around her.
Not just because of what she meant to Lucien—but because she was now one of their own.

Nerissa took over the duties of hostess with a brisk and inborn efficiency. The best doctors were sent for. Charles, Gareth, and Andrew took turns trying to keep Lucien off his injured leg—with little success—and Lucien never left the bedside of his duchess, now delirious with fever and, according to the doctors, quite unlikely to survive.

But they were only doctors, he thought savagely. He was the Duke of Blackheath, and he knew the power of his own will, the lengths to which it would go to serve him, and he had no patience for the dire predictions of the medical profession.

"I am sorry, Your Grace—unless we bleed her, she probably won't last the night."

"Bleed her? *Bleed her?* She's spent the last two days bleeding! Now get out," he snarled, glaring at the hapless fool who'd dared make such a ridiculous suggestion.

The physician fled. Another was brought in his place.

"Even if she survives, she is unlikely to ever conceive another child. You would do well, Your Grace, not to expect her to give you the heir you seek—"

One look from Lucien had frozen the man in midsentence. "Get out!"

And then a third doctor, full of his own importance, arrived. He bent over the duchess's battered body, his self-confidence rapidly draining as the duke loomed over him, not saying a word, not needing to, his eyes black and savage and cold. Finally he, too, had straightened, shaking his head. "I am sorry, Your Grace. There is nothing I can do for her except make her comfortable."

Lucien threw him out, too, and went into such a rage that even the servants steered clear of him.

He paced the floor, using his walking stick as a crutch, roaring at anyone who dared tell him he'd best stay off his leg until it healed. He refused meals, refused sleep, and existed on black coffee. He lost track of time. He forgot what day it was. He knew nothing except the shallow rasp of his duchess's breathing, the hot brow he continuously bathed, the scalding bath of his own bitter anguish.

It was obvious, of course. He loved her. He loved her, and he wasn't afraid or too proud to admit it. She had slipped under his defenses and claimed his heart, and now here she was, fading away before his eyes, taking his heart right along with her. Leaving him. Damn the fates that had done this to him! Damn the fates that had done this to *her*! He wanted his wife back; he wanted his duchess with her rare and beautiful courage, one of the few people on earth who wasn't afraid of him, the only woman who would ever be his match. But the woman who lay in the bed before him was no more than a pale, silent shell of what she had been, her hair caught in a single girlish braid over one shoulder, her skin as white and fragile as tissue.

She was dying. And it was all his fault. By trying to control her life he had killed her, just as he had probably killed Perry, just as he had certainly killed any chance Nerissa had for happiness. He had wrought unforgivable damage in the lives of other people; people who were not pawns to be moved about a chessboard, nor puppets to dance to his bidding—but people he cared about. People he loved. People who had the right to make their own choices, live their lives as they pleased, decide their own futures . . . without his interference.

He looked at the woman in the bed, and felt his chest constrict with grief. How colossal his arrogance now seemed, in light of what it had cost him, might still cost him. Even now her words came floating back to him, torturing him with their prophetic accuracy:

You need to consider the consequences of governing other people's lives, of making their choices for them, of imposing yourself upon their free will.

The consequences. Well, she was living—dying— proof of the consequences, wasn't she? He had imposed his will upon hers, with no respect for her thoughts, feelings, and wishes. He had imposed it because he had been supremely confident that he had known best, that his way was the only way, that nobody was as capable as he was of handling responsibility. And he had done the same thing with his siblings' lives—every one of them. His clever manipulations had all seemed like a game to him. How he had prided himself on his successes, the ease with which he'd ordered their lives! But now, with bitter remorse, he realized that life was no game.

And neither was death. He looked down at Eva's still, pale face.

I have learned my lesson. He buried his head in his hands, dragged them down his face, then hooked them around the back of his neck, elbows on his knees. He sat watching her with a brooding stare. Her ribs rose and fell beneath the coverlet, and he willed each laborious breath not to be the last. *I have learned my lesson, Eva, and never again will I try to play God with other people's destinies. If you live, my dearest, I will make it up to you. If you want your freedom, I will set you free. Whatever I can give you is yours. I swear it.*

Someone knocked gently at the door.

"Lucien?"

He unhooked his hands from his nape and looked up, blinking the fatigue from his eyes. It was Charles. He pushed the bedside candle back so his brother would not see the glaring evidence of the agony that ravaged him. "Come in."

His sibling entered the room with a tray. "Would you like me to sit with her for a while? You really ought to get some sleep."

"I cannot sleep. I will stay with her."

I will stay with her because I am terrified of leaving her.

Terrified that if I leave her, even for a moment, she will leave me and die, just like Papa did. Just like Mama did. I cannot allow it.

Charles nodded and, pulling up a table, set the tray down. The scent of strong coffee filled the air. He poured them each a cup, stirred milk and sugar into his, and, carrying it, went to stand before the fire. "I have been speaking with Nerissa," he said, sipping the steaming brew. "She's most distraught about Perry—and furious with us for waylaying her in Southampton, I'm afraid. I know you intend to resume the search for him, but at the moment, your going to France is out of the question. I will go in your stead."

"We are on the very brink of war with France, Charles. It is unsafe."

"I know. But some things must be done. This is one of them."

"When do you plan to leave?"

"In the morning."

Lucien opened his mouth to protest; he had spent his life protecting his siblings, making choices for them, *ordering their lives.* Charles wanted to go to France. *Who am I to prevent that?*

He took a deep, bracing breath, and clenched the protest between his teeth, giving his more-than-capable brother the respect he deserved, hating the out-of-control sensation of letting go. God, it was hard. . . . so very hard.

"How's the leg?"

His leg? Yes, of course. His leg. Lucien absently massaged the bandaged ankle and calf. "On the mend." He took another deep breath, then bent his head to his hand, kneading his brow and trying to find the right words. "Charles, I have an apology to make to you. To all of you. An apology that is many years overdue."

Charles turned and arched a pale brow.

"I want to say I'm sorry," Lucien continued gruffly. "Sorry for orchestrating your lives, imposing my will upon yours, stripping you all of the respect and dignity of making your own choices in life. I will not do so again. I have . . . I have learned my lesson, I think."

Charles merely looked at him, his pale blue eyes unreadable. And then he turned back to the fire, cradling his cup in his hands and watching the flames with a little smile. "Ah. That explains, then, why you didn't give me grief about going to France."

"Yes. I don't like the idea, of course, but I will not forbid you to go."

"It must be difficult for you."

"Excruciatingly so. But I'm trying."

Charles took another sip of his coffee, contemplating his cup for a moment, his thoughts his own.

"Charles?"

"Yes?"

"You've uh, been through all this. All of you have. Is this—" He swallowed, making a helpless little gesture with his hands as he tried to find the right words. "Is this the way it's supposed to feel?"

"Is this the way what's supposed to feel?"

Lucien frowned, his gaze sliding to the still figure on the bed. "I'm sure you know what I'm talking about."

"I'm sure I do." Charles smiled. "I must confess, however, to taking a certain satisfaction in wanting to hear you say it."

"Far be it from me to deny you, then." Lucien smoothed a stray tendril of hair from Eva's brow. "All these years, I have scoffed at the idea of my ever falling in love. Not that I didn't believe in it, of course; I remember how it was with our parents. I see how it is between all of you and your spouses. I just never thought it would happen to *me*. Never thought I had time for it, never thought my responsibilities to the dukedom would allow it, always thought I could . . . control my feelings such that I would never be plagued by it. And now it *has* happened to me." He shook his head. "Funny, how quickly it creeps up on a person—I never saw it coming."

Charles just stood there, smiling gently.

But Lucien was still gazing at Eva, his eyes deep and dark and sad. "Never saw it coming," he repeated, almost to himself. "And never expected it to—to feel like this."

"You mean, gloriously euphoric one moment, and as if someone is carving up your heart in the next?" Charles gazed at his brother's bent head. "Yes, Lucien, that is exactly how it is supposed to feel. At least, in the early stages. Things do get easier as time goes by, though. More . . . settled, I suppose you might say, as you grow into a friendship with each other."

"Even so, one must wonder why anyone would choose to even *be* in love."

Charles was still smiling. "I don't think most of us actually *choose*, Lucien. Sometimes love chooses *us*."

Lucien said nothing, his coffee going cold in its cup. Both brothers were quiet for a few moments; only the sound of the fire snapping in the grate and the wind sighing outside broke the silence. Both were lonely sounds. Mournful sounds. "I have much to atone for, Charles," said Lucien at last. "If she lives, I don't even know where I shall begin."

"Well, you could start by telling her how much you love her. Tell her you cannot live without her, that she means more to you than anything on this earth. It might give her the strength she needs to survive."

"I am not convinced she even wants to survive. I have treated her grievously, Charles. Forced her to do my will. For her, death will be an escape." He clenched his jaw. "An escape from me."

Charles finished his coffee and looked down at his brother's bent head. Never had he seen Lucien like this; never had he seen him laid so low, never had he seen him so humbled. Then he cast an appraising eye over the woman in the bed. Charles had seen enough men dying in war that he recognized the signs. And he knew, with a certainty that he didn't bother to question, that the Duchess of Blackheath was not going to die.

Not anytime soon, at least.

But Lucien didn't know that. And, given that love was already changing him in ways that Charles had never even begun to imagine, strange and wonderful ways that were preciously exciting, he decided not to interrupt its course. Love had a lesson to teach his brother. And Charles would not interfere. Let Lucien experience the full range of feelings that went with giving your heart to another person . . . including the frightening helplessness that often went with it.

For a man so used to control, it would be good for him to feel helpless.

He gathered up the tray and cups. "Well, I'm off to bed, then," he said. "Good night, Lucien."

"Good night."

He moved past his brother, whose head was bowed in anguish, dropping a hand on his shoulder as he passed. And then he exited the room, quietly shutting the door behind him.

Outside, Gareth and Andrew waited; they got immediately to their feet, frowning as they saw Charles's lips twitching helplessly.

"Well, what is it, man?"

"Lucien." Charles felt his grin broadening, until he feared he might actually burst into laughter. He looked at his two siblings. "He's fallen at last."

Some hours later, Eva opened her eyes.

It was dark in the room. Preternaturally still. She could hear the distant roar of the sea, the casements rattling in the wind, the first cry of a newly awakened gull. For a moment, her mind struggled to make sense of what had happened to her, knowing that something wasn't right.

That something was missing.

She felt a grinding ache that went deeper than physical, and into her very soul.

And then she remembered.

I've lost the baby.

Everything came back to her. The fight with Lucien. Her determination to leave him despite the storm. The accident. Oh, God—the accident. She had a dim memory of her husband coming for her. Rescuing her from the treacherous face of the cliff, even as the blood had oozed from between her legs, silent, endless, and terrible—as though her entire body were weeping for the baby's loss.

I've killed it. It's dead.

Dead.

She lay there, hot tears trickling from her eyes, moving in silent, meandering misery down her temples and soaking the pillow beneath her. *It's dead.* Her womb was empty now. So was her soul. She, with her pride and lack of faith, had killed her little baby.

Dead.

She wept soundlessly, staring up at the ever-lightening ceiling above her head, the distant sound of the surf tolling her baby's death with each mournful crash. It was getting lighter now; blackness was becoming gray, and around her, the still, silent shapes of furniture were materializing from out of the gloom. There, the highboy just visible through the parted bedcurtains. There, the darker shape of a painting on the wall. There, somebody in a chair drawn up beside the bed, so close she could hear his measured breathing.

She reached out and laid her fingers on his hand.

Lucien.

He stirred. His fingers closed around her own. He said nothing, just sitting there holding her hand, giving her a lifeline to his indomitable strength.

You are not alone, dearest. I am here.

She was unsure whether the words came from his lips—or from the deepest recesses of his soul. She only knew that he had said them. *I am here.* Her tears turned scalding, though she did not sob, did not make a sound. *I am here.* She squeezed her eyes shut, gripping his hand, the hot, salty droplets rolling down her cheeks in silent misery. *I am here.*

The bed sagged as he sat down beside her, holding out his arms in unspoken invitation.

A year, a month, a week ago, she would not have accepted the comfort he was offering, would have laughed in his face, would have shunned the desperate ache in herself that now made those arms the only place in the world she wanted to be. A place she never wanted to leave. A place that would always hold her, keep her safe from harm, offer refuge, comfort—

Love.

Without further hesitation, Eva went into them.

"Lucien," she sobbed brokenly. "The baby . . . oh, God, the baby. . . ."

He didn't say a word. He simply held her and let her weep until she had no tears left to cry, until the raw agony of grief began to subside, until exhaustion moved in to take its place. But she knew that he shared her anguish. That the solid, comforting strength that surrounded her would always be hers. That he had been with her by the bed all along, that he would always be with her. Her mind began to shut down, to seek relief in the deep oblivion of sleep. She was safe now. After all these years of distrust, resentment, and pretense, she was safe.

With him.

Chapter 28

In the days that followed, Eva slowly went about the business of healing. Grieving. Accepting not only that she had lost her baby, but any chances of ever giving her husband the heir that was so important to a proud and powerful aristocratic family like the de Montfortes.

She had failed him. She could never keep him now. Not in a million years. Annulment was sure to come. Day after day, she waited for his attentions to cool, to wander, waited for him to find some other pursuit than sitting at her bedside, encouraging her to eat when she had no appetite, joining her under the covers at night, his big body keeping her warm as he shared stories about his life, his childhood, those he knew and loved and cared about . . . and encouraged her to do the same. She was wary, waiting for the bubble to burst, waiting for him to realize that she was no good as his duchess now. Useless. But he did not go away. He did not leave her. And as the days turned into weeks, Eva's wariness faded to confusion, and then a fragile hope that maybe—just maybe—she had found that which her sisters-in-law had.

That which she had longed for all her life.

The deep and abiding love of a man.

God knew *she* loved him. How could she not? He was the antithesis of all she had believed the human male to be. He was powerful, intelligent, compassionate, devoted, caring, and worthy of the respect she had never thought she would give someone of his gender. She ached when he left her room, even for a moment. She glowed when he returned, knowing her smiles also lit him up, banishing the shadows from beneath his eyes, the severity from his face. He told her he loved her. He proved it in gesture, kindness, and word. But she could not bring herself to do the same. Not yet. It was the last threshold she must cross, and her inability to do so began to wear on her . . . in the form of frustration, in the form of guilt.

She determined to make it up to him. To do something—anything—that would atone not only for her failings as his duchess, but for her sins against his family. Something that would prove her love for him when she could not quite bring herself to utter the words. As her strength grew, she began to pace her room, and then the house, and then the gardens outside, looking out over a sea as restless as her own heart. . . .

And then one morning, a long-awaited letter arrived from France.

Nerissa awoke with the dawn.

Three weeks had passed since Charles had left in

search of Perry. Three weeks, of worrying not only about her brother's safety, but about the fate of her lost love. Three weeks—of watching, waiting, for word from France.

Oh, where was he? What had he found?

Please, Charles, come home. Come home and bring Perry with you.

The strain was showing on everyone. Gareth and Andrew, who'd elected to stay at Gingermere until Charles's safe return, were desperate to return to their wives. Gareth blew out his frustrations by taking long gallops across the dales; Andrew, much to everyone's dismay, occupied himself with his new explosive, the first earth-shattering detonation even setting the bells in the village to ringing the alarm until Andrew himself, fingertips burned and eyebrows singed again, had ridden over to explain the source of the fearful booms, reassuring the panicky inhabitants that no, the French were not attacking, and no, Britain was not at war with her age-old enemy across the Channel.

Yet.

But any day now, the dreaded news would come. It was a certainty. Nerissa feared for Charles's safety. She paced her room, constantly looking out over the sea, watching, waiting, worrying. And now, as she sat at the window and watched the sun rise in a fiery orange ball, sparkling like diamonds on the water, she wondered if today would bring the news that the two countries were at war once again.

There was a gentle knock on the door.

"Come in," Nerissa called, and turned to see her new sister-in-law enter the room.

"Why, Eva—good morning." She frowned. "Are you sure you shouldn't be resting?"

"Bah, I have had more than enough of resting. In fact, I'm feeling quite like my old self these days. Well enough, I think, to even go riding with Lucien this afternoon." Eva's green eyes sparkled, as they always did when she spoke of the duke. "Meanwhile, I thought we might have breakfast together."

Nerissa surveyed her with a critical eye. Eva was still thin and pale, but every day had brought healing, and the return of a little more of her old spirit. As Eva came fully into the room, bathed in the fiery glow of the newly risen sun, Nerissa sensed an inherent strength about her that even now seemed to have been enhanced, rather than beaten down, by all that she had been through. It was no wonder Lucien had fallen in love with her. No wonder he had barely left her side for the past three weeks. But was it Lucien's obsessive care that had brought a new softness to Eva's haughty features? Was it Lucien's love that now made her beautiful face glow with openness, something bravely vulnerable, as though all the hard edges had been razed off, leaving a glittering jewel in its place?

A maid came in behind her, bearing a tray of hot rolls and tea. She set it down, curtsyed, and left the room as quietly as she'd entered. Nerissa turned back toward the window. She stared out over the water, watching the gulls wheeling, diving, floating over the silvered sea as Eva came up beside her.

"My Perry . . . he is alive," she murmured, gazing out at the horizon. "If he were dead, surely I would have known. . . ." She placed a hand over her heart.

"Surely, I would have felt it in here the moment his dear heart stopped beating, the moment he took his last breath. Am I not correct, Eva?"

"You are correct."

Nerissa turned and looked into her sister-in-law's brilliant green eyes. "Do you know something I don't?"

"A letter has just come from Charles. Since Lucien is still abed, and I'm a perpetually nosy female, I took it upon myself to read it." She drew a folded piece of vellum from her pocket and, with a gentle smile, handed it to Nerissa. "Here."

Nerissa's breath caught as she stared at the missive. Hope and panic clawed for possession of her heart. What news would the letter contain? With shaking hands, she turned so that the fiery gold light streaming in from the window illuminated Charles's recently penned words:

Calais
3 February 1778

Lucien,

After countless inquiries, I have learned that the survivors of Sarah Rose *were transferred to a small gaol near here, which I took upon myself to visit under the guise of an American diplomat. I have found Brookhampton. Our friend, though alive, is somewhat the worse for wear. According to those with whom he is imprisoned, he was engaged in ship-handling when the vessel was attacked, suffered an injury that rendered him unable to speak for himself, and was taken prisoner along with the seamen. As his identity was*

not known to his companions, they were unable to tes-
tify on his behalf. Subsequently, our friend has spent
the first weeks of his incarceration trying to reclaim
his memory—and the last weeks, his freedom.

As you can imagine, the situation here is a precari-
ous one. Given the rather singular activities in which
he was engaged when the ship was taken, the French do
not recognize our friend as a peer of the Realm and sub-
sequently refuse to release him. The English authorities
with whom I have pled his case are reluctant to pursue
the matter, for fear of setting the fatal spark to already
hot powder and bringing about this war that looms
ever nearer on the horizon. The situation is beyond my
ability to rectify; I have taken lodgings at 22 Rue de la
Mer in Calais, and beg your presence here as soon as
you can grant it.

Charles

Nerissa lowered the letter, her eyes filling with
tears. "He's alive—oh, dear God, Eva, he's alive! We
must go to him at once!"

Eva gently took the paper from Nerissa's shaking
hands and, putting an arm around her shoulders,
guided her to the table where their breakfast waited. "I
have made a grave mistake, Nerissa. You see, when I
first visited the prisoners in gaol, there was a young
fellow lying on the floor, apparently near death. . . . He
was dressed like all the other seamen, and so I neglected to consider that he might be your lost Perry."
She poured a cup of tea, her eyes rueful. "Had I known
your beau was given to masquerading as a common
sailor, I might have taken a closer look at him."

Nerissa wiped at her tears. "I'm sure he was only doing it as a last way to have his fun, his freedom, before settling down to a life of boring domesticity with me."

"Here, now. You do not know that. After all, men"—she smiled—"they do such silly things."

That got a watery smile out of Nerissa. "Yes . . . and Perry *is* the leader of the Den of Debauchery, known for their outlandish pranks and outrageous deviltry. Or at least he *was.* I tell you, Eva, that is going to change the moment we get him back."

"I'm sure it will." Eva handed the cup to Nerissa. "Here. Drink up, while we decide what is to be done about this situation."

"But there's nothing to decide—we must get my dear Perry out of that horrible place at once!"

"Indeed, but you must hear me out first." Eva poured a cup of tea for herself. "As Charles has said, the political situation in France is dangerously volatile at the moment. I know this is going to be hard for you to hear, Nerissa, but you would serve Perry best by remaining here in England and preparing a loving homecoming for him—while I go to France and negotiate for his release."

"You? But Eva, you've been dreadfully unwell. . . . Why don't you let one of my brothers go?"

"Because this is something I must do," she said firmly. "I have much to atone for where your family is concerned, Nerissa. My conscience is burdened. Please, let me do this—for you, for Perry, for Charles." Her face grew shadowed for a moment. "And for Lucien."

"Lucien? He will never let you go by yourself."

"Lucien"—Eva affected a superior look—"will do as he's told."

An amused male voice cut through their conversation. "Lucien will do *what*?"

Both women jerked their heads up; there was the duke standing in the open doorway, one brow raised, his eyes gleaming as he took in the two startled faces. He strolled into the room, seated himself beside Eva, and wrapped an arm around her shoulders.

"I understand that a letter from Charles came for me this morning," he said conversationally. "Perhaps you'd like to share it, my dear?"

"How did you know that?"

"I know a lot of things, my love. Do hand it over."

Eva rolled her eyes, grinned, and relinquished the letter. She watched as Lucien quickly scanned it, his face going grave. "I must leave for France at once."

"I am going with you."

"No, Eva, I forbid it. You have been ill. I would not have you accompany me on such a perilous mission—"

"I beg your pardon?"

"It is too dangerous—"

"Now, look here, husband—"

Nerissa wisely chose that moment to intervene.

"Really, Lucien . . . you *did* tell us all that you're turning over a new leaf. That you're no longer going to control our lives. If Eva wants to go, I think you owe it to her to submit without argument."

Lucien's jaw tightened as Eva rose to her feet.

"Your sister's correct," she said. "Besides, I know my way around French diplomacy far better than you do. You would be well advised to let me handle this."

"But—"

"Lucien," Nerissa warned.

He thinned his lips. Took a deep, slow breath as he reined in his protests, and sought the calm both women were denying him. Oh, this letting go, this relinquishment of control . . . it was going to kill him, he just knew it. But Eva was right. She was capable. She knew her way around this situation far better than he did, and having her along in Perry's rescue would be an asset, not a detriment.

He exhaled, and looked bleakly at his wife. "I can't win," he murmured, shaking his head. "I just can't win."

"No," she said, grinning as she got to her feet. Linking her arms around his neck, she pressed her lips to his, kissing him until the bleakness left his eyes and they began to simmer with building heat. "You can't win, so you might as well stop trying."

Chapter 29

War was declared between France and England the following day.

While Eva, Gareth, and Andrew went to Portsmouth and prepared for the crossing to France, Lucien hurried to London, where he was granted an audience with yet another hapless soul who owed him a favor: the First Lord of the Admiralty. Within hours, he was on his way back to Portsmouth, where he informed his wife and siblings that they were to journey to France as guests of a certain Captain Christian Lord aboard the seventy-four-gun warship *Arundel*.

Predictably, the captain—a tall, austere man with pale gold hair and foggy gray eyes—was not at all pleased to have civilians aboard his ship, and even more irate when he learned that one of them was a powerful and famous duke. Still, Captain Lord graciously gave over his own cabin to the Duke and

Duchess of Blackheath, ordered his first and second
lieutenants to relinquish theirs to Lords Andrew and
Gareth de Montforte, and made his quarters elsewhere.

It began to rain shortly after the ship weighed
anchor and headed out into the foamy chop of the
Channel. Captain Lord, directing activities from the
quarterdeck with an eagle eye, waited until his command, and the little brig *Magic* that accompanied
them, was well clear of the vessels anchored around
Spithead, then invited the duke and duchess to join
him in his quarters for a conference.

There, the two men granted each other a wary
respect, each well aware of the other's power and influ-
ence in his given domain. Captain Lord had already
been briefed by his admiral about their mission: to
bring the Earl of Brookhampton safely—and quietly—
out of France. Though Lucien was accustomed to taking matters into his own hands, he conceded that this
was a military operation, and thus prepared to grudg-
ingly defer to Captain Lord's judgment.

The officer ensured that his guests had tea, coffee,
and some light refreshment before unrolling a map of
Calais. Spreading it out on his table, and using a sex-
tant to point out various parts of the coast, he began to
outline his plan to get Earl Brookhampton out of the
French gaol.

"My orders are to secure His Lordship's release
under terms as peaceable as we can manage, given the
circumstances. I hope we will not be forced to rely
upon *Arundel*'s guns to effect our mission, but if it
comes to it, we may have no choice."

He took a sip of coffee. "Admiralty has already
made contact with Lord Charles in Calais, who has

been briefed of our plan." The captain's gray eyes assessed his guests and the lieutenants who surrounded him. "Obviously, with war now declared, it would be unwise to take our ships within sight of the French coast. Therefore, we must fool the Frogs into thinking that this is an American, not an English venture. One glimpse of *Arundel* and that plan will be laid to waste."

Lucien saw Eva straighten in her chair. "I'm of the same mind, Captain. As I know the French coast well, and have contacts near Calais, I propose that I be the one to go ashore and, as part of the American contingent in Paris, negotiate for Lord Brookhampton's release."

"No," said Lucien flatly. "I will go."

"You can't go," Eva countered. "One look at you and the French will know immediately that you're English. Then we'll have to rescue you from gaol as well as Perry."

"I forbid it," Lucien said firmly. "It is unsafe. Besides, if Charles can fool them into thinking he's American, so can I."

"Charles served in Boston. He's married to an American. He can effect a passable enough Yankee accent if he so chooses, which is the only reason he's been able to deceive the French into thinking he's something he's not. I'm sorry, Lucien, but I don't think you're capable of pulling off the same deception."

"You have only just recovered from your injury, Eva. This is too dangerous!"

"And you," she said sweetly, nudging his ankle beneath the table with her foot, "have only recently recovered from yours."

Captain Lord just looked at the two of them, his cool gray eyes giving away nothing. At last he cleared his throat.

"With all due respect, Your Grace, I am in favor of the duchess's plan. With appropriate support from my own men, I would prefer that she go in your stead." He smiled dryly. "Besides, if I were to allow you—a duke—to go, and something happened to you, Admiralty would have my head."

Lucien's eyes went cold. "Are you trying to tell me that I can *not* go?"

Again, that hard, uncompromising smile. "Yes."

Lucien stared at the other man. Nobody—*nobody*— had ever tried to thwart him, let alone challenge his authority. Who the bloody hell did this fellow think he was? He turned his most chilling stare on the captain. "And you think your head won't roll if something happens to my *wife*?" His voice was dangerously soft. "Trust me, Captain, should one hair of her head be harmed, I will ensure that you—and your precious career—are ruined."

Eva rolled her eyes. "Boys—"

But Captain Lord was not finished. "I have my orders, and I will carry them out as I see fit."

"My wife is not going ashore."

"Oh, yes, I am," said Eva.

Lucien, jaw tensed, got to his feet. He knew the captain's word overrode his own here aboard ship, but he could not accept it. He knew Eva's reasoning was sound, but he could not condone it. And he knew that if he did not immediately remove himself from this cabin, somebody—he directed his blackest stare on the unflappable officer—was going to get hurt.

Very hurt.

He glanced at Eva. "I will see you at supper, my dear," he snapped, and, bowing, turned on his heel and stalked out.

Eva waited until the door shut behind him, then smiled at the unruffled captain. "Well, then," she murmured. "Shall we continue?"

Gareth and Andrew, fascinated by the workings of a warship, had stayed topside until they were well out into the Channel, watching the seamen running up the ratlines to set the sails, admiring the smart orderliness with which everything was carried out, enjoying the feel of the mighty vessel under their feet—and speculating on the reasons why Lucien, alone at the weather rail, looked about as furious as they'd ever seen him. But as the rain worsened and the ship settled on her course, Andrew retreated belowdecks, leaving Gareth still topside. Some time later, he joined Andrew in his brother's borrowed cabin.

"I say, Lucien's in one hell of a temper," he announced, as he went to the stern windows and watched the coast of England fading into the mist far astern. "I just met Eva going topside to try and console him." He grinned. " 'Twould appear that he and the captain didn't quite hit it off on the best of terms."

"Well, no surprises there." Andrew was scribbling in a notebook, a lead box resting near his elbow. "Two men used to absolute control are bound to clash."

"I was talking to one of the crew . . . a lieutenant named Teach. 'Sdeath, the bloke looks just like Blackbeard. Said the captain is one of the Royal Navy's finest and served for a time in Boston, so he must have a good understanding of the Yankees. Probably would get on well with Charles, if he were here."

"Yes, well, speaking of Charles, what I want to know is how we're going to get close enough to Calais to bring him and Perry out without the French sending their own warships down on us. One glance at *Arundel* here and they'll *know* she's British. And there was that fort the captain pointed out on the map, too. I'd hate like hell to get too close to *that*. . . ."

"Eva explained everything to me. The plan is to keep *Arundel* just out of sight of the coast and send *Magic* in, flying American colors, to report on things and land Eva and our men; that way, the Frogs won't catch on that this is an English operation."

Andrew never looked up from his notes. "Sounds good, but we all know that in wartime, anything could happen"—he curled his arm around the lead box— "which is why *I've* come prepared."

Gareth didn't pick up on Andrew's veiled implication. "Eva will go ashore tonight under cover of darkness. She'll rendezvous with Charles, who'll be waiting there with horses. Then they'll both go to the gaol tomorrow morning as representatives of the American contingent in Paris, obtain Perry's release— peacefully, it is hoped, but if not, that's why Admiralty sent this ship and its complement of marines—and meet us back at the landing point tomorrow evening." He shook his head. "No wonder Luce looked angry enough to commit murder when we saw him earlier!"

Andrew glanced up. "What, is he not going with her?"

"Captain forbids it. Says if anything happens to a

duke, his own head will roll, so Luce stays here with us."

Now Andrew was grinning, too. "By God, that *does* explain Lucien's foul mood. He'll not follow anyone's orders but his own. I predict fireworks, Gareth."

"So do I. But really, I'm sure Eva is more than capable of getting Perry out. Unless Luce and the captain kill each other, we'll be back in England by tomorrow night, no shots fired, no blood shed, everything done quite peacefully." Gareth suddenly noticed the lead box at his brother's elbow. "I say, Andrew, what do you have there?"

"My explosive."

Gareth went bug-eyed. "Good God, man, you'll get us all thrown off the ship if the captain hears of it!"

"The captain *won't* hear of it. Besides, it's wartime"—Andrew was all innocence—"and one never knows when a new, extra-potent explosive might prove useful, eh?"

Night fell.

As *Arundel* prepared to rendezvous with *Magic*, the Duchess of Blackheath stood on the lonely, wind-tossed deck, her hair hooded, a cloak protecting her against the harsh winter sea wind. Beneath her feet, the mighty ship rose and fell on the waves, its lanterns doused, its crew working in total darkness. In the ever-nearing distance, she could see the dark coast of France.

It was nearly time. She thought of Nerissa so many miles away, probably awake and praying for the safety of her loved ones. She thought of how she had struck Charles down and humiliated Andrew during the robbery. And she thought, too, of how she had hurt Lucien and forever denied him an heir, all because of her own damned pride. Sorrow filled her, and she raised her face to the wind. The time had come to make amends. To repay her debt to the de Montfortes. And yes, to prove herself worthy of that which she valued more than anything in this world—Lucien's love.

Suddenly she knew she was no longer alone. Knew that *he* had come.

"Lucien," she murmured.

He came silently up beside her, sliding an arm around her shoulders. She turned into his embrace, feeling his heartache, his anxiety for her safety.

"Forgive me, dearest," she said. "I know it's hard for you to let me do this, but please, Lucien, understand that I must."

"I don't understand. But I am also trying to tell myself that that doesn't give me the right to prevent you from going." He reached down and tilted her face up to his, blocking the wind and spray with his back so she would not suffer the full brunt of the elements. He cradled her jaw within his palms and gazed steadily into her eyes. "Will you not change your mind, Eva?"

She shook her head. "I cannot, Lucien. This is something I must do. For you. For your family. But mostly for myself."

His own eyes darkened and she saw the desperate ache and worry there before he concealed it behind a mask of pained resolve. Then he pushed her hood back and bent his head to hers, his mouth claiming hers with a desperate hunger. Wind lashed her hair across their faces. The timeless sound of the waves faded, and she heard only his breathing, felt only his hard, powerful body, sensed only his fear that this might be their last embrace. *Trust me, trust me*, she thought. And gave herself up to this sweet good-bye, pressing her body up against his, feeling the evidence of his desire against her pelvis and wishing, wishing, wishing she could have him inside her, because she wanted more. So much more.

"When I return, Lucien—"

"No promises, my love. Just come back to me, safe and sound."

"When I return, there is something I must tell you."

"Tell me now." *Because there might never be another chance.*

Eva pulled a deep breath into her chest—even as she heard someone coming up behind her. It would be so easy not to say it until she got back. So easy to put it off until she felt she had the right to its reciprocation. So easy to—

"Your Grace, the boat is ready; it is time to leave."

—just wait until she returned.

For once she would not be a coward when it came to matters of the heart.

She reached up and laid her hand against Lucien's cheek, her gaze meeting his, her heart constricting. The words were out of her mouth before she could stop herself from saying them.

"I love you."

He swallowed. His lashes came down, and he reached once more for her . . . but she knew that if she went into his arms, she would never leave. Steeling herself, Eva stepped back and turned away, head high as, swallowing the lump in her throat, she followed the lieutenant toward the waiting boat. She could feel her husband's anguished stare on her back. Could feel his love, his worry, his agony. Leaving him was the hardest thing she had ever done—but she had a job to do. The most important job she had ever undertaken. They would have a lifetime to spend in each other's arms.

Shunning the lieutenant's assistance, she climbed down into the boat . . . and looked toward the dark, menacing coast of France, trying to shake off the feeling of premonition that had nagged her all evening.

Of dread.

A lifetime.

She could only hope.

Chapter 30

Charles, wearing a black greatcoat and pacing fretfully, was waiting for her on the darkened beach. He stepped forward and helped her from the boat as it nosed against the sand, eyeing her in concern.

"You're sure you're up to this, Eva? We have a bit of a ride ahead of us."

She turned and gave the seamen the signal to depart. "Never felt better," she said, following Charles toward the three horses tied and waiting nearby. "Bodies heal. But other wounds take considerably more effort."

"Meaning?"

"That this is something I must do—for you, for your family . . . for myself."

He nodded, understanding. Then a smile softened his taciturn face. "In that case, I'm honored to have you at my side. I must confess, it's good to have a real

Yankee here, as I don't know how long I can carry on with this false American accent. It is only by virtue of the fact that English is not the primary language of those with whom I've dealt that I have managed to fool any of them."

"Have you seen Lord Brookhampton yet?"

"I have."

"And you're certain that this man we're about to rescue is indeed your friend?"

"I am certain."

"Did he recognize you?"

"No. He was asleep. I hadn't the heart to disturb him, to raise his hopes of rescue. Ah, here are the horses. I've brought an extra along for Perry—providing we are successful in bringing him out."

Eva tossed her head. "We will be."

Moments later, they were cantering along the road to Calais, the reins of the spare horse in Charles's capable hands. Trees, pastures, distant villages were becoming faintly visible in the gloom. It would be dawn soon.

They stopped and broke their fast at an inn just outside of Calais, where Charles's impeccable command of French got them immediate service and a table near the fire. By the time the sun was breaking through watery cloud, they were back on the road, the distant gaol looming upon the horizon.

They pulled the horses up just outside the gates.

"What condition is he in?" Eva whispered, dismounting as a guard approached.

"Bad. But between the two of us, we should be able to manage him well enough."

"And you got Captain Lord's message about the plan of action?"

"Yes. Get Perry out as diplomatically as possible, ride calmly away, spend the rest of the day out of sight, and meet the marines from *Arundel* just after dark."

"Providing this all ensues without complication."

"If it doesn't?"

Eva smiled grimly. "We're on our own."

The guard was swinging open the gates now, eyeing them suspiciously. "Your business?" he inquired in French.

Eva answered him haughtily in his own tongue. "I am the Comtesse de la Mouriére. This is my colleague, Charles Montvale. We are here as members of the American contingent in Paris, on orders from Dr. Benjamin Franklin. Our business is with your commander."

The guard, recognizing authority in Eva's manner, bowed low. "If you will leave your horses here and come with me . . ."

Dismounting, they followed him toward the building of dark gray stone. Behind them, another guard appeared, hauling the gates shut with an ominous clang that sounded frightfully final in the early morning stillness.

Eva and Charles exchanged silent looks, and then, tight-lipped, continued on. Eva, her nerves taut, reached down and touched the pistol hidden in the pocket of her petticoat. She told herself they were in no immediate danger, but her senses were on high alert.

"This way, *s'il vous plaît.*"

The guard pushed open another door, and then they were in the gaol. Eva blinked, trying to adjust her eyes to the sudden gloom. But it was nothing compared to the stench. She pulled a handkerchief from her pocket and pressed it to her nose as the guard led them deeper into the prison.

Its commander, a Monsieur Durant, was seated in an office well away from the stink of the main prison, eating a breakfast of eggs, sausage, and what looked to be a very dark ale. He was a large man, wide across the gut, with small, distrustful eyes set in a face pooled with fat. He looked up as Eva and Charles were shown in, nodding in recognition to Charles, and eyeing Eva with curiosity and undisguised lust.

Her skin crawled with revulsion. "I am the Comtesse de la Mouriére," she announced in haughty, Boston-accented English. "I am here on business of Dr. Benjamin Franklin, with orders to secure the release of one of the prisoners taken from the British ship *Sarah Rose* during her capture."

Durant pushed his plate aside, settled back in his chair, and with a dirty fingernail picked at a piece of meat lodged between his front incisors. "You have papers?"

Eva smiled, though she was well aware that those shrewd, ugly eyes were on her breasts, the flare of her hips beneath her riding jacket. "From Dr. Franklin himself," she murmured, producing the documents she herself had forged.

Durant's pudgy hand plucked them from her grasp. He eyed her suspiciously, then scanned the document.

"It all seems to be in order," he said, frowning as he handed it back. "But me, I cannot understand ze Americans' desire to have me release zis Briton. Why is he so important to you? He is crazed in ze head."

"Yes," Eva agreed, folding the paper.

"He says he is a British lord. Now, even if zis were true, why ze devil would ze Americans want a British lord?"

Eva gave him her most flirtatious smile and rapped his shoulder with the document. "Because, my good sir, if it *is* true, one British lord is worth a hundred American seamen when it comes to trading prisoners. You French are not the only ones at war with the despicable English. *We've* been fighting them for nearly three years."

"You hate ze English as much as I, no?"

"Loathe them," Eva seethed, meeting Durant's shrewd, piggy eyes.

"Zen I will take you to zis—how you say? obnoxious Briton who says he's a lord. He is difficult. Arrogant. We have had to punish him for his disobedience. Put him in ze solitary confinement . . . give him ze beating or two, you know? You will have your hands full with him, I zink."

He heaved his huge bulk up from the table, pushed his chair back, and, grunting with the effort of moving such a large mass through space, led them out of his office. Eva glanced at Charles. His eyes had hardened like ice.

Down through the dank halls of the gaol Durant led them. From behind blackened, dingy doors came noxious smells, and the sounds of despair: moaning, sobbing, futile singing, a tin cup clanging against the bars of a window.

At last they came to a door at the far end of the building. Durant took a ring of keys from his belt, inserted one into the lock, and, jiggling it, finally unlocked the door.

It swung open to reveal gloom.

Silence.

And a single figure slumped in a corner, his cheek pressed against stinking wet stone, his unblinking eyes turned heavenward toward the gray light streaming in through a window far out of his reach.

"As you can see, ze prisoner is in solitary confinement once more," Durant crowed, looking at the man, who half sat, half lay in a pile of damp, filthy straw, making no attempt to move or even look their way. "He struck at one of my guards last night. Ze guard— he had to strike back, no? But I zink we have finally broken *le Seigneur*'s spirit. He will not give you any more trouble."

Durant moved fully into the cell, Eva and Charles following just behind. Eva did not know Perry, but she knew he was a close friend of the de Montforte family, and she could only imagine how much pain the sight of him must be causing Charles. Filth and blood encrusted hair that was so dirty it was hard to discern its natural blondness. The cheeks, sallow now, were sunken beneath lifeless gray eyes, the mouth swollen and cut from a blow, the clothes hanging off a pathetically thin frame.

Eva's throat ached with guilt. This was the same man who'd been lying unconscious in the cell when she'd visited the *Sarah Rose* prisoners weeks before. Then, he had been unable to speak for himself. The others had not been able to speak for him. How had she misjudged the situation so badly?

"Take him, zen," Durant said. "I am well rid of him."

"Do you have a coat for him?" Charles asked, eye-

ing the skin, much of it raw and oozing with sores, that
showed through Perry's threadbare clothing. "It is
cold outside."

"Ah, you Americans, you are just like ze British—
far too compassionate for your own good. *Je regret*, but
I have no coat for him."

Wordlessly, his lips taut with anger, Charles
stripped off his greatcoat, then put his own coat of
dark, serviceable broadcloth over Perry's shoulders.
His friend showed no sign of recognition as the major
carefully bent his arms and coaxed them into the
sleeves, and finally wrapped the heavy woolen greatcoat over his gaunt frame.

"Has he been this unresponsive all along?" Eva
asked sharply.

"*Non*, only since last night, when ze guard hit him.
An improvement, if you ask me."

Durant stood back as Charles hefted Perry in his
arms, put him over one shoulder, and carried him
toward the door. Emaciated and beaten, he did not
appear to recognize the man with whom he'd grown
up. Eva, trying to veil all emotion—including fury that
an innocent man had been treated so brutally—
watched in despair, wondering how on earth they
were going to get —and keep—Perry aboard the horse
that awaited just outside.

Arundel, cruising somewhere just over the horizon,
had never seemed so far away.

Durant kept up a stream of chatter as they moved
down the dingy corridor, but Eva was not listening to
it. Her nerves were tingling once again; the tinny taste
of fear filled her mouth, and her heart was beating fast.
Too fast. Something was wrong.

Do hurry, Charles.

He *was* hurrying—though he was trying to conceal the fact from Durant so as not to raise an alarm. Eva broke out in a nervous sweat. *Hurry, Charles.* Her heart was pounding now. *Faster.* Ahead, two guards were leading a group of prisoners from a cell.

A group of British prisoners.

Those from the *Sarah Rose.*

Oh, no—

And then she realized what was wrong: that Charles, despite his ability to imitate an accent, could never conceal the fact that he was a trained soldier. It was there in the way he walked. In the set of his shoulders, in the way he carried himself. And it was just as they were stepping out into the fresh air once more, freedom agonizingly close within their reach, that a voice called out from behind them.

"I say! Is that you, Lord Charles?"

"*Don't stop,*" she hissed, for his ears alone.

"Lord Charles!"

Durant was turning around now. "I beg your pardon," he said to Charles, "ze prisoner—he mistakes you for someone else, *non*?" He raised his voice to address the man who had spoken and was now waving his arms, desperately trying to get Charles's attention. "You, zere! Quiet down. Zis is Charles Montvale from America, and we all know zere are no lords in America!"

"American? What do you mean, American? He's not Charles Montvale, he's Lord Charles de Montforte, and he's as English as I am!"

"Lord Charles de Montforte?"

"Aye! Met him in Boston, back in '75—I was in the Navy, he was a captain in the Fourth Foot!" The man was growing desperate now. "Lord Charles, take me, too! You can't save just one, you've got to take all of us!"

Some of the guards were frowning now, and even Durant was looking confused. Agitated. Eva, fighting her growing anxiety, gave a high peal of laughter, knowing each step brought them closer and closer to escape. "Really, Durant, what *is* going on with your prisoners? You've got our friend here claiming he's a lord, and that man over there claiming my country-man is a lord! Why must everyone be a lord, I ask you? I daresay there must be something in the water!"

But Durant's suspicions were raised. "Wait."

"Keep walking," Eva hissed.

"Nothing but a lead ball is going to convince me otherwise," Charles shot back under his breath.

"*Wait!*" Durant yelled.

And then Durant reached for his pistol and all hell broke loose.

"Run for it," Eva cried—and with a swift upward punch, knocked the pistol from Durant's hand. His howl of pain was cut short by her next blow, which caught him just under the chin and sent him toppling over backward. By the time she'd pulled out her own weapon, she and Charles were running for their lives.

Behind them, shouts rang out on the early morning air. Somewhere, a bell began to ring frantically. The alarm was raised.

"Bloody hell," Charles swore, as they bolted for the horses, who were fretting nervously just inside the gates. "I'm going to have to hold on to him, he's in no shape to ride. . . . Have a care, Eva, here comes the gatehouse guard—"

"Don't worry about him, just yourselves!" Something whizzed past Eva's ear; a moment later, a musket cracked behind them. And now the gatehouse guard was running forward, bringing up his musket and training it straight at Charles.

Eva paused only long enough to raise and fire her own pistol. With a scream, the guard collapsed, blood spurting from a hole in his side. Eva snatched up his musket, braced Perry while Charles swiftly mounted his horse, and shoved him up into the saddle before Charles.

"Mount up," he shouted.

"I'll hold them off—you just get yourselves out of here!"

"Mount up, damn it, and let's go!"

Another ball whined past Eva's head. Bark exploded from a nearby tree; an army of guards came pouring out of the prison, all of them shouting, some stopping to sight down the length of their muskets, and Eva knew that their time had run out.

Summoning her strength, she leaped aboard her wild-eyed horse, set her heel to its side, and, with Charles just behind, sent the animal flying out of the prison gates.

They had moments, only moments, before the guards would be mounted and in hot pursuit.

Moments—

Between life and death.

Chapter 31

L ucien was sharing an uneasy truce with Captain Christian Lord on *Arundel*'s quarterdeck when a hail from above claimed their attention.

"Deck there! Signal from *Magic*!"

Captain Lord immediately put down his coffee and was on his feet. "Report!"

"Gunfire from shore, sir! *Magic* reports two riders racing away from the gaol with guards in hot pursuit! It is the duchess and Lord Charles! *Magic* requests orders, sir!"

The captain turned to a midshipman who suddenly appeared at his elbow. "Send to *Magic* to make for the rendezvous point and hold off the pursuers as long as possible. And be quick about it!"

The young fellow dashed off to hoist the signal. The captain ordered *Arundel* to fall off and the big ship swung toward shore in support of the smaller brig.

Lucien barely had time to quell his rising panic when another cry drifted down from above.

"Deck there! Three sail off the starboard bow! Two frigates and a ship of the line, all flying French colors, sir!"

Gareth and Andrew, alerted by the shouts from above, came charging up on deck.

"Belay that last order!" shouted Lord. "Wear ship and prepare for battle!"

"What's happening?" asked Gareth, looking about in confusion.

Lucien, his hands clenched behind his back, stared over the water toward the rapidly appearing coast as *Arundel* fell farther and farther off the wind, her great stern already beginning to swing around. His face was as white as the foam that rode the surrounding waves. "The brig is on station near shore. It just signaled that two riders are fleeing the gaol with guards in hot pursuit. We're going in to rescue them."

"The hell we are," snapped Captain Lord, overhearing Lucien's tense explanation. "That fort I showed you on the map will be the first thing they'll man. I don't care how big *Arundel* is, she stands no chance against the guns of a fort, and neither does *Magic*."

"Are you telling me we're abandoning my loved ones?" Lucien all but roared.

"I'm telling you that if we don't get some sea room to fight off those vessels out there, we'll be trapped between a manned fort and three French warships. If you think I'm about to risk my ship and the lives of six hundred men for two people, you've got another think coming, Blackheath! Now go below—things are about to get hot."

"I'll be damned if I go below! You will head inshore to effect a rescue, Lord, or I can promise you this is the *last* command you'll ever be granted!"

"Deck there! Enemy running out her guns, sir!"

Lord grabbed a telescope from a midshipman. "Take in the courses."

A moment later, a low boom reverberated across the water like far-off thunder.

"They're firing on us, sir!"

"Starboard battery! Load and prepare to run out!"

" 'Sdeath, now what?" asked Gareth.

"We're about to get blown to kingdom come, that's what," snapped a lieutenant, racing past. "You three had best get below— splinters and hot iron'll be flying in a moment or two."

But the three brothers stood where they were, forgotten as the great warship prepared for battle. Men swarmed up into the rigging and out along the yards to reduce sail. Others ran to the boats in the ship's waist. The gun crews loaded the cannon all along *Arundel's* starboard side and, grunting and swearing, ran them up to their ports. Lucien, his jaw tense, glanced to windward; sure enough, the three French ships were bearing rapidly down on them, trying to trap them against the deadly guns of the fort and cut off their only means of escape.

"God help us," Gareth breathed— and in that moment, Lord brought his sword down.

"*Fire!*"

Arundel's broadside turned the deck beneath their feet into a shuddering platform of thunder, each reverberation roaring through their heads, deafening their ears, sending clouds of smoke billowing back into their faces. In a moment, all was confusion as officers and crew raced about, some shouting orders, others desperately hauling the cannon back in, sponging them out, and preparing to fire once more.

"Get below," Lucien yelled to his brothers.

"What?"

"I said, get below!"

"We're not going anywhere!" cried Gareth, and a second later another boom from the leading French warship roared across the water. A hail of iron rained into the sea a quarter mile away.

Andrew was watching intently. "They're almost within range."

And now, to leeward, they could easily see the French coastline—and the fort. Lucien snatched up a telescope and trained it on the shore. His guts seized up. Sure enough, figures, tiny with distance, were swarming all over the fort, readying its guns, preparing to fire upon *Arundel* and reduce her to floating rubble.

" 'Sdeath, they're going to fire on us!"

Lord raised his speaking trumpet and shouted an order.

Too late. Tongues of flame spurted from the fort and a storm of iron came screaming overhead like a swarm of angry bees, lopping off the fore topgallant mast like a scythe through wheat. Men screamed. The mast plunged into the sea, taking rigging and sail with it. *Arundel* faltered, then began to ease into the wind, trying to obey her captain's command. Lucien ran to the leeward rail—and spotted the riders, made small by distance, racing down the Calais road and fighting a losing battle to maintain the gap between themselves and their pursuers.

He shut his eyes in agony. And here he was, trapped and helpless aboard a ship that even now was turning its back on those he loved.

But Lord was not prepared to go down without a fight.

Lucien's ears exploded, and the deck shuddered beneath him as *Arundel*'s guns returned the fort's first challenge—but as the smoke cleared, it became apparent that the range was too great; even had their own iron been able to reach the towering stone walls, it would never have been able to penetrate them.

Never.

And here came the French ships, bearing down hard, while *Magic* tried desperately to rally to *Arundel*'s defense.

Gareth was there beside him. "We're about to be smashed between land and sea."

"Go below," Lucien snapped.

"If only we had the range that fort had."

"For God's sake, Gareth, get below!"

But Andrew was there, hands on his hips, excitement lighting his eyes. "I have an idea."

"An idea? What bloody good is that going to do?"

But Andrew was already rushing toward the hatch even as the captain, his face like a thundercloud, stormed toward them from out of the drifting smoke.

"I am ordering both of you to follow your brother below," he snapped, pointing his sword toward the hatch. "A warship's deck is no place for civilians."

Lucien didn't move. "You're setting our boats adrift."

"Yes, to lessen the chance of flying splinters impaling the lot of us."

Lucien's black stare challenged the captain's. "I will
not leave my loved ones to perish at the hands of the
French. You will give me command of one of those
boats."

Lord's face went even darker; another boom
sounded from the fort, and a storm of hot iron
screamed overhead, sending spars and rigging down
about them.

"I'll deal with *you, after* we get out of range!"

"You will deal with me *now!*" Lucien blazed, and
headed for the boats.

Just then, Andrew, lugging a leaden box, came
charging back on deck. "Captain!" he shouted, trying
to be heard over the roar of the guns, the muskets, the
barrage of orders that flew all around. "I'm an inventor—this is an explosive I've developed! It's far superior to gunpowder. . . . If we put it in the cannon, you'll
have range enough to hit not only the fort, but those
ships coming in from windward! It'll buy us enough
time to get Lucien to shore so he can save Charles and
Eva!"

"*What!*"

Lucien, with Gareth on his heels, was already at the
jolly boat as the crew prepared to swing it out over the
side.

"I implore you, just try it!" Andrew persisted, racing after the irate captain.

Lord waved a lieutenant forward. "Teach, summon
a dozen marines and send them off with the duke—
he'll need all the damned help he can get."

"Aye, sir!"

"But my explosive!"

Another crashing roar from the leading French

ship sent iron splashing into the sea just yards off *Arundel*'s bow.

"Fort's preparing to fire again, sir!" cried the lookout in the top above.

And then it came, in a murderous salvo so brutal that *Arundel* rocked on her beams with the impact. Andrew saw one of the cannon spin and then flip like a top, pinning men, screaming, beneath it. Spars and rigging came crashing down from above, bouncing off the rigged nets, falling into the sea. And now the big French warship was running out her own guns even as Lucien, Gareth, and the marines, all vulnerable, were lowered down in the jolly boat.

"Sir, I beg of you to at least *try* my explosive!" Andrew cried desperately.

Captain Lord halted, turned, and looked at him flatly. "Very well, then," he said. "The carronades have the most range. If you can buy time for the duke, then I'll eat my goddamned hat."

The jolly boat hit the water, the single sail was raised, and the craft veered toward shore, shielded, for the moment, from the guns of the incoming French ships by *Arundel* herself.

Lucien sat watching the two horses streaking across the ever-nearing countryside. "We're never going to make it. We're too late."

"It's not over yet," said Gareth, loading his own pistol. "By God, I'm glad I didn't enter the Navy. Don't think I could take too much of this sort of thing."

But Lucien was staring toward shore. He could see Charles in the lead, one arm around Perry as he urged speed out of the tiring horse. Just behind him was Eva, her hair flying behind her like a red banner. Their pursuers were gaining on them. Raising muskets. The pop of gunfire came from across the water.

Charles had seen them. He was sharply reining his horse, sending it flying off the road and down a muddy slope toward the shore. Lucien gripped the gunwale. Never had he felt so helpless.

"Head for the beach," he snapped to the man at the tiller.

Thank God the wind was in their favor, driving them toward shore. Thank God he had Gareth with him, thank God Eva and Charles had each other. Thank God—

And then *Arundel*'s guns flashed and the world exploded.

Metal screamed overhead in a sound so unnatural that the man at the tiller dropped the bar, two marines hurled themselves down into the hull, and for a moment the boat careened madly in the draft left by the wave of iron.

"God and the devil save us! What the bleedin' 'ell was *that*?" cried the nearest marine, his eyes wide with fright.

But Lucien was finally smiling.

"Andrew's explosive."

"There they are!" Charles shouted, holding desperately on to Perry as he sent his exhausted horse plunging down the muddy slope toward the beach. "Hurry, we've not a moment to spare!" Behind him, Eva was hot on his heels, the gaol guards rapidly gaining on them.

Shots whizzed past.

They were never going to make it.

Eva, too, saw the jolly boat driving forward to meet them, and farther off, the huge *Arundel* running her guns out, pointing them toward shore. The range was too great. Powerful as the British warship was, she could never land her iron this far, could do nothing to help them. She, Charles, and Perry were on their own.

"Well, it was a valiant effort," she cried, as the two hit the beach and thundered down the sand toward the incoming boat.

"Can't say we didn't try," shouted Charles, hurtling along beside her.

"If we're taken, I'm sure Franklin will negotiate for our release."

Gunfire banged behind them, and Charles winced as a ball sliced through the top of his sleeve, leaving an arrow of blood. "Taken?" he yelled back, as the French began to send their own horses down the muddy slope in pursuit. "At this point I'd be happy just to survive."

"Look! Lucien and Gareth are in the boat!"

And it was nearly to shore; already the marines were on their feet, muskets raised to their shoulders; oh, God help them, thought Eva, six marines to hold back the entire guard from the gaol? They were all going to be cut down like grouse at a hunt!

But at that moment *Arundel* coughed two puffs of smoke from her bow, and an unholy roar screamed across the water with a sound like all the demons of hell being unleashed at once. Eva's horse shied sideways, nearly unseating her; Charles's own mount reared in terror, spilling him and Perry to the sand; a moment later, it was bolting off down the beach, Charles was on his feet with Perry over his shoulder, and Eva was throwing herself off her own mount and running alongside him, both fighting to reach the incoming jolly boat before the guard was on them.

"What in God's name was that?" she shouted.

"Don't know—never heard anything like it in all my years of battle!"

She glanced over her shoulder. "Charles, look!"

He did—and saw what she had seen.

Half the guard lay smashed and dead on the beach behind them, and the rest were milling about in confusion, pointing out to sea toward *Arundel* and yelling madly in French.

"Andrew's explosive—it had to be!" Charles cried. "Hurry, they won't be long after us now!"

More shots banged out from behind them as what remained of the guard rallied. And now the jolly boat was through the surf, the marines already firing upon the guard to try and hold them off as Lucien and Gareth leaped out and ran forward to meet them.

Lucien saw that it was going to be a close thing. He threw himself in front of the three fugitives, took aim, and fired his own pistol at the Frenchmen charging down the beach.

"Get in the boat!" he yelled.

Lead whined all around. He saw Charles leap for the gunwales. Saw Eva turn to fire at their attackers. Reached for her—

And felt his side catch on fire. He clapped a hand to the wound, hot blood gushing from between his fingers, but it was too late. Through a graying haze, he saw Charles's stricken face, heard Gareth's cry of denial, saw Eva—his beloved, precious Eva—rushing forward to catch him.

Charles and Gareth hauled him into the boat, shots echoing all around.

And the last thing he felt was Eva's arms going around him.

Chapter 32

From far off came the sound of voices. Cries of pain. The distant, lingering boom of cannon. A rocking sensation . . . like being in his mother's arms.

"He's coming around," someone said.

Groggily, Lucien opened his eyes. For a moment he lay still, trying to discern his whereabouts. Trying to remember what had happened to him. He lay on a hard table. There was still that rocking sensation, and as he focused on the dark beams just overhead, a lantern swinging gently with motion, he realized that he was aboard a ship, and his cradle was the sea.

"Lucien?"

He turned his head and smiled weakly. "Eva."

"You had us all very frightened there," she said, stroking the hair at his temple.

"Are you all right?"

"I'm fine."

"And the others?"

"Right here," said Charles, moving into his field of view. His arm was bandaged, but he was intact.

And so was Gareth. "Welcome back, Luce," he murmured, joining Charles.

"Where is Andrew?"

"Right here."

"Your brother saved the day with his explosive," said someone else, and turning his head, Lucien saw the stern face of Captain Lord. "If it weren't for him, I dread to think of what might have happened."

"Yes, you've never seen three ships flee as fast as those Frenchies did when we put some of it in the guns and let fly," crowed Andrew, beaming.

Captain Lord gave a dry smile and then returned his attention to Lucien. "You've got a piece of lead lodged just under your lowest rib," he said gravely. "The surgeon is currently attending to the other wounded, but he'll be with you shortly."

Ah, then, so that explained it. They were in the ship's orlop. The surrounding cries, the stench of blood and death, were not just a nightmare—they were real.

"How is Lord Brookhampton?"

"Resting comfortably. He suffered a nasty head wound, but he's growing more and more lucid and seems most desperate to return to England."

"Can't wait to get back to Nerissa," Gareth explained.

Lucien smiled. Eva, Charles, Gareth, Andrew, and yes, even Perry, safe. . . . All was right in his world, then. He turned his head once more and stared up into the foggy gray eyes of the ship's captain. "No hard feelings, eh, Lord?"

"None." The other man smiled dryly. "But that's the last time I'm ever allowing a duke aboard my command. I'd sooner resign first."

Lucien laughed, but the pain was too much. He shut his eyes and willed his body to relax as the captain moved off to comfort his own men. He could sense his family hovering around, could feel their love for him, their concern. He was thankful that he was so blessed. But it was Eva's presence that was most precious. Eva, who stood by his head, stroking his hair, resting her other hand soothingly on his shoulder. Eva, whose bravery and determination had cost him his heart.

Eva. His duchess.

His love.

"The surgeon's coming," she said.

Lucien smiled weakly. It hurt too much to move. To breathe, even.

He felt someone slicing off what remained of his shirt. Competent hands, probing, palpating. Fingers pressed against his ribs, moved lower, pressed *there*; he sucked in his breath, his head swimming with the pain of it.

"Get him some brandy," said a gruff voice. "Lots of it."

Lucien, breathing shallowly through his chest in order to escape the daggerlike agony, opened his eyes. "I need my wife, not brandy."

"And I need *you* to be perfectly still as I'm cutting into you. One move, even a slight one, and it could cost you your lung, if not your life."

"I won't move."

"He won't move," echoed his brothers, who knew him well.

The surgeon only raised a brow and cleaned his scalpel. Gareth, Andrew, and Charles gathered close. Eva stood near his head, one hand still on his shoulder, her beautiful face close enough to touch. Lucien wanted nothing more than to do just that, but he had said he would not move, and he would not. Instead, he gazed up into her slanting green eyes, at the long lashes veiling the worry she could not hide. He focused on her lips, the lower one caught between her teeth as she watched the surgeon prepare to make the first cut. On the pale clarity of her skin, the purity of her complexion, the—

His breath stopped as the knife went in.

"I can't have you moving, Your Grace," said the surgeon, withdrawing.

"I'm not moving. I'm not even breathing," Lucien muttered, but he felt the dampness breaking out all along his brow and knew that he would be unable to keep his word.

The surgeon drew back, shaking his head. "I can't do it, then. It's too great a risk."

There was silence as everyone looked to each other for a solution. The surgeon prepared to move on to someone else. Again, Lucien tried to breathe, and felt searing pain where the ball rested under his rib. There had to be a way to do this. Had to be.

And then he felt Eva's hand, still lightly stroking his hair, his cheek.

Wordlessly, he reached up and caught it, his grip persistent enough to claim her attention. He stared up into her beautiful green eyes. She gazed back, trying to understand what he wanted of her. And then he placed her hand against the side of his neck, keeping it there, pushing it gently, firmly down. Their gazes locked.

She smiled then.

She understood.

"Doctor?" she called, as the surgeon began to move away.

The man paused, frowning.

"He'll give you no trouble," Eva assured the man. "Just give him a moment."

"One moment, then."

"All of you, give him one moment," Eva murmured to the anxious party that surrounded the table.

Lucien saw the exchange of puzzled looks, his brothers' worried frowns before they, too, moved reluctantly away from the table, revealing the darkened overhead beams, the lantern light flickering against a bulkhead, once more.

"What a clever girl I've married," he breathed, holding his own hand over her fingers as she expertly found the proper place on his neck. His gaze sought hers. "I love you, Eva. I've loved you from the moment you first thwarted me, I think."

"And do you know something, my beloved Blackheath?"

"What is that, dearest?"

"I love you, too." Her eyes grew luminous, and he saw her soul in them. A soul that was trusting where it had been suspicious. Open where it had been closed. Full of hope when it had been poisoned with cynicism.

"I love you, Lucien, and nothing on God's earth means more to me than you do."

He leaned his cheek against the inside of her wrist. Kissed it, tenderly.

"Are you ready, my love?"

"Yes," he said, turning his head so that he gazed up at her. "Work your magic, dearest, and work it well. I have said I won't move."

"And you won't," she assured him.

He gazed up into her beautifully mysterious eyes, wanting to hold on to the image for as long as he could. He could feel the gentle pressure of her hand against his neck now, the loving control of her fingers as she began to ease him down toward a place where there was no pain, no awareness. In a moment, he would be there. In a moment, the surgeon would be cutting into his flesh, digging beneath his rib, and he would not move.

The darkness gathered. He did not fight it. With a sigh of defeat, he gave in to it, relaxing beneath her skillful touch, sinking down into the depths of nothingness, his fingers twitching once, twice, before he lay as still as death beneath his duchess's hand.

Raising her head, Eva met the doctor's gaze. "His Grace is ready for you now," she said.

The scalpel went in. And true to his word, Lucien never moved.

Late that evening a war-torn *Arundel*, with *Magic* keeping station just off her rear quarter, beat her way past vessels of every sort, and dropped anchor at Spithead.

The sun was setting off to the west, blazing a trail, it seemed, all the way to America. Eva, standing at the rail with Lucien's arm wrapped possessively around her waist, leaned her cheek against his shoulder.

"A penny for your thoughts," he said, noting her distant gaze, her preoccupied smile.

"I was just thinking of America . . . and how in the end, we both wanted the same thing for it, but were too stubborn to see it."

"Peace?"

"Yes. I wanted it through war, hoping that France's intervention would put a quick end to things. You wanted it through diplomacy, hoping that negotiations and meeting my country's demands for fair treatment would satisfy its need for freedom. I only wish I'd realized we were both working toward the same end . . . just taking different routes to get there."

"Would you go back, Eva, given the chance?"

He was referring to that terrible night when she'd learned the terms of his will, his desire to keep her chained in England for the sake of his heir. A family responsibility that she now understood. And forgave. She smiled, and gazed up into his eyes. "No," she murmured, shaking her head. "My home is here now. With you. With my new family."

"I love you." He fitted his hands around her waist, drew her close, and kissed her, uncaring that they stood in plain sight of anyone who might be watching. "I am the most fortunate man in this world."

"And I love you, Lucien. I only wish I'd had the courage to tell you before."

"We have a lifetime to make up for our past wrongs to each other."

"Do we?"

He smiled, the gesture lighting up his whole face, transforming it into something boyish, eager, and charming. "I haven't had the nightmare for weeks now. I think it's gone."

"Ah." The corners of her eyes crinkled with joy. "That proves me right, then."

"Proves you right?"

"I suspected all along that the dream might be an analogy for something else. Think about it, Lucien. Every time you had it, you were impaled through the heart with a sword, mastered by something beyond your control. Do you not realize, now, what that sword really was? What it implied?"

"Love," he murmured, touching his fingers to her lips. "And the death I saw was the end of my lonely bachelorhood. My obsessive need for control."

"All ends lead to new beginnings."

"Indeed. And do you want to hear of yet another beginning?"

She raised a brow in silent question.

"I spoke with Perry a short time ago. He says he's had such a bellyful of adventure that the first thing he's going to do when he gets ashore is offer marriage to Nerissa."

"Oh, Lucien—it seems as if your last grand machination will bear fruit, after all!"

"Yes." He smiled. "My last grand machination. And now, my dear duchess, shall we go ashore, find our own rooms for the night, and"—he stroked her cheek, his eyes darkening with implication—"work on bearing fruit of our own?"

She sobered, her mouth turned down in a sad smile.

"You know what the doctors said . . . that I will never conceive another child."

"To hell with the doctors," he said, offering his arm and walking her slowly toward the entry port. "I never did put much faith in their dire premonitions."

Minutes later, they were in the boat that would take them into Portsmouth.

An hour later, they were holed up in a harbor inn, affirming their love for each other with words, with their bodies, with their hearts.

And nine months to the day after that, the sixth Duke of Blackheath—the miracle who was never to happen, the heir who was never to be conceived—was safely delivered in the ancient oak bed at Blackheath Castle, where every duke and every duchess before him had slept, and where someday he would bring his own beautiful wife.

As she and her proud husband gazed down at their newborn son, Eva couldn't help but feel a wave of love and satisfaction and the purest sort of joy she had ever known. She looked up into Lucien's triumphant eyes.

He smiled.

She smiled back.

And thought, as he picked up their little miracle and took him to the window to look out over the time-less downs that fell away toward the horizon, that some things would never change. There would always be twenty-four hours in the day. The sun would always rise in the east, and set in the west.

And Fate, it seemed, would always grant the wishes of the fifth Duke of Blackheath.

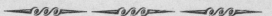

Avon Romances—
the best in exceptional authors and unforgettable novels!